What Readers Say About *Sylmar...*

"Rick Campbell takes the reader on a high-speed ride with colorful characters, a page-turning plot, and a strong message of redemption."
  JAMES WATKINS, author, speaker

"I absolutely recommend Sylmar to anyone on a spiritual journey. Sylmar takes faith beyond bumper-sticker answers right into the mess where Christian values meet the world."
  PASTOR GRANT FISHBOOK, Christ the King Church

"I couldn't put it down. It's a good read about real people. I'm putting a copy in the church library."
  DAVE CLINE, Retired Reformed Minister

"*Sylmar* is first-rate suspense. The characters are real, true to life. A successful confrontation of Christian values with today's social issues."
  PASTOR DENI STARBUCK, Christ the King Church

"You know all along there's going to be an earthquake, but you don't find out until the last pages how it affects this story. *Sylmar* is a lot of fun!"
  LIZ CHACE, Biblical Studies Student

SYLMAR

Rick Campbell

OakTara

WATERFORD, VIRGINIA

Sylmar

Published in the U.S. by:
OakTara Publishers
P.O. Box 8
Waterford, VA 20197

Visit OakTara at
www.oaktara.com

Cover design by David LaPlaca/debest design co.
Cover photo © 2007, courtesy John Lockwood, Pygmy Boats,
www.pygmyboats.com

Quote, pp. 107-108, from *The Reverse of the Medal* by Patrick O'Brian
(New York: W.W. Norton & Co. New York), 1986, p. 267.

Quote, p. 159, from *Experiencing the Depths of Jesus Christ* by Jean
Guyon (Sargent, GA: Seed Sowers), 1975, p. 35.

ISBN: 978-1-60290-045-5

Sylmar is a work of fiction. References to real people, events, estab-
lishments, organizations, or locales are intended only to provide a sense
of authenticity and are used fictitiously. All other characters, incidents,
and dialogue are drawn from the author's imagination.

Acknowledgments

A special thanks to my editors:
Una Cline, Jessica Juhl,
and my precious wife, Anne Campbell.

I hope this book encourages my children and grandchildren
to express the wonderful creativity
I see in all of them.

Author's Note

Sylmar is set in 1994 greater Los Angeles. Some of the events in the story really happened: the Northridge Earthquake was one of the costliest disasters in U.S. history. Earthquake data was summarized from newspaper accounts of the day and other studies of the quake. Numerous hospitals were severely damaged, including one in Santa Monica. It seems that the Golden Triangle really was destroyed as well; however it is much harder to confirm this report in the periodicals. Finally, sightings of dolphins in Santa Monica Bay are not uncommon.

Everything else is fiction. Any similarity to persons, places, or things, living or dead, is entirely coincidental and beyond the intent of either the author or the publisher.

1

He that will learn to pray,
let him go to sea.
GEORGE HERBERT

A rchie was feeling better today; a lot better. The pain in his ribs was down to a mild ache. *I wouldn't feel a thing with a couple of pain killers,* he thought.

As Archie finished the last of the physiotherapist's exercises lying on his back, he noticed a cobweb in the corner of the room near the ceiling. He got up, grunting, and headed for the kitchen. Archie had been doing the exercises every day for a week since he came home from hospital. At first they seemed to make his side hurt more, but over the last two days they were beginning to have the promised effect. He went to the kitchen sink, took two ibuprofen, picked up the condo's "do list," added the cobwebs, and put it back down.

Looking down at the boats in the marina from his third-floor window, Archie thought about how he came alive on the sea and how he often felt a little depressed on land, as he did this morning. He wondered if it had to do with the perpetual motion, some kind of return to the womb thing, but that wasn't all of it. Just going down to the dock perked him up. *Maybe it's the sounds and smells,* he thought as he opened the sliding glass door to the deck. A couple of noisy gulls wheeled by, as if to confirm his last thought. Turning quickly from the balcony he went to the computer and checked the marine weather and surf reports: 10 knots of wind and moderate swell out of the West, North West. Perfect conditions to take the *Mira Flores* outside the breakwater. *Only a mile out and a mile back. I wouldn't overdo it.*

Archie began going over checklists in his head and soon was

writing down what he needed: food, water, ballast, tie downs, cell phone, handheld VHF, and pocket wind gauge. He moved back to the kitchen and made breakfast: two poached eggs, cherry tomatoes, toast, and coffee. The vegetables were a concession to Luella. The fact that he didn't have to eat salad all the time was the only good thing about her passing. He liked this breakfast; it was simple and quick. He was waiting for the toaster to pop when he made his decision: he was going out.

After breakfast he set about preparing food to take along. He made up a freezer bag filled with stuff he could eat with one hand while he steered with the other. Archie filled two sport water bottles. Then he put all his food into a waterproof bag with a clip at the top to tie it down. Archie put his cell phone in a freezer bag in one pant pocket and his waterproof VHF radio in the other. With the wind gauge's lanyard cinched around his neck, he dropped the instrument inside his shirt. He went over his checklist again, deciding the rest of what he needed was at the boat slip. Putting everything in a duffle he headed for the dock.

Miller Post was sitting on the deck of the *Last Chance*. It was five after nine, but Miller already had a beer going. *Probably not his first*, Archie thought.

"Hi, Miller, how you doing this morning?" Archie asked.

"Just fine, Arch, just fine," Miller said as he eyed Archie's duffle. "Goin' out?"

"Yes, I am. Do you think you could help me launch the *Mira Flores*? I could do it myself, but I don't want a setback."

Miller got up and headed for the gate in his lifelines. Miller, whom Archie guessed was a hundred pounds overweight, had a way of puffing whenever he moved. Archie waited for the familiar sight of the large man steadying himself on a stanchion with one hand and holding his beer can out for balance with the other as he eased himself down onto the dock. Archie noticed how the *Last Chance* rocked after Miller stepped off.

2

"Weren't you just in hospital?" Miller asked as he moved along.

"They kept me in there for observation mostly. I'm fine."

"Well, I'll give you a hand, but you be careful out there," Miller said as the two made their way down the dock.

"I always am," Archie said. He knew Miller was right to warn him: the sea was absolutely unforgiving. "You know what they say, Miller, 'At sea, count on everything going wrong at the worst possible time.'"

Miller hardly ever went out, and then only if the sea was like a millpond, so he chuckled as Archie went on. "You have to have your routines in place, your gear in top shape, and back up for everything."

Archie also knew that sometimes quick action saved a lot of grief, but he didn't think the ribs would slow him down in a crisis. It was more a matter of pain tolerance, and at his age everything hurt anyway. However, he didn't tell Miller he was going outside the breakwater.

Miller set his beer down and clamped onto the stern of the tiny wooden boat while Archie took the bow. The *Mira Flores* was surprisingly light, an advantage of stitch and glue construction.

"Light as a feather," Miller said, puffing as he lifted. They turned her over and slid her into the water over the carpet-covered boards she was stored on.

"That's why the ballast is so important," Archie said as he opened the storage bin on the other corner of his slip. "Can you help me with these?"

Miller muscled the rectangular water ballast cans out of the bin one at a time, carried them around the end of the slip, and set them on the dock beside the *Mira Flores*. Archie got into the boat, and the two of them eased and locked the jugs into their frames beside the mast. Then Miller brought over the cast-iron centerboard and they slid it into its slot. Archie clipped the safety lock that held the centerboard in place if the boat capsized. Not only would this little device keep the board from going to the bottom, but also the leveraged weight made it easy to right her: Archie had made that happy discovery when he intentionally capsized her on a trial run inside the breakwater. Then Miller helped him step the mast and all the heavy work was done.

Miller picked up his beer and stepped back to survey the tiny craft. He admired her fine entry and hourglass stern. "How long is she, Arch?

Fourteen-fifteen feet?"

"Fourteen."

Miller took a pull on his beer. "Well, she sure is a pretty little thing."

"I have to admit she's stolen my heart," Archie said, looking at the boat. "Hey buddy, thanks so much. I couldn't have done it today without you."

"No problem. Give me a shout when you get in, and I'll help pull her out."

"Thanks, but I think I'll leave her in the water when I get back. You know me. I love getting out."

"All right then, but be safe out there."

"Will do. Thanks again, Miller."

Archie got the simple standing rigging in place: the forestay and two light port and starboard shrouds. He laid in the oars and dropped the tiller into the pintels. Then he secured everything loose in the boat—the food bag and another bag with flares, horn, and the first-aid kit—with a line to the eye bolt on the stern bench. Capsizing was always a possibility in an open boat as small as this, and he didn't want to lose any gear. The bailing scoop was permanently tethered to its own eye bolt. Then he put on his safety harness and life line and over that his life jacket. Finally he clipped the bitter end of his own lifeline to the eye bolt. He knew a lot of boaters would think he was overdoing it on such a mild day, but he had read enough stories about single-handers falling overboard and then having to watch their boat sweetly sail away. *Always stay with the boat* was a doubly good idea with the *Mira Flores* since he had added flotation chambers fore and aft. Unless she was absolutely crushed, she was unsinkable. He cast off and began to row past his Cal 40 toward the main channel.

Miller raised his beer as Archie rowed by the *Last Chance.* "Have a good one, Arch."

"You too, Miller."

The reach south down the fairway was uneventful. At the corner, where the channel turned west straight into the prevailing wind, Archie started on the first of several tacks to work his way upwind to the western breakwater. The *Mira Flores* wouldn't sail as close to the

4

wind as bigger boats with more leverage, but she did surprisingly well closehauled, much better than any other sailing dingy Archie had ever handled. She was very stiff as well. *Must be the centerboard.* Archie was pleased with the cast-iron modification he had designed. He ran as close to the rocks as he safely could on the first leg and came about. Back and forth he tacked.

The wind began to strengthen as the land heated up. He had decided to sail north first, up the coast, so he would have the easier leg of the sea trial on the way home with the wind slightly abaft the beam. He could see on this tack if she didn't take too much leeway, he would make it past the corner into the north-south channel. He headed her up until the little sail luffed, then backed off a point. The tiny boat dug in, sailed a bit slower this closehauled but made it past the corner—the rocks a biscuit-toss away. Archie felt no little satisfaction at this but could relish it only a moment, for now he could see and hear the breakers on the beach ahead to his right. He slid down farther into the sole of the boat with his back and most of his weight to the port side to counter the pressure on the sail. Soon he felt the roll of the waves from the west. As he rose on the first swell, he talked to the boat. "Well, darlin', there's nothing but ocean between you and China." Archie and his tiny boat entered the open sea for the first time.

Archie loved the little boat. He loved her for her classic lines. He loved her because he had built her and knew every inch of her. He loved her because the keel and ballast—his own modifications—made her a better sailor; he loved her because her name honored Luella. But now he loved her most because of how she took the sea quartering at her bow. As he had hoped, she held her course with little leeway. Light as she was, she cut bravely on. *Such tenacity*, he thought. Joy rose in his heart and then again as each successive wave went by the boards.

After 10 minutes of sailing the swells Archie was as happy as a man could be. He began to sing his favorite sea shanty, "The Sailor's Alphabet," in a raspy baritone:

> "A is the anchor that keeps us in place,
> B is the bowsprit that stands out in space,
> C is the capstan we wind our chain round, and

D are the davits we haul our boats on."

Archie cleared his throat, spit downwind, and carried on with the chorus, most of the rasp gone from his voice.

"How merrily, how merrily, how merrily are we,
There's no life on earth like a sailor at sea,
Blow high or blow low as the ship sails along,
Give a sailor his grog, and there's nothing goes wrong."

He remembered the happy times sailing with Luella and the girls, how the girls laughed when he would make up verses toward the end of the alphabet. On he sailed with pure joy in his heart.

Back at the marina, Primo felt jumpy. He tried to calm himself with a little pep talk about how well this was going to go as he went through his pre-trip check on board the *Cobra*. He knelt down beside the open engine compartment, checking the oil in each of the three inboard/outboards and then the seawater exchange hose that gave him trouble last summer. Primo succeeded in keeping his white shorts and navy blue sweatshirt clean as he handled the dipsticks and the grimy hose. Everything looked shipshape.

"Hello, we're here!" Summer called out from some distance up the dock. Primo popped his head up, closed the engine compartment, and watched the three girls approach. He stood up to allow them to admire his athletic build and deep tan and was immediately disappointed that the women were covered from head to foot in warmup suits instead of wearing the short shorts he had fantasized. But Summer had been out before and knew it could be chilly in the breeze. Primo cursed the coastal cloud and willed it to burn off so the women would take off their unisex outfits. He hid his disappointment perfectly, however, with his winner's grin as he called back, "Hi, gals! Ready for a big adventure?"

"We sure are," said Summer, looking pleased.

The other two guests, Danielle and her daughter, Shanti, didn't speak, but their eyes got bigger and their step slower as they stared at the *Cobra*. Its low-profile deck and flat transom made it look like it was going fast tied to the dock. Primo chuckled. He could see his "pick up" rig was working again.

Without looking away from the *Cobra*, Shanti asked, "Momma, is this the boat that's taking us for a ride?"

"It sure is, Shanti," Primo answered, beaming at the little girl. "Welcome aboard, ladies," he said, flashing his winner grin again and holding out a big paw of a hand to steady them as they stepped down into the cockpit.

"Thank you so much for inviting us for a ride," Danielle said over Shanti's head as she steadied Shanti from behind.

Primo took the little girl under the arms with both hands and swung her into the cockpit. "There you go," he said in his cheeriest voice. "Danielle, it's my pleasure. When Summer told me you two liked fun rides, I said, 'They have to come out on the *Cobra*.'"

Primo was good at making people believe he was completely sincere. He continued to chat them up as he got their gear stowed and showed them the tiny head in the cuddy below decks. The two were impressed and delighted with everything.

Summer, knowing the drill, waited on the dock to cast off the lines.

Primo fired up the three 500-horsepower inboard/outboard engines. The 1,500 horsepower rig was the most power available in this model and made Primo's boat one of the fastest in the marina.

Danielle had been worried that Shanti would be hard to handle in the confined space of the boat. Instead, once the tour was over, the four-year old seemed content to sit on the back bench and carry on the fantasy play she had begun in the car with her two favorite stuffed animals. It was Shanti's way of coping when she felt shy, and clearly she felt shy around Primo. Danielle saw she was "talking" Sweetheart the cat and Pardner the pony. In the ongoing drama, Pardner was playing the role of a handsome prince trying to rescue Sweetheart, a fair maiden, from some terrible fate. Danielle guessed she was OK and thanked Primo when he helped Shanti into her life jacket and fastened the seat belt over her lap.

"No problem ma'am," Primo said. "It's safety first on the water. Now I want you to come up here to the driver's seat, so I can show you how to run this thing."

"Oh no, I couldn't do that. I...."

"Now come on," he said, taking her slender arm in his big hand. "When we get out away from everything, we'll slow her down and you can get the feel; then speed up as much as you want, as long as the Captain thinks it's safe."

"Oh my gosh," Danielle said as she slipped past Primo, got behind the wheel, and eyed the array of instruments and controls.

"Hey guys, I'm making a quick stop at the ladies' room right over there," Summer said from the dock. "Anyone else need to go?"

"No, we're fine," Danielle said. She had made sure the two of them had taken care of business just before they left the house.

"OK, I'll be back in a sec."

Usually Primo got steamed whenever Summer held him up like this. But in the rush of the first close encounter with the exotic beauty beside him, he couldn't be bothered. Out of habit he said, "Don't be long, Summer. The fun is all out there," but it lacked the usual irritation.

Everyone lost track of time for the next few minutes—Summer in front of the mirror in the ladies' room, Shanti in her make-believe world, and Primo and Danielle in their intense discussion over how to run the boat.

Like most mariners Primo had a funny story about every aspect of boating, and the two of them were having a lot of laughs. Most of the controls and gauges seemed similar to any land vehicle Danielle had driven, except for the dead-man switch. "The driver fastens this little alligator clip to himself before he starts out so if he passes out or has a heart attack, the plug pops out and the engines shut down. It's especially important when you are alone in the cockpit to clip it on."

"I see," said Danielle. "The boat would keep going without it."

"Right. The worst-case scenario has happened more often than you would think. The operator falls overboard, and the boat motors off into the sunset."

8

"That would be a bad thing," Danielle said.

The *Cobra's* powerful engines idled in the confined space of the slip and little of the light, offshore breeze made its way to Primo's dock. The exhaust hung in the air around the boat.

"OK, Captain, ready to cast off," Summer called in a perky voice as she dropped her bag in the cockpit.

Primo let Danielle slide over, then he got behind the controls. "Cast off," he said. Summer slipped the bow, stern, and spring lines off the dock cleats and stepped nimbly onto the deck. She stowed the lines in the cockpit as Primo brought the *Cobra* into the main channel.

"Here we go, Shanti," Danielle said, smiling over her shoulder at the little girl, who was now looking over the side at a large gull sitting on a dock post.

"Here we go, Mama," she replied, holding Sweetheart and Pardner in a way that they could see out too. She said something about the three of them watching the bird, but her words were drowned by the sound of the engines as Primo brought the *Cobra* up to the five-mile-an-hour limit to make his way down the channel.

The *Cobra* cut through the chop in the east-west channel as they turned straight into the ten-knot breeze. Primo had the two women sit upfront with him. Danielle, beside him, was carefully watching everything he did, anticipating her promised stint at the wheel. Now and again she checked Shanti over her shoulder. Later in the ride she'd go sit back with Shanti. But the child seemed happy for now as she continued to hold Pardner's head up so he could see out over the side of the boat.

Shanti was enjoying the ride, but at the same time she felt nauseous and had a headache. But she didn't want to tell. Once she had told her mom she didn't feel well when they were going to the rides at the beach and her mom had made them go home. She had been looking forward to this boat ride for days, so she kept quiet.

Primo turned north at the outer breakwater and, as soon as he cleared the channel, he kicked the power full on. Quickly the *Cobra's* nose came up and then down again as she reached planing speed. And just as quickly they began the exciting ride over the three-foot swells. Heading north in a west-to-east sea, the boat made a kind of corkscrew motion as she sped ahead. Occasionally she was airborne, returning to the sea with a *whumph.* Danielle and Summer put their arms up and screamed each time they lifted off.

Shanti however, was not doing so well. Her symptoms had progressed: more nausea, a worse headache, and now a degree of dizziness. Suddenly Pardner, whom she was still holding up to see out, was ripped from her hand by a gust of the combined offshore breeze and the boat's speed. She shouted his name as she followed his backward flight. Somehow one of his legs caught under a stern cleat.

"Mama, Pardner!" Shanti shouted, but her voice was covered by the roar of the engines and the women's gleeful screams. Shanti was strong-willed and resourceful. She knew how to unbuckle seat belts. Someone had to save Pardner. She popped her belt open, stood up on the seat and reached for the pony just as the *Cobra* hit the biggest wave of the day. Shanti floated upward and then abruptly shot backward as the slipstream caught under her life jacket and carried her past the *Cobra*'s stern into the sea.

After riding the swells for over an hour in the *Mira Flores,* Archie was more than convinced of her seaworthiness. He had stopped wondering if the tiny boat would capsize long ago and for some time had been daydreaming about crossing the Pacific in her. Being a weekday, only a few other boats were out and only one powerboat had passed nearby so there was little distraction to break his fantasy. He had read about a guy who crossed the Pacific in a small open boat; was it sixteen feet? Archie wondered if he could set a new smallest boat record. Even though his mind was elsewhere, he stayed focused on the waves ahead in order to steer a straight course. The data from his vision, touch, and experience at the helm translated without thinking into little corrections on the tiller. His mind, split between these two worlds of fantasy and sense perception, suddenly focused exclusively on the sea.

It was a familiar sound rather than visual or tactile data that broke off the fantasy: *Pfouff.* The lone dolphin seemed to come up from behind him and was now abeam not 10 feet away.

Archie's spirits lifted another notch. "Hi buddy. How ya' doin'?" he said in the same high voice he used to talk to dogs.

The light was such that Archie could see the dolphin's eye looking back at him. Archie had seen lots of porpoises in the San Juans; once he even got into a super pod of Orcas. The porpoises would sometimes swim around and around the Cal 40, when they were under sail, but wouldn't come near when the engine was running. But this was the first dolphin he had seen in Santa Monica Bay.

"What ya' doin' in L.A., buddy?"

The dolphin took one more blow and then swam off to the northwest. Archie followed the fin, beside himself with happiness. Suddenly he glimpsed something on a crest near the dolphin that shouldn't have been there, but it disappeared into the next trough before he could be certain.

Archie riveted his gaze on the area where he expected to see it when it came up out of the trough. He also began calculating how he could bring the boat alongside the...*the body*? On the next swell the dolphin was circling a person in a life jacket, floating face up. At first the size didn't make sense as the person seemed farther away than it should have been given the amount of detail Archie could perceive. Then another shock of adrenaline hit his already charged system. "God help us!" he cried. "It's a child!"

The child was about 30 yards ahead of him, but 10 yards upwind. Archie feared the *Mira Flores* leeway might make it impossible for him to get there this tack. In that case he would miss the pick up on the first pass and have to double back. He considered dousing the sail and rowing to the child but ruled it out for the risk of capsizing. As well, there would be lost time and distance downwind getting the sail down and oars deployed.

He made a decision and brought the bow into irons. The sprit sail luffed as he hardened the sheet as much as he dared. *Mustn't break anything.* Three more inches of sheet came free of the grab cleat. He put the tiller over and eased her off until she was sailing as close to the wind as she possibly could. Her forward motion was greatly reduced, but she was making more upwind headway. Green water joined the spray coming over the bow. There would be time to bail later; all that mattered now was to get upwind to the child. Archie strained with every fiber to will the boat to the motionless body. Now he could see more detail; long hair streamed out behind the child's head. *It was a girl*, he thought as she crested the wave ahead. "Jesus, have mercy on us!" he cried.

Her eyes were open. Without movement he couldn't tell if she was alive or dead. With all his heart he wanted her to be alive. He was just a couple of boat lengths from her now but also one trough downwind. He had little room left to cover the last few feet upwind. He made another snap decision, turned off the wind momentarily to build speed, timed the wave, and then just as the crest was at the bow he turned the boat into the eye of the wind. She slid down the back of the wave into the same trough as the little girl, now just a boat length away. He brought the bow off the wind and the *Mira Flores* shot toward her.

Archie held the tiller in his left and the main sheet in his right. The moment the child was abeam he popped the sheet clear, dropped it, and reached for her with his free hand, his left still on the tiller. His fingers closed on the loose end of a life jacket tie that was drifting ahead of her. As he pulled her alongside, her eyes rolled to look at him. "I've got you, darlin'! I've got you!" he cried. He eased her round to the stern and with both hands hauled her up and over the transom into the tiny boat, then propped her up on the ballast near the mast. He noticed neither the sail flogging in the breeze nor the roll of the swell. But even neglected, the tiny boat did not fail him.

Archie bent over the little girl and looked into her still open eyes. "You're safe now, darlin'. You're safe. We're going to get you to shore quickly, and you'll be fine." As he spoke to her he wiped the wet hair away from her face. *Such a beautiful child.*

"Pardner," Shanti moaned.

"Oh," Archie said. "Yes, I'm your partner, honey, I'm your partner." He looked away, squinted the tears out of his eyes, and scanned the sea around him. *I've got to get her ashore.*

He missed the look Shanti gave him when he said he was her "Pardner." *What a funny man,* she thought. *He can't be my pony.* But she felt too tired to explain to him, so she lay back in the tiny boat looking at the sky as she had been doing in the water. She hoped her headache would go away.

Archie studied the beach perhaps a mile downwind. He briefly considered calling an ambulance to the water line and beaching the boat. But he decided he might wreck in the surf...out of the question with her on board. *Better get help,* he decided quickly.

Archie turned the handheld on and the LED screen went automatically to channel 16, the one the Coast Guard monitored. Archie keyed the mike: "Mayday, Mayday, this is the *Mira Flores.* Mayday, Mayday, this is the *Mira Flores.*" In 22 years of sailing it was the first time Archie had ever made the ultimate distress call.

Immediately the little handheld crackled, "Roger, *Mira Flores,* this is Coast Guard Dispatch. I read your Mayday loud and clear. Switch to channel 27, go to channel two, seven, over."

Archie knew this was proper procedure to get off the hailing channel and answered back quickly. "Roger, Coast Guard, I'm switching to channel 27." Archie turned the channel selection knob from 16 to 27 and immediately heard the dispatch saying: "*Mira Flores,* this is Coast Guard Dispatch. Give me your position and situation, over."

"Roger, Coast Guard Dispatch. This is Archie Douglas. I'm single handing a 14-foot sailing skiff without auxiliary about 300 yards south of the Santa Monica Pier and maybe 100 yards west of it. I just pulled a small child out of the water. She is alive, but not talking much. I'm unable to determine the extent of her injury. Request assistance, over."

"Roger, *Mira Flores,* roger position, roger sea rescue. Standby, I'm patching you through to the Santa Monica Lifeguard Dispatch."

"Roger, standing by," Archie said.

This time there was a bit of a delay. Archie imagined the Coast Guard was giving the information already gathered to the lifeguards. He looked down at the little girl now shivering under his windbreaker. He wished he had brought more dry clothes or a heavy blanket. He thought about holding her on his lap and warming her with his own overheated body. She still lay with eyes open, but had a glazed look. Archie sensed there was something else wrong with her beyond the wet and cold. He wondered whether she had a concussion.

"Honey, my name is Archie. What's yours?"

"Shunty," he heard her say.

"Oh wonderful! Your name is Shunty," he said with rising hope, knowing how important it was that she was oriented to person. "How do you feel, darlin'?"

"Headache," Shanti replied just as the radio crackled.

"*Mira Flores*, this is Santa Monica Lifeguard Dispatch, over."

"Lifeguard Dispatch, this is the *Mira Flores*, over."

"I have your location at 300 yards south of the Santa Monica Pier and 100 yards west of it. Is that correct? Over."

Archie glanced around to check his bearings again as he keyed the mike. "Umm, yes, darned close," he said. "Over."

"All right, *Mira Flores*, I've got a surf patrol boat in that area, just north of the pier. You should see him coming to you any moment, over."

"Oh, thank God. I mean...uh...roger that," said Archie as he looked toward the pier.

"That's all right, skipper, we thank God a lot in our line of work," Dispatch said.

Archie saw a white powerboat bearing down on him, throwing a wide bow wave. "Sorry, I'm pretty hyped here. I see a boat coming dead on...guess she's about a 30-footer, over."

"That should be our crew. By the way, my name's Frank. Now tell me what you can about your rescue, over."

Archie regained some of his composure as he looked down at the little girl. Her shivering had increased. He slid further down into the bottom of the boat, pulled her onto his lap and wrapped his arms around her, holding the VHF in one hand. "Roger, Frank. I'm Archie Douglas, and the little girl's name is Shunty."

Shanti was shivering so hard Archie couldn't tell she was also shaking her head at the mispronunciation of her name.

"She started shivering hard just a minute ago, Frank, so I'm holding her close to counter the hypothermia. She seems in one piece...about a four-year-old little girl. But something's not right. She's conscious, awake, but looks glassy-eyed and complains of a headache. She knows her name though, right, honey?"

Shanti didn't respond to the last question, but to her more pressing

14

problem. "C-cold," she said.

"Yeah, honey, I know." Archie realized he still had the mike open and apologized again.

"You're doing great, Archie," Frank said. "Do your best to warm her up. Stand by while I talk to the boat crew."

Archie bent over the little girl, hoping his heat was going into her as much as her chill was going into him. At the same time he watched the lifeguard boat bearing down on him. He noticed how skillfully the operator slipped through the swells, but he feared the wake could sink the tiny *Mira Flores*. Archie willed them to slow down just as the bow wave abated.

The handheld crackled. "OK, Archie, the boys are ready for you. They will take you aboard, stabilize the girl, and get you both back to our dock ASAP. I have an ambulance on the way. Now, getting back to Shunty's condition, was she a swimmer, boater, or fell off the pier? How do you think she got there? Over."

"She is dressed in a...what do you call it...a jogger's warm-up suit and is wearing a new-looking PFD. I put my money on her falling off a boat. She was upwind of the pier when I found her. No way she could have come from the pier. Over."

"Roger that, Archie. Standby." Frank switched channels and called the lifeguard boat. "Chad, Dispatch, over."

"Go ahead Frank," the boat operator said.

Frank repeated Archie's description of Shanti's symptoms and added, "Sounds like the little girl fell off a boat. Better take CO counter measures as well as everything else."

"Roger, we'll put her on oxygen first thing," Chad Gier said. The lifeguards were well aware that carbon monoxide was the most common form of poisoning in the US and boaters were particularly vulnerable in certain circumstances. "Billy," Chad shouted to his crewman, "get the O2 ready. Possible CO poisoning."

"Possible head injury, possible anything," Billy shouted back.

Chad nodded and shrugged. They both knew how vague CO symptoms were. Chad had the *Dolphin* right on top of the *Mira Flores* now and eased the 28-foot boat along the windward side to protect the smaller craft from the swell. Chad was an experienced operator. With the two 357 inboards he could hold the *Dolphin* motionless, backed right down on the surf line, as his crew rescued floundering swimmers. Maneuvering this far from shore in this gentle swell was a piece of cake.

Billy clapped on to the *Mira Flores'* gunnel and pulled her quickly to the *Dolphin's* swim platform as Chad turned gently to starboard to protect the stern from the wind and waves.

Archie noticed the name of the boat and thought of the "fish" that led him to Shanti.

Billy and Chad moved the shivering child carefully onto the rear deck. Archie scrambled aboard himself and fastened the skiff's painter to a cleat. They could make her more secure for towing in a minute. First the girl had to be stabilized.

Billy toweled off her face. "Got a headache, hon'?" he asked her.

Shanti nodded.

Billy said, "This will help you feel better" as he slipped the oxygen mask on, explaining to her gently what he was doing as he went. He could see she was wearing shorts under the warm-up suit. He took off the one-piece suit, her shoes, socks, and T-shirt, and wrapped her up in one fluffy towel, then dried her face and hair with another. He checked the temperature in the heated hypothermia bag, tossed the wet towels aside and eased the bag around her, finally zipping her in. Then he began checking her vision, blood pressure, and the rest of the emergency response protocol.

Archie admired the way Billy worked quickly and gently over the little girl. Archie was trembling now too but could tell his body was far from hypothermic.

Chad noticed that Archie held the coffee he'd been given in both hands to steady it. Frank had told him Archie seemed like an old salt. Now that Chad saw the tiny boat up close, he marveled at what the old gentleman had done.

"Mr. Douglas, do you think you could hold her steady on this course and speed for a minute while I secure the skiff for a fast run into port?"

"Ooch, I'd be happy to do anything to help. Chad, the centerboard is held down with a clip," Archie said over his shoulder as he slid behind the wheel and Chad scurried to the stern. Chad quickly furled and secured the sail and brought the tiller into the bottom of the wherry. When he pulled the heavy cast-iron centerboard he realized how Archie could sail such a small boat in unprotected waters. He thought of running a tow line from the Samson post to the *Mira Flores,* bow but instead decided they could make better time if he slid her aboard. He draped a towel on the swim platform and pulled the skiff aboard as far as she would go, lashed her down, and hurried back to the controls.

"All right, here we go," he said as he eased the throttles forward. The big inboards responded.

On the fast run back to the marina, Chad guided the *Dolphin* with casual ease through the swells and troughs now quartering astern.

"Nice boat," Archie said.

"She gets the job done," Chad replied as he steered with one hand and held his mike with the other. "Dispatch, this is lifeguard boat 22 reporting, over."

"Wait one, Chad," Frank replied.

"Frank must be having a busy day," Chad said.

"This is so much fun," Danielle said as the *Cobra* flew over the swells, giving her the butterfly stomach she loved when they went weightless. She looked back to see how Shanti was enjoying it, and her happiness turned to the worst kind of panic. At first she couldn't speak, couldn't breathe, couldn't believe what she saw and didn't want to. She gripped Summer's arm so hard it hurt. "Summer, Summer, Shanti...."

Summer turned, saw the look in Danielle's face, followed her gaze, and immediately screamed, "Primo! Shanti's not in the boat!"

Primo looked back in disbelief, then anger as he quickly pulled back the throttle and brought the boat to a stop. Danielle stumbled to the stern looking frantically about and calling Shanti's name over and over.

"She was there just a minute ago," Summer said.

Primo turned the boat around and began retracing their course. "We'll go back the way we came. Only we'll have to go slow."

The two women stood precariously on the seat, holding onto the windshield. Danielle was crying and shaking; she couldn't see clearly. Summer tried to comfort her and at the same time keep a lookout. As soon as they were settled into this search mode, Primo called the Coast Guard.

After a minute or two the *Dolphin*'s radio crackled. "Dispatch to lifeguard boat 22. Chad, this is Frank, over."

"Frank, we have the little girl, Mr. Douglas, and his skiff on board. We're on our run for the Del Sur dock, ETA seven minutes, over."

"Roger sea rescue. Chad, is the little girl conscious? Over."

"She is conscious, but Billy says her responses seem a little slow, over."

"I think I may have found the boat she fell off. Ask her if her name is Shanti Jackson; mother's name Danielle, over."

By now Billy, who was good with kids, had a pretty good rapport going with the little girl. She nodded and even smiled a little when he pronounced her name properly.

"OK, Chad, I'll have the ambulance at the dock and probably the mother too when you pull in, over and out."

"Great."

"Chad, I like the way you boys do business." Archie said.

"Well, we do this all the time. But you should get a medal for what you did today in that tiny skiff."

Archie hunched over his coffee, feeling embarrassed and proud at the same time.

"You know, we do ride-alongs," Chad continued. "If you ever want to come out for a shift with me on surf patrol, give me a call." Chad handed Archie his card. "My phone number is on the bottom of the card there."

"Yes, definitely; you'll be hearing from me."

"This is Santa Monica Lifeguard Dispatch calling the *Cobra*, over."

Primo keyed the mike, "Go ahead, over."

"We have your little girl, Shanti Jackson, on a lifeguard boat headed to the dock at Marina del Sur, ETA six minutes from now. Confirm the girl's mother is aboard and request you meet them at the dock, over."

"Is that ever good news," Primo said into the mike, smiling weakly at Danielle.

"Is she OK? Is she hurt? How is she?" Danielle asked, still shaking.

"Uh, the mother wants to know how she is," Primo said.

Frank was used to boaters not following radio protocol, especially under stress; he didn't miss a beat carrying on with the conversation. "Shanti is conscious and oriented. Is she normally talkative or quiet? Over."

"Quiet at first with strangers, and then she will talk your ear off," Frank heard Danielle say and Primo repeat.

"Well, the lifeguards say she is still in a quiet phase. We are taking her to Santa Monica General for further assessment and would like the mother to attend. Captain, can you get your boat to the Del Sur lifeguard dock as soon as possible? Over."

"Uh, yeah, sure," Primo said into the mike.

At the same time Frank could hear another woman's shrill voice in the background saying, "Go, Primo, just go!"

Chad noticed that Archie continued to shiver all the way in. *It could be post-traumatic shock*, he thought. He mildly proposed that maybe Archie could go along to the hospital to keep the little girl company. He figured the old salt would balk at any suggestion he needed attention himself. Archie agreed to go and when they reached the dock, Chad alerted the medics that it wouldn't be a bad idea to give Archie a quick exam and keep him around for observation for a while.

They put Archie up front with the driver and were loading Shanti's gurney when the *Cobra* cut around the corner and whipped up to the dock. Chad helped fend them off and tie them up. He picked out the dazzling dark-haired woman who looked more like Shanti than the cute blond and said, "Ma'am, are you the girl's mother?"

"Yes?" Danielle said expecting the worst.

"You can ride to hospital in the back there with your daughter and the paramedic," Chad said as he held out his hand to help Danielle onto the dock. Chad led her to the ambulance and introduced her to Edgar Flores, who was busy getting Shanti secured. He quickly helped Danielle up next to Shanti. Edgar pulled the oxygen mask off for a few seconds so they could talk.

"Oh darling," Danielle said as she fought down her own panic, "are you OK? I'm with you now. I'll stay with you, sweetheart."

"Pardner," Shanti said.

Summer and Primo were standing at the back of the ambulance looking in. "Is she OK? Danielle?" Summer said in a pleading voice.

"I don't know. She's in one piece. She wants her horse. Can you look in the back of the boat? Better bring the cat too," Danielle said to Summer.

Summer ran back to the boat and saw Chad holding the stuffed horse. "It was stuck under the rear cleat," he said as he held it out to her.

Summer came back with both stuffed animals just as the driver was closing the back doors. The ambulance pulled away, siren blaring.

Chad walked up to Primo and Summer. "You folks don't mind if I ask you a few questions, do you?"

They both shook their heads.

"Was there any time when the girl could have breathed exhaust fumes? Say, like idling at the dock? We are particularly concerned about carbon-monoxide poisoning."

The attending ER physician, Dr. Ahmed Jihad Hazim, moved quietly through the closed curtain into Shanti's cubicle. "Mrs. Jackson?" he said in his gentle bedside voice.

"Yes?" Danielle looked through swollen eyes at yet another white coat.

"I'm Dr. Hazim, the attending physician. I'll be in charge of Shanti's treatment. How is she getting on?" The question was quite ordinary, but Hazim's soothing, reassuring tone had an effect on Danielle.

"She seems to be resting quietly, Doctor but she..." More tears. "She isn't herself. I'm so worried, Doctor."

"We are going to help her get well, Mrs. Jackson; completely well."

Dr. Hazim handed Danielle a fistful of fresh tissues and held out the wastebasket for the used ones. Hazim was a fine doctor: well liked by the staff, unflappable in a crisis, and especially good at the doctor-patient relationship. The ER at Santa Monica was the kind of work environment where everybody had a nickname. It eased the extreme pressure that often came upon them. One of the admitting nurses picked up on Doctor Hazim's middle name and started calling him "Doctor Jihad." The name stuck, and soon most of the staff used it, out of earshot of the patients. of course. Doctor Hazim took the name as a sign of acceptance and received it good-naturedly, spinning it into "the one who wages holy war on sickness." His spin stuck, too.

However, for all his strengths, he had one weakness: beautiful women. Danielle, even in her tear-stained disheveled state, was all a man could ask for in that department. Hazim could hardly take his eyes off her, and it took a good deal of willpower to stay on task.

"I have the results back from the bloodwork, Mrs. Jackson." He glanced at the girl in the hospital bed for a moment and said, "Shanti, the nurses told me you were very brave when they were here earlier."

Shanti looked over the plastic oxygen mask at Doctor Hazim and said nothing. By now she knew no one could understand her with it on. She liked the soothing sound of his voice, however, and was interested in his stethoscope.

"Mrs. Jackson, could we take a short walk together? There's a treatment regime for Shanti I would like to discuss with you, and it would be easier to explain if we could go to that area of the hospital. It's just down the hall."

"I don't want to leave Shanti alone," Danielle said, taking Shanti's free hand in both of hers."

"Of course you don't, nor should you," he assured her. "How about I ask a nurse to stay with her? We will be away just a few minutes."

"OK," Danielle whispered.

Doctor Hazim stuck his head out of the curtain. "Katie, could you come here for a moment?"

Katie Piorek, in her third year of nurse's training and already well on her way to becoming a competent caregiver, was especially good with kids. "Yes, Doctor, how can I help?"

Hazim pulled the curtain back to let her into the cubicle. "Could you stay with Shanti for a few minutes while I take Mrs. Jackson down to the hyperbaric chamber to explain our treatment plan to her?"

"I would love to stay with Shanti," Katie said in a way that was both enthusiastic and comforting. She moved to the little girl's bedside and gave Pardner a squeeze. She patted Danielle's arm. "You go on. We'll be fine."

Katie's sincere kindness produced another gush of tears as Danielle got up. "I'll be right back, honey," Danielle said in a tiny voice as she paused at the curtain. Looking back she could see that Katie was talking with Shanti about Pardner.

Dr. Hazim had already organized his thoughts. He would start with the good news, slip the bad news in the middle, and finish with the promise of successful treatment, which in this case was completely true. He got them headed down the hall toward the hyperbaric room and began his summary. "Shanti seems unhurt from the fall off the speedboat. There are no broken bones, no lacerations—no apparent injuries of any kind. Her vital signs are good, and we foresee a complete recovery."

"Oh, thank you, Doctor. That is wonderful news." More tears flowed at the first good news Danielle had heard in hours.

"However, in order to completely recover, Shanti will have to undergo a painless course of treatment."

"Treatment? I thought you said she was fine."

"She is well in every way but one. Shanti is suffering from mild carbon-monoxide poisoning."

Danielle's hands involuntarily covered her mouth, her eyes went large, and she stopped walking.

"Do not despair, Mrs. Jackson. The malady is completely treatable. We have the best equipment for it and, thanks to her rescuers, we have early intervention. All factors point to an excellent prognosis. May we resume our walk?"

"I'm sorry Doctor. It's just, she is so important to me," Danielle said, falling into step and breathing again.

"Of course she is, of course she is. Now, as I was saying, the lifeguards confirmed that there was a time in your recent boat trip when she could have been exposed to carbon monoxide. At any rate, the bloodwork was conclusive." While Doctor Hazim carried on through the clinical protocol, another part of his mind was consumed with how strikingly beautiful Danielle was. He found himself saying, "I give you my personal assurance you will receive the best possible care...I mean, of course, your daughter will." Dr. Hazim stopped in front of a closed door. "Ah, here we are."

The name over the door read HYPERBARIC TREATMENT.

Dr. Hazim, well into his presentation now, thought it best to get to the meat of it and then field Danielle's questions. "As I was saying, the state-of-the-art treatment for carbon-monoxide poisoning is the hyperbaric chamber. It is completely safe, painless, and has no side effects other than popping of the ears when the pressure changes. The chamber was developed for deep-sea divers to safely equalize pressure on the surface after a deep dive."

"Shanti and I have seen that on the Nature Channel."

"Excellent, excellent. Perhaps we can present it to her that way—make it more familiar and at the same time an adventure."

"Well, she is adventurous all right...too much so for her own good sometimes. But how does it help carbon-monoxide poisoning?"

"You are reading my mind, Mrs. Jackson," Doctor Hazim said, unable to hide his pleasure of being with this extravagantly beautiful and—at first impression—quick-witted woman. He liked beautiful women, but the combination of beauty and intelligence made him weak in the knees. "I was about to say that the problem we face with CO poisoning is twofold. One, of course, is that in high doses, it is fatal. We can already rule that out," he said quickly, holding up his hands in a double-stop sign to her anticipated concern. "Thanks to her timely rescue, the lifeguard's immediate use of oxygen, and her probable mild exposure. The second problem, which we do have, however, is if the carbon-monoxide molecules are not completely, as it were, driven out of the blood and body tissues, delayed neurological damage can occur. The hyperbaric chamber is by far the best way to do that."

At this point, Dr. Hazim held the door open for the two of them to enter. When she passed close by, the smell of sandalwood wafted over him and his legs turned to jelly. He held the door with one hand and gestured toward the chamber with the other, "This treatment allows the patient to breathe 100 percent pure oxygen while lying inside the pressurized chamber."

"It's just like the one on the nature show—only bigger," Danielle said.

The chamber was a royal blue cylinder about 15 feet long and 7 feet in diameter with a door in one end big enough to wheel a gurney inside. *It looked very heavy, to withstand the pressure*, Danielle thought. The outside was studded with boxes and gauges of various sizes and shapes.

"Precisely the same," said Doctor Hazim, realizing this was going to be easy, and liking Danielle more and more. In fact he was beginning to wish he had met her outside of the strict intimacy taboos of the doctor-patient relationship. As attractive as she was, it wasn't worth losing his hard-earned status as a board-certified physician in the great state of California. Doctor Hazim's career was well established. He had visitation rights at SMG and a thriving private practice just down the street. He had inherited it from old Doc McFarland, who had taken him on seven years ago and then retired four years after that. Hazim had done well building up the practice on skill, hard work, and an excellent way with patients, especially women patients. It didn't hurt that he had movie-star good looks. But no, he wasn't going to risk losing all.

To extinguish further fantasy about her, he focused his visual attention on the chamber, a sobering sight. "Mrs. Jackson, the treatments are ninety minutes daily, five days a week."

"For how many days or weeks?" Danielle asked.

"That depends on the patient's recovery rate. As soon as the lab determines there is no more CO in her system, she is done. I imagine with a mild case like this we're looking at less than 20 treatments." He anticipated her concern about the little girl holding out for so long. "It won't be so bad. A nurse trained in hyperbaric medicine will be with Shanti at all times; you can chat with her through this portal and the sound system and, oh yes, this model comes with a TV so she can watch her favorite videos."

"Oh, that will make a big difference. Shanti loves to watch movies."

"There you have it: the best method for reversing the effects of carbon-monoxide poisoning ready for Shanti's first treatment."

"You want to get started right away?"

"Yes. Just as soon as you sign the release, we'll bring her down for her first treatment," Hazim said, handing her the clipboard with another form to sign.

Minutes later, back at Shanti's room, Danielle swept up beside Katie and, in the most positive tone she could muster said, "Shanti, you are about to have a big adventure."

Shanti took her mom's hand. "What, Mama?" she asked through the mask.

As Archie entered the ER, one of the nurses who had taken care of him after the car accident saw him in the hall. "Archie, you bad boy; you must be hangin' with the wrong crowd."

"Ha, ha, ha, Laurae. Yeah, it's rough out there," he said as he waved and followed the EMT into an examining room. Filling out the forms took longer than the examination. But waiting his turn took the longest. Well before they got to him, his pulse had returned to normal and all the shaking had subsided. The ER doc checked him out and was primarily concerned about his previous injuries. Archie admitted his ribs hurt more, and the doc wasn't impressed with his story of how they got strained. In the end the doc said Archie was fine and could go.

He asked at the desk if he could see Shanti, the little girl he had rescued. Archie was a deacon at Westside Community Church and often did hospital visitation at Santa Monica General. The nurse he approached at the desk remembered him from previous visits. "Sure, no problem, Mr. Douglas. Come on. I'll take you over."

Archie's spirits lifted as they walked along. He loved children and already felt attached to the little girl he had pulled from the sea just a few hours earlier.

He arrived just as Dr. Hazim, Danielle, and Katie, the nurse, were wheeling Shanti down the hall for her first hyperbaric treatment.

"Mrs. Jackson?" Archie started to introduce himself, but as soon as Danielle saw him she grabbed his arm and pulled him to Shanti's side.

"Shanti, look who's here! It's Mr. Douglas, the man who rescued you."

Dr. Hazim and Katie smiled as Archie bent over the little girl. "Hi Shanti. How you doin', girl?" Archie asked, smiling down at her.

Katie had pulled the oxygen mask off for a moment so the two could have a word. Shanti looked Archie in the eye, held up her stuffed horse, and said, "Pardner."

"Ooch, awe!" said Archie. "So this is your Pardner. Ha, ha, ha!" He was happy that the little girl still had spunk after all she had been through.

Katie put the mask back on, and they resumed their walk down the hall. Archie explained how he mistook himself as Pardner and how Shanti must have thought he was a goof. Danielle said that she figured Pardner was the reason Shanti fell in. The adults discussed her condition as they walked down the hall. When they arrived at the chamber and turned Shanti over to Lois, the hyperbaric nurse, Dr. Hazim, and Katie congratulated him on the sea rescue.

Hazim said, "Your quick intervention may have saved this little girl's life."

"Well, it was providence, Doc—me being in the right place at the right time. Totally a God thing as far as I'm concerned," Archie said, shaking the doctor's hand.

"Yes," Dr. Hazim said. "What other satisfactory explanation is there? Now, if you will excuse me, Mrs. Jackson, you are in the most capable hands with Lois...."

Inside the chamber Shanti settled in to watch one of her favorite movies and said her ears were fine when Nurse Lois asked her. She found the chamber interesting but still didn't feel well enough to get excited. She did like it a lot that she could have the mask off, however, and watching a TV in the ceiling was a new experience.

Outside the chamber Danielle wanted to hear all the details of how Archie had rescued Shanti. Of course Archie, used to telling sea stories, described the action in great detail, pausing from time to time to explain nautical terms. When the story got to the ambulance, Danielle slipped her arm through Archie's and gave him a side-to-side hug. "Oh Mister Douglas, how can I ever repay you for saving my little girl?"

As she was hugging Archie, he looked up. A man in the hall was peering through the window.

"Go right in," Nurse Katie told the man.

"Here's Shanti's dad," Danielle told Archie. "He will want to meet you."

Upon hearing the news about his daughter, Tom Jackson had dropped everything at the lab and sprinted across the UCL.A. campus to his parking space. The traffic in Westwood was always bad, but today it was near gridlock. Tom was a seismologist developing earthquake-resistant building designs with Bill Bixby, a structural engineer. The two of them worked in a dingy back room at the UCL.A. School of Engineering and Applied Sciences. Often the 405 was backed up this time of day. He decided to take Wilshire straight west instead of the 405 to the 10.

Tom was a practicing Catholic. After stewing through the first few stoplights, he remembered to pray. He prayed desperately. At the next light, he asked for help from St. Anne, the patron saint of little girls. He always included her in his prayers for Shanti. At the next light he asked Jesus to heal her. Danielle had been vague in her communication, only saying Shanti wasn't herself. At the next stoplight he prayed the "Our Father" and in this way he arrived at Santa Monica General more or less in his right mind.

Upon racing into the ER, Tom identified himself. Katie, who happened to be near the desk, came over when she heard him asking for Shanti. "Mr. Jackson, come with me. I'll take you to your little girl straight away."

"Tom, oh Tommie," Danielle said, embracing him.

Tom felt an ache inside when she held him close. He was still in love with her, but this wasn't the time to go into all that. He pulled back. "How is she? Where is she?" he asked as he and Danielle held each other's arms.

"She's going to be OK. She practically is already. Look in here," Danielle said, turning to the chamber's viewing porthole.

Tom looked in. Shanti's little face was right on the other side.

"She's watching *Mary Poppins*," Danielle said.

The nurse explained she was getting a hyperbaric oxygen treatment for carbon-monoxide poisoning.

"So this how they do it," Tom replied. "How bad is it?"

"The doctor said it was a mild case," Danielle answered.

Tom was torn between chatting with Shanti and finding out how she was from Danielle. After her first happy greeting, however, Shanti resolved his dilemma, wanting to get on with *Mary Poppins*.

Danielle answered all of Tom's questions with detailed descriptions. She seemed to understand thoroughly what was going on. For her part, repeating the treatment and positive prognosis to Tom calmed her own fears as if for the first time her heart heard the good news. When she got to the part about the importance of Shanti's timely rescue, she reached out to Archie and introduced him as "Archie Douglas, the man who saved our little girl."

Tom grabbed Archie's hand and shook it vigorously. "Thank you, thank you, Mr. Douglas. How can we ever repay you?"

"Well, seeing her here still full of spunk and knowing she will recover completely is the best reward for me," Archie said as he looked through the window at Shanti. "Would it be OK if I look in on her from time to time? I spent some time here a few weeks ago myself, and I know how boring it can get. Having a visitor can really cheer you up." Archie had taken one of his Westside Deacon cards out of his wallet and handed it to Danielle. "I sometimes do hospital visitation with the pastors from our church, so I know the protocol with kids, to have a nurse or family member present and all. Here's Pastor Jim's phone number at the church office. He can give you a reference about me. Oh, and please call me Archie. Mr. Douglas makes me feel geriatric."

"Oh Archie, that would be sweet of you," Danielle said, squeezing his arm again. "But you don't have to...."

"No, I want to. You know that thing about when you save somebody's life you, uh, feel connected to them. Shanti is the first person I have ever rescued. I headed off a few suicides and abortions when I was a therapist, but this is different."

"That would be great, Archie," Danielle said.

"How did you end up in hospital?" Tom asked.

2

"Would'st thou," so the helmsman answered,
"learn the secret of the sea?
Only those who brave its dangers,
comprehend its mystery!"
HENRY WADSWORTH LONGFELLOW

At 67, Archie Douglas was in hospital for the first time in his life. "Cracked ribs and various lacerations" was Doctor Delson's diagnosis. It didn't matter which way Archie turned or even if he held his breath, everything hurt. On top of the pain was deep humiliation. As he lay in his bed, unable to sleep, he obsessively replayed the accident, trying to find a way to make it not totally his fault.

He was driving to the grocery store, actually the Venice Food Co-op. Archie had begun shopping at the co-op in Seattle; it had sheep and goat cheeses and other products that didn't set off Luella's food allergies. They had also grown to savor specialty items, not available at the regular supermarkets. Archie was delighted when he found a co-op in Venice, not far from his Marina del Sur condo. Archie usually went straight from the marina to the store, necessitating a stop and a left turn at the co-op corner.

But that day he had made a trip to the post office first. That meant he approached the co-op parking lot from a different direction—instead of turning at the corner he went straight through. He was in a hurry; he planned to sail that afternoon. He was also preoccupied because his daughter, Bets, had just called to tell him her husband, Mark, was so hobbled with stiffness in his joints he couldn't keep up with Janie, Archie's two-and-a half year-old granddaughter. They were afraid it might be rheumatoid arthritis that had so crippled Mark's dad and—

Kaboom! Archie's Volvo was T-boned in the co-op intersection just 40 yards from his destination. The airbags and seat belts saved both drivers, and fortunately there were no other passengers. But both cars were seriously damaged. Archie was pretty banged up and a little dizzy right after the accident; the paramedics insisted he go to hospital. He had been in for three days now for tests and observation, and so far everything looked like he was going to recover. The worst seemed to be a couple of cracked ribs. It took longer to heal at this point in life, Dr. Delson had reminded him.

His next replay of the accident was broken when his friend Sonny Milan entered the room. "Hey Arch, how are you this morning?"

"I wish I could say better, Sonny, but still the same. It's good to see you, though. The boredom is the worst part of being here now."

Since the accident, Sonny had come to visit every morning right after Buck's workout at the beach. Sonny would tell Archie all about the border collie's feats that morning catching the Frisbee; how he was a great dog if he got worked every day and an impossible one without it. Archie tried to keep his mind on the conversation, but nothing Sonny said distracted him from the pain in his ribs. Soon Sonny ran out of news and the friends sat in silence, a silence that would have been comfortable for both of them if it weren't for Archie's injuries.

Archie began to ponder the history of their friendship. The two had met at a grief support group held in a bungalow across the alley from Sonny's place in Venice. Archie had found the small group of men through a flier tacked up on the co-op bulletin board. One of his pastors had suggested he try a support group and this one was only five minutes away. These thoughts catapulted Archie into a memory that did make him forget about his pain....

Bill, the support group leader and a retired schoolteacher with eyes that always looked sad, said, "Why don't we go around the group tonight and share how our spouses died. I think we have been together long enough to trust each other with this, but as usual you can pass if you don't feel ready to talk about it. Let's go around this way." The first two men reported briefly their wives died of cancer and heart failure, respectively.

Then it came to Sonny. He seemed reluctant to talk at first, but once he got started he had a lot to say. "Anna and I ranched in Northern Nevada. She loved the scenery—painted a fair amount of it. She was an oil painter, well known in the San Francisco art world. Maybe you've seen some of her work—she went by her maiden name, Anna Mikela Chorlinka."

One of the guys said, when it came to his turn later, that he owned one of Anna's oils. The rules were no cross talk when somebody was sharing.

"Anyway," Sonny continued, "she died after a fall from a horse during a cattle drive—head injury." He paused, waiting to regain his composure before he went on. "After that, I couldn't go on ranching. I sold out and moved to the coast, just across the alley, in fact. I had some dirt-cheap desert land on the outskirts of Vegas and about that same time the developers needed more land for subdivisions, so I sold that off too. I'll never have to work again, but I'd give it all back to have her still with me." Sonny turned and looked at Archie, indicating he was finished.

It was Archie's turn. Before Sonny had shared, Archie had decided to pass, but he couldn't now that Sonny had been so open. "It's hard for me to talk about Luella's death." Archie put his head down, searching for the words. "Luella"...he faltered..."Luella was murdered."

One of the men gasped as Archie faltered again. "Murdered in the Gulf Islands...on a sailing trip. That's all I can share right now."

"That's OK, Archie, we have all the time you need," Bill said….

Archie's mind popped back now to the hospital room and the pain in his ribs. Sonny was resting his right hand on the bar at the foot of the bed. Sonny was one of the most powerful men Archie had ever met. He was only five-eight but what strength. Sonny had grown up on the Lazy M and had the kind of power and endurance that comes from a lifetime of hard work.

Archie looked at his own hands, soft from years of office work; Sonny's were tough as saddle leather. That wasn't the only difference in the two men. Aside from the bonding similarity of the tragic loss of their wives, and their commitment to their children, Sonny and Archie were about as different as two men could be. Comparing these differences kept Archie's mind off his aching ribs a little longer. First there was their appearance. Archie was of average height, build, and strength; Sonny was short and powerfully built. Archie had the dark hair—now graying—and fair complexion common to the Douglas clan; Sonny's olive complexion was deeply tanned. Neither man would say he was handsome, but women generally found them attractive—something Archie took no advantage of because of his Christian values. He found it hard not to inwardly criticize his friend for his opposite approach with women now that he was a widower.

In terms of personalities, Archie was cautious, analytical, and liked routine. Sonny was adventurous, intuitive, and liked spontaneity. After Luella's death, Archie had moved south to be closer to his children and grandchildren. Buck was the only living thing Sonny knew when he came to Venice—his kids all lived up north in Nevada and San Francisco. Even so, Archie smiled as he thought of Sonny's dedication to his family, and their frequent visits.

Sonny Milan was a third-generation Italian-American and a lapsed Catholic. Archie's ancestors were Scottish, but he had been unable to trace his family tree past a homestead in western Pennsylvania in the early 1800s. Archie was a Protestant evangelical and very active in his church. Archie had found out about Sonny's spiritual life—or lack of it—at the launching of Sonny's new Bay Liner. Sonny's grandson, Mike, backed Grandpa's Land Rover too far down the boat ramp into about two and a half feet of salt water. The tail pipe went under and, before Mike reacted, the engine stalled.

"Mother Mary, have mercy!" Sonny muttered.

Archie produced an old, slightly frayed dock line he always had along and doubled it from his Volvo to the Land Rover. He towed the Rover, boat, and trailer back up the ramp a few feet. "So, Sonny, are you a Catholic?" he asked when the excitement died down.

"I was raised Catholic."

Archie knew what that meant. "So you don't go to mass anymore."

"Naw, I don't have any use for it, Arch. It's fine that you're a believer and all and my mother is still devout, but not me."...

Archie's reminiscence was interrupted when another visitor popped his head in the hospital room door. "Hi, Arch, how you doing?"

"Hi, Jimmy! Come in and meet my friend Sonny Milan. Sonny, this is my pastor, Jim Mitchell."

Jim and Sonny shook hands, and Sonny winced a little.

"Sonny, is that tennis elbow acting up again?" Archie said, gritting his teeth as he pushed himself up in bed.

"Yeah," Sonny said. "That dog is going to be the death of me."

"Sonny here has a border collie he taught to catch the Frisbee," Archie explained to a smiling Pastor Jim. "The dog works him so hard he has inflamed ligaments in his elbow from the reps."

"I had to teach myself to throw it with both hands," Sonny said.

"You know," Jimmy said, "My Uncle Bob had one of those dogs when he lived in cattle country. Every winter he would go up the ridge behind his house to cut a small fir for their Christmas tree. He always took the dog with him wherever he went, but one time when he called the dog to go home with the tree, Scooter was gone. Well, he called and waited as long as he could, but you know how early it gets dark in December, so all he could do was drag the tree down the hill and go home. The next morning he was back up there looking for his dog at the crack of dawn. As he got near the spot where he lost him, he looked up and saw Scooter driving 40 head of cattle toward him through the woods."

Jimmy's story triggered one from Sonny about Buck that was equally noteworthy, but Archie noticed Sonny avoided telling Jim about his lifelong experience in cattle ranching.

Sonny finished his story, said he had to go, and quickly moved to the door. "I'll be back the same time tomorrow, Arch."

"Thanks, Sonny. It means a lot."

After Sonny left, Pastor Jim moved the chair a little closer and sat down. "How did you two guys get to be friends?" Jim asked.

"We met in a grief support group two years ago," Archie said.

"He lost his wife too?"

"Yeah, in a ranching accident."

"Wow, that's tough. Is he a believer?"

"Lapsed Catholic."

"Hmm, which makes it harder, I imagine."

"He seems to be getting through it."

"So how are the ribs today, Arch?"

"Not good Jimmy, but I decided to ease off the pain killers; they just make me goofy and don't really touch the pain anyway."

"So you're going cold turkey."

"Yes, you could say that. So how are you doing?"

Jimmy was senior pastor at Westside Community Church, a large, seeker-friendly church in West L.A., and Archie was his friend and mentor. As Jim talked, Archie thought how good it was of him to spend so much time away from his busy schedule. Yet Archie knew by now their meetings were just as stimulating for his friend as they were for him. True to form, Jim was getting animated, having drifted onto their favorite topic—Augustine…on the double knowledge. "So I said to him, we can only truly know ourselves when we know God, and we can only truly know God when we know ourselves," Jimmy said.

"Just in the last few months, maybe since I got back from Italy," Archie responded, "I've had a new sense of peace, even through this mess. I have a feeling it isn't going away. I'm even able to have some peace about being a man who needs to pray for forgiveness every day."

"You know, when Luther was in seminary, he went to confession about five times a day before he figured out the whole 'grace alone' thing," Jimmy said. "It was so bad, a priest finally told him, go away!"

"Man, that sounds like Monty Python."

"Run away, run away!" Jim said quickly, in a high voice.

All of Archie's aches hurt worse when he laughed.

"Sorry, sorry," Jim said, involuntarily imitating Archie's scrunched-up face.

Archie steadied himself and carried on. "What's different for me now is I'm able to live with two opposite dimensions of myself at the same time: the part that's dedicated to God and the part that isn't. You know, when I was younger I could get carried away in worship or whatever, and completely forget about my dark side. Or I could get caught up in temptation and forget completely about God. Now I seem to be able to be aware of both my brokenness and God's goodness, and it's giving me a lot of peace."

As soon as he said this, Archie regretted it. He had overstated it, he knew. Of course he still forgot about his love for God and sinned. Of course he wasn't perfect. And what about all the obsessing he had been doing about the accident? But something had changed in his soul in Assisi, and he did feel more inner peace—not so conflicted—and he wanted to share that with Jimmy. Still he regretted his exaggeration because he knew from experience the Lord never let him get away with it. He feared he would be tested on this one if he didn't make it right with Jim.

But before Archie could clarify, Jimmy set off on a lengthy description of three scholars he was reading who were from completely different backgrounds: Greek Orthodox, Catholic, and Protestant. They agreed on the central importance of the double knowledge and the tremendous life-changing impact it had on the soul over time. Archie hadn't heard of any of them, but was delighted to see his friend so excited. Jimmy was a deep thinker and a passionate believer. *Maybe that's why I like him so much*, Archie thought.

Archie had started mentoring Jim when he was a younger, associate pastor at a church in Seattle. When Jim said he was trying to overcome a gambling addiction, Archie had volunteered his services. It was old stuff for Archie, being a psychotherapist by profession, and he was able to point Jim in the right direction. The rest was done by Jim's sincerity and his close encounter with God at a healing conference. Yet Jimmy was still grateful after all these years and was very happy when Archie followed him to Westside.

But since Jim's initial problem had been dealt with, mentor seemed a less accurate description of their relationship than friend. Over the years Jim had proved he wasn't lacking in wisdom, and Archie often sought his advice. Still, Archie knew how important a confidant was to a senior pastor, who can so easily become isolated from any relationship where he can be real and vulnerable.

Archie followed Jim's animated telling of the three theologians' like-mindedness with a personal memory. "You know, Jim, your Catholic and Protestant theologians' agreeing on something reminds me of an amazing conference I went to in New Mexico years ago. Five hundred people with healing ministries—therapists, medical doctors, pastors, and priests—together for five days. There were Catholics and Protestants, monks and lay people. Not only that, the local bishop had given a special dispensation so we could all have communion together. The presence of God was amazing every time we got together. You were either laughing or crying. It was just amazing."

"God can't resist showing up whenever He sees unity happening in His church," Jim said, and off they went on the unity theme.

Soon it was time for their visit to end and Archie thanked Jim for coming.

"I'll stop by again in a few days, Archie."

"You still have time for hospital visitation with all the rest?"

"I always have time to visit you."

"Well, call first because I may be out of here."

"All right, let's pray together, and then I have to go." It was only after Jim left that Archie realized he had forgotten to tell Jim about the exaggeration; he had left himself in a vulnerable position. Lying there, not long after Jim had left, Archie's thoughts about the accident started again: *how could I have missed the red light!*

Archie tried to stop obsessing. He began practicing the presence of God. The thoughts stopped for a moment. Then he remembered what God had said to him in Assisi, *"You have to let go of the responsibilities you have taken on and focus on me."*

"If I hadn't been worrying about Mark, I would have seen the red light," he mumbled to himself. "Ooch, I'm at it again." Once more he tried to turn his obsessing mind from the accident to practicing the presence. He began repeating the name of Jesus with each inhalation. He let go of the self-recrimination with every exhalation, and focused on God's imminent presence in the space between the breaths. After several backtracks his mind finally quieted. Then it dropped into a memory of his closest encounter with God.

He had been counseling at a non-denominational church in Seattle where he had hooked up with a great referral network: a lay, inner-healing ministry. They all sent him the cases over their heads. One of them was an aircraft engineer from Ballard who was having marriage problems and a lot of self-doubt. He remembered how—what was his name? Frank?—how much Frank benefited from prayer. Archie would pray with him at the end of each session.

On one occasion, after a major breakthrough with a lot of tears, Frank said God had really been talking to him about his issues, but also told him to do something. "What was that?" Archie asked.

"He says I'm supposed to take you with me to the Spiritual Warfare conference in Anaheim."

"Really, ah, you know, I would love to go, but things are a little tight financially right now."

"No, you don't understand. I'm supposed to take you, pay your airfare, hotel room, and conference fee—the whole nine yards."

"Ooch, I can't let you do that. That would be a bundle."

"Now Archie, you're not going to put old Frank in a position where he disobeys the Lord are you?"

"Uh, I'll pray about it, talk it over with Luella, and let you know next visit."

"Great!" Frank said.

"You're going to like it here, Arch. Marcie and I stayed here last year for a golf holiday," Frank said as they entered the hotel.

"You have to try their Chicken Caesar," Marcie chimed in.

The Bay Water was plush, but as soon as Archie identified himself, the perky receptionist said, "I'm so sorry! Your room's been double-booked somehow, and the other guest has already checked in. With the conference on, we are completely sold out."

Frank and Marcie, horrified at the mixup, started to protest. But Archie really didn't mind; he was too amazed at being in Anaheim in February—first the conference and then two nights with his oldest girl, Betsy, at UCL.A. He was happy to move to a hotel down the street. It was not plush, but the rooms were clean and he liked the Vietnamese cooking smells coming down the hall. He decided to make the best of being isolated from the other conference goers; he would make these four days a time of turning inward, of seeking God's presence and direction. He studied his Bible for an hour before bed, made a general confession, and went to sleep practicing the presence of God. In these ways he prepared his soul for the conference in the morning.

However, nothing prepared him for what happened next. He awoke from a sound sleep in the semi-darkness of the hotel room. He remembered seeing the time—2:37 AM. But what really stunned him was that he awoke sobbing…tears streamed down his face. The crying had begun while he was asleep, he realized, and continued now that he was awake. He was weeping because God was talking to him. It wasn't an audible voice, but it seemed so loud and distinct in his head. He couldn't say exactly how he knew it was God, but he knew for sure it was. He felt powerful waves of love surge through him. At the same time he was gripped with fear. He also had the sense that what He was saying was extremely important.

Archie grabbed a pad and pen he kept at his bedside and wrote as fast as he could. His hand was shaking so much he could barely read his writing later. Also, from time to time God's words pierced his heart so gravely that he would break down completely and be unable to write. This went on for about 20 minutes. God talked in such a gentle tone about things he had done wrong and in the same way about things he had done right. God knew the most intimate details, the most inward thoughts, some of which had never clearly formed before in Archie's conscious mind, yet he knew them to be completely true. God knew everything about him and Archie waited for the ax to fall, the judgment to come, but it never did.

Instead God shifted to the future, in the same, gentle, loving tone: *You are about to be a part of something truly great in the Kingdom. Something so awesome that people will say, "I have never seen anything like this before." Surely, I say to you, not many days hence, the day of the Lord will come and all will be filled with awe.*

That was the end of the message. Later Archie thought he might have asked what the great thing he was going to do was. But he realized he was too undone at the time to think to ask anything and, even if he had thought to ask, he was sure that he was too afraid to say anything.

It was so intense to feel so loved and at the same time so afraid. Afterward he had no doubt about the prophecy; he felt unworthy, but also excited and sure that he was going to be a part of something amazing.

But that was 20 years ago and now, looking back, he wasn't sure if it had happened. He had helped a lot of people in counseling and had been present on many occasions when the Lord healed someone. He was sure many of them would say that was really great. But he wasn't sure he had ever done the thing that the Lord was talking about in Anaheim.

Archie decided to bring it up at Jimmy's next visit. Jimmy would help him sort it out. That thought made him smile, and he was able to roll over on his good side and sleep for a while.

Danielle and Shanti Jackson lived in a low-rent area of Venice on the edge of the Oakwood black community. Their neighbors were a mix of ethnic backgrounds—mostly Chicano, a few blacks, Sikhs, and Vietnamese. There were also a good number of counterculture people like Danielle, who rented an apartment over a garage on a back alley. Her landlady, Mildred Johnson, was in her 90s, and appeared financially independent. At least Mildred wasn't too concerned about the rent, and that was good for Danielle who was often late with it. Mildred never seemed to mind and was delighted to have the young woman and child around. Danielle valued the older woman's support and care.

Danielle, like Mildred, didn't care much about money. She did care about her spiritual path, about Shanti, and about Munchie. Munchie was a large, old, black-and-tan mongrel dog. Munchie had a terrier beard and eyebrows, but she was way too big to be a terrier. That combination made people chuckle at first sight of her. Another thing that Danielle cared about was that her house was a few blocks from the beach, and that was where she, Shanti, and Munchie were headed. Danielle's long, fluid strides were interrupted intermittently by Shanti's tug on her arm. The four-year-old skipped or trotted happily at her side, slowing for various distractions—a beetle, a dandelion, a particularly interesting crack in the sidewalk—which Danielle accepted. She would not let Shanti come to a complete stop, however; that much purposeful movement toward their goal she held onto. Danielle saw the late-model sports car slow down and then speed up again out of the corner of her eye, but paid little attention.

Primo looked hard at the striking woman. He glanced at the little girl and dog, then looked hard again at the woman. He wanted her. He wanted her for himself, but even more for his business. A more insightful man might have recognized that Danielle was full of life and that's what attracted Primo so strongly. But he could never have said why he wanted her, nor had he ever thought much about why other things attracted him. Primo wasn't much good at introspection, but he was good at getting what he wanted. From past experience with "hippie chicks," he knew they needed to be approached in a certain way.

He flipped open his cell phone and drove on.

"*Mande.*"

"Chucho, how fast can you be at *Lucky's Pizza* on Ocean?"

"*Dos minutos.*"

"Good. Meet me there, I'm in the BMW."

Chucho knew Primo could speak Spanish fluently. Chucho thought that Primo always talked to him in English to remind him of his lower social standing. It was something Chucho resented, but he also sensed insecurity on Primo's part in it. Perhaps he could exploit it later, he thought.

Chucho, formerly known as Aurillio Rodriguez, was an illegal immigrant from Mazatlan. As tough as life was here, it was nothing like the grinding poverty he had known in the *colonias*. Before he came north, Chucho had survived by being a foot soldier in the Sinaloa drug-trafficking business.

Primo had guys like Chucho around the neighborhood to run his errands. He paid them a few bucks here and there and everybody was happy, but he relied on Chucho for important jobs. He was loyal, very resourceful, and had quickly become Primo's go-to guy. He could handle anything Primo had for him, even murder.

Chucho slid into the passenger seat while the girl was still a block away. Primo was sure she hadn't seen them; he had stopped in front of a parked delivery van.

"There's a chick walking this way on the other side of the street. I want you to find out where she lives, where she shops. Go through her trash, bring me her mail receipts…you know the drill." Primo shot a hard look at Chucho. "I don't want her to know you are following her. Got it?"

"*Si, Patron.*"

"All right. She's a hippie chick with a little girl, maybe four, and a big, goofy looking dog. Get out, and when you see her, give me a nod. And call me as soon as you have the info."

Chucho got out and immediately nodded.

Just then Primo's cell phone rang. It was a customer. As Primo turned quickly to step on the gas his bad knee hung up, and pain shot through him. He gritted his teeth and cut around the corner, staying out of her line of sight.

Primo had blown his knee in the middle of his senior season at San Diego State. He was good, fast, and liked to hit. He was known as a fearless, slashing runner, willing to stick his head in anywhere. He still had the highlight film at home of the run that won the conference title his junior year. It was a routine off tackle play that should have gone for no gain, but Primo bounced out of the grasp of a 320-pound all-state lineman and shed two more defenders on a 70 yard TD run that won the game and the championship in the dying seconds. He put the video on whenever he needed to pump himself up. He'd had pro scouts looking him over throughout his senior year, but the blown knee had ended all that. He still wondered if the hit was intentional. The sports reporters always attributed the injury to the player injured, never mentioning the fact that it was the blitzing free safety who hit him low just as he planted to cut up field.

His football career was over. The doc said it was the worst knee injury he had ever seen—severed both cruciate ligaments completely and nearly severed the interior collateral. Primo never finished his degree in sociology either, even though he was just a few credits short of graduation. He already knew his way around the neighborhood—supplying friends with marijuana—so when football went south, it wasn't hard to expand his business.

Now he dealt in a lot of product lines. Drugs and gambling were his mainstays, but he also had a sweet connection with the movie industry in Sylmar. You could say he was a talent scout, and that chick had talent. He popped a couple pain killers for the knee and drove on. He had business to take care of.

Archie and Jim were deep in discussion. Archie had gotten the small talk out of the way quickly—he told Jim at the door he was probably getting out tomorrow and then as soon as the how are you feeling today was over, he went right into the Anaheim prophecy.

Jim was fascinated with Archie's account—he loved Holy Ghost stories. "Wow," Jim said. "That's amazing stuff. Why didn't you ever share it with me before?"

"Honestly Jimmy, it never came to mind. We always have so many intense things to talk about. Maybe this memory surfaced for a reason just now. But I want your input. I don't know if I ever did the thing God said I would do, and I don't know what I should do with this."

Archie had written out the prophecy; Jim read it over again.

"You are about to be a part of something truly great in the Kingdom. Something so awesome that people will say, 'I have never seen anything like this before.' Surely, I say to you, not many days hence, the day of the Lord will come and all will be filled with awe."

"OK, sure," Jim said. "Let's see. Of course, 'not many days hence' could mean any length of time in chronological time. Look at the time lag for Isaiah's messianic prophecies."

"Right, good point," Archie said.

"So it's possible that it is still yet to happen. Have you prayed about it? You know, asked God what's up with this time thing and did it already happen or whatever?"

Archie felt embarrassed when he admitted he hadn't ever prayed about the Anaheim prophecy. But at the same time he felt excited and hopeful that prayer would make a difference.

"Well," said Jim, "let's pray into this right now."

Archie bowed his head as Jim prayed. "Father, we ask You to make it clear to Your servant, Archie, what this prophecy is about, whether it has been fulfilled, and if not, then when and how it is going to be fulfilled. Give him signs in the natural, Lord, that will lead him into Your truth. Father, heal him quickly and completely so he can continue serving You in full capacity. In Jesus' name, amen."

Archie thought about calling his friend Sonny to pick him up at the hospital but instead, in a rare moment of spontaneity, decided to take a cab. He had to battle his Scottish nature most of the way home. It was only a few miles from the hospital in Santa Monica to his condo at Marina del Sur. He figured the cab fare would be under 10 dollars and it was. Archie was a funny guy with money. He liked to pinch his pennies, but when it came to tipping cabbies, he liked to go high. He had driven cab a bit himself when he was in college, so he knew how important the tips were. On top of that Bets, his oldest, had worked as a waitress and once added a couple bucks to a tip he had left for a lunch they had together. After that he always tipped 20 percent or more. The cabbie went away happy when Archie dropped a fiver on him for an eight-dollar fare.

Archie loved his condo: on the top floor, plenty of light, plenty of room, and best of all, it looked right down on the marina. He couldn't see his own boats, a Cal 40, and the 14-foot Wherry he had rigged for sailing, but he could see the others coming and going, and it gave him joy. He opened the sliding glass door to the deck to let in the nautical sounds and smells. He had picked up the week's worth of mail from his neighbor, Estelle, who had collected it for him and now plopped in his favorite overstuffed chair in front of the open deck window to sort through it.

There beside the window on the small bookcase were his Patrick O'Brian novels, all 20 of them. He pondered how much he loved the sea and sailing and the O'Brian novels, and then missed Luella his first mate. *She knew how to have fun*, he thought.

But he had too much to do to let himself drift into grief. He pulled the open cardboard box of mail closer. It was easy for Archie to forget things. His memory had always been bad, but it got worse when he entered the "wonder years." There was a benefit to this, however: he could start the 20-novel series over with *Master and Commander* as soon as he had finished *Blue at the Mizzen* and, for the most part, found them fresh.

His "forgetory" had also served him well; as a therapist as he was able to engage with his client's pain in the moment but didn't carry it with him for long. He still marveled at the psychiatric social worker he had known when he was first starting out in Seattle. He was a type A and had a photographic memory. He couldn't forget a thing. He always gave Archie a hard time because Archie didn't work 80-hour weeks, but the social worker burned out completely in three years. The staff psychiatrist put him on anti-depressants, sent him home, and told him he would have to get into another line of work. Archie had chugged through 40 years of listening to people's problems before he decided he had heard enough. Of course, his unreliable memory could cause problems, but he had learned to compensate with a minimalist approach to the details of life. Simplicity and routine were essential.

It was with this approach he sat down to open his mail. He quickly sorted the junk mail from the important stuff and then cut the ends off all the envelopes with scissors. He went through the good mail pile to see what he had besides bills. There was a letter from Jeanie, his youngest, a grad student at UCSD. Her fall term had started well; she liked her classes and had a new guy friend.

"Well, that deserves a phone call," Archie said to himself and put the letter in his shirt pocket so he wouldn't forget to call. He was so proud of his girls.

The next letter was from Tricia Knox, one of the members of the worship team at church, whose day job was working wonders as Pastor Jim's administrative assistant. Archie had been meeting with Jimmy once a week for years and had gotten to know Tricia pretty well through scheduling appointments and doing music together. Archie thought about how cute Tricia was and wondered if her affectionate hugs were any more than Christian love. *Probably Christian charity. Ha ha!*

When the worship team found out Archie had played the mandolin and violin with a psychedelic band in the '70s they insisted he sit in with them. His riffs between verses added color to the simple choruses, but he felt too old to play with the kids. As well it was a lot of work: moving gear, setting up, interminable sound checks, and lengthy practices for a few minutes of actual worship leading every week. He also feared that the 90 to 100 decibels of amplified sound was damaging his hearing. Truth be told, he really didn't like light rock that much. He could play it alright—the little hooks and tags—but he preferred quieter, contemplative music at this point in his life. He was really into Hildegard von Bingen's music. The medieval mystic's contemplative style was a great help in centering on God. Of course Archie also liked sea shanties. The young musicians knew his different tastes in music. They would always respectfully say they liked the songs Archie had on when he had them over for the occasional lunch. For his part, he agreed to play with the band on special occasions like Christmas or whenever they decided to cut a CD.

Archie now opened Tricia's letter, wondering why she would be writing to him.

Dear Archie,

As soon as we heard you were in hospital, we wanted to do something for you. So guess what? We all chipped in and got you a ticket to the Flame of Worship Conference next month.

Archie stopped reading, looked out the window, and groaned before he went on.

> *We are all commuting together in Bill's camper van, and you can lie down and rest in it any time you need to. Anyway, we love you and hope you can come.*
> *Love, Tricia*

There were about 20 other signatures: all the band members, tech support, and their spouses had signed. He was touched, but really didn't want to go.

Immediately he heard Luella's voice: "Oh come on, Archie, it will be fun!"

He quickly, reluctantly determined to go. He realized some time ago he had to take over Luella's initiator role now that she wasn't with him or his world would shrink to nothing. He also knew, as she often pointed out, he hesitated at every new thing. Partly because it disrupted the routine he liked so much and partly because he always feared failure. Archie had done a lot of therapy to become a therapist, and he knew why he hesitated. Archie's father was cold, hypercritical, aggressive, and competitive. Archie's milder, gentle nature got criticized a lot. Nothing he did was ever good enough. So he had become hesitant in starting new things, thinking he wouldn't be able to do them well.

He took a breath. "I can't let my dark side win," he said to himself.

Archie looked at the brochure Tricia had sent along with the registration. It had bios and "hits" from the usual collection of "big name" worship leaders and one name he didn't know, Mark O'Brian, who was evidently well known in the "Taking the Church to the Streets" movement in Ireland. Archie had a vague recollection of something happening in Ireland. He wondered if Mark O'Brian read Patrick O'Brian, Archie's favorite author.

Archie skimmed the brochure with mild interest until he came to the venue: Anaheim Convention Center. A jolt of electricity went up his spine as he flashed back to the Anaheim prophecy given at that same place 20 years ago.

"Ooch," he said to himself as he looked at the map to the Convention center. "Jimmy prays for a sign and *boom*, I get this a few hours later."

Archie said "ooch" and "awe" when he was excited because he had grown up working in his dad's shop around diesel mechanics. By the time he was 12 he knew every swear word in the book and some not in it. When he became a Christian he was determined to clean up his language. It was hard to teach an old dog new tricks, however, and he had many setbacks. The most horrific was the Mother's Day sail with Luella, her elderly and very proper parents, and all three of his girls. His old diesel ran away on him in a stiff breeze. It took him about 10 minutes to get her under control and for that time he wasn't aware of much of anything he said or did.

Luella told him later he was swearing like a sailor. "You said over and over, F— me. F— me."

"Oh no," Archie said, putting his hands to his head.

"Yeah, Dad," his twelve-year-old prosecuting attorney said. "You need to apologize to Granddad and Grandma!"

"Apologize!" said the entire jury in one voice.

The in-laws were very gracious, accepting his apologies. But Archie felt like a fool. It wasn't long after that he got help with the language problem in an unexpected way. He was reading a series of historical novels about his ancestors carrying on in the Scottish borderlands. In the Middle Ages the Douglasses were fierce warriors, constantly at war with England. There even was an Archie Douglas, "Archie the Grim." The author had them saying "ooch" and "awe" whenever they were animated. These exclamations stuck in his psyche and began to replace the profanity.

"Well, it could be coincidence, or it could be God," he said aloud, placing the brochure and the letter in the "needs further attention" pile. He would have to write the dates in his daytimer and on the kitchen calendar. He also made a note to call Tricia to ask her to remind him in case his other memory aids failed and of course to thank her. *Redundancy, redundancy—that's the key in sailing and in life*, he thought.

He plowed through the rest of the mail, paid a few bills, and dropped the junk in the recycling bin. Then he stood out on the deck surveying the marina. After he opened the mail and paid the bills, he always went outside for a while. He was trying to decide how much exercise his old battered body could stand when the phone rang.

It was Sonny. "Hey Arch, I called the hospital but you were gone."

"Yeah. I'm feeling better, and they had completed all their tests and observations, so they let me out."

"How did you get home?" Sonny asked.

"Taxi."

"You paid for a taxi?" Sonny's tone was incredulous.

"Come on now, it was under 10 bucks."

"You know I would have come to get you. I was waiting for your call."

"Yeah, I know, but I came down, the cab was sitting there, and I just got in."

"Wow, Arch, you did something impulsive."

"Everybody says I'm so methodical, but I'm not really."

There was silence on the other end, but Archie could tell that Sonny was laughing. Finally Sonny said, "So, how would you like to go for a little sail around the marina in *Mira Flores?*"

"I don't know how much I can do. You've seen how banged up I am."

"*No problemo*," Sonny said. "I'll do all the work—make ready to sail, work all the lines—and you can just sit by the tiller like Captain Jack."

Archie had some serious concerns about this proposal. Sonny's eagerness reminded him of the first time out with his friend and Sonny's teenage grandson, Mike. With perfect conditions—eight to 10 knots and a small swell—Archie had put Mike on the tiller. They were sailing along nicely when a mini-squall kicked the breeze up to 15 to 20 knots. It took only about 10 minutes to pass over, but the *Dawn Treader* with the 150 percent Genny and full main was suddenly carrying too much canvas. Without the feel of the tiller Archie figured out what was happening too late: being a good sailor she just headed up into irons. Before Archie could get control of the situation other mistakes were made and they ended up hove to with the foresail backed against the main, a bit of an embarrassment, but certainly not a crisis.

"While we're here," Archie said, "let me point out that this is a good way to hold a boat in place with a man overboard."

They both looked at him blankly; he continued to explain how one sail counteracted the other so that the boat wouldn't sail away from the overboard, but would drift at pretty much the same speed and direction as the person in the water.

When Archie solved a problem in seamanship like this with his "crew"—most often Luella—he liked to think through the steps out loud. She also had good input, and between the two of them they got along fine. In this case it was also a way to teach novice sailors how to solve a problem and get everyone on the same page so when he gave the command, they all could work together. Or as Captain Jack Aubrey would say, "Do it handsomely."

However, the moment Archie pointed and said, "See how the foresail sheet is on the wrong side of the mast?" Sonny sprung from the cockpit onto the lee side of the boom, putting himself unnecessarily at risk of being knocked overboard if anything should let go. Then as Archie was saying, "Sonny, never go up the lee side of the boom—always to windward," Sonny grabbed hold of the foresail sheet with both hands. Before Archie could say "one hand for the boat," Sonny manhandled the foresail around the mast.

"Whoa," Archie exclaimed. He knew the kind of brute strength that would take in this kind of wind. At the same time all the things that could have gone wrong with this maneuver spun through his head: loss of a finger, a torn foresail, or Sonny tangled in the sheets and banged about. Or, worst case, Sonny swept overboard when the sail cleared. Then he'd have a heavy man in the water, the boat out of control, and a novice fourteen-year-old on board.

"Ooch," Archie said.

As it was, Sonny got a nasty burn on both palms from paying out the sheet.

When Sonny was back in the cockpit, Archie said, "Well that's one way to solve a problem." He wasn't happy, but he didn't want to say anything to Sonny in front of Mike.

50

He thought about it later on the way in. *The next time I talk Sonny through a problem, I'll have a firm grip on his safety harness.*

Of course, that was two years ago and Sonny had rounded into an able seaman since then. But the problem at the moment was Archie wasn't sure of his own strength if any emergency might arise.

"I'll tell you what—it's about lunch time," Archie said. "Why don't you come on over for a bite and, after lunch, we'll walk down to the *Mira Flores* and see if I'm strong enough to go to sea."

"Ha, ha! That's the spirit, Arch, and don't fix any food. I've got pasta ready to go."

3

The Lord does not subtract
From your allotted days on earth,
Those that you spend on your boat.

Sonny's penne with pesto sauce was over the moon delicious—a perfect homecoming meal for Archie after a week of hospital food. The two old friends caught up on local news and soon were ready to make their way down to the dock.

The main gate was about two blocks away. Since the coastal cloud had lifted, Archie said, "Let's walk." He felt a lot better with the pasta under his belt, and the fresh sea air was wonderful—there was practically no smog this time of year. Both men wore ball caps clipped to their collars, sunglasses, and Archie put on 30 sunscreen.

As they neared the gate, Archie noted the breeze was light. Maybe they could go for a little sail. They walked along the docks to the berth where Archie kept the 40-foot *Dawn Treader* and the 14-foot *Mira Flores*. Archie stored the *Mira Flores* out of the water on planks that ran diagonally across a forward corner of his slip. But today she was bobbing on her painter next to the dock with her mast stepped and the heavy centerboard locked in place.

"Well, Sonny, I guess you were pretty sure I would want to go out," Archie said.

"Yep. This is the best thing for you, Arch."

Normally, Archie worked just as hard as Sonny making ready to sail, but today he was happy to just sit on the dock and watch his friend. His vision habitually swept the rigging on the two boats in front of him. The *Dawn Treader*, a classic Cal 40, was Archie's second. The first *Dawn Treader* remained in 120 feet of water at the bottom of

Active Pass. The name came from C.S. Lewis' ship that sailed to the end of the world. Archie's family loved Lewis's *Narnia* stories. They used to read them aloud at bath time, with Luella doing most of the reading. It was the easiest way to get the kids in and out of the tub and into bed. The reading reinforced good behavior and was such a wonderful time of family togetherness.

Archie had bought his second Cal 40 used, for a bargain price, but, like all boaters, had put a lot of money into her. The Cal 40 was a flat out great sailor. The production boat first came to fame in 1965 when *Psyche* took overall honors in the Transpac. It's a rare thing for a mass production boat to win any race, but the 2,225 mile Los Angeles to Hawaii race was quite a passage. Not only that, *Psyche* was the first of four Cal 40s to take the overall Transpac honors. The *Dawn Treader* sailed true to her class: weatherly, fast, good on any point of sail, and with the right amount of canvas, she liked a good blow.

Archie's gaze returned to the tiny *Mira Flores*. He had wanted to do something to pull himself out of the depths of grief for Luella after a year of it and settled on building a wooden boat. He had always wanted to do it and found a kit for a beautiful, 14-foot Wherry with a classic hourglass stern. It was put together with stitch and glue, epoxy, fiberglass, and really fine wood. Everything came pre-cut, and the salesman assured Archie that even a guy without any particular boat building skill could do it.

The *Mia Flores* had turned out all right. Of course there were some real mess-ups, but nothing structural and nothing that hindered her making way through the water. It took him most of a year to build the hull and rig it for rowing. Then for one season he used it as a tender for the *Dawn Treader*. He also rowed it about the marina for exercise. Sonny had a good rowing dingy too, and the two of them got their miles in three times a week.

Then Archie broke down and bought the sail kit and hardware and took another five months rigging the boat to sail. He thought with a few modifications she would sail pretty good. He wanted something that would be stiff in a good blow, so he asked a guy in Venice who fabricated garden ornaments to make a duplicate centerboard out of cast iron instead of mahogany. The cast-iron board was a little narrower, resulting in less drag, but it weighed over 60 pounds. Archie reasoned that the leveraged weight underwater would stiffen her up and his theory proved out. Of course, it was too heavy to pull up anywhere but at the dock, so he just left it in downwind. He glassed in a metal plate for the iron to sit on with a snap-lock to hold it in place if she capsized. Then he built two shallow, open boxes near the mast and added two flat, rectangular, polyurethane water containers for additional ballast when he sailed her alone. He adjusted the amount of water ballast by trial and error. Finally he boxed in the bow and stern seats and filled them with styrofoam so that even with the heavy centerboard in and the boat submerged to the gunnels, she wouldn't sink. In the end he had a good little sailor that booted right along with the 60-squarefoot sprit sail that came with the kit.

He had been sailing her for about four months in the marina and had planned to test her in the swell beyond the break water the very day of his car accident. The naming of the *Mira Flores* was quite another story....

Archie had Tommy, his three-year-old grandson, over for the day while his mom was at a conference. She worked part-time for a big pharmaceutical firm and shared childcare with her part-time schoolteacher husband. Tommy saw Grandma's picture while they were eating their quesadillas for lunch and wanted to know where Grandma was. Since all the children and grandchildren lived in Southern California—Archie and Luella had planned to move south one day together and had bought a plot a few years ago in the area even though they still lived in Seattle—Archie explained she was buried nearby. Tommy wanted to go see. Archie hadn't been to the cemetery for a while so they drove over. Hand in hand, they walked from the car to the plot.

"This is it, Tommy. This is where Grandma took her final rest. Of course, her soul is with God in heaven," Archie said.

"With the angels, Granpy?"

"Yes, with the angels, darling."

"Granpy, look—flowers!"

Archie looked. Tiny white daisies were growing in the grass on the plot. They were scattered all around the area, but definitely seemed more concentrated here. Archie's lip quivered as he thought how Luella was such a gardener and how it was just like God to put flowers here for her.

"Are you crying, Granpy?" Tommy asked, looking up into his face.

"Yeah, honey, I guess I am." Archie knelt beside the little boy. "I'm remembering how much your grandma loved growing things, especially flowers."

"Did you really love Grandma, Granpy?"

"Yes, I did, sweetie, and I love you." Archie gave the boy a hug. "I only wish you could have known her; she was so good with children."

When Archie told the story at his grief support group, Miguel Armado translated Tommy's exclamation: "*Mira Flores!*"

At last Archie had the name for his Wherry, which was under construction at the time….

"Come on, Arch," Sonny said. Sonny had made ready to sail, put on his life jacket, and eased himself onto the forward bench, facing backwards, ready to row them out into the channel. He held the boat firmly against the dock, waiting for Archie to get in. Archie had his life jacket on too. He preferred the regular jackets to the inflatable because they gave a nice padding to lean back against. True, the inflatables looked sharper and were more comfortable on a hot day, but the price difference was intolerable.

Archie, sitting on the dock, gingerly swung his feet into the boat. He got a grip on the transom with his left hand and on the gunnel with his right and pivoted himself onto the back seat without too much discomfort. "Well, that wasn't so bad," he said, adjusting his ball cap. "All right boys, cast off your lines and man the sweeps."

"Aye, Captain," Sonny rejoined. Both men delighted in the Aubrey-Maturin stories that Archie had insisted Sonny read if he was going to become an able-bodied seaman. So whenever the two men got on the water, they couldn't help imagining it was 1810, and instead of rowing out into the Marina del Sur channel, they were rowing out to the *Surprise* in Mahone. Heroic Jack Aubrey rowed to his square-rigger to weigh anchor and sail away to another adventure in the Med.

"I wonder if she would carry a small bow chaser," Archie said as he eyed the bow over Sonny's shoulder.

"A small one for sure," Sonny replied. "She'd be perfect for a cutting out expedition."

The *Mira Flores* made her way easily through the narrow channel between the familiar sail and powerboats along Archie's dock, gliding a long way, Archie thought, after each of Sonny's powerful pulls. Archie noticed a couple of things going on in the neighborhood. *Blackguard* had her mainsail off. *Getting new canvas*, Archie thought. Miller Post, the live-aboard owner of the *Last Chance* was teak oiling her bright work again. That meant he would have a case of beer on board. Sure enough, he stopped to take a long pull just as the Wherry reached his stern.

"Hey Arch, Sonny, how you doin?"

"Just fine, Miller, just fine. Don't fall in putting that oil on," Sonny said.

"Now come on, when did I ever? You boys goin' out?"

Like many powerboaters, Miller hardly ever moved his own boat and was quite interested when somebody else did.

"Yeah, just going for a little turn," Sonny said. "Arch here got banged up in a car accident and this is his first time out."

"You don't have to tell everyone, Sonny," Archie hissed at the same time as Miller yelled back, "Hey have a good one!" Both men waved to Miller as they moved out of easy conversation range.

"Sorry, Arch. I didn't know you wanted it kept quiet," Sonny said, chuckling.

"Awe," said Archie.

A moment later he forgot his embarrassment as they popped out from the lee of *Intrepid,* a 60-foot, three-decker powerboat moored at the end of the dock. The steady, light, off-shore breeze lifted Archie's spirits as little else could.

"Ship your sweeps, mate. We can make way now," Archie said, as he eased himself down into the bottom of the boat, keeping one hand on the tiller.

Sonny boated the oars and quickly slipped the square knot on the line that held the sprit sail to the mast. He let the little sail out on the port side, got down off the seat and hardened the sheet. The little boat heeled, stiffened, and accelerated. Archie was pleased with the seamanlike way Sonny had handled the rigging and the ballast—Sonny himself being the ballast. Sonny had rounded into an able seaman, and Archie pondered how much easier it was to work with someone perhaps overly quick than someone overly slow.

He chuckled to himself, remembering Tyler, one of Bets' ex-boyfriends, who wanted to go for a sail. Bets knew how sometimes you have to be quick at sea and had warned Archie about Tyler. But Archie loved the idea of having an able-bodied young man to help him sail the Cal 40. Archie could single-hand her with foresail only, but she was a real performance boat with the main up.

Archie and Tyler were about 10 minutes out of the harbor with full sails rigged for a ten-knot breeze when a rain squall cut toward them at a fast clip. Archie figured it would be blowing over 30 knots in about 10 minutes. He didn't want to get soaked at the start of their outing, so he suggested they put on the rain gear. Archie got his on in about two minutes, but the squall went over with Tyler still below complaining of how the boat heeled suddenly. Archie took measures so the 40 didn't get knocked down, but he was relieved when Bets moved on and married Mark, a man who could get things done in a timely manner. As for Sonny, Archie had hit the "lose not a moment" jackpot.

Away from the bigger boats lining the sides of the fairway, Archie was able to get a read on the wind. They were on a beam reach with the wind a bit astern.

"Try easing that sheet a little," Archie said.

Sonny let out a few inches of line, and the *Mira Flores* picked up the slightest speed and flattened out a little.

"Good, good, that's about right," Archie said.

They sailed smartly down the middle of the wide channel between all the boats. Archie was quickly caught up in the wind on the sail, pressure on the tiller, and himself in the middle. *I love this*, he thought for the thousandth time. He saw the same satisfied expression on Sonny's face that he felt in his own heart.

"Why do we love it so, Sonny?" he asked.

"*La dolce vita*," Sonny replied, holding his face up to the warmth of the winter sun.

Primo stood in front of his favorite Mexican takeout eating a "Macho Burrito." He had just moved 10 kilos of marijuana when his cell phone rang again. "Yeah," he answered.

"*Tengo informacion sobre la Hippy Chica.*" It was Chucho.

Pretty quick work, Primo thought. "Did she see you, or notice anything?"

"No, patron."

"All right, all right." Primo drove the few blocks to where Chucho waited.

Primo took the manila envelope Chucho handed him and pulled out a couple of twenties for Chucho while he held half the burrito in his mouth.

"Gracias, patron," Chucho said but couldn't understand Primo's reply around the burrito. "What did you say, *patron*?" Chucho could speak English but didn't like the way Primo made fun of his accent.

Primo took the burrito out of his mouth with one hand as he put the Beamer in gear with the other. "Watch her and call me when she goes out. I want to meet her in a public place."

"*Si patron.*" Chucho put the money in his pocket and noticed Primo's eager look as the Beamer pulled away. *Who wouldn't be eager with a woman like that?* he thought.

Primo drove straight to his place on the beach. He needed a little space to sort through the papers and the cut-glass dining room table in front of the sea-view window would do fine. He saw that his Mexican house keeper had tidied up. He spread out the papers.

"Let's see," he said to himself, "Danielle Jackson, 271 Gardena." He went through the rest of the papers and learned that: Danielle got mail from Tom Jackson, who lived in West L.A.. *Probably her ex*, he thought. A diagram Chucho had drawn showed she lived over a garage on the back alley. "Hmmm, she shops at the Venice Food Co-op," he said to himself, finding the co-op newsletter and receipts.

Best of all, he found a credit card number on a discarded bill. He called a hacker who was one of his drug clients and asked him to do a background check on Danielle. An hour later he knew she was born in Korea, her father was US Army, her mother Korean, and knew when they all moved to the States. She had a valid California driver's license but neither owned nor maintained a vehicle. Primo upgraded his first impression from "hippie chick" to "hardcore hippie chick." *Hardcore,* he repeated to himself. Then he noted she had been at Long Beach State for two years.

He thought maybe he just got lucky and called Summer, one of his girls. "Hey babe, it's Primo."

"Oh hi, got some work for me?"

"Could be...maybe something in the recruiting line. Didn't you spend some time at Long Beach State?"

"Primo, I got a fine arts degree from the Beach," she said, not trying to hide her irritation.

"Sorry," he said. "In Drama, right?"

"Right."

"Well look, did you ever know a chick named Danielle Jackson...no, her name then would have been Blakely."

"Yeah, seems familiar. What did she look like?"

"A real knockout—tall, willowy, dark hair, a killer figure, has that Eurasian look. She's half Korean."

"Yeah, I knew her. She hung out with a geeky science guy all the time...uh, what was his name?"

"Tom Jackson?" Primo read off one of the letters.

"Yeah, Tommie. I think they got married and he transferred to UCL.A.."

"Look—I'm going to recruit her for the movie business. I want you to be ready to meet her in the next couple of days. I want the meet to look accidental. She shops at the co-op, so that could work as a place where she won't suspect anything. You bump into her and then introduce her to me. You're an actress. You can do this."

"Sure, I'm up for it." Summer knew there was money in anything you did for Primo Carreta and she always needed money.

"All right. I'll give you a heads-up and pick you up when it's on."

"Sure Primo, I'll be ready. Just one thing, though. She pronounces it *Danielle,* like Dante...not the way you said it."

Archie got back to his condo in time for supper. Sonny said he would get the *Mira Flores* up on her boards and promised to stow all the gear. He sent Archie home to take a painkiller. Archie's spirits were greatly lifted by the little sailing trip inside the marina's main channel, but he had forgotten to bring along the ibuprofen, and his cracked ribs were hurting. In the bathroom he looked for his glasses—he didn't want to take the wrong pills. He patted all his pockets and found the letter from Jeanie. He carried it around while he looked for his glasses, fearing that if he put it down he would forget about it. Finally he found his glasses in the windbreaker pocket in the hall closet. He remembered taking them off when the spray started coming over the side. The big powerboats always kicked up some chop even when they stayed below the five-mile-an-hour speed limit. He had a lot of leftovers in the freezer compartment and put some stew in the microwave.

Soon he settled at the breakfast nook table with his dinner, Jeanie's letter, and the portable phone. He got her on the third ring. "Hi, hon. How are you?"

"Hi, Dad! How are *you* is the question?"

"Well, they let me out of hospital this morning, and I'm feeling pretty good. Ribs hurt a bit, but at my age something always hurts."

"Awe, I wish I could be there to take care of you. Are you sure you can manage?"

"Yeah, I'm doing OK. It sure beats being in hospital, and I've got friends and neighbors to help if I need it. Sonny stopped by for lunch, and uh, we uh—"

"You two didn't go sailing, did you?"

"We didn't go out beyond the breakwater; just a little flat water sail in the *Mira Flores.*"

"Dad, you should be more careful, just out of hospital."

60

"Well, it really picked up my spirits, you know, and Sonny did all the work. I just rode along like Captain Aubrey on the quarterdeck."

Archie's girls knew how much he loved sailing, but they weren't too sure about this new tiny boat, the *Mira Flores*. "Well, as long as you stay in the marina, I guess you'll be safe."

"Safer than driving! Ha, ha! Anyhow I called about your letter. Sounds like you're enjoying your courses this term."

"Yeah, I'm getting more into the subjects I really like, but the workload is increasing too. You know how it goes."

"Yes, I do. And you've got a new guy friend?"

"Yeah. Michael Lamb is his name. He's a grad student too. We met one Saturday night at The Inn."

Archie remembered that The Inn was a Christian coffeehouse in La Jolla near the campus. "So, he's a Christian?"

"Yes, Dad, he is."

"So are you two, you know, going out?"

"Well, we aren't dating yet, but he seems pretty interested."

"You like him?"

"I do. We seem to have a lot in common, and he's got a great sense of humor; makes me laugh a lot."

"That's a good thing."

"Daddy, I'm so glad you called, but I have to go. I'm supposed to meet Michael at the library in a few minutes."

"Oh, good, good. Well, God bless you, honey. I'll be praying for you, and I'll add Michael to my prayer list."

"OK, Papa, and I'm praying for you. Have you told Bets and Julie you're home?"

"I'll call them as soon as we're off the phone."

"Bye Dad, I love you."

"Bye sweetheart, love you too."

Archie left a message about his recovery on Julie's machine and had a nice chat with Bets, his oldest. They were all relieved that he was out of hospital and had no serious injuries. Bets wanted to bring him home to her house in Orange County while he recovered, but he assured her he was doing fine where he was.

Archie had a lot to be thankful for that night as he said his prayers.

He was thankful that no one was seriously injured in the crash, thankful that he was out of the hospital, thankful for his good friend Sonny and for their sail in the *Mira Flores* today, and thankful that he had such a wonderful family. He lay in bed hoping he could fall asleep. But after an hour of finding no comfortable position, he took one of the sleeping pills they had given him at the hospital. His last thought before he drifted off was a memory of Luella. He missed her.

Primo tapped the steering wheel with his championship ring and was cursing under his breath when Summer finally got in. She was always late, and he always got steamed. He checked his watch; they could still beat Danielle to the co-op if she wasn't walking too fast. He threw the BMW in first and shot out of the loading zone where he had been waiting.

Primo sped the few blocks to their destination. He turned the Beamer into the co-op parking lot, cursing the speed bumps as he carefully maneuvered the low-slung sports car over them. As soon as he parked, he jumped out of the car, but Summer didn't move from her seat; she was checking her makeup in the vanity mirror.

"Summer, get out of the car!" he growled, fighting to control his temper. The combined aggravation of the speed bumps and Summer's dawdling was pushing him over the edge. At the same time he realized it wouldn't do to have her upset at the first encounter with Danielle.

"Primo, I really don't see why we have to be in there before she is and..."

"Summer get out of the car and just...just..." He really wanted to tell her off but instead flapped his arms up and down in a jerky motion and turned red in the face.

"Don't have a coronary, Primo. Look—I'm out of the car, OK?"

"Fine, fine. Let's just take a breath and start shopping," he said, forcing a smile. He was impressed when she finally emerged.

Summer had a fresh, perky look that Primo thought would perfectly compliment Danielle's smoldering beauty. The short shorts made her long tanned legs look even longer. The halter top covered by a loose filmy blouse showed off her figure without making her look like a streetwalker and the makeup and hair were not overdone either. In spite of his frustration with her, Primo had to admit she looked good. But Summer was a little nervous and giving Primo the gears for pressurizing her gave her an outlet. She was still giving him an earful about it when they got to the shopping carts.

"Summer, it's showtime. Now you're a professional actress, and you know how to put all this behind you."

Flattery worked where pressure had failed, and Summer quickly became her usual cheery self. Primo and Summer were putting some tortilla chips in their cart when he saw Danielle enter the store.

"There she is," Primo said.

"Hey, she still looks good, and you didn't tell me she has a little girl. What a cutie pie!"

Danielle was pushing a cart with one hand and holding Shanti's hand with the other. Clearly Shanti wanted to ride in the cart. Actually, she wanted her mom to drive the cart crazily with her in it—she liked wild rides. Danielle bent over to speak to Shanti, and when she did, Primo clamped on to Summer's elbow and started to maneuver. "You're getting to be a big girl now, Shanti. You can walk alongside your mom. We'll go to the rides at the park after we shop."

A few minutes later Primo and Summer approached the pair while Danielle was studying a label in the vitamin section.

"Hey, I know you," Summer said, smiling broadly. "Danielle!"

"Summer Jensen!"

They gave each other a little hug while they both talked at once.

"Is this your little girl?"

"Yes, Shanti this is Summer, a girl I knew in college."

"Hi. Oh my goodness, you are so cute. You must be so proud of her. She looks just like you!"

"Yes, she is getting to be a big girl now," Danielle said, looking down at Shanti. "So is this your boyfriend?" Danielle whispered to Summer.

Primo had been standing aside, beaming his winner smile and trying to follow the machine-gun-paced conversation. He wore his best Hawaiian surfer shirt—the one with faded blue floral pattern on a lighter background, knee shorts, and tire sandals. He looked very fit and he knew the scar on his knee often got a sympathetic response from the ladies that he thought turned into admiration when he told his football story.

"Oh, no," Summer said, "sorry! This is Primo Carreta, my agent. Primo, this is Danielle...well, is it Jackson now or Blakely?"

"It's Jackson. Primo, glad to meet you," Danielle said, extending her hand.

"Glad to meet you, Danielle." Primo wrapped his big paw around her slender fingers.

"If Primo is your agent, does that mean you're an actress?"

"Yeah," Summer said in a valley-girl voice. "Well, nothing big. You probably haven't seen any of the stuff I've done—mostly B movies, that sort of thing, but it sure pays the bills," Summer said giving Primo a quick look. "So what happened in your life? You and Tommie got married and..."

"Married and had Shanti, but he lives in West L.A. now and works at UCL.A. in seismology research. He takes Shanti every other weekend and stops by, usually once a week."

"So where do you live?"

"Oh, just a couple blocks from here."

"No kidding. I live in Ocean Park; we're practically neighbors. Let's exchange numbers and get together for lunch sometime."

Danielle's attention was now on Shanti, who was kicking an empty box quite a way down the aisle. She wrote the number, returned the ballpoint to Summer, and scurried after the four-year-old.

In the checkout line with Summer, Primo could see Danielle had moved to the back of the store. "That was a good start," he said to Summer under his breath. Now I want you two to really get tight, before you bring up any details of the movie business. Then emphasize the easy money and—"

"I'm not a two year old, Primo. Let me handle it."

"Fine, fine," he said as his cell phone rang. It was a drug deal. Primo always tried to think positive about his business deals. He repeated, "Envision success and it will come to you," a phrase he liked from one of the self-help books he had read.

Summer recruiting Danielle was going just the way he pictured it. Once the friendship was solid, the new girl would be easy to bring along. Primo believed that hippie chicks were easily influenced by their peers. Their choices were all a matter of who they happened to be with at the moment. To them all choices were equally valid. *So why not do a porn movie? Summer likes the work and likes the easy money.* Primo cast a vision for Danielle that couldn't miss. For Primo it was all about making money, a lot of money. He dropped Summer off at her place and shot away in the silver Beamer to wrap up the waiting drug deal.

Danielle welcomed Summer's interest in renewing their friendship, but not for the reasons than Primo imagined. Primo was right that friends meant a lot to Danielle, but what he didn't realize was how hard it was to keep up adult friendships and adult activities while taking care of a four-year-old.

Summer seemed perfectly happy to watch cartoons instead of adult programs and laughed at the same jokes that amused Shanti. She was particularly taken by the beautiful little girl—perhaps even more beautiful than her mother; but unlike Summer, whose profession constantly called her attention to her physical appearance, Shanti was completely unaware and unconcerned about how she looked. That fresh lack of self-awareness gave a breath of life to Summer. The recruiting money Primo paid her helped Summer buy groceries until she got paid for the movie she had just finished. But she also sincerely liked Danielle, her beautiful little girl, and the family feeling she had with them.

As well, all three of them liked to hang out at the beach, where they were again today. Shanti liked playing in the sand while the women talked, but best of all she liked the rides at a little kid's park set up in the soft sand near the boardwalk. Summer and Danielle took turns pushing the merry-go-round.

"Shanti likes rides; the wilder the better," Summer said, panting.

"Just like her mother," Danielle said.

Both women took a breather, having grown a little dizzy with so many turns on the merry-go-round.

"You liked rides too?" Summer asked.

"The wilder the better," Danielle said. "Shanti can't wait to go on Indiana Jones at Disneyland. That's my favorite. But she isn't tall enough yet so we do the tea cups until I feel sick."

"Hey, Primo has a speedboat and he likes company when he takes it out. Now that's a wild ride when the swells are big; it's like a roller-coaster. I'll call you next time he asks me; I'm sure you and Shanti can come too."

"Oh, that would be wonderful. Shanti and I like to go down to the marina and look at all the boats, but we've never gone out on one."

"Summer, Summer, push me!" Shanti cried as the disk began to slow.

"Game on," Primo said, when Summer told him about the boat ride. With a couple more calls back and forth they worked it out for the day after tomorrow. Summer would pick up Danielle and Shanti and meet Primo at the *Cobra*. Primo pictured himself with the two girls roaring over the swells: Summer a pert blond and Danielle a willowy brunette with that exotic Asian look. He imagined how his producer would drool over them together. He began working on a stage name for Danielle that would complement "Summer Storm" and that would somehow convey exotic Asian beauty.

4

My boat is so small
And thy sea so big.
Lord, have mercy.
MARINER'S PRAYER

Danielle screwed up her courage and phoned Westside. The receptionist seemed relaxed and friendly and said she had caught Pastor Jim at a good time; she would put her right through.

"Hello, Jim Mitchell, speaking."

"Hello Pastor Mitchell, this is Danielle Jackson calling."

"Oh hi, Danielle. Archie said you would call; he wants me to be a character reference for him."

"Well, I hardly think he needs a character reference, having saved my daughter's life, but he insisted I call you before he would visit Shanti in hospital."

"How is she, Danielle?"

"Dr. Hazim said she's going to be fine, and she seemed pretty much herself last night. But she has to stay in hospital for treatments for carbon-monoxide poisoning. I worry she'll go crazy cooped up like that. She is such a lively child."

"Well, I'm glad to hear she is going to be OK. Archie has the whole church praying for her, you know."

"No, I didn't. That's good, thank you."

"Hey, that's what we do. I think having Archie visit regularly should cheer her up. He is a visiting deacon, on call for hospital visitation two days a month. As well, he was a Christian counselor for years and he is my personal mentor. I give him the highest recommendation, without reservation. Danielle, I can't tell you how much Archie means to me…."

As soon as Danielle finished with Pastor Mitchell, she put a call through to Archie. "Hello, is this Deacon Douglas?" she asked.

"Ha, ha, speaking," Archie answered.

"Hey, why didn't you tell me you were going to have people pray for Shanti? That's sweet of you, Archie."

"Well, I didn't think of it until I got home yesterday. By the time I had the arrangements made, it was pretty late. So you talked to Pastor Jim?"

"Yeah, he thinks you're the greatest."

"OK, good. So I can start the visitation tomorrow if you like."

"That would be fine, Archie."

"Now with this visiting deacon thing I can come anytime, not just visiting hours. So when would be best?"

"Shanti's in the chamber from 10:30 to 12 and she gets up at the crack of dawn. Do you think you could come between nine and ten?"

"Sure, let's try it out tomorrow. There is one more thing you should know, Danielle, about the car accident I had a couple weeks ago. I was totally at fault and lost my license. So my friend Sonny will be driving me. He's a grandpa too and loves kids. He wanted me to ask you if he could stop in with me sometimes—you know, to cheer her up."

"Of course! Shanti will love all the attention."

"Well, if you're going to be there tomorrow morning, I'll introduce Sonny to you. I think you will like him."

"Oh, I'll be there and, Archie, Shanti is up in the children's wing now, room 327."

"That's good. It's so brightly decorated."

"Yes, and Tom has a good health plan so she's in a double room."

"Great! I'll see you there at 9:00 tomorrow."

Sonny was very excited to see the little girl Archie had plucked from the sea. *Perhaps too excited,* Archie thought.

As they entered the hospital parking lot, Archie said, "You can come in, but you have to be on best behavior—no swearing and no sudden movement of any kind."

"Aw, come on, Arch, I know how to act around kids."

"It's not the kids I'm concerned about, Sonny. It's hospital protocol."

Their first visit was going very well. Shanti was definitely more herself and proved to be quite a conversationalist.

Archie's concerns about Sonny's impulsiveness seemed groundless. Late in the hour-long visit Sonny was delighting Shanti and Danielle with a story about Buck, his Frisbee-catching border collie, the smartest dog in the world. As he pulled out his wallet picture of Buck, Archie excused himself and slipped out to the men's room. When he opened the heavy bathroom door to return, he heard shrieks of laughter coming from the direction of Shanti's room. As he approached he could see all the nurses on the ward smiling. Suddenly the head nurse came popping out of 327 just as Archie was reaching for the door.

"Oh, excuse me," she said.

Archie noticed her trim figure, bowed slightly, and said, "Carry on, Nurse."

The moment Archie entered Shanti turned to face him and, with the wildest look in her eye, caught her breath, pointed at Sonny, and shouted, "Dr. Bobo, Dr. Bobo!"

Archie's gaze followed her arm to Sonny, who stood at the foot of the bed. A bright red, plastic ball covered his nose; silver-rimmed sunglasses covered his eyes. He had frizzed the hair at the side of his head. Through a goofy grin he was saying, "Yeth, oh yeth, I am Doctor Bobo, and I am here to examine thith paish-i-ent." At that he shot out his wiggling fingers toward Shanti, who screamed and dived away from his awkward passes.

Archie worried that the racket would disturb other patients. He worried that a nurse would soon come in and shush them. He thought of asking why the head nurse had come in but instead in a lull in the screaming he said, "Danielle, isn't it time for Shanti's treatment?"

"Oh my, so it is, Archie."

"Well then, I'm afraid it's time for the two old guys to leave. Come on, Sonny, let's tidy up here."

"Can you come see me tomorrow?" Shanti asked breathlessly.

Archie glanced at Danielle, who looked pleased and nodded. "I can come," Archie said.

"I have to take care of some business tomorrow," Sonny said. "But I'll come see you later in the week."

"Oh goody," Shanti said.

They completed their good-byes, and Sonny and Archie moved down the hall, past the meaningful looks at the nurses' station. While waiting at the elevator, Archie could hear Shanti and Danielle talking excitedly and giggling.

On the way to the car Archie was trying to think of the most tactful way to ask Sonny to dial it down a little, but Sonny spoke first.

"So, Arch, it's just the little girl you're visiting, hmmm?"

"What do you mean?"

"Come on. Don't play dumb with me. That Danielle is drop-dead gorgeous. Or I suppose you're going to tell me you hadn't noticed."

"Sonny, Sonny, Sonny. There's more to life than beautiful women."

"Aha! See, you *are* attracted to her."

"Sonny, I've just lost some memory—not my sight. But come on: it's Shanti who's cooped up in hospital forever. Danielle doesn't need anything from an old reprobate like me."

Sonny laughed and laughed as he unlocked the SUV and swung behind the wheel.

Once inside the car Archie asked, "So you think we could make these visits regularly?"

"Absolutely. And, like you, my focus is entirely on the girl; for the mother, nothing. Ha, ha!"

"Ooch, awe," Archie said, turning to ease the pain in his ribs when the SUV ran stiffly over a speed bump on the way out of the parking lot. As they neared the marina, Archie decided to just come out with it. After all he and Sonny were close and Sonny would understand. "Sonny, you're still OK with our arrangement of coming in with me a couple times a week and just dropping me off the other days?"

"Hey Arch, I have a life you know. I really don't plan on going to the hospital every day or anything. But it sure was fun today, wasn't it? Did you see the gleam in Shanti's eye? Man, is she a live wire."

Archie was working around to tell Sonny how he was concerned with the racket disturbing the other patients. But he knew to present the positive feedback first. "Yeah, Sonny, it was just great. You know, there is research that laughter actually speeds healing."

"No kidding. So Doctor Bobo is the real deal. Did you know Nancy asked me if I would visit some of the other kids next time and do the Bobo thing?"

"Who's Nancy?"

"Nurse Hollings, the head nurse."

"Really? No, I must have been out of the room. That would be nice."

It wasn't that Archie didn't see the value in Sonny's method; it just wasn't what he was used to in hospital visitation.

Archie's next visit alone to the hospital was quieter and more comforting, he thought. Danielle asked him to tell Shanti the rescue story. Archie loved to tell sea stories and had few that came close to the drama of this one. It took him nearly all of the hour.

Shanti seemed most interested in the dolphin. "How did you know his name was Buddy?"

"Well, I didn't. I just called him Buddy."

"It's a nice name for a dolphin. I saw him when he swam around me."

"Did you? How wonderful."

"Um-hmmm, he bumped me with his nose. Did he talk back when you talked to him?"

"She's seen the dolphin show at Ocean World," Danielle explained, "where they make those clicks into the mike and the trainer tells you what they are saying."

"He didn't say anything I could hear, but he did look right at me for quite a long time. He did tell me something, though, without words.

He told me where you were, Shanti."

After a pause Shanti said, "Do you think he was an angel in disguise?"

"What a remarkable child," Archie said quickly as an aside to a smiling Danielle. "You know, Shanti, it is entirely possible he was an angel. Or maybe God asked Buddy to lead me to you. God can use animals in His plans, you know. There's a whale in the Bible."

"Can you tell me that story?" Shanti asked.

"Yes, I can; I even have a picture book about it at home that I read to my grandchildren. How about I bring it tomorrow?" Archie was pleased that the visits were settling into a pattern.

The next day the reading of the Jonah story went very well, and Archie could tell from her questions that Shanti was an extremely bright child. He remembered that his youngest daughter, Jeanie, was about Shanti's age when Luella started reading the *Narnia* stories to her older sister. Jeanie wouldn't miss a reading and loved every minute of it.

The following day Archie introduced Shanti to *Narnia,* and she too couldn't wait for the next episode.

Archie's deacon duties had brought him to the children's ward a few times before this, but he had never come day after day. By now he was getting to be on a first-name basis with most of the nurses, including the head nurse, Nancy Hollings. He had resolved to make the best of Bobo the Clown's chaos, so on Thursday morning, when Sonny asked him to tell the hospital staff he would be in the next day, Archie did it with equanimity.

"Good morning, Nancy," he said to her at the nurses' station. "Dr Bobo will be coming in with me tomorrow."

"Good morning, Archie," she said, smiling, "that's wonderful. We have selected kids for him to visit who have been in for a long time or who most need a lift."

While they were talking about Sonny's visit, Archie noticed she had her wedding ring on her right hand. He also noticed again what a sweet disposition she had and how fit she looked.

"You do the visitation for Westside, don't you?" she asked.

"Yes, I'm one of their visiting deacons."

"We'll have to talk about our faith sometime. I attend a little Presbyterian church not far from here. Could you tell Danielle we are trying to keep the other bed empty in Shanti's room? She has so many visitors we thought it would be easier for everyone."

"Oh, thanks, Nancy. I'll tell her and, yes, let's talk." Archie chuckled to himself as Nancy excused herself and hurried away to tell the other staff about Dr. Bobo. He decided to let them find out for themselves about setting boundaries for Sonny. Especially in the rooms with multiple patients, shrieks of laughter would make it impossible for others to read or concentrate on anything. That morning Archie, Shanti, and Danielle laughed together in anticipation, imagining what Dr Bobo would be up to the next day.

As Archie had anticipated, Sonny took it farther than anyone had planned. This time he brought along some of his props and visited every room in the ward. When he had covered the children's wing, he headed for the doors to the adult wing, saying they needed some cheering up too. But Nancy headed him off, explaining that was a different department, and walked him back into her territory.

On Saturday, Archie arrived at nine as usual but found Shanti's room empty. He caught up with a weekend casual nurse in the hall and asked her what was up.

"We had to move Shanti's treatment up an hour because there are four smoke inhalation cases in the ER. They will need the chamber throughout the day."

Archie thanked her, wandered down to the treatment room, and found Tom sitting beside the chamber. They greeted each other warmly. Archie waved through the porthole at Shanti, who waved back but quickly returned to her movie.

"Tom, can I buy you a cup of coffee? Mocha Joe's just down the street."

"That would be great," Tom said gratefully. "I've been here since seven. Let me give you some cash to get me a donut or something."

"It's on me, Tom."

When Archie got back with the coffee and sinkers, he and Tom sat on the chairs provided in front of the tank and fell into easy conversation.

"I'm covering for Danielle today and tomorrow so she can have some time off," Tom said through a mouthful of donut. "She has to do laundry and stuff like that. I wish I could have come over during the weekdays to give her a break, but I work during the day. So I come every night after work."

"What line of work are you in?"

"I'm a seismologist at UCL.A.."

"Wow, that sounds interesting. Are you teaching?"

"No, not right now. I'm doing research at applied sciences with a guy named Bill Bixby from engineering. We're refining a contraption that simulates earthquakes so we can test what happens to various structures— buildings, dams, bridges."

"Really...that's fascinating." Like most people in southern California, Archie had more than a casual interest in earthquakes.

"My training is in geology," Tom said, starting another donut, "with a specialization in tectonics."

With a mouthful of donut, Archie shrugged and shook his head.

"Tectonics is the study of bedrock motion," Tom explained, "which builds mountains, creates sedimentary basins, generates volcanoes, and causes earthquakes."

"Ah," Archie said.

"Bill's a structural engineer. The two of us are going for grant money to develop a program that tests structures and then makes building code recommendations to local municipalities. Our department has already done quite a bit of this since the Sylmar Quake in '71. But Bill and I think we can do an even better job. You know, if you're really interested, you could come over to the lab and see what we're up to."

"I'd love to do that."

The two of them got out their DayTimers and arranged to meet the next week. Tom gave Archie careful directions where to park and how to get from the lot to the lab. "Westwood traffic is always heavy so give yourself plenty of time coming and going."

"Will do. What about you, Tom? How far is your commute?" Archie avoided mentioning he couldn't drive.

"It takes me about fifteen minutes from West L.A."

"West L.A. huh?"

"I have a little two-bedroom just south of Wilshire: one room for me and one for Shanti when she comes for the weekends. Where do you live?"

"At Marina del Sur. My condo looks right out on the boats."

"Cool."

"Tom, you and Danielle seem to get along pretty well. How is it that you aren't living together?"

"Oh man, where to start." Tom took the last bite of donut and another sip of coffee and told Archie it was good before he settled into his story. "Danielle and I were both going to Long Beach State. I was in geology and she was in psychology. We met at a mutual friend's birthday party, fell in love, and were very happy at first. After a couple years of study I got more interested in tectonics but Beach's geology department is focused on sedimentary geology. So I put in to transfer to UCL.A., which emphasizes tectonics. I got accepted and got a grant. I told Danielle I wanted to transfer and asked her to marry me. When she said yes, it was the happiest day of my life."

"What's your marital status now?"

"We're still married but legally separated. I'm Catholic, so divorce isn't a good option. Anyway, I don't want a divorce. I know I'm a fool, but I still love her and pray every day we'll get back together."

"Oh no, Tom, I don't think you're a fool at all. I always tried to do everything I could to keep couples together whenever I did marriage counseling. All the studies show most people are unhappier after divorce than they were before."

Archie and Tom paused for a moment as Shanti looked at them through the portal, briefly smiled, and went back to her show.

"Why did you separate?" Archie asked.

"It wasn't my idea, that's for sure. After we moved to Venice,

Danielle decided to go to work, instead of carrying on with her studies. She has an IQ over 130, you know, but she went to work as a waitress in a high-volume restaurant. It did help pay the bills, mind you, but Danielle needs more than that. Then she tried LSD. After that yoga, and from there she got into a whole different way of thinking about reality."

"How do you mean?"

"Well, take science for example. All of a sudden it became a big issue. She started talking about how science was exploiting and polluting the environment—scientific imperialism, she called it. At the same time I was getting excited about how tectonics could improve the quality of life for everyone. Not just in California, but around the world."

"So the two of you started arguing about your calling."

"Yeah, but there was more to it than that. She also started to take exception to my faith. I'm a practicing Catholic." Tom stopped, looked at Archie, and fidgeted with his coffee cup.

Archie gave Tom a sympathetic look, a nod, and an encouraging "um-hmmm."

Tom rallied and went on. "She started calling me an ideologue. She would say stuff like, 'It's intolerant to think that the teachings of the church are right and everybody else is wrong.' When I tried to reason with her, she would say I was using logic to gain power over her... turned it into a male dominance thing. She would say, 'Why hasn't there ever been a woman pope?' "

"So it was the religion thing that eventually killed it."

"Religion, science, woman's liberation—it got so everything became contentious."

"And through it all you felt like an innocent victim."

"Well sort of. I wasn't totally innocent. I got hired to do research right out of undergrad, and I was working on my masters at the same time. I admit I wasn't around much. That became a big issue, too. She started saying things like, 'Why do you even bother to come home at all?' That idea seemed to gain momentum, and it wasn't long before she was saying she needed her own space. It was never a final 'we're through' type of thing, though."

76

"What do you think God wants for the three of you?" Archie asked as he looked through the portal at Shanti.

Tom followed his gaze. "I've been praying that He would reunite us. But to tell the truth, I haven't got much faith for that after all this time."

"You know, it always seems that about the time I've run out of faith God does something to keep me going. Saving Shanti's life is one of the most important things that has happened in my life. But maybe He has even bigger plans."

"What are you saying?"

"God's up to something here. I don't know exactly what, but I know it will be good in the end."

The two men sat in silence for a time, Tom imagining what God might be able to do and Archie working out what his part might be.

"Would it be all right if I joined you in your prayers for God to reunite your family?"

"Yes, of course. Oh please do, Archie, please do."

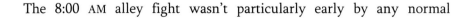

That night Archie was reading Ephesians chapter one and was moved to kneel and pray beside his bed.

"Father, in Your tender mercy You sent Jesus to pay the price for our sins and to show us how to forgive. Through Him You can heal the brokenhearted and make all things new. Father, here are three broken hearts I lift up to You now: Shanti, Danielle, and Tom Jackson. Oh Lord, pour out upon them forgiveness and reconciliation. Heal their marriage and restore their family to an abundance of love and joy in Jesus' mighty name. And Father, in Your good and perfect will, bring Shanti and Danielle to faith in Jesus so that the Lamb who was slain might receive the reward of His suffering. Amen."

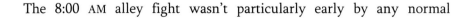

The 8:00 AM alley fight wasn't particularly early by any normal

standard, but Primo had gotten in only hours before and had a massive hangover. The cats knocked over a garbage can lid to add percussion to their yowling.

Primo got up, swearing bitterly. He was tempted to get his piece and start blasting away, but no, blowing his cover would never do. He sat on the edge of the bed, thought he might be sick, and staggered to the bathroom. He had a strict rule to never use his own product as he had seen so many dealers ruin their business that way, so he had quietly passed on the drugs going by at the poker table. But he had no reservations about drinking and there was, as always, plenty to drink. The game usually started mid-afternoon and ended whenever you wanted to leave. Primo's routine was to cash in around midnight as it was quite a drive from Ventura. But last night Primo had some luck along with his usual skill and just couldn't leave the game. He walked away with over 17,000 dollars. *Not chump change,* he thought as he leaned over the toilet bowl.

Primo was a good poker player. He'd picked it up as a way to kill time on away games for San Diego State. Soon after he started playing, he read and committed to memory a book on poker by a professional. That knowledge, a near photographic memory, and a head for numbers gave him a big edge over the amateurs he played with. His memory also served him well in his business: he kept all his accounts in his head, wrote nothing down, left no paper trail. It never occurred to him that his gifts could have served him well in a legitimate business.

The nausea passed. He took three aspirin and went back to bed.

The phone rang. He swore again as he picked up the receiver.

Summer's perky voice made his head pound. "Hi Primo. I didn't expect to get you so early; thought I'd just leave a message. I didn't wake you, did I?"

"Naw, cat fight woke me up a few minutes ago." Primo held his free hand to his pounding head. "What time is it?"

"It's a little after 8:00."

"So what are you calling about?"

"Well, I was thinking we should go up to the hospital today and pay a visit to Shanti. I was just on the phone with Danielle, and she and I are going around 1:00 and I thought it would be good if you came along too."

Primo's hangover didn't affect his clarity about business. It would be bad practice to pass up a chance to salvage this deal after he had put so much time and money into it. "Yeah, I'll go."

"OK," Summer chirped. "Want me and Danielle to pick you up?"

"No, I'll meet you at the hospital at 1:00. What room is she in?"

After he hung up the phone, Primo got up and began his hangover recovery ritual. He mixed a potion in the blender that usually settled his stomach and gave him some energy. He remembered to put his 500-dollar stereo earphones on to dampen the sound before he turned it on. Then he hit the shower for as long as the hot water lasted. He came out with a towel around his hips and began to drink the mixture right out of the blender. He started feeling a little human. As he put on the clothes his maid had laid out for the day, he went back to the excitement of his winning hands. He remembered how he'd suckered the others in on the betting when he had good cards. He felt contempt for the man he had taken most of the money from, "Triple X," a hard-core porn producer and a pretty big fish in cocaine.

"Trip," he said out loud. "Maybe you were a big man with the Hell's Angels, but you sure are a terrible poker player!"

Archie ran into Tom in the hall just outside Shanti's room. "I prayed for your family last night after church," Archie said.

"Thanks Archie. You go on Saturday night?"

"Yeah. At Westside they encourage us old-timers to go at odd times to keep the Sunday morning services open for those who are just starting."

"Interesting. Well, I went to mass at 6:00 this morning and then came straight over."

"Good man, Tom. Look, since it is Sunday and all, I brought along this picture Bible to read to Shanti. My grandchildren really like it. Do you think it's OK if I read her a story from it?"

"Please do," Tom said. "I've been talking Barbie dolls for two solid hours."

At first Shanti seemed disappointed that Archie hadn't brought *The Lion, the Witch, and the Wardrobe,* but she quickly became interested in the story Archie had picked: Paul's shipwreck on the way to Rome. Archie had introduced it to her and Tom as one of his favorites.

As usual, Shanti had lots of questions about the story—one of them being, "Why was Paul going to Rome?"

Archie guessed that Tom had a good answer and gave him a little nod.

"On the one hand he was going there because the Romans were taking him to jail," Tom said. "But on the other hand he was going for God, to start the church in Rome."

As Tom was speaking the door opened slowly and Danielle stepped into the room.

"Mommy," Shanti cried as she jumped off the bed and ran into Danielle's embrace.

"Hi guys," Danielle said between kisses. "How's your morning going?"

"Fine," the men said in unison.

"Summer and Primo are here. They want to say hello and wish you well, Shanti. Can they come in for a few minutes?"

Shanti hesitated. "OK, Mama."

"You know, my hour is up. I'll just say goodbye for now," Archie said.

"Oh no, Arch, they want to meet you; they know you rescued Shanti. I've told them all about you. Please stay."

"Alright, I'll stay a bit longer." Archie smiled weakly at Danielle who, without further ado, opened the door.

A man and woman stood in the doorway. They were smiling brilliantly, carrying gifts, and were better dressed than the Jacksons or himself. Summer wore a colorful loose-fitting blouse and tight, white, pedal pushers, while Primo wore spiffy shorts, sandals, and a Hawaii surfer shirt. Summer held a large stuffed dolphin toward Shanti.

Shanti hesitated, then shyly accepted the dolphin.

"He's real squishy," Summer said as she knelt beside the little girl.

"Yeah, he is," Shanti said softly as she cuddled the dolphin.

"What do you say to Summer, Shanti?" Danielle prompted mildly.

"Thank you, Summer," Shanti said in a little voice.

"We have a vase for those, right over here," Tom said to Primo, taking the bouquet.

While visiting Shanti, Primo kept his graduated lenses on. His eyes were still very light sensitive. He realized he was sweating. He hoped his breath mints were working.

"Let me introduce everyone," Danielle said. "Archie, this is Summer Jensen and Primo Carreta, the friends who were taking us for a boat ride that day. And, of course, you two know who Archie is."

"We are so grateful to you, Mr. Douglas," Summer said as she pressed Archie's hand in hers.

"Yeah, I don't think I've ever felt so relieved in my life as when the dispatch told us you had rescued Shanti," Primo added. "But I have to tell you the truth: when I saw the size of your boat and no motor, I couldn't believe it. Good going, man!" Primo flashed his winner smile as he gripped Archie's hand, but he knew his grin lacked some of its usual dazzle this morning. He also noticed the children's Bible in Archie's other hand.

"It was providence that I was in the right place at the right time," Archie said.

"And this is Tom, Shanti's dad," Danielle went on, gracefully.

After a few minutes Summer said, "We're so glad you're going to be OK, Shanti. But we better be going now." She looked at Danielle and made a scrunched-up face. Danielle followed Summer and Primo into the hallway.

At Primo's suggestion, Summer gave the keys to her car to Danielle, who needed to run some errands, and caught a ride back in the BMW.

Primo swore under his breath all the way from the hospital door to his car. At the same time his calculating mind was at work strategizing. It wasn't until they reached the car that he shared with Summer what he was fuming about. "Did you see what Archie had in his hand?" He swore, then continued. "A Bible—that's what. Summer, the next time you are alone with Danielle, I want you to undermine that guy. Find some way to discredit him. He's a threat to this deal."

"Where are you coming from?" Summer said in an exasperated tone. "If it wasn't for Archie..."

"I know, I know, he saved Shanti and saved our bacon, but he will try to discourage Danielle from taking up the porn business, and I don't like it."

"Primo, you don't know anything of the kind."

"Mark my words, Summer. We have to neutralize his influence."

"Danielle is a very independent woman. She'll make up her own mind." Primo's head started to pound again. Driving south into the winter sun was killing him. He let Summer have the last word.

Archie had a strange feeling in his gut. The six of them had carried on with conversation in Shanti's hospital room, but Archie felt awkward. Was it just Shanti's shyness that put a damper on it, or was there something more? When Danielle had gone out in the hall with Summer and Primo, Archie and Tom had exchanged a look but said nothing. Was Tom feeling the same thing?

"I'm going now too, sweetheart," Archie said to Shanti, giving her a little hug.

"OK, Archie. Are you coming to see me tomorrow?"

"Yes, I am."

"Can you bring the other book we were reading about *Narnia*?"

"Good morning, Nancy," Archie said on his way past the nurses' station the next morning.

"Good morning Archie," Nancy replied.

What a pleasant woman, Archie thought as he continued down the hall to Shanti's room. Dr. Hazim was there for a visit. Archie excused himself and began to back out.

But Hazim insisted he come in. "Your timely rescue has a lot to do with Shanti's recovery."

"Is she better?"

"Yes, much better. It's safe for us to finish the treatments on an outpatient basis."

"She's going home this afternoon, Archie," Danielle said, beaming.

"Wonderful!" Archie said.

"But Archie, will you still come and visit me at home?" Shanti asked.

Archie looked at Danielle; he wanted to come, but it was up to her.

"Could you come for dinner tomorrow night?" Danielle asked. "I want to do something for you after you have done so much for us, and Tom says I'm a good cook."

"Oh, well yes, I would love to."

"Yeah!" Shanti shouted, jumping up and down in bed.

"Do you like Thai food?"

"Do I—" Archie couldn't finish his sentence as tears came to his eyes. In a moment he recovered and said in a raspy voice, "My wife, Luella, made the best chicken satay with peanut sauce you ever ate. I miss her."

"Archie, you are the sweetest man," Danielle said, slipping her arm through his and pulling him close.

Shanti hugged him from the other side.

He wiped his eyes with the back of his hand. It felt good to be held.

"Please excuse me," Hazim said, slipping his stethoscope into his pocket and patting his little patient from the other side of the bed. "I must continue my rounds."

The adults thanked Hazim and Shanti said, "Bye for now."

Hazim hurried down the hall. A wave of envy swept over him as he imagined just how Danielle would repay her debt. But then he comforted himself somewhat with the thought that deacons must have the same ethical restraints with patients and their families as medicos.

Summer knew that Danielle would be up early with Shanti, but she waited until eight to call. "Hi Danielle, how you guys doing?"

"Hi Summer, it's good to be home. Shanti is already in the backyard."

"I was just calling to see if I could give you a lift to the hospital for Shanti's treatment today?"

"Girl, you are a true friend. Treatment's at 10:00, but why don't you come over now for breakfast? I'm making *huevos rancheros* and there's something I want to discuss with you."

"I would love to come over and hang out with you."

A short while later Summer climbed the steps to Danielle's apartment with mixed emotions. She really liked Danielle and Shanti and always looked forward to being with them. But the more she liked them, the more she dreaded having to con Danielle into Primo's scam. She had pretty much decided to come clean and forget the whole thing by the time she got to the top step.

She called hello through the screen door.

"Come on in, Summer. Your timing is perfect," Danielle said from inside.

As Summer pulled the screen door open an aluminum baseball bat beside the door caught her eye. "Are you a ball player, Danielle?"

"No." Danielle grinned. "That's my low-tech security system."

"Right," Summer said, thinking there was more to this woman than meets the eye. The table was set for two. Shanti had already eaten.

"Did you see her in the yard?" Danielle asked as she checked on the little girl through the window over the sink.

"Oh yes. Shanti and Munchie gave me a royal welcome. But Shanti was deep into an imaginary play she had to get back to."

Danielle shook her head, chuckled, and said, "That girl," as she served the eggs.

Soon the two friends were enjoying another delicious meal.

"What gives it that extra kick? It's not hot sauce?" Summer asked.

"Could be the fresh cilantro you're tasting. Here's a whole leaf. Is that it?"

"Yes, that's it. I learn something every time I come over here," Summer said, smiling at Danielle. "So what is it you want to discuss?"

"It's about Shanti's hospital bills. Tom has an adequate salary and most of the cost is covered under the university's healthcare plan. But some things Shanti needed were not covered."

"And I'll bet you were shocked at how fast it adds up."

"Summer, just between you and me, we are talking thousands of dollars here." Danielle sighed.

"Really."

"It isn't fair to saddle Tom with all of this; I'm looking for a way to cover the additional expenses. Let me be totally up front with you. I think Primo's interest in me is more business than personal."

"OK, let me be totally up front with you. Number one, you're right. Primo has had his eye on you from the get-go; he says you have 'star quality.' Number two, I do soft porn."

A bite of egg froze in space in front of Danielle's open mouth.

Summer couldn't help but laugh. "You're surprised."

"No, not totally. I had a feeling it was something a little off…but soft porn, wow." Danielle's fork and egg lowered slowly to her plate. "What exactly does soft mean?"

"It means we don't actually have sex with the guy, we just act like we are. It's only in triple X where they really have sex, and believe me, with AIDS and all the other STDs you don't want to be doing triple X films these days."

"So you just act like you're having sex with the uh, other actor," Danielle said as she finally put the forkful of food in her mouth.

"Yeah. I mean, you have to get out of your clothes and you get touched, but no…you know…no sex."

"What about Shanti?"

"What do you mean?"

"I wouldn't want her to know this was going on. I wouldn't want her influenced by this."

"Hey, not a problem. Neither Shanti nor any of your friends will ever have to see the movie. You would act under an assumed name—

mine is Summer Storm—and you don't have to tell anyone what you're up to. The main thing is, it's good cash money. Quick and easy money. That's just what you need."

Danielle pushed the rest of the eggs around on her plate; she had lost her appetite.

Summer cleaned her plate with a tortilla as she thought about her own cash reward—the finder's fee for bringing Danielle into the business. But at the same time she wanted to make sure her friend knew exactly what she was getting into. "So, what do you think, Danielle? I guarantee with your looks you're not going to be turned down. And hey, look at me. I've done a bunch of these flicks, and I'm better than ever."

"I don't know, Summer. I do need money but...well, I just can't imagine myself doing this. I've never even seen a porno movie."

"What do you say we rent one I'm in, and I give you a kind of running commentary on what's going on behind the scenes?"

"Oh, oh dear. OK, as long as we do it after Shanti is asleep."

"Of course, honey, of course."

That night Danielle and Shanti watched with rapt attention as Archie ate his first few bites. He seemed to be enjoying it, but the two cooks just had to know. "How is it, Archie?" Danielle asked.

"Ladies," Archie said between mouthfuls, "I feel like I've died and gone to heaven."

Shanti looked confused, as if she hadn't heard that phrase before, but the pleased look on her mother's face told her it was a compliment.

"Where do you get the fresh ingredients for the peanut sauce around here?" Archie went on.

"There's a little store about two blocks south on Ocean, next to the dry cleaners that has everything," Danielle replied.

"You know, I still have Luella's recipes. With the right ingredients, I could get into this."

The three of them enjoyed the meal immensely. The food was

gourmet quality, the wine Archie brought fit it perfectly, and the conversation was delightful although certainly geared to topics that were of interest to a four-year-old.

Afterwards Danielle let Shanti watch her favorite cartoon while she and Archie cleared and washed the dishes. Over the sink Archie said, "Danielle, consider us even. That meal was life-changing."

"You must let me decide the value of saving my daughter's life, Archie."

"Ooch, you have quite the way with words my dear…most persuasive." Danielle said nothing more but looked pleased with Archie's acquiesces. "Oh, how the time has flown. I must give Shanti a bath and put her to bed. Can you stay a little longer, Archie? I'd love a bit of adult conversation after she's down."

"Sure. I'll finish up here in the kitchen."

"Watch some TV if you like—we have cable."

Archie put the last dish in the drying rack and was wiping down the counters when Shanti returned from her bath for a good-night hug. He knew from years of experience with children not to do anything exciting at this juncture or she would be awake for hours. He hugged her briefly and wished her a good sleep. Danielle looked back at him over her shoulder as she trundled Shanti off to bed.

Archie moved into the living room, picked up the remote, and started surfing channels. He stood in front of the TV with the volume low so it wouldn't bother Shanti. He came across a Billy Graham crusade. Archie liked Billy and left it on low. A few minutes later he heard Danielle enter the room quietly behind him and turned toward her. Danielle yawned and stretched. Archie knew how sleepy an adult can get putting kids down.

"She is out," Danielle said, leaning on the door casement.

"Good—she seems to go full throttle all day."

"Tell me about it."

The crusade was building to the altar call and caught Danielle's attention. "You like Billy Graham?" She gestured toward the TV with her chin.

"Yeah I do," Archie said.

"Can I ask you a question? If you say Jesus is the answer, and everyone has to believe the same way, isn't that exploitive? One person imposing their beliefs on another?"

"I understand that argument," Archie said. "If I'm right, then you're wrong; but I think you can take it too far and end up with everyone paralyzed, afraid to believe in anything uplifting because it might offend someone else."

"Archie, how many times in history have people thought they were right, gone off on a crusade for their beliefs, and later found out they were wrong?"

"Plenty of times. But the gospel has stood up over centuries, proven its value age after age."

"How do you know that? How do you *really* know that for sure?"

"Look, all I want is to make a positive contribution to society. I want to make things better for the people around me as much as I can."

"That's fine as long as you don't try to convince me I should believe the same things you do."

"But what if I think it would make your life better?"

At this point Archie fully realized, although he had been somewhat aware from the start, that each time Danielle spoke she moved a step closer to him. It wasn't that many more steps before she would be...

"That is a judgment you have no right to make, Archie," she said stepping closer again. "My values are just as valid for me as yours are for you. And didn't Jesus say we're not supposed to judge?"

"You've got me there," was all Archie could say. His cognitive powers were overwhelmed by the effect of her proximity. Danielle was so close he could smell her: a mixture of four-year-old, sandalwood, and beautiful woman. No further argument came to his mind, but he realized he was smiling and so was she.

"You like debate," he heard his voice say.

"Yes, I find it...stimulating," Danielle said, moving closer still. A dozen thoughts and emotions whipped through Archie's soul: how utterly beautiful she was, how ridiculously young she was, how good it felt to be so close to such a woman, how preposterously old he was, and feelings he couldn't capture in words...his desire, his loneliness, his missing a good woman.

She slipped her arms around him and held him. It wasn't one of those Christian hugs either, he told Jimmy later—you know, leaning in so only the shoulders touch—but a full, frontal embrace.

Archie put his arms around her too. What else could he do?

"Oh Archie," she said, "you'll never know how grateful I am for..." and her voice caught in her throat.

"That's OK...it's OK," Archie whispered, his mind racing. Was this just a grateful, sexually uninhibited mother thanking him for saving her precious child's life? Was it more than that? Was he a fool to think that it could be more? What should he do if it was?

Then another line of thought began. If he acted on this temptation, he would be sinning with a capital S. If anything happened between them, his good standing at Westside would be ruined: no more Deacon Douglas. He would come under church discipline and perhaps, worst of all, it would be a blow to Jimmy's leadership. Imagining telling Pastor Jimmy made him feel nauseous. *No, Archie Douglas*, he thought, *you are not going to do anything with this young woman.* But how could he end it without hurting her feelings?

Suddenly Billy Graham's voice broke through his cascading thoughts: "If you want to say yes to Jesus and make him your personal Savior come forward now." *Forward*, Archie thought and his upper body leaned forward, pushing Danielle ever so slightly away. "I'd really like to hear about your spiritual journey, Danielle."

She followed his lead, pulled back from the embrace, and said, "Sure. People say it is pretty interesting." Danielle turned and sat on the couch as she spoke and patted the cushion next to her for Archie to sit as well.

Archie sat, his inner world a turmoil of checked desire, nausea, and relief.

"I do yoga and occasionally go to Satsang, and I guess you could say I dabble in other stuff—a soft form of Tai Chi, meditation. I haven't settled on any particular school."

"How did you get interested in the spiritual side of life?"

"When we moved to Venice from Long Beach, I met some interesting people in the neighborhood. Tom was away a lot, working or studying, so I set out to make some new friends; all of them were into consciousness-raising stuff. But my spiritual quest really took off when one of my old girlfriends from Long Beach State stopped over for a few days' visit. She had some 'window pane' and said it was really good. We split a tab one summer morning. I had an experience that I knew went way beyond the acid."

"So many people in my generation started their journey that way. What happened?"

Danielle closed her eyes, thinking back to that beautiful summer day. "We dropped at different times so one of us would be able to take care of the other if we spaced out while we were peaking. I felt really heavy at one point and went in to lie down on the bed. You know how it is often foggy here near the coast in the summer? It was a morning like that. I lay down and then I really started to trip. There was a lark outside my window singing, and in the distance I could hear a foghorn intermittently. I became fascinated with the call and response of the lark's high song and the horns *baso profundo* reply; I guess it was a sort of yin-yang thing. What happened next is hard to put into words. The best I can do is to say my awareness of myself as a separate being began to dissolve: first I merged with the sounds outside the window; then in a few moments with all of nature; finally I felt I became one with God. Throughout this I had a building sense of ecstasy and then I passed out."

Danielle paused to see how Archie would respond; he was listening intently, smiling thoughtfully, waiting for her to go on. "The next day—completely sober—I felt strongly that the experience went way beyond the influence of psychedelics. I knew that there was something important outside everyday reality; I wanted to find out more about spirituality. I guess you could say the LSD opened a door and I went on from there."

"So, you don't do acid anymore?"

"I tried it a few more times, but found I was getting closer to my first experience through meditation. So no, I haven't done acid for quite a while."

"I haven't done any drugs for over 30 years."

"You used to do drugs?" Danielle looked shocked.

"I started my spiritual path in the same kind of dabbling you're describing. In fact, Luella and I met while she was visiting the

90

meditation center I lived in up in Seattle. Truth be told, there was as much drugs and sex as meditation. About the same time we got married, though, we got involved with a form of yoga that put a lot of emphasis on purity: no drugs, no alcohol, no sex for singles, no meat, and so on. We stayed with that for seven years until the guru was exposed as a fraud."

"Really? What happened?"

"It turned out that Mr. Purity was having tantric sex with just about any woman or girl he could get his hands on. The younger ones were traumatized by it, so his foundation set up counseling for the girls. Of course they kept the whole thing under wraps for as long as they could, but eventually it got exposed."

"So, what did you and Luella do then?"

"The timing was pretty amazing. Right in the midst of the crisis with the guru we got zapped by the Holy Spirit at a Christian conference and eventually gave our lives to Jesus."

"And you have been a Christian ever since?" Archie nodded and shifted his position on the couch; his ribs were aching a little.

"So what's it all about, Archie?" Danielle said dreamily, yawning.

"What's what all about?"

"Life."

Archie took his time to answer. "That's deep." Danielle's question brought a specific memory to mind. "I took it really hard when Luella died; it was so sudden. I went into profound grief; I tried a lot of remedies but couldn't shake it. Somewhere in the second year of it I had a waking dream. Ever had one of those?"

Danielle nodded.

"Well, in the dream, I saw myself as a little boy, maybe five, sort of draped over this coffin. I knew it was Luella's. Then Jesus came to me and took my hand and led me up a rise to a ridge line. We looked down the other side where the light was different, kind of glowing. And then I woke up. I thought and thought about that dream for days. It was like an icon for me; I studied and pondered it. Finally I made a decision. I wrote it out, like a motto for life in my prayer journal: *I want to give life to life.* Then I took it up to Luella's grave site and read it out."

Here Archie paused. "Maybe that's why I like sailing so much. I feel more alive at sea. On land, though, especially with others, I have to keep making that decision: to give life. I'm an introvert—I get energy from being alone and often feel drained with people. But not you, Danielle," he added quickly. "Also, there's a lot of stuff you can do everyday—meaningless tasks that have to be done—that have nothing to do with life. Then there are the problems of not knowing how to give to someone else or not having the capacity to do it. But in the end I keep choosing to give life to life."

"You sure hit a home run with my family," Danielle said as she snuggled closer and kissed him on the cheek.

5

A rchie arrived at the lifeguard boat dock a little before 8:00 AM for his ride-along. He was interested in anything to do with the sea but was particularly excited about going out with the man who had delivered Shanti to the hospital in time.

Chad invited Archie aboard. "Make yourself at home. There's coffee at the station; want me to bring you back a cup?"

"No thanks. I just had some with breakfast."

"All right. I'll be back in a second, I have to take care of some paperwork and then we can make ready to sail."

As soon as Chad was off, Archie began to look the boat over. At 28 feet the *Dolphin* was 12 feet shorter than his Cal 40, but the boat, designed and equipped to be a working platform at sea, had a lot more deck space. Archie was drawn to the most unique feature of the aft deck, the Sampson post. *No doubt named for the strongman in the Bible,* Archie thought with approval. The heavy metal post was about three feet tall, four inches in diameter with a T about three inches from the top. Archie could see how easily and quickly the crew could fasten a line to the post for towing disabled craft or for clamping on the bitter end of a life ring line. He noticed there was a second shorter post near the bow as well. His attention was drawn to all the life-saving equipment, life rings, life slings, life-saving buoys, floating lines, and two inflatable life rafts. He noted that everything looked heavy duty and everything floated. Archie was examining the rapid inflation device on one of the life rafts when Chad came back on board.

"OK, I'll check the engines and away we go. Come on, Arch, you'll be interested in these beauties."

Indeed Archie was a bit awed by the two Chrysler Marine 357 inboards.

Chad kept up a tour guide commentary as he checked the oil, hoses, and belts. "We need the power not only to get to the rescue in a hurry but also to hold the boat steady in the surf. Most of our rescues are of swimmers who have been pulled out by a riptide. The lifeguards on the beach spot them, then call us over to haul them out of the water. It's a lot better than trying to get them back to shore through the surf."

"So you actually run the boat into the surf?"

"We back right up to it. The trick is to get close enough to the victim to throw them a line or for my swimmer to go in after them. Our basic maneuver is to back up to the surf line and hold there."

"Could get dicey."

"A good operator can do it day in and day out, but it's definitely not something your average boater should try. Worst case would be to have an engine fail at the surf line. That happened to Louie Champas last year. He got out of it on one engine but had to call in another boat to complete the rescue. We try to keep everything about the engines shipshape as possible; we keep regular maintenance schedules, just like an airliner."

Archie said nothing but thought, *They intentionally draw near to the very thing every seaman, for all time, has carefully avoided: the dreaded lee shore.*

Archie cringed as he remembered his lee shore. He was single-handing the Cal 40 in the San Juans, approaching a narrow opening to a small anchorage behind a sand spit. The lee shore was on his starboard side with very shallow ground at the current high slack, fully exposed for 200 yards at low tide. The 25-knot wind was blowing straight onshore; Archie was making five knots with nothing but a closehauled jib. He failed to notice that the stopper knot had worked loose on the sail's weather sheet; when he let the sail go to furl it, the sheet blew out into the water. He had the presence of mind to kick the engine into neutral before the sheet trailed aft and tangled in the prop, but he had to recover it before the wind blew him aground. He ran forward along the plunging deck, pulled the sheet aboard hand over hand, then ran it back aft and threw it down the companionway—salt water and all. He got underway just seconds before he would have grounded.

Chad moved on to inspect the second engine, and Archie recovered from his memory. "I've never seen cleaner engine compartments," Archie said.

The boat creaked and rolled slightly. "That will be my swimmer coming aboard right on time. Good morning, Art," Chad said without taking his head out of the engine compartment.

"Morning, Chad. Looks like we could get some action today."

"Yeah, what's the surf report?" Chad asked as he closed the engine compartment.

"Four to six-foot waves out of the northwest. Rip should be running pretty strong."

Chad and Archie made their way onto the after deck. "Archie, this is Art Shaw, my partner today. Art, this is Archie Douglas, our ride-along."

"Good to meet you, Mr. Douglas. Chad told me how you hauled out that little girl with CO poisoning."

"I was blessed to be in the right place at the right time," Archie replied.

Chad had moved on to the control panel and called Archie over. "See here are the twin throttles and twin gear shifts that enable the operator to hold the boat steady in the surf line."

Archie cut short any reply as Chad hit the starter button and first one, then both big engines roared to life.

"We'll let them warm up while we make sure everything is good to go on deck."

Archie watched the two men complete their checks. Art cast off the lines, and Chad maneuvered the *Dolphin* away from the dock. Archie noted how Chad could move her sideways by running the engines in different combinations of forward and reverse. Chad made it look easy, but Archie knew one false move in these tight quarters would mean almost certain collision. Just the other day he had watched a powerboater coming in for a haul out run his bow right up on the dock. The floating dock sank momentarily, and the skipper was able to back off with only cosmetic damage, but Archie could see there would be none of that sort of thing with Chad at the controls.

Chad continued his "tour guide monologue" while they sped to their patrol area. "This time of the year we don't get many locals in the water—too cold for them. But we do get people from inland who think this is warm for late November. Now most of your locals know the riptide, but the out-of-town folk don't see the danger until it's too late. On the other hand, sometimes we have to rescue experienced surfers. Go figure."

Archie was taking it all in and loving it: Chad's generous chatter, the casual efficient way he handled the swells, and the exhilarating feeling Archie always had when he left the marina behind. Today, as most days, he fantasized about not coming back—of leaving for an endless sea voyage— with a sweet longing in his soul....

"Some people describe lifeguarding as hours of boredom punctuated by minutes of panic; not today!" Chad said as they entered their third hour. The three men had not been bored today, not at all. The boat operators liked to take ride-alongs because they got to tell their stories again—stories of bizarre happenings at sea. This ride-along was even better as Archie also had plenty of sea stories to tell. Art had them in tears with "The Naked Lady" story; Archie's "Coastal Navigation in Fog with Depth Gauge Only" wowed the boys, and Chad got on a roll with a series of stories of equipment failures forcing improvised rescues. Then each one had their own version of "Struck by Lightning."

From time to time they scanned the surf with their high-powered German-made binoculars. So far they had none of the action Art had predicted. They were just about to break out their bag lunches when the radio crackled. "Patrol boat 22, this is Dispatch, over."

"22 responding, over."

"Beach patrol reports three swimmers in trouble near the south edge of your patrol area, over."

"We're on our way, Frank."

Art and Archie began scanning the zone with binoculars while Chad got the *Dolphin* up to planing speed. "Quick response is everything in sea rescue," he said to Archie as the *Dolphin* flew over the swells.

"Got them," Art said. "About a mile ahead, just outside the surf line."

"Dispatch, this is 22, over."

"Talk to me, 22."

"We have a visual on the swimmers. ETA three minutes, over."

"Roger, 22. Beach patrol has revised the count to four in the water, over."

"Roger, four in the water."

"Art, you better run Archie through the rescue drill. With that many in, we may need all hands." Art fastened the bitter end of four life ring lines to the Sampson post. He also put several other loose rings and buoys in a stern corner. As he worked, he explained the drill to Archie. "Our first choice is to get close enough to throw the attached ring to the victim, then haul them up to the swim platform. But if they are in bad shape, I go to them with a buoy. If we can't get close for any reason we want to get something that floats to them right away, then I can swim them to the boat."

"I understand," Archie said.

"Now if I go in, you stand by, ready to do whatever Chad says, OK?"

"Right," Archie said. He had practiced man overboard drills in his boater safety course and everything Art said made perfect sense. However, all of his preparation had been for rescuing people at sea. He had never imagined pulling someone out of the surf. Now they could see the four heads in the water without the binoculars.

Chad brought the *Dolphin* down out of her plane and proceeded toward the swimmers at a safe speed. They were right at the surf line, still trying to get back to the beach. One of them turned and saw the boat approaching and alerted the others. The boy on the left turned just as a swell broke over his head. He came up thrashing and went under again.

Art immediately strapped a buoy over his shoulder and shouted to

Chad, "We got one climbing the ladder. I'm going in. That guy on the left is drowning," Art said as he moved onto the swim platform.

Chad closed the gap, spun the *Dolphin*'s bow into the oncoming swells and began backing down to the swimmers and the crashing surf line. Archie fought down his emotions as Chad intentionally put them in a position every seaman dreads: a lee shore in pounding surf.

In seconds the situation onboard 22 changed dramatically. Chad's attention was absorbed with the swells coming toward him and the surf crashing behind his open stern. He constantly adjusted the throttles to hold the boat close to the swimmers as the *Dolphin* pitched up and down in the steep waves that became surf a few feet later. Art dove and swam powerfully toward the boy on the left who, by Archie's count, had gone under a third time. Archie's fear of the surf diminished a little: he could see that Chad was able to control the boat so close to the breakers, but Archie's throat went dry when he thought of engine failure.

"All right Archie, start throwing the attached ring buoys to the other three...hold on, HOLD ON," Chad said. At the top of a crest he saw a big comber coming: "Outside break—have to get farther out! THROW IN EVERYTHING LOOSE THAT FLOATS. NOW!" Chad's voice boomed.

Archie began throwing rings and buoys at the three heads in the water as fast as he could. When they were all in he held the Sampson post with both hands; the last thing he wanted was to add to the problem by falling overboard.

The *Dolphin* plowed forward as Chad gunned the engines; a second later the big wave broke right under their stern. The *Dolphin* hung in the balance, her engines roaring as their props spun in thin air, spray and green water washed over the side and over Archie, who was thrown against the Sampson post as the boat shot down the back of the breaker. Chad moved them farther out, waiting for the second and third waves of the big set to pass. Archie grabbed a towel from one of the closed compartments and wiped his face. He could see each of the three boys on the right bobbing on a flotation device.

Art had made it to the swimmer on the left, but he seemed to be struggling with him. Then the two went under for several seconds;

when they came up again the victim seemed cooperative. "If they won't do what you say, you dunk 'em," Chad commented dryly as his head swiveled back and forth between the action astern and the incoming swells ahead. Archie swallowed hard as he saw Chad was drifting the boat closer to the surf line again.

"OK, Arch, now you can throw the rings attached to the post. Try to get one to Art first, as we probably need his muscle to get the others out of the water."

Archie noted that Chad's voice had returned to its usual laid-back tone. Archie fired the rings off quickly and not inaccurately.

"Good work, Archie. Now, as soon as Art is clamped on, haul him and his rescue up to the swim platform." With all the swimmers hanging on to a ring and line attached to the Sampson post, Chad gently towed them all out away from the crashing surf line.

"Well, that was a bit gnarly," Chad said to Archie when they were a safe distance from the white water.

"Was it then?" Archie replied, grinning with relief at not having messed up in the moment of crisis.

"I usually don't cut it that thin," Chad went on. "Well, let's get these boys on dry land, where they can contemplate their misadventure."

Archie and Jimmy were well into their weekly mentoring hour, and so far Archie was doing all the talking. Jimmy could see his old friend was upset about what had happened at Danielle's, so let him carry on.

"Jimmy there's no fool like an old fool, and I'm one three times over: a fool to be tempted by a woman so much younger than me, a fool to think she would be attracted to an old reprobate, and a fool to be outdone by her in the debate." Archie finally seemed to run out of words at the point where Danielle kissed him.

Jimmy, who had been following the narrative closely, picked up on the intensity of Archie's agitation and asked a definitive question: "So then you slept with her?"

"NOOOOO! Jimmy, NO! How can you say that?"

"I wanted to rule out a worst-case scenario."

"But Jimmy, you haven't seen her. Even the pope would be tempted."

"You didn't sleep with her?"

"No."

"So the problem is...?"

"She's still married to Tom, and I really like him, and they should be together, and I love their little girl like she was my own, and I think I love Danielle too; that's the problem."

"Are you in love with her, or do you love her as a friend?"

"Good point. Good point. As a friend...but it's hard to keep the boundary from blurring because she is so beautiful, Jimmy."

"What do you want, Archie?"

The question stopped Archie cold. He recognized that it invited solutions instead of being stuck in the problem. "Ooch, that's a good one, Jimmy. That's a good one."

"I learned it from you," Jimmy said, trying not to laugh.

As Archie thought about Jimmy's question, clarity began to come to his troubled mind.

Jimmy smiled behind his hand, waiting to see how his mentor would resolve his dilemma with the beautiful Danielle.

"I want Tom and Danielle to get back together, for Shanti's sake as well as theirs. I want Danielle and Shanti to get saved." Archie stopped, but Jimmy sensed there was more and waited. "And I wouldn't mind meeting someone more my own age."

The final "want" was hard for Archie to admit, but he trusted Jimmy as much as he could trust anyone.

"It all sounds good to me, especially the part about you meeting someone." Jimmy grinned. "Why, I could have a dozen Westside ladies lined up for coffee with you in no time. And good Christian women too."

"I suppose you could," Archie said. "But seriously, Jimmy, I feel I've been a terrible witness to Danielle. She is so good at debate, and I don't think quickly enough to get the right points across."

"Don't worry about it, Arch. In all the time I've known you, you have been kind, gentle, and honest. Haven't you been the same with her?" Archie shrugged and Jimmy went on. "Those qualities will witness to her better than anything you could say."

"Maybe so, maybe so."

Jimmy smiled at his old friend. "As far as the temptation goes, you mustn't be alone with her for any length of time—you know, where something could happen."

Archie nodded. He knew Jimmy was giving him the usual sound, pastoral advice about temptation. At the same time he felt foolish for having to get the talk at his age.

On the way home, however, he realized that everyone is tempted and remembered it was also a sin to judge, even yourself. He hoped that being honest with Jimmy and putting the whole thing under his authority would squelch the temptation.

November 25th was the day Luella and Archie—and now just Archie—always put up the Christmas decorations. Right after breakfast he started bringing the boxes out of the storage shed in the underground parking. He was particularly keen to get them up today as he had invited Danielle and Shanti for lunch the next day. It was Shanti's last hyperbaric treatment, and Archie wanted to do something special for her. Dr. Hazim said her bloodwork had been clear since Wednesday. He added the two days of treatment to be absolutely certain she had no carbon monoxide in her system. Danielle told Archie Shanti liked turkey burgers, so Archie planned to barbeque on the deck.

He lined up the boxes of Christmas decorations in the living room; each one had writing on it, identifying its contents. He found the lighted swag for over the sliding glass door first. Archie had cut down a lot on the quantity of decorations Luella used to put up. She worked from the philosophy that more is better; Archie was a less-is-better person. She also had an artistic flair that he lacked, but he carried on the tradition, keeping it simple. Archie had left little hooks above the sliding glass door so he could get the swag up quickly. He plugged it in straight away. The tiny lights seemed dim as the morning sun flooded through their window. Nevertheless, Archie was pleased with their effect and the efficient, minimal effort it took to get them up. The lights reminded him of Christmas music. He had a special CD holder with nothing but Christmas songs. He loaded some of them and fired it up.

Next he opened the crèche box. Archie had built the crèche with Julie and Jean when they were little, out of some rough cedar boards left over from one of Luella's gardening projects. Archie set it down on a low table in the corner of the living room and plugged in the little light he had wired inside the peak of the roof. He intended for Shanti to be able to get at the figures. Knowing how she loved fantasy play, Archie bet she would find the Holy Family, the wise men, and the shepherds great characters to build a story around. Luella had acquired quite a cast of Fontini figures over the years, too many for the space on the table. Archie put a few of the figures on a window ledge as if they were coming from a long way off.

Archie pulled the artificial tree out and assembled it. He couldn't bring himself to buy a real tree in this Southern California climate. He put two strings of lights, some garlands, and finally the various balls and other decorations on it. The last box contained a variety of decorations, candles, and the front door wreath. Archie got the whole room finished well before lunch. He paused to take in the overall effect. He was doubly pleased: it achieved the desired Christmas atmosphere, and he wouldn't miss his afternoon sail in the *Mira Flores*.

He looked out onto the marina and checked the tell tails on the sailboats. The offshore breeze was filling in nicely. He got excited when he remembered he could bring Danielle and Shanti down for the Christmas sail-by in a couple weeks. Many of the boat owners decorated their rigging with lights, and it made a beautiful scene as they went up and down the main channel.

It was already past noon the next day. Archie tried not to get upset. They were only 20 minutes late, and Summer was driving. He doublechecked his food list, trying to keep busy to pass the time: in the fridge turkey burgers seasoned and ready to go, the mayonnaise, deli potato salad in a serving bowl, and a relish platter; on the table ketchup, plain and horse-radish mustards, and the hamburger buns; two kinds of soda pop in an ice chest, and apple crisp and vanilla ice cream for dessert. He worried that Danielle's cooking was too exotic for her to enjoy this simple fare, but reassured himself that, after all, it was Danielle who had requested the menu for Shanti.

He was about to adjust the volume on the Christmas music when the doorbell rang. Archie's worries vanished the moment he gazed upon his guests in the doorway. They wore matching bottle green pants and sparkling white blouses, and Danielle had obviously spent some time on their hair and her makeup. The technical details of these dress-up preparations escaped Archie, but the overall effect did not. He felt an actual physical palpation of his heart as he gazed upon their dazzling beauty.

"Archie, aren't you going to invite us in?" Danielle said.

"Come in! Come in!" Archie said as he reached out and drew his treasures into his home. "You both are so radiant I was dumbstruck," he said as he bent to hug Shanti first and then stood again to hug Danielle.

Each returned his embrace warmly and gave him a kiss as well.

"Welcome, my good friends," he went on. "Make yourselves at home while I get the burgers on."

"Archie, it's Christmas!" Danielle said.

"Look, Mama, the baby Jesus, just like at Daddy's house!" Shanti cried, going straight for the crèche.

Archie saw Danielle's look of concern as Shanti began handling the figures. "Danielle, I put the crèche down there at child level on purpose. My children and grandchildren always act out the story with the figures. The Fontinis are very sturdy and, of course, replaceable."

As the two adults watched Shanti examining the figures Archie remembered Ginger the cat. "You know Shanti, we used to have a calico cat named Ginger. She would always climb into the crèche and lie down inside it purring. She filled the whole thing end to end and toppled the figures again and again. The children adored her for it. They said she loved the baby Jesus."

Shanti gazed at the crèche, imagining the cat in it, and Danielle relaxed. Archie went out on the deck and ignited the propane barbeque.

"Anything I can do to help?" Danielle asked.

"Yes, bring out the turkey burger platter from the fridge, if you please, and turn down the music a bit."

"Thank you," Archie said as he began to put the burgers on the grill. "Everything else is ready."

The meal went well. "Simple food, but plenty of it," Archie said.

"It tastes great, Archie," Danielle replied from behind a burger with the works.

The potato salad was a hit, too. "Quite filling," Archie said.

"I'm stuffed," Danielle replied.

"Me too," Shanti chimed in.

"Oh," Archie said, "I have something for you, Shanti, to celebrate the end of your treatment." He handed her a card and a gift-wrapped shoebox. He had left the envelope unsealed so she could open it easily, which she did. On the front the card said "Congratulations" in big red letters. Inside Archie had drawn a picture of a little girl riding on top of a pony with her hands raised high above her head.

Danielle read the caption: "Three cheers for our brave Shanti, who successfully completed the 'Chamber Treatments'! November 26, 1993. All my love, Archie."

"Thank you, Archie," Shanti said, looking again at the picture.

"You're welcome," Archie replied. "Now open the gift."

Shanti worked slowly, trying to preserve the wrapping paper as she had seen her mother do, but to no avail as it started to rip diagonally.

"Don't worry, there is plenty more of that stuff," Archie encouraged.

From then on she pulled it off quickly and opened the old shoebox. Shanti inhaled sharply as her little hands reached into the box. "Oh Mommy, look, it's a pony." She held up a palomino horse with a white mane.

"I thought Pardner would like to have a partner! Ha, ha!"

"Thank you, Archie," Shanti said without prompting.

"Now I propose a toast," Archie said, raising his glass and waiting for the others. "Here's to the bravest little girl in all the world. May she be happy, healthy, and safe for the rest of her days."

"And here's to Archie Douglas, the man who saved my little girl!"

Danielle added.

"And here's to my mom, the best mom in the world!" Shanti said.

Archie was delighted with how well the party was going and once again amazed at the alacrity of the four-year-old.

Danielle began clearing the table with the speed and sure hand that comes from years of waiting tables. "You two hang out for a while. I'll clean up."

Archie started to protest but realized she would be done in a fraction of the time it would take him and that it was good for Shanti and gave Danielle a break.

"What do you think you will name the new pony?" Archie asked as the two of them made their way into the living room.

"I'll have to think about it," Shanti said.

"Of course you will."

"Archie, can we talk the dolls in the crèche?"

"We can. We can tell the Christmas story with them. Would you like that?"

"Yes!"

Archie pulled an easy chair over and the two of them settled down in front of the crèche. They were quickly engrossed in the characters: Mary, Joseph, the innkeeper, the shepherds, and wise men. After a few minutes, Shanti asked Archie to talk in his normal voice. She didn't like it when he put on voices to play the different characters. Shanti played Mary, giving the story some interesting twists and turns which Archie gently and creatively, he thought, brought back to the biblical narrative. She also brought her new pony into the play, oblivious to its improper scale.

Danielle drifted into the living room. It seemed to Archie that she finished cleaning up in seconds. Archie was very slow at washing dishes—thorough, but slow. He noticed his complete collection of Patrick O'Brian's novels caught her attention. She picked one of the 20 books at random and eyed the cover. It depicted a woman in a pink, full length dress standing on a quay with a variety of square-rigged ships at anchor behind her. O'Brian's name was in larger print than the title, *The Reverse of the Medal*. The back cover outlined the plot and included a glowing critique that described it as a "great novel," Archie knew. She opened the book and began reading.

Archie came to the usual stopping point in the Christmas story—the end of the wise men episode. He had no intention of going on to Herod's slaughter of the innocents.

"Is that the end of the story?" Shanti asked.

"Yes, it is."

"Can we tell it again?"

"Why don't you play with the figures yourself for a while dear? I would like to spend a little time chatting with your mom."

"Okay, Archie, but will you play with me again later?"

"Of course I will."

"Are you familiar with O'Brian?" he asked as he moved across the room and sat in the easy chair near hers.

"No, I'm not, but I can see you like him."

"I have to admit, I'm addicted to the series."

"What's the big attraction?"

"Well, of course, the sailing of the big ships before the days of auxiliary engines is utterly fascinating to me. When I pull into port in the Cal 40 I furl all sail and motor in. They had to either sail in or come in with the tide or tow with their rowboats or drop anchor and then haul themselves in on the winch."

"It's all beyond me, Archie."

"Yes, I suppose, there are a lot of nautical terms. But I also like the themes of courage, friendship, and the nobility of the heroes Aubrey and Maturin and the lengths O'Brian goes to to develop their character. They are people I would like to know in real life."

"Could you read a bit of a favorite passage? You know how little adult stimulation I get." She smiled.

"Yes, of course, you poor dear. Let's see what book you have there." Archie was so taken up with thoughts of his favorite reading, he forgot completely that the last "adult conversation" with Danielle was quite distressing for him. "Ah yes, *The Reverse of the Medal.* This has one of my favorite scenes. It left me breathless when I first read it."

Her eyebrow lifted. "Do you mean you have read it more than once?"

"I confess I read them over and over. You see, with my memory, by the time I finish the 20th novel, I can go back to the first and I have forgotten many of the details, so it's still interesting." The admission of his addiction made Archie blush. He hoped she didn't notice, but suspected from the hint of a smile she did. "I can read only a few pages at a time, of course, as I keep pretty busy with church work and sailing."

"Yes, of course you do," Danielle said.

"There are much worse addictions, I can tell you."

"As I well know. Please, read something."

"All right, let me set the scene. Jack Aubrey is skillful, cunning, knowledgeable, and wise beyond measure at sea, but absolutely hopeless on land. He makes fortunes at sea and loses them on land. He is a good judge of character on his ship, but forever being taken by con artists on land. Get the picture? In this story traitorous double agents set him up for a stock-exchange scandal—he is totally innocent of any wrongdoing—but they actually get him tried, convicted, and sentenced to be pilloried."

"Put in stocks?"

"Yes. Imagine—a captain of His Majesty's Royal Navy publicly humiliated in such a way." Archie was only vaguely aware of how animated he had become telling the story. "But Jack has been in the Navy for his whole life," he went on. "His kindness, good humor, the way he knew how to keep discipline without being harsh and his valor in battle endeared him to his shipmates. The word spreads around the fleet and on the day of the execution of his punishment hundreds of sailors and scores of officers assemble in front of the pillory."

Archie began to read.

"Babbington was there immediately in front of the pillory, facing him with his hat off, and Pullings, Stephen of course, Mowett, Dundas....he nodded to them, with almost no change in his iron expression, and his eye moved on: Parker, Rowan, Williamson, Hervey...and men from long, long ago, men he could scarcely name, lieutenants and commanders putting their promotion at risk, midshipmen and masters mates their commissions, warrant officers their advancement.

*" 'The head a trifle forward, if you please sir,' murmured the
sheriff's man, and the upper half of the wooden frame came down,
imprisoning his defenseless face.*

*"He heard the click of the bolt, and then in the dead silence a
strong voice cry, 'Off hats.' With one movement hundreds of
broadbrimmed tarpaulin-covered hats flew off and the cheering
began, the fierce, full throated cheering he had so often heard in
battle."*

Archie had forgotten what effect the passage had on him. Tears
were rolling down his face halfway through, and he had to stop several
times to get the last sentences out. Danielle reached out to comfort him,
and Shanti came over to give him a hug.

When he had regained his composure he said, "I don't know what
touches me so deeply about this—the nobility of the scene, of course,
but also something about the skill of the writer. He communicates such
deep meaning in such a straightforward description of events."

"Yes, he does have economy of style," Danielle said softly. "But
Archie, don't you think you give the meaning to the passage?"

Like most men, Archie couldn't feel powerful emotions and think
clearly at the same time. Danielle's comment escaped him.

Seeing his blank look she went on as Shanti went back to the
crèche. "Well, you're a psychologist. Don't you think it's the reader
who gives meaning to whatever passage he is reading? The author is
trapped in his particular cultural context and can't communicate
meaning to the reader at all. He can only tell his story and leave it up to
the reader to give it meaning."

Archie was startled. "But O'Brian is a great communicator—all the
critics agree."

"I would say even O'Brian isn't aware of the meaning of his own
writing. He, like all of us, is driven by inner motivations that are
beyond his own awareness. It's up to each reader to interpret the text
through their own perceptual filter."

Archie knew a great deal about perception and thought, since
those topics had always fascinated him in grad school and were the
underlying theory behind much of his success over the years as a

therapist. But this application was new to him. "Perhaps you could give me an example of what you are saying."

"Love to," Danielle said, warming to the "adult conversation." "You're a man; O'Brian is writing about men predominantly, yes? And you interpret the meaning of what he writes through the filter of your male outlook on the world."

"OK."

"But how would a liberated woman feel reading these books? For example, in this scene, there are no women cheering for Jack. Do women have no part to play in noble acts? What role are they assigned in the telling of these tales?"

Archie was dumbfounded; Aubrey and Maturin were his heroes, and O'Brian a genius in his estimation. Moreover, he had never heard or read anything but praise for the great writer and was completely taken aback by Danielle's criticism. At the same time he realized he had never viewed the books through the eyes of a feminist. And he realized she had hit upon a vulnerable point. He cringed as he remembered the superstitions of the crews and even officers of O'Brian's Navy: having a woman on board was usually considered bad luck. "But these are historical novels; he is writing about the Royal Navy in the early 1800s. Wouldn't it be a revision of history to put feminist values into the stories?"

"Perhaps, but my point is there must have been some women at that time who were heroic and noble. Does O'Brian include them in any of his stories? And if not, isn't he creating an ideology that says men are noble, men are brave, women are not?"

Archie had a terrible sinking feeling as Danielle went on; he hated to admit there was some truth to what she was saying. At the same time he knew there were counters to her arguments but he was feeling too raw emotionally to think clearly.

"Mama, Mama," Shanti called from behind the crèche.

"What is it dear?"

"I'm stuck."

Danielle rolled her eyes and shook her head as she moved over to Shanti. Archie followed. Shanti's finger was stuck in the knot hole in the back of the crèche. Because of the way the hole tapered, her finger went in easily but would not come out. Archie got the liquid soap dispenser from the bathroom and with a couple of well-placed squirts and some tears they were able to pull the finger out.

"I'm so sorry for the mess here, Archie," Danielle said.

"Not a problem, Danielle. It was my idea to put the crèche where the kids can interact."

Archie's assurances had no calming effect however; suddenly Danielle was a blur of motion as she picked up after Shanti. "We have to go," she said. She stopped, holding Shanti's new pony in one hand and her handbag in the other. "I was wondering after our talk at my place if you would ever like to go to Satsang with me at the yoga center. They have introductory meetings every Wednesday night."

Archie watched her stuff the pony in the bag. "That would be a very interesting thing to do. I'll get my DayTimer." Archie looked at the following Wednesday. "Tom has invited me over to see what he's doing at the earthquake lab, or whatever you call it, next Wednesday in the afternoon. But I could come over after that."

"Yeah, that should work. Maybe Tom could bring you over and hang out with Shanti while we go out."

"Sounds like a plan."

"OK, I'll set it up with him. Thanks so much for a wonderful lunch."

"Thank you, Archie," Shanti added.

"All right, see you guys later. And Danielle," Archie called after them as they moved down the hall, "forget about the stuck finger; that's what kids do." 1

Danielle frowned just before they turned the corner for the elevator.

Archie closed the front door and went out on the deck. He gripped the rail with both hands and took several deep breaths. He was looking at the boats in the marina, but he didn't see them. Instead his mind replayed the conversation, adding all the things he could have said in a cascade of thoughts. *How does she do it? How does she seize moral authority in these debates? I should have held the high ground. Of course an author can communicate his meaning to his reader; both are sentient beings. The whole purpose of language is to communicate. Yes,*

110

O'Brian comes from a particular culture and is writing about another particular culture, but isn't the essence of being human the capacity to transcend culture?

Archie remembered something of his own transcendent experiences in Latin America before the thought cavalcade resumed: *There is more to man than a bundle of conditioned responses. We are not prisoners of our personal history; love compels us to reach across the barriers to the other. True, each of us has a particular perceptual filter, but that doesn't mean we can't understand each other! That's the problem with these amateur psychologists; they latch onto one theory about one aspect of the mind and ignore all the rest. Furthermore, the whole feminist critique doesn't apply to courage and nobility. These are transcendent qualities. Men can learn nobility from women and women from men. What we need are role models who live out good values regardless of their gender and that's what O'Brian gives us.*

Archie concluded that at the deepest level, the spiritual level, there is the potential for unity. How did Paul put it? "We are neither male nor female, Greek nor Jew, slave nor free but all one in Christ." All these thoughts made him feel worse, however. He realized she had beaten him again, far worse this time, and he despaired of her ever coming to faith. He shuddered, thinking of what Danielle would do with Scripture. He felt the turkey burger sitting in his stomach like lead and he felt depressed, almost too depressed to go for his afternoon sail.

As Archie sailed down the main channel sometime later, he realized how much he missed Luella. Being naturally extroverted, she was so much better at talking to people about Jesus. She would have had a way to turn the conversation with Danielle away from debate toward faith. He lamented his own tendency to freeze in any kind of conflict.

I am not a good witness, he thought. *Maybe I'm not good at anything.* Then he recognized that as depressive thinking and fought to eject himself from the downward spiral he had fallen into. *I so often feel like a stranger on land these days.* That thought, together with all the loneliness that it brought, stayed with him all the way down the main channel.

For the most part, Archie had made peace with himself: he accepted his weaknesses. Yet when conflict arose with another person, he lost his inner tranquility and fell into the obsessive thinking—either endless rehearsing or endless replay—that had so plagued him throughout his pre-Christian life. The constant vigilance required at sea, however, forced him to concentrate on the present, moment by moment, at times with all his skill, strength, and intelligence. That focus on external reality took the wind out of feeling guilty about the past and anxious about the future.

After the corner, after he started the series of tacks toward the western sea wall, he began to gain in the battle with the negative thoughts. Now he was helped by upwind sailing, which was more intense in an open boat than the easy broad reach he had just completed down the first leg of the channel. With each successive tack he became more at one with the wind, the pressure on the tiller, and the performance of the tiny boat that pleased him so much.

A sweetness began to seep into his body, mind, and soul, and a modicum of peace returned. Archie jibed at the western breakwater and began the downwind leg. He let the sprit sail out to starboard to catch as much of the wind as possible coming now just behind his left shoulder. He wondered if the boat would go faster downwind with the centerboard up. Probably a little, he thought, but then she wouldn't steer a straight course so effortlessly nor would she be so secure against capsize.

The sun warmed him as he moved along in the almost still air of downwind sailing. He remembered times in the *Dawn Treader,* when Luella fell sound asleep in similar circumstances. His mind stopped obsessing.

When Archie got back to the condo, the answer machine had three messages. The first was from his oldest daughter. As usual, Bets and Mark were hosting the family gathering for Christmas dinner. She wanted to chat about the arrangements. The second was Tricia Knox, reminding him about the worship conference on the 28th. Archie wondered why they were having a conference between Christmas and New Year's. *Perhaps they are hoping the high school and college age musicians will be more likely to come during the holidays,* he thought. The third message was from a secretary at WCC, reminding him that he was on call for hospital visitation this weekend. Archie hoped he wouldn't get any more calls tonight as he was looking forward to having a quiet evening at home. *There's no rest for the wicked and darn little for the righteous,* he thought, realizing how pleased Luella would be at his activity level today.

Yet as the evening progressed the apartment seemed almost too quiet, after all the action of the afternoon. He found himself wondering what it would be like to have a companion again, but decided it was too much trouble to start dating at his age. He picked up his current O'Brian novel and settled into his favorite chair.

When Sonny had moved from the ranch to Venice, he'd been challenged to find something that would take the edge off his border collie's energy. Then one evening, a few weeks after they had moved in, Sonny saw a show about Frisbee dogs. Sonny went right out and got a Frisbee. There was a bit of a learning curve at first for Sonny and the dog. Sonny was not much good at throwing the disk, and Buck would wait for it to land before he clamped on. But on the morning of the second day, everything clicked. Sonny knew Buck would pick up a bouncing ball on the dead run so he tried to roll the Frisbee. On the third attempt the offshore breeze held the disk on its edge as it cut along the wet, packed sand. Buck snared it with ease and brought it right back. He dropped the plate at Sonny's feet, then made a false start in the direction he wanted Sonny to throw it, lowered his head, and made fixed eye contact with Sonny until he threw it again. "The eye" was one of the ways cattle dogs controlled a herd, and Buck knew how to use it. Sonny hoped he could skim the Frisbee just a foot off the ground and Buck would snare it just the way he grabbed the roller.

"Now don't let it hit the ground, boy, catch it in the air." Sonny took a long stride forward to lower his toss and succeeded in launching a low, flat trajectory.

Buck caught up to the disk in a few strides and this time, instead of letting it float to the sand, he took a little leap forward and caught it in mid-air.

Sonny was ecstatic. He shouted, "Good dog, good dog!" over and over. He tried to catch the dog up in his arms, but Buck would have none of that. He dropped the Frisbee at Sonny's feet and resumed his position, head lowered, eyes fixed, waiting for the next toss. From that moment Buck caught it in the air every time no matter how badly Sonny threw it.

Soon a crowd gathered to watch the show: families with children, other dog owners and their pets, and beautiful bikini-clad women. Sonny instantly turned the whole thing into a circus act, not letting on that they had just figured it out. "Ladies and Gents, appearing today at Venice Beach, Buck the Wonder Dog, the smartest dog in the world!"

After that the early morning exercise sessions became part of their routine. Buck was tireless, especially with the occasional foray into the sea to cool off. Sonny wondered how long the dog could keep it up, but never found out because he would always give out first. He had to train himself to throw the Frisbee with both hands as he developed "tennis elbow" from too many reps with his right. Today's morning toss had the usual routine catches and a few fantastic ones. Sonny particularly enjoyed it when joggers would come into play, and Buck would have to dodge around them to get to the floating disk. They set a record this morning with Buck weaving through no less than four runners on one throw.

On the way back to his bungalow, with Buck running circles around him, Sonny remembered he had promised Shanti she could meet the dog and, on the spur of the moment, decided that today was a good day to go visiting. He took Buck to the outside shower at his house. When the dog was toweled dry, Sonny said, "Want to go for a ride in the car, boy?"

Buck tipped his head to one side and pricked his ears.

"We can go to Shanti's house." As soon as Sonny finished toweling him, Buck ran to the keyholder, sat, and looked back at Sonny, panting.

Shanti and Danielle were hanging out in the garden, when Sonny and Buck arrived outside the iron gate.

"Look, Shanti, Sonny brought Buck to see you," Danielle said as she greeted Sonny.

"Now Danielle, I have to warn you that Buck has a way of inciting other dogs to behave badly, so maybe you should put a leash on your dog there so we can control them."

Danielle looked over at Munchie. The old dog was lying in the sun, eyes half closed, paying little attention to the friendly visitors. "Oh, I don't think we will have any trouble from Munchie," she said, sure of Munchie's ever-present good nature.

"Trust me on this one, Danielle," Sonny said.

Danielle laughed as she clipped the leash on Munchie, who stood up, expecting to go for a walk. Sonny came through the gate. Buck sidled up to the bigger dog innocently enough, but Sonny saw the eyes lock and dug in his heels for the charge.

"Brace yourself, Danielle," he said too late as Munchie shot forward. In a split second the two leashes were hopelessly tangled and had to be abandoned as the dogs spun round and round each other, Munchie making terrible growling, squealing sounds, Buck silent. But once Sonny and Danielle were able to pull them apart, they seemed happy to carry on as if nothing had happened.

Shanti insisted both dogs be inspected for injuries. Sonny knelt down and examined the panting dogs while Danielle stood behind Shanti with her long arms draped over the little girl's chest.

"Summer is coming over for Belgian waffles in a bit. Want to stay for breakfast?" Danielle asked.

"Yeah, Sonny, stay for breakfast," Shanti said.

"I would love to, but I have a 9:00 with my broker in Santa Monica. We can stay for just a few minutes; I came over on an impulse."

"Well, can I fix you a waffle for the road?"

"That would be great! Anyway, let me show you a few tricks.

Shanti, one thing you have to know is Buck won't do any tricks if you don't say please," Sonny said, looking at Shanti, who made a funny face. In fact the 'please' had nothing to do with it. Buck was trained to hand signals: he would move, sit, lie down precisely as ordered at almost any distance away as long as he had line of sight; but it didn't matter what you said if you didn't give him a hand signal.

"All right," Sonny went on, "Let the games begin. Ladies, I give you Buck, the wonder dog, the smartest dog in the world!" Sonny ordered Buck to circle the house.

Buck remained motionless, looking intently at Sonny.

Sonny feigned frustration, put his hand on his hip, raised his voice, and repeated the order: not a twitch. Finally, Sonny said please and made the subtle hand gesture for a circle run.

Buck took off like a shot. In seconds he came tearing around the other side of the house and slid to a stop right in front of Sonny. Sonny then had him run out precise distances and sit, or lie down, or retrieve objects—all with the game of not doing it without the "please." Shanti was delighted; Danielle suspected something else was going on, but couldn't figure it out.

Munchie—on leash, but not going for a walk—began whining, so Danielle took her inside while she fixed Sonny's waffle.

Summer arrived in the middle of the show, to Shanti's shouts of delight. Shanti ran to her at the back gate, grabbed her hand, and began tugging her over to Buck and Sonny. "Summer, Summer come see. Buck won't do it unless you say please."

"Hi, Sonny, how you doing?" Summer asked in her usual cheery manner.

"Hi, Summer. I'm just showing Shanti some of the things Buck learned when he was a working dog at the ranch."

"You lived on a ranch?"

"Yeah, in northern Nevada." Sonny felt uncomfortable with Summer and, as he often did, he began to tell a story to mask his uneasiness. "Buck here saved my life one time."

"Really? How could a little dog like that save your life?"

Just then Danielle came down the stairs with Sonny's waffle wrapped in a napkin. The two women greeted each other warmly while

Sonny took a bite, said how delicious it was, then began his story. "Well, Buck and I were checking on a water hole when an old bull came out of the brush and took a notion to charge. There I was out in the open, 30 feet from my horse, no gun, and no way to escape. I thought I was a goner when suddenly I saw a blur of black and white fly across the bull's path. Buck grabbed that bull right by the nose and threw him to the ground."

"Unbelievable," Summer said, looking at the little dog.

"I know. I wouldn't have believed it myself if I hadn't been there. How can a 30-pound dog throw a 3,000-pound bull."

They all looked at the dog who was holding his position in front of Sonny, waiting for the next command.

"The thing is," Sonny went on, "if he had grabbed him anywhere else it wouldn't have worked. Buck had never thrown a bull before nor ever seen it done. How did he know to grab the nose?"

The four of them stood there awhile, looking at Buck, pondering Sonny's question.

"He is the smartest dog in the world!" Shanti finally said.

Sonny said his good-byes, thanked Danielle for the delicious waffle, and headed for the gate, Buck at his side sniffing the waffle.

"Come and see us again, Sonny," Shanti said.

"Yes, you and Buck are always welcome," Danielle said.

Shanti returned to playing make-believe with her dolls in the garden while Summer and Danielle headed upstairs for breakfast.

"Isn't Shanti going to join us?" Summer asked.

"She had her breakfast a while ago. Since she was in hospital she has been getting up at a ridiculous hour."

"And you have to get up with her."

"Yup, I'm not much good for night life." Danielle poured batter into the waffle iron and served orange juice, coffee, and a warm waffle to Summer.

"I was surprised to see Sonny over here so early," Summer said.

"He promised Shanti when she was in hospital that he would bring Buck over and show us his tricks. I guess he's an early riser too."

"You feel safe with Sonny and Archie?"

"Yeah I do. First of all, Archie saved Shanti's life and then, when he suggested the hospital visits to keep her spirits up, he made me phone his church to get a recommendation. His pastor practically said he was a saint."

"So they seem like pretty reliable guys?"

"Yeah, why, do you know something here I don't know?"

"No, not at all; it's just that I care about you two and these guys that you don't know from Adam are suddenly a big part of your life."

"Maybe it's just karma, Summer; it was meant to be."

"What about Archie being a Christian? Has he tried to convert you yet?"

"We've had some discussions. But I don't get the feeling he is pushing his faith onto me. In fact, I win most of the arguments," Danielle said, smiling.

Summer was holding her waffle in both hands, having just taken a bite. She pointed at Danielle with both her little fingers, the only ones not engaged as she said, "I wouldn't want to get into an argument with you, sister!"

Danielle laughed and went on, "He used to be into Eastern religions before he became a Christian."

"No kidding? That's a trip."

"He's coming to Satsang with me next Wednesday."

"Maybe you'll convert him," Summer said, taking another delicious bite. "Oh, I almost forgot to tell you. Primo has your screen test all set up."

Archie was having his usual breakfast, two poached eggs, toast, orange juice, and coffee, reading the *Tribune,* and wondering if he should call Sonny to see if he wanted to take the Cal 40 out for a day sail. They were catching the back side of a big storm system off Mexico and it would soon be too windy to take out the *Mira Flores.* The *Dawn Treader,* on the other hand, liked a good blow and really showed her stuff on just about any point of sail once the wind got over 15 knots. He was putting the paper down to reach for the phone when it rang.

"Archie Douglas speaking."

"Hi, Archie, this is Marcie calling from WCC."

"Hi Marcie. How are you today?"

"Fine. You're on call for hospital visitation?"

"Yes, I am."

"OK. Timmy Gonzales, age nine, fell off his skateboard yesterday; they are holding him over for observation at SMG. I guess he banged his head or broke his arm, or maybe both. Anyway, the Gonzales family is new at church and a visit would probably be a good thing."

"Right," Archie said as he continued writing a note to himself. "Is Timmy in the ER or in the children's ward?"

"You know, I don't have that info. But if you're going over, I can get it and call you right back."

"Thanks, Marcie, that would save me some time." Archie didn't say why he was in a "lose not a moment" mode: that he wanted to go sailing and hoped to get the visit in as soon as possible. He ruled out calling Sonny for a ride, and certainly ruled out biking to the hospital; instead he called a cab to give him more time for sailing later. He changed into slacks and a decent shirt, ran the electric razor over his face and got the call back from Marcie: Timmy was in the children's ward.

On the way over he wondered if he would see Nurse Hollings but realized it was Saturday and she would have the day off.

The visit with Timmy and his mom went really well, Archie thought. The poor little guy had both a broken arm and a mild concussion. They were Guatemalan refugees with an uncle in Santa Monica who had sponsored their immigration. Timmy spoke perfect English but not his mom. The fact that Archie was able to chat with her in Spanish made everyone feel more at ease. They had the usual debate—whether her English was better than Archie's Spanish—and Archie sincerely encouraged her to keep after it as she was doing really well.

"Most adults find it hard to pick up a second language," he told her. "But if you stay at it, eventually it kicks in," he told her in both English and Spanish. Mrs. Gonzales shared that she liked the Spanish-speaking service at WCC. Archie asked her if it would be all right if he prayed for Timmy's healing. The mother's approval was quite animated.

"Are you OK with me anointing you with oil and laying a hand on your shoulder while I pray, Tim?"

"That would be all right," the little boy said.

Archie put a dot of oil on his index finger and made the sign of the cross on Timmy's forehead saying, "In the name of the Father, the Son, and the Holy Spirit." Archie then prayed in a straightforward and simple way for God to heal Timmy's injuries. The Westside motto about prayer was: "Ordinary people, praying simple prayers, getting miraculous results." Archie liked the idea that his part in the transaction was very small; most of what went on when prayer worked was God's doing.

Archie came out of the room feeling good about the visit. He liked the Latino culture and the warm feeling he had when he reconnected with it. He hurried down the hall, thinking about how the Cal 40 would do in the gale that was now blowing outside but was stopped in his tracks about 20 feet from the nurses' station.

There, dead ahead, was Nurse Hollings. She was wearing sandals, faded jeans, a brightly colored blouse, and was engaged in an intense conversation with an on-duty nurse in uniform. It was the first time Archie had seen Nancy in civilian clothes and he liked the way she looked.

"Hi Nancy," he said, having slowed his fast pace.

"Hi Archie. Visiting Timmy Gonzales, I bet."

"Yeah, they just started coming to WCC. Don't you get the week-ends off?"

"Yes, I do, but I had a little 'admin' crisis here today; I live nearby so I just popped over. It's all taken care of now."

Archie couldn't believe how uptight he felt talking to Nancy. He realized he wanted to ask her out. He kicked himself for feeling anxious. He had counseled so many young men about how you just ask them out for coffee—no one will ever turn down a cup of coffee. Yet here he was with the fear of rejection gripping his heart.

"Can I buy you a cup of coffee?"

"That would be lovely, Archie, and I know just the place." Nancy didn't take them to Mocha Joe's just down the street, as Archie had expected, but to Pasquali's, a tiny place on an alley in downtown Santa Monica. The espresso machine on a back counter and selection of pastries under the glass in front of them transported Archie back to Italy.

"How did you find this place, Nancy? It is so much like one Luella, my wife, and I liked in Bologna. It was the only no smoking place in the whole city."

"Oh my goodness, the one just west of the leaning tower?"

"You've been there?"

"My friend Beatrice and I spent a month in Italy just last fall."

"We were there six years ago." Archie realized the server was smiling at them and waiting for a break in their nonstop conversation that had been going on from the moment they left the nurses' station.

"*Provo en Italiano. Due café, perfavore*," Archie said.

"*Bene, molto bene*," the server replied and then rattled off a phase that went by too fast, but Archie guessed correctly by her gesture and one word that seemed familiar that she was asking them if they wanted a pastry too.

Nancy put her hand on Archie's arm. "These cream-filled ones are to die for, Archie."

"We'll have two of those," Archie said, smiling at the server but thinking neither about the pastry, nor the woman behind the counter, nor his dairy allergy; his total awareness was taken up by the light pressure of Nancy's hand on his shirt sleeve. As the couple made their way to a tiny table near the window, it started to rain and, as so often is the case in southern California, if it rains at all it pours.

"Well, that wasn't in the forecast," Nancy said.

"It's a sign," Archie said, still looking out.

"Of what, Archie?"

"Well, I was going to go straight from the hospital to my boat to go for a sail. I don't mind getting caught out in the rain; I have all the gear for it. But I'm not so desperate that I'll start out when it's pouring like this."

"So, it's a sign you aren't to go sailing?"

"Yes, and that it's a good day to be here, inside a coffee shop that transports us to *Italia*. What a good choice, Nancy." The phrase that went through Archie's head was *"it's a sign to be here with you,"* but he left out *"with you,"* thinking this would sound overly bold at their first meeting.

"Thank you, Archie, it's one of my favorite places. So you own a sailboat?"

"Two of them actually—a Cal 40 sloop and a 14-foot sailing skiff. I was in the skiff when I rescued Shanti."

"You know I've heard bits and pieces of how that happened. I'd love to hear the whole story."

Archie told the story briskly, having been over it so many times by now. As he was telling it, he noticed how interested and overall delighted she seemed; a need to know welled up in him whether Nancy might like to sail and, perhaps more important, whether she was prone to seasickness. "So what about you? Are you nautically inclined at all?"

"I've never been sailing, but I would love to give it a go. Most of my experience on the water was fishing the lakes in Minnesota and Northern Ontario when I was a girl. My dad was quite the sportsman."

The rain pelted on the window.

Archie looked out. "The waves will be building now. Ever get caught out in conditions like this?"

"As a matter of fact, we did." Nancy became quite excited as she told about being in a 24-foot runabout on Lake of the Woods when a thunder and lightning storm hit.

Archie was fascinated with the story, but even more with her. She seemed so lively and energetic telling it. Her big, brown eyes flashed, and every now and then she tossed her auburn hair. When she said, "You know, thinking back, I believe I actually like life on the water more than on land. I don't know what it is—the constant motion, perhaps, but out there I feel more, more..."

"Alive." Archie finished the sentence for her with a lump in his throat and hope rising in his heart.

"Yes, that's it exactly, more alive," she said, beaming at Archie.

He so much wanted to seize her hand and tell her he thought they were soul mates but restrained himself: too much too soon. He also had to be sure about the seasickness. He looked for every clue in her narrative that she wasn't prone to *mal de mar* and as she described how the land disappeared each time they entered a trough on the way back to the fishing lodge he thought she wasn't, but he had to know for certain. "And nobody got sea sick?" he said, pleased at his subtlety.

"Oh no. The Dowds all have cast-iron stomachs."

"Excellent, excellent," Archie cried. Then, seeing her slightly puzzled look, he tried to cover his excitement: "Dowd was your family name?"

She nodded behind her coffee cup.

"I had a friend in college named Dowd from Northern Ireland."

"Yes, our family emigrated from there about four generations ago. We've traced our roots back to a small coastal town called Larne on the North Channel."

From there the conversation swept on to their trips to their ancestral homes, hers at Larne and his in the Scottish borderlands just across the Channel. That brought up their mutual fascination with how Christianity spread from Ireland to Scotland and their shared delight with the Abby on Iona. They plunged into the depths of their faith. They talked about their families: the deaths of their spouses, their children and grandchildren.

Hours passed; the rain stopped. Archie suggested they stretch their legs. They walked and talked their way onto the pier. The sun came out and the wind died as the conversation sailed on. The areas of common interest, activities, and shared points of view seemed limitless and their dialogue was punctuated with, "You're kidding me, I had the same reaction," and "Get out of town, you haven't been there?" They became hungry and ordered fish and chips from a stand on the pier.

The afternoon was soon over. Neither wanted it to end, but Nancy had to babysit her grandchildren that evening and Archie had a Saturday night service to attend. Each had duties to fulfill at their church the next morning as well but they agreed to meet for Sunday lunch.

6

She knows she bears a soul that dares
And loves the dark rough seas.
More sail, I cry, let her fly,
This is the life for me!
ELIZA COOK

Archie was glad that his previously arranged visit with Tom at U.C.L.A. fell on a day when Nancy was working. Archie took the bus from the marina to U.C.L.A. A bus route map, an L.A. street guide, and Tom's directions got him to within a few blocks of the earthquake simulation lab. The driver let him off at a likely corner, and he was happy to walk the rest of the way. He was pleased that he was able to do the whole trip on one fare: two buses with a transfer. The bus trip reminded him of some of his adventures in Europe, where public transportation was the way to go. L.A. Transit wasn't as fast as London, but not as slow as Rome. Rome: what a difficult city to get around, but on the other hand, who cares with something interesting on every corner?

As he walked across campus he gave Tom a call on his cell phone.

"Hey, Arch, are you on your way?"

"Yeah, I think I'm getting close. I'm in front of something called Norton Hall."

"Tell you what. Just wait there about two minutes. I'll come over and get you. You're coming in from the opposite direction I imagined. It will be easier to meet you there. I need some fresh air anyway.'"

Archie passed the time waiting for Tom in one of his favorite activities: people watching. He hadn't been on a college campus for some time and found the youthfulness and variety of folks going by fascinating.

"There you are; good to see you," Tom said as the two shook hands. "Come on, it's this way. My partner is out in the field today, so it's perfect timing for your tour."

From the outside, the lab was just another nondescript building. Inside, the first thing Archie noticed was a strange contraption made up of electric motors, pistons, clamps, and a heavy metal frame. Wires and cables ran away from it to what appeared to be a control console. Behind that were various gauges and one thing he did recognize: a seismographic recorder.

Tom picked up on the direction of his gaze and launched into his explanation. "What you're looking at is our Earthquake Simulator. Bill and I call it ELVIS—as in 'a whole lot of shaking going on.' We inherited ELVIS from the last team that was working on this, but we made some modifications and improved his durability and life expectancy with these shock absorbers. Before that he had a tendency to self-destruct."

"Not unlike the singer," Archie interjected.

Tom grinned. "Never thought of that. I'll have to tell Bixby. What we're working on now is developing, or really better said, *refining* sensors that can monitor dozens of different conditions in the structures we are testing, like acceleration, strain, and displacement. Through manipulation of these bars and clamps, and different settings on the motors, ELVIS is capable of producing a variety of shaking motions and intensities—small, moderate, even significant structural vibrations. Make sense so far?"

"Yes, I've always been a fan of applied science. It's not unlike therapy, where we are always looking at how theoretical breakthroughs or technological advancements can be applied to help our clients."

"Good stuff, Archie. OK, now over here is the computer programming area, where we are developing software that will uplink all the data we generate. That way researchers around the world can join in the fun."

"Brilliant."

"Yeah, well, we hope that piece makes the project more attractive for funding sources down the road. More bang for your buck sort of thing. Another phase that's on the drawing board is to export the sensors to real structures, dams, bridges, freeway interchanges—hook a mobile ELVIS on to them and then monitor the effects. Understand, Arch, all of this has been going on for some time; Bill and I are just refining the technology."

"I know there have already been a lot of improvements in building design," Archie said.

"I'd say the whole thing really got rolling in our area after the San Fernando Earthquake in '71. I guess the press called it the Sylmar Quake because of the very destructive surface faulting that occurred in Sylmar. After that the people responsible for building codes started paying attention to our input. I know the Sylmar Quake had tragic outcomes for the people living in the area, but at the same time it provided an immense amount of data that should prevent loss of life and reduce property damage when the next big one comes in a metropolitan area."

"I notice you're saying when, not if."

"Archie, earthquakes happen every day in our state; most are small and cause no damage, or if they are big, the epicenters aren't near a heavily populated area. It's just a matter of probability when the next one will be under a city. But there are other factors that make certain areas higher risk. I'll show you. Come on in the reference room. I've laid out maps, photos, and other data to give you an idea of why we're doing this."

"I love maps," Archie said.

They moved into a smaller adjoining room lined with file cabinets and metal bookshelves filled with file folders and other nondescript documents.

Tom went straight to several piles of papers laid out on the large rectangular table in the middle of the room. "I thought we could start with the data you're probably most familiar with—the surface damage—and then work our way down into the depths." Tom went to a map first, following Archie's interest. "Most of the damage in a quake is caused by surface breaks, which in turn are caused by faulting or cracks in the sub-strata during the quake. In the San Fernando Quake the breaks started here in the Bee Canyon area, went east through

Sylmar here, and ended up in the Big Tujunga wash over here."

"That must be over 10 miles."

"Yep, about twelve and a half." Tom sensed Archie's interest and comprehension and forged ahead into the more technical issues, trying to keep to layman's language as much as possible. "Most of the breaks on the surface are caused by thrust faulting: in the Sylmar Quake, land on the north side of the break was lifted and 'thrust' toward the south over the land on that side of the break. Does that make sense?"

"Very scary," Archie said nodding and thinking of the force it would take to do that and the damage such movement could cause. "So it's not just the shaking that causes damage?"

"Right. Well, that depends on how hard the shaking is versus how major the thrust faulting is. We haven't seen a metropolitan quake where shaking out did faulting for damage, but it's a scenario we can't rule out, and if it happens it could affect a much larger area. In '71 the most damage was caused by thrust faulting. Here—look at these photos taken near the intersection of Hubbard and Glenoaks in Sylmar. See how the surface breaks went right through a heavily populated area?"

"Yikes!" Archie said, looking at photos Tom handed him of destroyed buildings, collapsed freeway interchanges, and cracked dams.

Tom gave Archie a few moments to take it all in. "OK, now let's start looking at underlying causes. Check out this topographic map of the Valley. See how the San Gabriels rise thousands of feet above the heavily populated regions here in the north east end of the valley?"

Archie nodded as his finger traced the closely packed topographic lines indicating the steep rise of the mountains. "Two factors come into play here: first, the relative stability of this region." Tom's hair fell over his eyes as he bent over the maps and documents. "Few quakes occurred here recently. You see, other areas have small quakes frequently." He pointed to several recorded quake sites on another map. "The theory is that when a region is stable, pressure has to build before something lets go; the accumulated strain results in a bigger quake. *Comprende?*"

"*Si,*" Archie said gravely.

"Now, a second key factor." Tom ran his hand along the map. "These mountains on the north side of the valley are, relatively speaking, young mountains, still on the way up as evidenced by their ruggedness and abruptness—no time for much erosion yet. These mountains have been raised by fault movements countless times during the past several million years. And every time a fault moves there is an earthquake."

"All these factors point to Sylmar as a high risk area?"

"Yes, really the whole northeast valley, anywhere along the south side of the San Gabriels all the way over into L.A.; wherever there is population density."

"Man, there's been a lot of construction in those areas lately." Archie eyed the topographical map.

"I know, I know. The final piece of the puzzle is my first love: tectonics. Are you still with me?" Tom said, looking at him intensely.

"I would call my current state of mind a kind of horrified fascination, Tom."

"Good, good," Tom went on. "The mountain ranges that surround the San Fernando Valley, like the San Gabriels on the north and the Santa Monica Mountains on the south, have an east-west trend that makes them traverse ranges. These ranges are actively deforming because of folding and thrust faulting that's occurring here in the 'big bend' of the San Andreas fault. See here how the San Andreas changes course to a more northerly direction?"

"Yes, I see the bend, but I don't understand much of what you just said."

"OK, OK, I tell you what. Let's start from the other end of the story, the big picture, then all these smaller pieces will make sense." As Tom spoke, he opened an illustrated textbook that was laying beside the maps. "You know how ice floats on top of a lake in winter. It can be several feet thick and solid enough to support thousands of pounds."

Archie nodded, remembering stories of ice fishermen driving their pickups right out on the ice.

"The earth's crust, also known as the lithosphere, floats on the planet's molten insides. Unlike the ice on the lake however, there is no shore to act as a boundary to keep it in place. So the whole crust is in slow but constant movement." Tom could see Archie was tracking with him now; Tom's hands shook with excitement as he demonstrated the next point. "The whole of the Earth's crust is broken into 16 pieces, or what we call plates. These slabs of rock are around 60 miles thick and thousands of miles wide and they are all moving."

"I think I see where you're going with this."

"Excellent!" Tom's passion increased another notch. "They are all moving, and along their edges, where two plates meet, is where most of the surface action is produced. Sometimes two continental plates converge and collide: the Himalayas were formed when the Indian subcontinent pressed inexorably into Eurasia. Sometimes they spread apart like right now in the mid Atlantic—the North Atlantic Plate and the Eurasian Plate are moving apart as much as eight inches a year. Here on the west coast the North Atlantic and Pacific Plates are sliding against each other, the Pacific moving roughly south to north."

Tom put his hands side by side, palms down and slid the left along the right to illustrate. "Fault lines develop where they slide against each other. They don't slide smoothly; edges catch, pressure builds, and then lets go. The plates move in little jumps usually but sometimes, as in '71, the pressure has built for a long time and the larger jump results in a larger earthquake."

"So the quakes, which seem cataclysmic to us, are really just the tail of the dog of a much bigger process going on beneath the surface," Archie said.

"Exactly!" Tom was glowing at his new friend's comprehension. "Now let's get back to the 'big bend' issue," he said, pointing to the map that showed the curve in the San Andreas Fault just north of L.A.

"I think I got it," Archie said. "That bend curtails the north by northwest movement of the Pacific Plate."

Tom held his breath and nodded rapidly.

"That creates greater pressure, which in turn increases the likelihood of bigger quakes on the surface."

"You got it, Arch. Now just to not oversimplify, there are actually faults running all over the place in this region—see here, here, and here, for example. Beyond that we're sure there are many faults we haven't identified yet." Tom paused, again studying his maps. "You know, there is even an east-west fault running right under the hospital in Santa Monica where Shanti was. See here?"

"Yikes," Archie said.

A short while later, he was reflecting on his afternoon. It had been very interesting—one of his best outings yet. Since his travels in Europe, he had learned that every neighborhood has points of interest, even fascination. The key was to find the right person to uncover the hidden mysteries that most folks aren't aware of. Tom was a treasure trove for the L.A. basin. The plan was to catch a ride back to the beach with Tom and have a quick supper with the three Jacksons. Then Tom would spend the evening with Shanti while Archie and Danielle went to Satsang.

But first Tom needed an hour to finish up some paperwork. Archie welcomed the opportunity to have a little rest before his next big adventure. He went out to a grassy area in front of Tom's building, found a sunny spot, and lay down with his backpack under his head as he had seen a couple of students doing earlier. He realized he was hungry and brought out his usual peanuts and raisins snack, a banana, and a juice box. Archie nibbled, dozed, and pondered the visit with Tom. He realized he hadn't thought once about Nancy the whole time he was in the lab. He wondered if she would be interested in tectonics. He was unaware that he was smiling. A coed must have noticed, however. She smiled back and said hello as she walked by.

Supper had gone well with Shanti carrying the conversation and the three adults happy to follow her interests.

"All right you two, go on to your meeting," Tom hollered from the kitchen. "Shanti and I will clean up."

"Starts at seven?" Archie asked.

"Yes, we better get going," Danielle replied. "Thanks, Tom. We should be home before ten."

They all said their good-byes, and Archie marveled once again at how much goodwill there was between the estranged couple. He couldn't help asking about it in Tom's car. "You two seem to get along so well; ever think about getting back together?"

"You sound like my mother, Archie."

"I don't mind confirming her observations."

Danielle frowned. "It's for Tom and me to work out, and don't say anything about what's best for Shanti."

"How did you know I was going there next?"

"That's where she always goes next. Any more questions?"

"Where's Satsang?" Archie said.

Satsang was in a little house in Ocean Park, just a few minutes away. They arrived at 6:55. The people who lived there, the Coalingas, had moved all their living-room furniture into the dining area, hung glass doors between the two rooms, and did all their eating in the breakfast nook. The living room had meditation pillows scattered around the floor, a harmonium in the middle of the room, and not much else. Guru Rahndananda smiled down on the whole scene from a picture over the fireplace which now served as an altar. A votive candle flickered beneath the picture, and sandalwood incense burned at one side of the mantle. The living-room windows were hung with heavy, blackout draperies. The men sat on one side of the room; the women on the other. Fifteen people were there; it looked like the place might hold 25.

It was all familiar to Archie, much like his grad-school days. His immediate concern at this stage of life was sitting on the floor. At his age, he wasn't sure he could last for the duration, but he found a place against a back wall on the men's side. He made himself as comfortable as he could, turning both legs to one side and started his favorite activity—people watching. *The usual suspects,* he thought until he came to a girl in the back row on the opposite side. She was unremarkable in every way but one: emblazoned across her white T-shirt in day-glow pink letters was "I HAVE ISSUES." The message made Archie laugh, made him want to know what they were, and made him wonder if she had some clever follow-up for all inquirers.

While pondering her issues he flashed back to the conversation with Danielle in the car. Danielle had not said an outright no to the question of getting back together with Tom. *Jimmy and I will have to keep praying,* Archie thought. He had discussed coming to Danielle's Satsang with Pastor Jim and had asked him to intercede for the outing.

His thoughts were broken off when an attractive 30-year-old

woman wearing a sharp-looking business suit stood beside the altar and began speaking. "Welcome to Satsang. My name is Diane Coalinga. As you can see, my husband, Phil, and I have turned our living room into a meditation hall. A special welcome to our first-time guests. If you haven't already, be sure to fill in the requested info in our guest book; that will get you on our mailing list for upcoming events. This evening, as every Wednesday, we will have a short talk on meditation, about 20 minutes of chanting and then a few minutes of meditation. What is meditation? Why do we meditate? How does it work?" Diane swung into her talk.

Archie was impressed. She spoke well and without notes of any kind. Danielle had told him Diane was a lawyer with a big firm in downtown L.A. She came across as a polished and confident professional. The last few minutes of the talk she demonstrated how to meditate—integrating the mantra "Om, Rama Krishna" with the breath, "Om" on the inhalation, "Rama Krishna" on the exhalation.

"Don't force the breathing; let the body lead you. In fact, don't force anything; whatever happens during meditation is what is supposed to happen. Relax, enjoy, and just return gently to the mantra when your mind wanders. Now Phil will lead us in some chanting. The words are on the cards. Danielle, could you pass them around? Thank you."

Archie's attention turned to Phil as Diane sat down gracefully. Danielle had said that he was a schoolteacher in West L.A. Unlike his wife, he must have changed after work as he wore a loose-fitting, East Indian style white shirt and navy blue sweatpants that looked comfortable for sitting on the floor. Phil sat in a full lotus in front of the harmonium. He began to squeeze the bellows at the back of the box-shaped instrument with his left hand as he touched the keys with his right. The gentle notes of the natural wind instrument carried the melody in a pleasant, unbroken sound. Archie had forgotten how soothing the instrument's sound was. A woman on the other side began to pluck a tall, four-stringed, drone instrument. *What was its name?...murdung*, Archie thought.

The chanting was familiar to Archie. They played two songs starting with one he didn't know, but the second was the familiar "Hare

Rama, Hare Krishna." As Archie remembered, the chant started slowly, then accelerated with each repetition. At one point Diane and another woman joined in with finger cymbals in a pleasing, syncopated beat. At the end, Phil played a slow, brief salutation to the guru while someone dimmed the lights. The room fell silent.

Archie was glad he had the Jesus prayer for his meditation: "Lord Jesus Christ, have mercy on me." The prayer was first passed on to him in his early days of being a Christian. When one of his mentors found out he had practiced new age meditation, he gave him a book on the desert fathers. Archie was amazed to discover that Christians had worked out a way to meditate on Jesus since the third century. He prayed, "Lord Jesus Christ" on the inhalation, "have mercy on me" on the exhalation, and practiced waiting before the Lord in the space between the breaths. Archie was having a good prayer time, centering on Jesus, when Phil played a long note on the harmonium and then the salutation again.

Without getting up, Diane began speaking in a mellow, low register: "Take your time coming out of meditation." Then, after a long pause, she went on, "If you have questions or would just like to hang out and get acquainted, we have coffee and cookies in the other room. But this ends the formal part of the evening. Thank you for coming."

Archie saw her hand move behind her as the lights came up. *Cool,* he thought, *a rheostat under the pillow.* This low-tech device reminded him of the afternoon spent with Tom and ELVIS. He regarded the gap between Tom and Danielle's lifestyles. *Ah well,* he thought, *that's why we pray, "Nothing is impossible with God."*

"So how was it for you, Archie?" Danielle asked as they made their way down the street to the car.

"It was all very familiar, Danielle, except for the girl in the 'I Have Issues' T-shirt."

"Oh, she was a first-time guest."

"Aha," Archie said, and then a moment later asked, "Speaking of first-time guests, do you think I stood out as much as she did?"

"Possibly Archie, but did you feel uncomfortable being there?"

"No, actually I didn't; it was very similar to what I was doing before I became a Christian."

"Why did you make the switch to Jesus?" Danielle asked as she unlocked Tom's car.

Archie tried to remember his state of mind at the time of his conversion as he got in the passenger side and Danielle slipped behind the wheel. She put the key in the ignition but didn't start the engine.

"It's hard to remember exactly what I was thinking or feeling at the time or the exact order of events. I do remember at some point early on it made sense to me. I came to the conclusion that it was reasonable to believe in Jesus because it gave ultimate value to my life and the lives of others and because it gave me good values to live by. And then around that same time we discovered the guru wasn't living the pure life he claimed. I think I told you how he was having tantric sex with women and girls in the Ashram. Many of the girls were seriously traumatized by it." Archie looked at Danielle as he was saying this to see how it went over. *Not great*, he thought.

After some hesitation Danielle said, "We're friends, right?"

"Of course we are."

"And you know how much it means to me—how much I owe you—for rescuing Shanti."

Archie nodded.

"I want to tell you something that I know will test our friendship—maybe end it."

Archie couldn't imagine what it could be and then remembered the punch line of a bad golf joke: "You're really a man?" But he had learned over years of experience with Luella it was better to say nothing than to say the wrong thing at a time like this.

After a pause, Danielle went on, "You remember my friend Summer? She makes her living making movies. She and Primo think with my looks I could make some money acting in movies. And I need some extra income to pay for Shanti's hospital bills that weren't covered by Tom's insurance."

"There are always some things not covered, aren't there," Archie said, shaking his head.

"It adds up to thousands. There's no way Tom can come up with that kind of money, nor is it fair to put the entire burden on him."

"I think it's honorable for you to want to help out, Danielle. What makes you think this would be a problem in our friendship?"

Danielle turned sideways in the car so she could look right at Archie. "OK, I have two words for you: pornographic movies."

Danielle waited for Archie's reaction. But Archie couldn't respond, not in words, not outwardly. His first response was physical; his body went hot then ice cold. He felt his viscera tighten; he was gripped by fear. After a few moments he wanted to say this would not be pleasing to God, but he censored that as too inflammatory.

All Danielle could see was Archie staring down the street. "So what's your response, Archie? What are you thinking?"

"I have a bad feeling about this, Danielle. I don't want you to do this."

"Are you trying to control me? I can tell you right now, that is not going to work."

"No, no, you have it all wrong. I don't want to control you. I'm just trying to protect you, to protect my friend. The porn industry uses women, it degrades women. The producers, the men who buy the videos, they are all going to use you."

"Look, Archie, maybe you live in a world where that's the way it is, but that isn't my world. In my world if it's good enough for Summer, it's good enough for me."

"Summer seems like a nice friend for you, sweetheart, but..."

"Don't you sweetheart me. I'm not your daughter, Archie."

"Look, Danielle, I have money. Let me loan you the amount you need to pay off the bills; or I'd be happy to pay them outright, I..."

"I'm not a charity case, Archie," Danielle said as she started the engine and quickly pulled out of the parking space. "If you want to end our friendship over this, go ahead," she said looking over her left shoulder. "But I am doing this, Archie. The screen test is already set for next week." She looked at him for a moment. "If you want to stay friends with me and Shanti, you have to accept that."

Archie didn't respond. He felt terrible. He regretted that once again their conversation had gone a direction he didn't want. He felt worse about the direction Danielle's life was headed. He didn't like the choices she gave him, but he understood and respected her right to set boundaries. Danielle was also silent all the way to the gate of his condo where she pulled over with the engine idling.

With his hand on the door handle Archie said, "I still want to be friends, Danielle. I can't think on my feet as fast as you. I need some time to mull this over and pray about it.

"Sure, Archie, take as much time as you need. I'm sure it's a lot for you to deal with."

Archie got out of the car. "Good night, Danielle, and thank you for Satsang."

Archie and Pastor Jim's mentoring session was following its usual course, but it took a lot of willpower for Archie to let Jim talk all the time since he wanted to unload about last's night's turn of events with Danielle. The two men talked as they walked around the neighborhood, their preferred way of passing the hour; it was especially good for Jim to get out of the office. They had worked out a route that looped through a small park, a pleasant residential neighborhood, and then back onto the strip mall where Westside was located.

Archie was doing a good job of staying focused and helping Jim work through a tough decision until they passed the corner video store. "Ooch! Awe!" he exclaimed, horrified by the thought of Danielle in the porn section.

"What's wrong, Arch?"

"It's Danielle," he cried. "She's made a decision that could ruin her life and says I have to live with it!"

The men switched roles as Archie summarized last night's revelations interspersed with comments that beat him up for never managing it well with Danielle.

"Come on, Arch, she's a handful. I don't think anyone would do better than you."

"Luella would; Luella always knew the right thing to say."

Jimmy did not reply but did stop walking and fixed his friend with a look that said "I'm waiting for you to tell me what's wrong with this picture."

"All right, all right, I know, this kind of thinking is getting me nowhere. I should move on to problem-solving."

The two resumed their walk.

"But that's just it; she's put me in a position where I can do nothing!" Archie gestured wildly with his hands as he spoke.

"Nothing?" Jimmy repeated.

"You're right, I can always pray. It's just that I know this course is heading her straight for the rocks."

"Well, maybe you can be a port in the coming storm," Jimmy said, trying a sailing analogy of his own.

Archie phoned Danielle that night with his decision. "I want to be a friend to you and Shanti no matter what. And I will keep praying for you." He left off the part about being there for her when her ship founders—as it would certainly do.

"Good, Archie, I was hoping you would say that," Danielle replied. "And you know, it's not like I'm going to make a career of this. When the bills are paid, it's over."

Primo had arranged the screen test for noon Wednesday, December 8th, between movie shoots. Summer told Danielle it would just be the two of them and the cameraman. They would work a scene that set up the entrance of the male actor and would go through various stages of undress. Summer assured her the cameraman, Jake, was totally professional. The whole idea was to see how Danielle looked on camera, how she responded to the demands of acting and so on. Danielle felt a little nervous about it but was determined to go through with it. The only problem she had was Tom couldn't take Shanti as he had an important presentation at one o'clock. Danielle tried all her regular baby sitters with no luck. The only person left was Archie. She realized the ethical dilemma it posed for him—he would be facilitating something he morally opposed. She hoped he could find some other way of looking at it as she picked up the phone.

After the initial pleasantries she came straight out with it. "Archie, I have my screen test tomorrow at noon. Tom and all my baby sitters are tied up. Could you watch Shanti for maybe three hours?" After a pause of a few seconds she said, "Archie, are you there?"

"I'm thinking," he said. "What would you do if I couldn't do it?"

"Well, I guess I'd have to take her with me."

Archie knew how strong-willed Danielle was and didn't doubt she meant what she said. The idea of Danielle going to a porn studio was bad enough, but Shanti going was intolerable. "OK, I'll watch her, but you know I don't have a car."

"Thanks, Archie. Summer is picking me up. We'll bring Shanti over around 11, if that's all right. She loves your place."

Archie's reluctance melted the moment Shanti shot through his open door and wrapped her arms around his neck as he bent over to pick her up.

"Archie!" she cried.

Archie had determined before they arrived to keep his focus on the little girl, but he had to look at Danielle when she handed him Shanti's backpack and explained about a few of the necessary items inside. Clothes and makeup were not one of Archie's strong suits. On the other hand, he knew a beautiful woman when he saw one and Danielle was stunning. For all his resolve to avoid looking at her, he gazed upon one of the most beautiful women he had ever seen. But her perfection only deepened his already present sense of doom. He was sure the porn producers would put her to work in a heartbeat. Sandalwood wafted over him as she kissed Shanti good-bye and swept out the door.

Archie fought the terrible sinking feeling by focusing on the child. He had several activities planned for their time together, including a walking tour of the marina, lunch, and reading. But Shanti went straight to the crèche and wanted him to talk Joseph, the wise men, and shepherds, while she took up the role of Mary and the baby Jesus.

What better way to pass through this perilous time, Archie thought. Forty minutes later, Archie realized his play-acting was becoming disjointed as his mind fogged over with the ongoing make-believe. He was about to beg for a change of activity when the phone rang.

"Hey Arch, good day for a sail."

"Sonny!"

"Is Sonny coming over? Can he be Doctor Bobo again?" Shanti cried as she ran to Archie at the phone.

"Is Shanti over for a visit?" Sonny asked.

"Yes she is; I'm entertaining her for a couple hours while her mom, uh, explores a job opportunity. Shanti wants to ask you something."

"Can you come over and be Doctor Bobo?" Shanti asked without hesitation.

Archie could tell from her delighted expression the answer was yes, but Sonny must have had a few more things to say before Shanti handed him back the phone. Shanti seemed too animated now for make-believe, but she was interested in the peanut-butter sandwiches Archie had made for their lunch. They were just finishing when the doorbell rang.

"That should be Sonny. Do you want to let him in?"

Shanti ran to the door, flung it open, and squealed with delight. Archie laughed too; there in the door stood Sonny in a long, white doctor's coat, stethoscope, and Dr. Bobo nose. Beside him stood a smiling Buck with a ruffled clown collar around his neck. The dog towed Sonny into the room as he made a beeline for Shanti, determined to give her a good face-licking. The visit now kicked into high gear with Sonny and Buck doing—and at Shanti's insistence repeating—some clown tricks that Archie thought were as good as any he had seen in the circus.

The phone rang again. It was Danielle. "Archie, the screen test is over, but Summer's mother called all freaked out about a high cholesterol report she just got from her doctor. Summer said she was crying on the phone. Summer wants to go over from here. I don't want to spend the rest of the day in Glendale, but I can catch a ride back to Venice around seven or I can call a taxi right now if you have plans for the afternoon."

"Just a second," Archie said, "I may have another option." He turned to Sonny and whispered, "It's Danielle. Her ride fell through. Are you up for a little road trip?"

Sonny jumped up, "I'm all over it, Arch! Where is she?"

Buck, even more excited than Sonny, led the way down the stairs to the Land Rover, circling them at the landing to keep the little group bunched. Hundreds of years of breeding had honed the dog's instinct to keep the herd together. Archie grabbed snacks and soft drinks and threw them in Shanti's backpack.

As they were loading Shanti, the pack, and the dog into the back seats, Sonny asked, "So what kind of a job is Danielle going for in Sylmar, Arch? That's quite a commute."

Archie didn't answer until they had Shanti belted in, and Buck sitting properly next to her, albeit leaning against her. Archie closed the back door and spoke hurriedly. "Sonny, I don't know what Danielle has told Shanti about this, so you must promise you won't say anything about it in front of her."

"I promise."

"I mean it now," Archie said, giving Sonny a withering look, which Sonny returned with one of complete innocence. "Danielle just had a screen test with Summer to make pornographic movies."

Sonny's eyes went wide. "Mother Mary, have mercy."

"Shush, she will hear you," Archie said as he grabbed Sonny's powerful forearm. "Believe me, I did everything I could to talk her out of it, but you know how strong-willed she is. Anyway, don't say a word."

Sonny didn't bring it up. Instead he pointed out sights along the way until they reached the freeway, then the three of them launched into the "I spy" game. Traffic was light for the 405 and they approached the exit Danielle had given them in 50 minutes.

Wild Bill Chase was not your everyday Christian. He was an ex-Hell's Angel who had a radical conversion experience 15 years ago in the CMA tent at the big Sturgis, South Dakota Rally. He gave up the drugs, sex, and rock-and-roll lifestyle, and began to ride for the Christian

Motorcycle Association. He had led a number of bikers to Christ over the years, but his most recent passion was to bring down the local pornography industry. When he lost his baby sister to teen porn two years ago, he vowed he would do whatever it took to shut them down. He joined Families Against Porn and soon became one of FAP's most outspoken leaders. Some thought his ideas of dawn to dark picket lines ineffective. Others said it was just a publicity stunt for "Wild Bill's Chop Shop," his motorcycle customizing business.

But Bill was sincere, and his tactics did increase media attention from time to time. And whether successful or not Bill's commitment to the cause was personal and deep: he did not waver in the face of adversity. By 1993, 90 percent of all pornographic videos were produced right in Wild Bill's hometown: Sylmar, California. The big three producers formed what was known in the industry as the Golden Triangle. They churned out low-budget pornographic videos as fast as the market demanded.

Wednesday afternoon, two to six, was Wild Bill's shift on the picket line. He usually brought a few of his CMA buddies with him.

Archie and Sonny drove slowly down the street of nondescript buildings, looking for the correct address. Sonny passed several parked cars, then pulled into a large opening across the street from Valley Productions where six tough-looking characters were walking up and down the sidewalk. Each one carried a hand-stenciled placard: "SAY NO TO POR-NO"; "CHILD PORNOGRAPHY: AN ABOMINATION TO GOD; and "FLEE THE WRATH OF GOD: SHUT DOWN PORN" were three signs that Archie could read at first glance.

"Sonny, why don't you and Shanti stretch your legs over here on this side of the street? I'll cross over and look for Danielle."

"Come on, Shanti; let's take Buck for a walk. I'll bet he would like to check out that vacant lot we passed."

Buck shot a glance toward the lot, then leapt over the front seat and out Archie's open door. Sonny called him back and grabbed the trailing leash. Archie helped Shanti out the back door and in a few moments the trio headed up the street with Buck heeling properly on Sonny's right and Shanti skipping along on his left.

"Yeth, oh yeth," Sonny was saying, "we are the 'Explorers of the Valley.'"

Archie took a deep breath and headed for the picket lines.

With all the commotion ahead of him Archie paid little attention to the black stretch limo parked a few cars behind Sonny's Land Rover.

Of the three "Explorers of the Valley," only Buck noticed the limo. The dog didn't like what he sensed there and pushed against his master's leg to steer him away from possible danger.

Sonny staggered a bit but was too engaged with Shanti to pick up Buck's meaning.

Inside the limo, Triple X's attention was riveted on one of the trio as they walked past his heavily tinted windows: the little girl. "Paulie," he said to his driver, "Stay here until I tell you to go."

"Whatever you say, Boss."

X had come down from his lair in the Ventura foothills to give a little personal touch to solving some post-production problems with editors who worked both the soft and hard porn side of the street. He had satisfied himself that the problem had gone away with the usual application of incentives—greed and fear being X's stock in trade. X prided himself in knowing how to push all the right buttons. His business completed, he had just settled back in his limo when he saw the two scruffy looking senior citizens and the beautiful child get out of the Land Rover.

His breathing was the only sound inside the limo. X watched the trio pass on his right and the other old guy cross the street to his left. Only X's eyes moved; his massive frame was motionless. Although obese, X was still a powerful man beneath all the excess. He saw the old guy who crossed the street enter Valley Productions and picked up his cell phone. "Chuckie? It's Trip. I need you to do me a favor. Stay on the line and come to the front window. There's somebody I want you to I.D. for me."

In less than a minute X saw the old guy come back on the street with a chick on his arm. He noticed the stunning young woman's face was stiff as she looked away from the picketers; in contrast, the old guy seemed to be trying to read all the signs and smiled and said something to one of the picketers who nodded and said something in return.

As they made their way across the street, Chuckie, X's post-production editor who had been in the limo a few minutes ago, appeared in the window of Valley Productions with a phone to his ear.

"Who are the people crossing the street right in front of you: the babe and the old geezer?" X said into his cell phone.

"Uh, her name is Danny Delicious," Chuckie immediately replied. "She just came in for a screen test with Summer Storm and judging by the reaction here I'd say she got the job hands down. The old guy I never saw before."

"Who's her agent?"

"I think it's Primo. Want me to double-check on that for you?"

"I would appreciate it very much if you would do that for me." X wheezed. "I'll call you back in 10." X had an unlisted number that not even his closest lieutenants knew. There were some things he did himself for security reasons, and setting up the cell phone under yet another pseudonym and paying the bill through an offshore credit card account was one of them.

Now the old guy and the babe were standing right beside the limo. The woman called the girl, who came running into her arms. X could see the family resemblance and figured the little girl was her daughter. He couldn't hear what they were saying as the dog was barking; he seemed to be barking at the limo.

So that two-bit hustler Primo is her agent, X thought as he gave Paulie a signal to drive on.

Triple X wasn't the only person studying the comings and goings at

Valley Productions from behind tinted windows. A few parking spaces further back a new, nondescript mini-van went unnoticed by all. Inside, detectives Jedediah Lincoln and Charlie West were on stakeout duty. They worked for the L.A.PD Child Exploitation Branch of the force's Sex Crimes Unit.

"Get the limo, Jed," West said.

"I'm gettin' it, I'm gettin' it," Lincoln said as he focused his telephoto lens and got four clear, quick shots of the car pulling out of the parking space.

Detective Jed Lincoln—a career officer, 17 years on the force—was also an amateur photographer who took great satisfaction in his work with a camera. He had dozens of shots already of vehicles and people going in and out, including the old geezer and the young Asian beauty and the guy with the sheep dog and the cute little girl.

His partner, Charlie West, was a lot younger and was recently promoted to detective. He brought a love of research and advanced computer skills to their work together.

Their objective in the five-day stakeout was to increase their database on individuals connected to child pornography. They knew Valley Productions was a likely place to find some overlap with the harder-to-find bottom dwellers they were after. Charlie had logged a description of the limo, would get a year, make, and model number from a computer search, and would add the info to a long list of data they were compiling.

"That's the first limo we've seen up here," Charlie said.

"Could be something," Jed said.

"I'll make a note to check out ownership on that puppy."

"We have to check them all out, Charlie."

Archie put Nancy to work as soon as they hit the dock. He gave her the tasks of removing the sail cover and dodger window covers while he went below to check the engine. She had all the covers in a neat pile when he came back on deck.

"What else can I do?" she asked with enthusiasm.

"You can hook on the main halyard if you like. You'll need a bit of help with the finer points." Archie talked her through the steps and was pleased at how fast she caught on. *She must have a high mechanical aptitude,* he thought. "You know," he said, "On this boat a person can advance from swab to able-bodied seaman real quick; if you keep this up, you're going to break the record."

Outside the breakwater, the Cal 40 was up to her usual performance in the steady breeze. It was a high-pressure day so the wind hadn't filled in until around 11, but that was fine. It gave Archie time to check out Nancy on the equipment. His main concern going out was whether she could sail a straight course or not. With her on the wheel, he was free to work the sheets whenever they had to come about. He had tried the maneuver a few times in the light airs of the earlier morning and was surprised and delighted at how fast she learned everything. The precision she showed making the 90-degree turn on the tacks amazed him. Of course, a wheel is easier to learn than a tiller where the steering motion is backwards, but even so she showed a steady hand, not overcorrecting and not losing her bearings mid-tack, like so many first-time helmsmen.

Now the breeze had filled in nicely at 10 to 15 knots; they were pelting along closehauled but off the wind enough to be in the *Dawn Treader's* best point of sail. Archie liked to sail upwind at the start of a day and then take it easy coming in. Having Nancy out gave added incentive to taking the upwind leg first, as most people were more likely to get seasick with a following sea. With all of his heart he wanted her not to get sick. Closehauled for a couple of hours would give her time to get her sea legs, he hoped.

"How am I doing?" Nancy asked.

"Like you were born to it."

"Really?" she said, beaming.

"Yep, I'd say your North Channel ancestors are very pleased. How do you like sailing?"

"Oh Archie, I love it! You feel so connected to the wind and waves. The boat seems alive, and there is so much to do. I had no idea there was so much to do on a sailboat."

Archie had to look away; he pretended to scan the horizon for other boats. There was no doubting the sincerity of Nancy's response. Her delight pierced the most secret place in his heart, the place where hope came from, and now he was overcome with emotion. Her words set off a chain reaction: all his hope turned into a deep, unbridled affection for this woman and an even deeper longing for her. He hadn't thought it possible that he could find another good woman who could be a good sailor too.

God, he prayed silently, *why are you so kind to me?*

Archie broke out the ham sandwiches Nancy had made and the apples he had brought. He took the wheel for lunch, and the two nibbled and talked as the *Dawn Treader* cut effortlessly through the three-to-four-foot swells she was designed to handle. As usual the conversation was easy.

When they got started talking about their faith, Archie wanted to tell her about Danielle. He'd had another sticky conversation with Danielle and hadn't been able to see Jimmy yet. Besides, he thought it was time he worked this out some other way. Jim would be getting tired of the same complaint week after week.

"How are you at sharing your faith with non-believers, Nancy?"

"Hmmm, you know I think Presbyterians have it a bit easier than you evangelicals in that department. We put more of an emphasis on letting our actions speak for themselves."

"That's what Pastor Jim always says to me whenever I share my frustrations with him. 'Just be yourself, Archie. God will do the rest.' "

She's not just a pretty face, Archie thought, admiring Nancy's wisdom. He didn't say it, though, suspecting it might sound chauvinistic. Stuff like that could wait until they knew each other better. He hoped she was self-assured and would find it funny, not hurtful.

Instead he went on. "But it's daunting for me. I'm really an introvert."

"Are you talking about a specific situation here?" Nancy asked, taking a bite of apple.

"Yes. You know the mother of the little girl in your ward a few weeks ago for hyperbaric treatment?"

"Of course. Shanti's mother. So you have been sharing your faith with Danielle?"

"Well, that's just it. The first few times we talked about spiritual matters, I ended up on the defensive. Then I would think of all these great things to say *after* we talked. She's very bright. Tom, her husband, says she has something like a 130 IQ and it really shows when we have these debates. I can't keep up. So yesterday I was determined to make my case and at the first opportunity I went right to the central issue: faith."

Archie paused as white water from a particularly large swell came off the bow and nearly made it into the cockpit. He wondered if the wind had picked up a notch. *No point in getting wet*, he thought and eased her off slightly. "Nancy, let out about three inches on that main sheet and maybe two on the jib. That's good—right there. Now, where was I with Danielle?"

"Faith. You brought up the issue of faith."

"Right, so I said to Danielle, it is more rational to believe in God, the Father of Jesus Christ, than it is to not believe because believing in Him gives ultimate value to life—mine and everyone else's—and gives good values to live by."

"Oh, that's well put, Archie."

"I think it's the best argument for our faith I have ever heard. I got it off a guy who used to go around debating atheists and agnostics to packed halls on college campuses. The deal was at the end he would have the audience vote. I forget his name, but he claimed to win the debate every time."

"So you thought that would work well with Danielle?"

"I thought it couldn't miss with an intellectual like her."

"I have a feeling it was otherwise."

"Ha, ha. Right again." Archie noticed another sailboat about half a mile ahead of them and asked Nancy to lean out and check the blind spot behind the foresail before he went on. "Danielle said, 'I don't have a problem with faith, I just don't get how you can narrow it so completely to one set of beliefs. It seems just as reasonable to me to have faith in Buddha or Krishna as in Jesus.' "

"How interesting."

"So I said, 'What about the values part of it? Christian values are revealed by God, mostly through the Bible. Here in the States we have an underlying values system—like every life is as important as every other life—that may not be a part of the value systems of Buddhism or Hinduism. We assume they share our values, like equality for women, but find out later they don't.' I thought I had her there," Archie said, taking a bite of his apple.

"How did she counter this one?"

" 'Archie,' she says, 'you just turned the truth on its head. Your values are yours alone. Your truth is yours alone. It is only true within your particular cultural paradigm. It doesn't apply to other cultures. It's so backwoods to claim to have all the answers for everybody.'

" 'But if there isn't one true set of values, there would be moral chaos,' I said.

" 'No, Archie,' she said. 'Respecting other value systems results in tolerance, freedom of expression, and inclusion of all peoples.' "

"What an interesting and articulate argument," Nancy said.

"Once again she had the last word. It was only later I thought of asking her, 'What about mass murderers, rapists, and pedophiles: do we tolerate their value systems? Do we give their morality equal weight? Would it be backwoods not to include them?' But, as usual, I didn't think of it at the time."

"I can see this whole thing is very frustrating for you."

Was it that obvious how much it bothered him? Perhaps Nancy had noticed the set of his jaw, the turning down of his mouth, and how he glared at the coming sea. "Awe, let's just sail," Archie said, and the two fell silent for a while.

Archie's report of the conversation was accurate, and overall he was correct that he hadn't made any headway with Danielle except for one moment, which he had left out of the telling because he had no idea how really important it was. When he and Danielle were talking about absolute values versus situational ethics, Archie had said, "Compassion is the driving force of Christianity and an absolute value for me:

compassion always ends up in the highest place whenever I think it through and I see it often compels me to act."

This rang true for Danielle; she could see it in Archie's life, and it held a high place for her too. She remembered how she had been touched last year at a talk on compassion by a Tibetan Buddhist monk. Archie's words went right into her heart and stirred her thinking.

With all the other issues flying in the conversation, it's no wonder that Archie missed the significance of the moment. It was the first time in their debates that he gained the weather gauge, or upwind advantage in a battle of sailing ships, and he never knew it.

The wind and motion of the boat and Nancy's presence brought Archie's good humor back quickly. After all, here he was, doing his favorite thing with a very able and attractive companion.

Soon it was time to jibe and head for home. The wind from the south usually died in the evening, and it wouldn't be much fun motoring in. On the way back, Nancy invited Archie to her church the next day. He agreed to go without hesitation. He could call Jack McClelland, a friend and fellow deacon, to cover his duties at Westside.

After a few minutes Nancy said, "You know, Archie, I've been thinking I would like to get to know Danielle better. I chatted with her a few times when she was in my ward with Shanti but mostly small talk. I wonder if it would be good for her to get to know a mature Christian woman."

Nancy's proposal surprised Archie completely and threw him into inner debate. On the one hand it made perfect sense and, in fact, he himself had counseled other men in his exact position to bring a woman like Nancy into the picture. After all there were issues Danielle might need to discuss that she would never bring up with a member of the opposite sex. On the other hand, he was suddenly wary of the dynamics of the triangular nature of the proposal—he didn't want to be caught in the middle. He also couldn't imagine how he would propose the meeting to Danielle.

"It would be a good thing, Nancy, absolutely. I'm just trying to imagine how I would suggest it to her."

"Well, give it a little time. I'm sure you'll think of something."

After that weekend Nancy and Archie were together every possible moment. Only the most serious prior commitments, including Nancy's work, kept them apart. Archie realized it wouldn't be so difficult to tell Danielle he was "seeing" Nancy and to present the idea to her that he wanted his two friends to get to know each other better. As well, Jimmy's input was that Nancy was absolutely right and Archie should do everything possible to set up the meeting.

So Archie phoned Danielle. He told her he was seeing Nancy and suggested they get together.

"Archie, how wonderful! Of course I remember Nurse Hollings. She was so kind to us during Shanti's stay at the hospital. I'm so happy for you both. I even said to Shanti once that the two of you would make a cute couple. How about we get together Saturday? Tom is taking Shanti to Disneyland, and I would love to have some adult time."

"Great, Danielle, wonderful," Archie said with immense relief and some wariness. He knew by now what "adult time" meant and worried how Nancy would handle it. "Do you like Mexican food?"

Don Pepe's on Culver Boulevard was one of Archie's favorite places. From the street it didn't look like much, but a side alley led to a tree-shaded parking lot in the back. From there, it became apparent that the Ordonez family had created another world. The restaurant sat on about two acres of land that Grandfather Ordonez had developed into a lovely garden patio surrounded on the front by the restaurant and on the other three sides by high adobe walls. Strategically planted eucalyptus and palm trees, climbing vines—most notably a huge, ancient wisteria on the back of the building—and a natural-looking rock fountain in the middle of the patio turned it into a magical place of semi-tropical beauty in the midst of the arid cityscape. It was a favorite place for wedding receptions.

But Archie's main reason for going wasn't the setting or the excellent food. It was the mariachi band. He knew four of the guys: Luis, lead trumpet; Paco, second trumpet; Juan, first violin; and Miguel, second violin. The four musicians attended Westside and played on the worship band in the Spanish-speaking service. Archie admired their musicianship, loved their singing, and enjoyed chatting them up in Spanish.

Last year they had asked him to come to the Sunday afternoon Spanish-speaking service to give his testimony. It was a challenge putting together his talk in Spanish, but Luis, the lead trumpet player, went over it with him and got the idioms right. The 10-minute talk went very well, and after that Archie was considered an honorary member of the congregation. From then on he attended several times a year and tried to catch all their special events.

The boys were belting it out near the hostess desk and greeted him and his party with nods and looks as he entered with the two very attractive women. The hostess led the three of them to a table near the wisteria after only a five-minute wait. Archie got them in during the lull between lunch and dinner; by the time they were eating, the line waiting for a table stretched out of sight, into the shaded parking lot.

The conversation was going very well. The two women hit it off famously with Danielle making no attempt to hide her delight that Archie and Nancy were "going out," and Nancy making it clear she truly liked the younger woman. In fact, the women's talk flowed so fast Archie couldn't keep up with all the tangents, back tracks, and what seemed to him incomplete thoughts. After a while he became irritated with his, "Who said 'I don't think so?'" types of questions and their patient but superior replies. He gave up trying to be a part of the flow. He was happy to listen to the band and eat his rice and beans.

As they reached the point where none of them could eat anymore, however, the band moved inside the packed restaurant itself and the volume of their music outdoors diminished to a level that Archie couldn't enjoy. At that moment Archie heard Danielle saying, "It's so good for me to get to know you better, Nancy. You're self-confident, a professional, and yet, well, you're a Christian."

"And you didn't think a Christian woman could also be a liberated woman."

"Exactly," Danielle said, squeezing Nancy's arm. "I've had the impression for some time that the church is, shall we say, behind the curve on women's lib."

"Well, that isn't the case in my life, but I know what you mean. Male chauvinism is definitely an issue in church leadership. But I believe that comes from the existing culture or cultures in which the church happens to find itself—not from the gospel."

"Really? Why do you say that?"

"Well, historically the equal rights movement is rooted in the gospel. The early Christians seriously challenged the existing values of Mediterranean culture because they taught there is no favoritism with God. How does the apostle Paul say it? 'There is neither Jew nor Greek, slave nor free, male nor female, but all are one in Christ Jesus.' One result of this radical view was a lot of the early conversions to the faith came from the huge slave population in the society of the day. It really was Christianity that got the whole liberation thing started by declaring God values every person. I think an accurate history of ideas would have to say that the gospel was the beginning of the end of suppression of women and of slavery for that matter."

Nancy took a sip of water while Danielle chewed her taco salad.

To Archie, neither seemed upset or agitated. *They could be talking women's fashion for all the world*, he thought. He looked hard at Nancy, who seemed totally calm. *How does she do it?*

"So how do you explain 1800 years later slavery was still going strong in the U.S., a supposedly God-fearing Christian country?" Danielle asked.

"You're in good company making that judgment. President Lincoln said—and I think it was during his second inaugural address, but check that out—he said he thought the appalling casualty rate during the Civil War was a result of God's judgment on the nation for supporting slavery while claiming 'liberty and justice for all.' Also, don't forget the abolitionist movement was led by Christians," Nancy answered.

At that point the conversation went off on one of its inexplicable tangents that Archie didn't even try to follow because he was still relishing Nancy's erudite presentation: *Lincoln's second inaugural, for all the love...where does she get this stuff?* He realized that his mouth had dropped open during that last bit; he closed it quickly, but continued to marvel at how well this was going. He pushed away a thought about what an idiot he was to not handle these hot topics with the same dispassion as Nancy. No, he wouldn't go there. After all, he was the one who brought the two of them together.

Then their conversation took a turn that amazed him even further: somehow Nancy brought the whole thing back to the Bible. "Have you studied the Bible much?" Nancy was asking.

"No, never. My mother was into a kind of ancestor worship, and my dad was a hard-drinking army sergeant. So that's a big no on the Bible question."

"Well it would be fun to get together and look at some of the passages that relate to what we've been talking about. In a historical context it's very interesting stuff."

Danielle didn't miss a beat. "Would you be able to come over to my place? I don't get to go out that often with Shanti not in school yet."

Archie sat back experiencing total cognitive dissonance—he heard what they had just said, but he couldn't believe it. *At their very first meeting, Nancy is already going for Bible study. And she says she isn't an evangelist.*

Nancy spent Christmas Day with her kids and Archie with his. The two of them had had a romantic Christmas Eve together listening to music and watching the lighted boats parade in the marina from Archie's balcony; so each was able to attend the family gathering the next day without missing the other too much.

In Archie's family, Bets, the oldest, had assumed the role of convener when Luella was suddenly no longer there.

Bets greeted Archie warmly when he arrived and noticed the change in him at once: the ease in his manner, a renewed joy in little things and, most obviously, how often he talked about Nancy. Archie wasn't good at keeping secrets and, although he never said as much, everyone, even the older children, knew he had fallen in love long before they sat down for Christmas dinner. It was the first time his three daughters had had a chance to interrogate him face-to-face, and all were extremely interested in this new and unexpected development.

The conversation started in the kitchen during the last-minute preparations and carried right through most of the dinner. Their endless questions—How did you meet? How far along has the relationship progressed? What does she look like? What is her personality like? How is she like Mom and not like Mom? Had he met her family yet? When can we meet her?—got Archie telling a series of stories. Archie started his favorite, the one about their first sailing trip on the *Dawn Treader*, just before Mark said the blessing. They all said a hearty amen and then encouraged Archie to carry on. They noticed how he chuckled and sometimes laughed out loud at various things Nancy had said. Everyone else smiled politely, but soon they realized that most of what so amused Archie wasn't really funny.

During one of Archie's longest laughs, Bets saw Mark lean forward to begin to say something. "Mark darling," she said, and when he looked to the other end of the table he froze.

Mark had been busted by Bets many times over the course of their marriage for his acerbic wit. He didn't want trouble; he bit his tongue. He picked up a half-empty pitcher and made his way to the kitchen past Bet's chair. As he passed, he leaned over as if to give her a kiss and hummed the first line of "People Will Say We're in Love" so only she could hear.

Bets popped up and followed him through the swinging door into the kitchen. She gave him a playful spank on his backside. "Now don't you say anything, Mark. This is wonderful for Dad; you know how long he has been grieving."

"All right, all right, I'll be good," he said as he put down the pitcher. "But what about us?" he said, catching her up in his arms. "Love is in the air."

Back in the dining room the children were getting bored with Archie's story—nothing like the usual funny or exciting ones he had told at previous gatherings which he, in fact, directed at them for their entertainment. Left to their own devices there was soon a little scuffle involving Luke and Janie. Bets and Mark hurried back and while they were settling things down, Archie realized he had been neglecting his grandchildren. "Anyway," he said, "that's enough about me. What about you kids? What did you get for Christmas?"

7

His rule will extend
From sea to sea.
ZECHARIAH 9:10

Archie was in a grumpy mood, riding in the back of the camper van. *I would much rather be sailing, or be with Nancy, or be sailing with Nancy than go to this conference,* he said to himself.

Music had been a big part of his Christian life in the past, but since Luella's death, it just didn't give him a lift the way it used to. But even as these prickly thoughts arose he remembered the Anaheim prophecy. In the end he resigned himself to do his Christian duty and make the best of it.

After all, he thought, *Tricia and the rest of the kids had been kind to me; I don't want to put a damper on their experience.* He'd had a bunch of them over the evening before for dessert and coffee and the view from his deck of the boats lighted up for Christmas. They were a nice bunch of youngsters, and Tricia had seemed particularly interested in his collection of 19th-century nautical music. He had played his favorite medley for her: "Jack's The Lad," "See The Conquering Hero Comes" and, of course, "Britannia Rules the Waves." Tricia gave him a hug when she saw he choked up on "Britannia."

"It gets me every time," he said weakly.

"Aw, Archie, you've got a soft heart," Tricia replied.

These memories now gave him a short respite from his "I don't want to do anything new" mood. A few miles down the freeway, he remembered to repeat the Jesus prayer as a way of fighting off the negative thinking.

By the time they reached Anaheim and parked near the convention center, he was in a decent frame of mind. The three-day conference was laid out with plenary sessions in the morning and evening and workshops in the afternoon. Every session, even the workshops, had a worship portion at the start and prayer ministry at the end. Archie signed up for "When God Takes Over," a workshop with Bryce Meadows—a songwriter he knew and respected—and "Worship Intercession" with Mark O'Brian, the Irish kid who was having such a big impact across the pond.

The group of seven who had traveled down from Westside found seats together about halfway back and settled in for the first plenary session. Archie found the worship very good for his soul and tearfully repented for his negative attitude in the van. He realized he needed a close encounter with God and vowed to keep his focus on the Lord throughout the conference.

Archie found the afternoon teaching by Bryce Meadows most interesting. First of all, it fascinated him how so often guys like Bryce, who wrote the most evocative melodies and intimate lyrics, seemed so flat emotionally when they spoke in public. Archie didn't object; in fact, he preferred speakers who just laid out their material without hype. The lack of tonal change in Bryce's speaking voice, however, was in such contrast to his emotionally charged singing voice, that is was almost startling. After Archie got past that, however, he realized that Bryce's material was excellent.

Bryce's thesis was that sometimes corporate worship goes to another level where we enter a profound sense of God's presence. "It's as if all our efforts—to play and sing and to press in to intimacy—all our self-effort ceases and God takes over." He drew on one of Archie's favorite mystics, Jeanne Guyon, on "abandonment." He talked about how important it is for every Christian to live a disciplined life, to practice the spiritual disciplines to make a daily effort to do the right thing. But he said, "It is equally important to understand that our Christian life is one of cooperation with God. He is the principal actor in every Christian's life; at least He wants to be. Thus it is essential that each of us practice abandonment: we lay aside all of our personal cares, we drop our personal needs, and we give ourselves over entirely to the

Lord. We engage entirely with what He is doing. This, I think, is a key element in worship often omitted in teaching young worship leaders how to go about it. So much of our energy goes into mastering our instruments or improving our vocal technique."

Heads nodded in the audience.

"You know the drill. But listen to what Madam Guyon says—and I recommend you read this book *Experiencing the Depths of Jesus Christ*," he said as he held it up. "What is abandonment? It is forgetting your past; it is leaving the future in His hands; it is devoting the present fully and completely to your Lord." Bryce paused and looked around the room of 100 or so worship leaders who all knew and respected him through his songs and CDs. Some had been on worship teams with him. "What I'm trying to say to you guys is this: what Jeanne Guyon said about devoting ourselves to the Lord on a moment-to-moment basis is essential for leading worship if you want to get to the place where God takes over." Bryce went on to give the group some ideas about how to do this, including practicing the presence of God.

Archie greatly appreciated the talk and went up to see Bryce afterward to encourage him. "That was great, Bryce; Madam Guyon is one of my favorite mystics. She communicates the depths of mysticism more clearly than anyone else."

"Thanks, Archie, that means a lot. How are you doing? I haven't seen you since Luella's funeral."

"Yes, that was almost four years ago. I'm doing well. I have a very full life." Archie almost told Bryce about Nancy but felt uncomfortable with the jump from Luella's funeral to "I have a girlfriend." Other workshop members pressed around them, and Archie drew back to give them a chance.

The plenary sessions that evening and the next morning were also times of excellent worship and teaching, so much so that by the afternoon of the second day Archie felt like he already had gotten his money's worth. Over lunch at a Mexican food takeout, he made a point to speak to Tricia Knox. "Tricia, I can't thank you enough for bringing me along. This has been wonderful. I feel like a new man."

"Archie, that's great! And we still have a ways to go. Which workshop are you going to this afternoon?"

"I signed up for that Irish kid, Mark O'Brian; he has the same last name as my favorite author. What about you?"

"I'm going to that one, too." Archie wondered why the worship intercession workshop was in the main hall, but as soon as he and Tricia entered he saw O'Brian and seven other musicians on the stage. Archie realized this was the only hall that could accommodate so many players.

Tricia ran up to the platform to chat up a friend in the band. Archie found seats in the middle section about 10 rows back, not in line with the big speakers. He worried his slight hearing loss may have been worsened by too many decibels from past forays into amplified music. He looked around and figured about 300 people were attending this workshop. Tricia got in her seat moments before the session started.

Mark O'Brian seemed about average height, had a very round face, and a sunny disposition. He explained that the best way to teach worship intercession was to do it, so the formal teaching segment in this workshop would be only about 20 minutes; then they would give over the rest of the time to trying it out. "It will be a learning laboratory," he said.

Most of his talk was setting up what they were going to do during the lab segment. "We will play several sets of worship songs, interspersed with read Scripture and spoken prayers. After each prayer the band will try to pick up on the themes just spoken and convert them into sung prayers. During the spoken prayers, the band will continue to follow a simple chord progression—three or four chords— laid down in the previous song. The tricky part musically comes after each spoken prayer. The band has to improvise a melody line using some of the words or concepts just prayed. Once you get the hang of it, it's not as hard to do as it sounds," he said with a shy smile. "We asked several pastors attending the conference to lead us in prayer today. They met for an hour this morning and agreed on several areas of concern. Each one will lead out in a particular area, but all of the topics have to do with the local region. Are you ready to give it a go? Let's stand for the first set."

Archie was impressed that O'Brian spoke as briefly as he promised. The band swung into a moderate tempo worship song, and Archie knew after a few bars they had selected the best musicians for this one. They played the simple songs with just the right amount of color, but for the most part kept it simple. Archie always thought the band should try to get out of the way as much as possible and let the people commune with God, and that's exactly what began to happen even before the first song was over. Archie sensed God's presence before the end of the set. He knew that good worship had a way of clearing the mind so one could experience God. Three hundred people pressing in to God at the same time developed a momentum that swept the willing individual worshiper along. On top of all that, this was their fifth session of worship—they hit the ground running. Archie considered all these things in one part of his mind while in another he was experiencing and surrendering to the sweet presence of God.

The band reached the end of a worship song, but kept playing softly. One of the pastors came to the mike. "We felt on each round of prayers we should focus on the three counties of Orange, Los Angeles, and Ventura. Our first prayers are for the churches in these three counties: that their devotion to Christ would increase; that their lives would be sanctified, set apart for His service; and that they would make powerful witness for the Lord. But before we begin to do that, we should dedicate ourselves to the task. So let's pray."

The nameless pastor prayed a brief, general prayer of confession and forgiveness with a time for silent, personal prayers at the end. "Most merciful God, we confess that we have sinned against You in thought, word, and deed, by what we have done, and by what we have left undone. We have not loved You with our whole heart. We have not loved our neighbors as ourselves. We are truly sorry and we humbly repent; for the sake of Your Son, Jesus Christ, have mercy on us and forgive, that we may delight in Your will, and walk in Your ways to the glory of Your name. Amen." Without further direction, he began to pray through his list. He would read a short Bible passage and then pray the Scripture for the three counties.

Archie heard murmurs of agreement all around him and found himself wanting to kneel. His old body wouldn't allow much of that so he bent over instead. He opened his eyes to bend over—so he wouldn't hit his head on anything or anyone—and was deeply moved to see people all around him kneeling.

When the first pastor reached the end of his prayers, Mark O'Brian came to the mike. "Let's sing call and response. I'll sing a line, and you repeat it."

Archie felt a wave of electricity go through his body. He knew the power of call and response, of alternating active and receptive prayer. He remembered the Bach Motet Number Five, set for two choirs, that he had sung in college and the powerful effect it could have.

The band filled in as O'Brian sang out a phrase that the first pastor had spoken: "fill our hearts with love for Jesus." O'Brian had a strong, clear, lyrical voice, and found a sweet melody that fit the chord progression, then 300 voices repeated the phrase. O'Brian repeated it again and then, like a good songwriter, expanded it to include our mind, our will, and our lives. Each time the workshop attendees followed O'Brian's lead. The concept of praying for the three counties added another meaningful layer of repetition to the sung prayers, so they progressed through the prayers. The pastor would pray on a subject, O'Brian would pick up the theme, and the body of worshipers would sing their heartfelt agreement. It was powerful. After the first set, it seemed to Archie that the whole assembly was unified into one will, one desire that progressed from theme to theme.

Archie remembered the verse in Judges: *As one man they stood before the Lord at Mizpah.* So it seemed here. The presence of God was palpable. Archie's faith soared. He imagined if he opened his eyes, he would see angels. *This is not a workshop*, he said to himself. *This is the real deal.*

Archie, like most of those there, was too caught up in the Lord's presence to notice much of the comings and goings on stage. He missed the host pastor talking to O'Brian while the third designated pastor was getting ready to pray. Almost everyone there was surprised when O'Brian came to the mike and said, "We have come to the end of our workshop time and you are dismissed to go catch a wee bite. However, the conference steering committee feels that the Lord wants us to go on through the supper hour. I guess we are going to keep going until somebody decides we're done," he said, grinning and looking around at the host pastor, who grinned back and nodded.

Archie decided on the spot to pass on the burrito and stay; he knew how rare and precious these visitations of the Lord were. He didn't expect everyone to stay. He couldn't help looking around a bit. No one, not one soul, headed for the exits. Just then he heard O'Brian say, "We have one more pastor ready to pray from the last set and then the guys tell me they have a lot more material to cover as well."

Good news travels fast. The conference goers who had attended the other afternoon workshops had heard that God had come to the intercession workshop while they were eating supper. Many cut short their break and started drifting into the main hall well before the evening plenary session was scheduled to start. As a result, the number of intercessors grew steadily. Their number doubled and then swelled to over 1200 hundred by the time the evening session was supposed to begin. The assembly now included a number of people who weren't attending the conference but somehow got word that a move of God was underway.

Soon the steering committee decided—and had O'Brian announce—that the plenary speaker would be held over to tomorrow morning. The worship intercession, now at four hours, would continue. Archie opened his eyes after O'Brian began his announcement and stretched his back. *Bumping a headliner for a workshop—that doesn't happen every day*, he thought.

The "holy ground" sense of the room was not lost with the gradual assimilation of the additional people. At the same time, those who came in the evening came fed and rested and added a new wave of physical energy to the group that had been there since three in the afternoon.

A little after seven the prayer cycle started over with the pastor who had started them off in the afternoon coming to the mike again. They had agreed the band would not play during what they were about to do next.

The lead-off pastor began, "The prayer team feels we're called into some areas of intercession now that require us to make a diligent effort to get right with the Lord before we go there. So I'm about to lead you all through prayers of confession and repentance. If any specific un-confessed sin comes to your mind, deal with it one-on-one with the Lord. We all know He is here in power, and is able to reveal our sins and to forgive us and cleanse us. If you can't get through it one-on-one with the Lord, there is a room near the back left entrance where a prayer ministry team is waiting to help you. So now I'll pray in general, and you pray in specifics if need be."

He collected himself and went on. "Most merciful Heavenly Father, we know that we have not always loved You as we should, nor have we always loved our neighbor as we should. We ask now that You would reveal to us the darkness in our own hearts, that we might confess our sins to You." He paused.

Archie prayed that God would reveal his heart and waited. He had a clear memory of his impatience with Sonny and his judgment of his dear friend. He felt a deep sorrow in his soul. The expression of that sorrow was aided by a building sound of sobbing around him. Soon the meeting was engulfed with weeping, even wailing voices coming from every quarter.

The lead pastor waited in silence still longer. Then, as the sound seemed to have passed its peak, he said, "Merciful Father, for these sins we have committed against You and our neighbor we are truly sorry." He had to pause as another wave of tears swept over the room. Then he went on. "Yet we believe that our Savior, our precious Jesus—" He lost his composure when he said the name and had to pull out his already used hankie before he could go on. "We believe that You, Lord Jesus, have conquered sin. Because of what Jesus has done, we ask now, Heavenly Father, that You would forgive us our sins as we forgive those who have sinned against us."

This last concept came out somewhat unexpectedly, as he slipped into the Lord's Prayer. The idea of forgiving others launched the already repentant assembly into another wave of forgiveness such that the speaker could not go on for some minutes. Archie turned Luella's murderers over to the Lord yet again in this power encounter.

Finally the speaker was able to carry on. "Father, it is written that if we confess with our lips and believe with our hearts, You are able and just to forgive us our sins and purify us. Come, Holy Spirit, and purify us. Set apart a people for Yourself, O Lord. Sanctify us now for Your purposes and Yours alone." He had to almost shout the last of this into the mike as the din increased again.

He stepped back, bowed his head, and waited. After what seemed to Archie a very long time, the speaker turned to O'Brian, who led the band into "Unending Love."

"Father we come to you,
lifting up our hands,
in the name of Jesus,
by your grace we stand.
Just because you love us
and we love your Son
we know your favor, unending love."

So began the evening session of intercession. The pastors leading the meeting cycled to the mike in briefer but more intense appearances; it seemed everything they prayed had greater urgency. An overall theme began to emerge. They were praying for the kingdom of God to come in the center of the worst sins, the greatest darkness of the region: alcohol abuse, drug abuse, and domestic violence. They prayed for God to come to the jails, prisons, and high-crime areas. They prayed about the sins that have plagued mankind for all time, but in ways that focused on specific manifestations in the three counties.

At around 10:30, Archie felt someone take hold of his elbow. He opened his eyes to see Tricia Knox's tear-stained face. She leaned close to his ear. "Other musicians have been sitting in for the original band."

As she spoke, Archie looked at the band and could see what she meant. O'Brian was there but had given his guitar to Bryce Meadows. Archie recognized other changes as well. When he saw Bryce, the memory of his now-prophetic workshop was stunning: *God knew what He was up to,* Archie thought, *He knew He was going to "take over," and He led Bryce to teach on it.*

Tricia went on, "Mark's fiddle player can't play anymore. His hand is cramping. Could you sit in for him?"

Archie's usual hesitation at doing anything new or unusual did not appear. Instead he took Tricia's arm. "Lead me to him, little sister."

Tricia led Archie up the steps and over to the fiddle player, who was sitting down and not playing. "This is Archie, the guy I was telling you about."

The fiddler handed Archie the violin and bow without hesitation. "Carry on, friend."

The two exchanged goofy grins and pats. "Ain't this grand," the tired musician said in Archie's ear in a thick Irish brogue. Then he made his way past Archie, off the stage. They made the change while one of the pastors was praying.

The band was playing a four-chord progression, quietly waiting for O'Brian's cue to lead into the sung prayers. The lull gave Archie a chance to check the tuning, which was fine and to get into the flow. He immediately felt how locked in the band was. After a few bars he sensed some progressive jazz background in the base and keyboard player. They weren't playing any jazz chords; it was just the way they extended a phrase occasionally. Most of all, he felt the presence of God: the spiritual atmosphere on the stage was even more electric than where Archie had been sitting. The combination of the anointing and the band's expertise quickly took Archie's own musical abilities in some very creative directions. His discipline did not fail him, however. He knew that in an ensemble of eight, less is more. Each one has to keep his part simple or the band creates a wall of sound, not music. Still, he threw in a couple of licks that clearly perked up the others; the rhythm instruments were waiting for a melody line to soar on their solid foundation. Archie fit right in.

The next pastor at the mike said he was going to pray for God's kingdom to come to the pornography industry. He told the intercessors about Sylmar—how most of the pornographic videos consumed in North America were produced there. Archie wondered if he knew Wild Bill. Then Archie thought of Danielle and began to intercede with even greater intensity, thankful that he was able to play the violin and pray at the same time.

Archie was stunned when the praying pastor read from Haggai, chapter 2. He said he felt led to this text for this time and this region: "'In a little while I will once more shake the heavens and the earth, the sea and the dry land. I will shake all nations, and the desires of all nations will come and I will fill this house with glory, says the Lord Almighty.' Oh yes, shake us, Lord, shake Your church to take personal leadership in this battle against pornography. We ask for nothing less than a revival to come out of this epic struggle for moral integrity."

But all Archie could think of was his visit to Tom's earthquake lab three weeks ago. *Yikes! Does this guy know that the fault line runs right under Sylmar? You have to be careful what you pray for.* Then Archie kicked himself for being such a worrier and kicked himself again when the 1200 powerfully agreed with the pastor's prayers. Archie cursed his tendency to worry and tried to overcome it by pressing into the music. After a few cycles with Mark leading the mass choir, Archie's worries dissolved in the sublime power and joy of the moment.

O'Brian was particularly inspired. He led them to pray light where there was darkness, compassion where there was cruelty, and holiness where there was sin. As on other subjects, he seemed to be able to emphasize positive outcomes, though he didn't shy away from the worst of the topic. He emphasized the Lord's strength, wisdom, and love in dealing with the evil man can do.

The pastor jumped back in and prayed about child pornography. He wasn't asking now; he was proclaiming, "God will take back His children"—such was the presence of His authority and the certainty of faith. O'Brian carried on in a triumphant tone even through this darkest evil. The band's fatigue dissolved; they soared above their musical capabilities into uncharted areas of creativity and expression. Near what proved to be the end of the set Archie found himself playing two bars— just a hint—of "The Wonderful Cross" as filler in a gap between sung verses. It was a jazz technique to play a totally different melody that fit the chords; the keyboard and bass players looked at him with faces filled with delight.

Suddenly O'Brian turned away from the mike and, looking right at Archie, said, "Go with that."

"Now?"

"Yes now!"

Archie played the melody to the verse once through, naming the chord changes as he went along. The band locked in after two bars. Then O'Brian began to call out the words with that beautiful Irish lilt and told his choir, "Sing with me now!" as he extended both arms to them. There was something overwhelming about coming back to the cross at this point in the intercession. People loved the old hymn. Archie could see many were overcome, unable to sing.

"When I survey the wondrous cross,
on which the Prince of Glory died.
My richest gain I count but loss,
and pour contempt on all my pride.

See from his head, his hands, his feet,
sorrow and love flow mingled down.
Did e'er such love and sorrow meet?
Or thorns compose so rich a crown?

Were the whole realm of nature mine,
that were an off'ring far too small.
Love so amazing so divine,
demands my soul my life my all.

Oh the wonderful cross,
Oh the wonderful cross,
bids me come and die
and find that I may truly live.
Oh the wonderful cross, oh the wonderful cross,
all who gather here by grace
draw near and bless your name."

Then near the end of the chorus O'Brian turned away from the mike again and said to the band, "Modulate up one." The higher key gave the hymn a victorious edge. O'Brian fell to his knees, head bowed, as the congregation got their second wind and belted out the chorus one more time. No, twice more. At the end of the second chorus everyone stopped. O'Brian didn't tell them to, they just did. The room was filled with silence, the first complete silence for nine hours.

After a little while, Archie saw the host pastor wobble to the mike, visibly shaken and at a loss for words. He stood there for a while and then said, "This seems like a good place to stop. People need to get some sleep for tomorrow morning's session. I'll just pray a closing prayer. Father, we thank You for taking over this meeting. We ask You to seal everything You have done and bring us all back safely for tomorrow. In Jesus' mighty name, amen."

On the way home Archie and Tricia realized they hadn't eaten since lunch. One of the kids in the van was happy to share his trail mix and bottled water. They agreed it was a perfect way to end their fast. There wasn't much conversation for a few miles. Then, after a pull on her water bottle, Tricia said, "I have never seen anything like this before."

Everyone agreed. The others all talked at once about how incredible it had been, but not Archie. At Tricia's utterance, a bolt of lightning shot through him, and the fear of the Lord descended upon him: it was the Anaheim prophecy. She said what the Lord had told him would be said. The precise words of the prophecy replayed in Archie's memory: *You are about to be a part of something truly great in the Kingdom. Something so awesome that people will say, "I have never seen anything like this before." Surely, I say to you, not many days hence, the day of the Lord will come and all will be filled with awe.*

Archie was glad the darkness of the van hid his trembling.

Triple X was in a very dangerous mood. He shuffled up and down the cabin floor in his slippers, alternately swearing bitterly and slugging expensive scotch from a large tumbler. His usual sidemen—two hulking bodyguards and a small pock-faced man, his bookkeeper—had taken up positions near a window ledge. They were intent on giving him as much space as possible in the upscale log house. All three hoped saying nothing was the best way to weather the storm.

X shouted out, to no one in particular and interspersed with obscenity, "What the—is the—U.S. Coast Guard doing in—Ecuador?"

Mickey, the bookkeeper, had just told X that the U.S. Coast Guard had seized 14 tons of cocaine, his cocaine, off the coast of Ecuador.

X drained his glass and held it out to one of the body builders for a refill. He waved his other huge arm at his bookkeeper. "All right, Mickey, give me the details."

"Well, Boss, our connection at the wire service said they took 138 bales, the fishing boat, and the crew into custody."

X resumed his pacing and swearing nonstop.

After waiting a few moments, Mickey spoke again. "Uh, Boss, it's Saturday."

"I know what day it is!" X shouted, laced with more obscenity.

"I mean, in light of these developments, do you want me to cancel the poker game tonight?" Mickey doubled as the dealer, banker, and convener of X's card games. In fact Mickey had worked himself into a near consigliore position in the three years he had been with X. The poker work was a natural for Mickey, who had been a dealer in Vegas before X brought him into the business. Mickey had gotten into a little trouble at the Casino, and X's offer was a way out. If he had known then what he knew now—how perverted and violent X was—he would have turned himself in to the gaming commission and taken his lumps; but he didn't, and his natural abilities were just what X's huge, cash-rich empire needed. Mickey hoped he was more secure with X depending on him for so many facets of the operation and therefore was a little bolder than the other two, who were more expendable.

"No. The game is definitely on."

The three men heard the change in X's tone, knew something was up, and waited, saying nothing.

X held the ice-filled tumbler to his temple. "I need to talk with you alone, Mickey. You boys go for a walk," X said, waving the back of his hand at the two giants.

The game ran its predictable course that night. X bought his usual 30,000 in chips and played as recklessly as he always did, winning two pots through dumb luck, but mostly losing. Everyone knew—or at least had heard the stories—that he had houses, campers, boats, even warehouses full of bales of unlaundered cash.

Primo figured it was true since he had his own hidden compartment in a camper parked at a secure storage facility near Santa Monica Municipal Airport. He also had an offshore account in the Cayman Islands and an expensive arrangement with one of his flying drug dealers to move suitcases of cash there on return flights.

Primo liked the simplicity of the arrangement; it was just a matter of filing a flight plan with the FAA to anyplace near the Gulf, then dropping below the radar while still in U.S. air space and diverting to the Caymans. He had instructed Chucho to always wear gloves when handling the suitcases to leave no prints, so the cash left no paper trail. *Primitive but effective*, he thought. He wondered if Chucho had figured out that there was more money going south than payment for product required whenever he brought the suitcases to the small plane. Anyway, it made sense that with X's huge operation, he could have a problem laundering money. Primo and the other players had long since concluded that it was this overabundance of cash that made X such a careless poker player.

Tonight, however, everyone noted an additional element of surly impatience in his play. He had come to the game already smelling like a distillery and continued drinking heavily hand after hand. X's dark mood worried Primo as he thought about taking his usual early departure. Primo was up about 7,000 and anticipated X might object more strongly than usual to his leaving the game early and ahead.

Around 10, Primo went out on the porch to stretch his legs. One of the guards was there, scanning the perimeter with night glasses. "Paulie, what's up with X tonight?" he asked.

Paulie liked Primo. The two had swapped football stories on occasion; he thought of him as a fellow athlete. "I'll tell you, Primo, but you have to promise you won't say anything to anybody."

Primo nodded, pressed his lips together, and shrugged. "I'm as silent as the grave, Paulie."

Paulie looked over his shoulder, then leaned close and lowered his voice. "He's in a bad mood because he just lost a bundle on a Coast Guard seizure off Ecuador."

When Primo returned to the game, he sat down quietly and eased into the next round, making as little fuss as possible. He made a mental note to check on that seizure; it would be a way to size up the competition.

When Primo had started to get involved in the porn business, he'd heard about X's poker games from a cameraman who was shooting Summer's first film. For a hundred bucks the guy put in a good word for Primo, and he never missed a game after that.

X had asked Mickey about Primo's play after he first sat in over a year ago. Mickey said, "Primo isn't a pro, but he handles himself well. I'd rate him with the best amateurs."

Even though X consistently lost to no other player the way he lost to Primo, X let him stay in the game because he liked the feeling he was playing against the best.

Primo played from natural ability, honed from years of taking five-dollar pots from his friends in college. He had also committed to memory professional players' pointers on odds and tactics. Primo was generally good at reading people; with a little practice he easily picked up *tells*—the way a player's subconscious body language reveals his intentions. Primo's photographic memory and a head for numbers allowed him to quickly calculate the odds of beating every other possible hand in the "Texas hold 'em" game X preferred. No one else at the table had these skills. Primo routinely won thousands, and X was his biggest victim. Primo kept to himself that his winnings had paid for the BMW parked outside.

Mickey ran the game as dealer and banker and made life easier for Primo. Mickey ran an honest, well-organized game and, like Primo, had an ability to keep a mental tab on how much everybody was down or ahead. There were never any arguments about who owed Primo money at the end of the night. The only ceiling on the betting was the house rule that everybody had to settle up when they cashed in their chips. There were usually six to eight players in the game. Tonight a lucky seven bellied up to the table. There were some hangers-on too—a few women, X's guards, of course—and there were lots of drugs. Primo never used his own product, but he prided himself on being able to win drunk; he even used it as part of the hustle. He drank little tonight, however, figuring he would need all his wits to mollify X if he got out of hand.

At midnight, as usual, Primo leaned back from the table and said, "Well, gentlemen, it's been a pleasure. I've got a long drive ahead of me and a big day tomorrow so I'll...."

The table feet squeaked on the wood floor as X lunged awkwardly against it, swearing bitterly. "One more hand, Primo," he growled. The cigar stub in the side of his mouth fell onto the card table. One of his bodyguards whisked away the mess. X didn't move; he simply glared at Primo.

"All right, Trip," Primo said, flashing his winner smile. *One more hand*, he thought. *I got off easy.*

X had won one big hand earlier in the night, filling an inside straight late in the betting—all seven players had had pretty good cards and stayed in to the last. That big pot put him ahead for a while, and now he was second in winning chips behind Primo. But with his bigger initial buy-in, X had the most chips to bet.

"All right, everybody, ante up," Mickey said, poised to deal the next hand.

Primo was dealt two kings, X a single ace. At the start of the betting, X had the only hand with a hope of beating Primo. It was Primo's turn to bet first. He checked to draw in the others. Two folded on the first round, but when it got to X, who bet last, he put up 5,000 dollars. Primo called, but the other three folded.

Now it was just the two of them. Neither hand improved as the face-up cards were dealt, but X kept betting large and Primo kept "cautiously" calling. There were tens of thousands in the pot when, just before the last card was dealt, X went all in.

Primo waited. *Is he bluffing?* He knew he didn't have enough cash if he lost, yet if he folded now he would lose all his winnings and most of his stake. He had never left the game a loser. He could see the only chance of beating his two kings was two aces. It all came down to whether X was bluffing or not. Primo needed an edge. He waited to see if X would give it away. With only one hand that could beat him, a pair of aces, he knew the odds were in his favor if X was bluffing. Primo sat motionless, expressionless, looking through his progressive lenses at X, studying his eyes and sweating face. *Come on, X, give me a tell.*

"Man up, Primo," X finally said in a challenging tone.

When Primo didn't react, X leaned his bulk over in front of Mickey, who was squeezed between them, "Man up!"

Mickey cringed visibly, but now Primo knew. He was certain. *Primo's bluffing.* The tell was plain as day: X had a weak hand. "Call," he said.

Primo had read X right. He held only the ace of hearts. But when Mickey dealt the last card, he turned up the Ace of Spades.

X leaned back in his chair and casually turned over his cards. "Can you beat two aces?"

Primo was shocked. Beads of sweat popped on his forehead.

X leaned back farther and laughed at him. "*Now* you can leave, Primo...once you pay up."

X's sidemen followed the boss's lead, and laughter rippled around the room. There wasn't a person there who was sorry Primo got beat. Primo looked at the size of the pot and swallowed hard. Mickey began his count to cash him out. Primo knew he would come up way short. He knew he didn't have that kind of cash with him. He tried to stay calm outwardly as the panic rose. He desperately tried to think of a way out. The last thing he wanted was to give the already drunk and bitter X a target for his rage.

Mickey finished his count. "All right, Primo, you started with ten, you were up seven and change, but you lost 54 on this pot. You need to pony up 37,000." Mickey delivered his report with a complete poker face. There was something about his hard, pocked face so close to Primo that made him feel nauseous. He feared he was going to get sick.

"Look, X," Primo said, unable to mask his nervousness, "I don't have that kind of cash on me, but I can get it for you tomorrow. I just have to visit my stash in—" Seeing X's growing fury he quickly added, "I'll drive it back tonight if you like. You know I'm good for it." Primo tried to flash a winner smile.

X shouted a string of obscenities. "You're—happy to take our—money night after night and now you think you can lose and not—pay up? You know the house rules; pay the—up!" X rolled his new cigar from one side of his mouth to the other, his gaze never leaving the sweating Primo.

Primo knew this wasn't about money; X had more money than he knew what to do with. It was about challenging X's authority. He decided to beg. "X, all I'm asking is that you do me a favor. Just three hours, X. I can be back with the 37 in three hours and I'll bump it to cover the inconvenience."

"Let me get this straight," X said. "You want me to do you a—favor, you—miserable—"

Primo recognized the rhetorical question and realized anything he said now would only make it worse. He just shook his head.

"You should be doing me a favor, punk."

"Sure, X, anything you say," Primo said, lunging at the first glimmer of hope.

X leaned forward and put both of his huge, hairy arms on the poker table. "I hear that new Asian-looking girl...what's her name, Mickey?"

"Danny Delicious."

"Yeah, that one. I hear she works for you?"

"That's right. I'm her agent," Primo said, fighting for self-control.

"All right then." X took the cigar out of his mouth and made a casual, sweeping gesture at Primo. "I'll give you 48 hours to bring me the cash you owe me and the little girl Danny Delicious had with her the other day at the studio in Sylmar. Then we're even, wouldn't you say, boys?"

The other players nodded, but Primo felt punched in the gut. He froze for a moment, then shot to his feet, his chair falling behind him. "Please no, X. Not that. I—" As soon as he stood, he knew it was the wrong move. He saw X's face turn to rage.

The huge man pushed himself to his feet and, never taking his eyes off Primo, extended his right hand to his bodyguard, snapped his fingers, and said, "Paulie, your piece."

Paulie pulled a machine gun pistol from under his leather jacket.

X, weaving on his feet, grabbed the gun and waved it at Primo, punctuating his threat with profanity. "Get me the—girl and my—money or I'll kill ya right now, you—two-bit punk!"

The onlookers behind Primo scrambled out of the line of fire, the poker players leaned as far back from the table as they could, but Primo stood frozen, like a deer in the headlights. He held his hands out toward

X, as if to stop the hail of bullets. "OK, OK, I'll do it. Just put the gun down."

X wavered for a moment, then tilted the gun up and away slightly, taking Primo out of the direct line of fire. "Fine. You've got 48 hours. But...Primo, I'm not happy about this, after all the money you've taken out of this game."

Primo saw the rage returning to X's face, and thought he was going to lose it and kill him anyway.

Then suddenly X laughed. "Get out of here, and don't come back until you have the girl and the money."

Primo stumbled for the door. When his feet hit the gravel at the end of the porch, he could not help running for his car. He vaulted over the side, slid behind the wheel, and sped out of the compound.

As he hit the main road, his panic subsided somewhat—he wasn't going to die. His mind ranged back and forth between what had just happened and what he had to do. He prided himself on always projecting a confident image and was appalled at how his façade had crumbled in front of X and all the others. He was equally sickened at the thought of kidnapping Shanti and taking her to that scumbag. Selling drugs to consenting adults was one thing, but kidnapping a child? He chilled at the thought of the penalties if caught. He considered packing his bags and disappearing. He had just under a million in the Cayman accounts. Properly invested, it was enough to live well in several Central or South American countries.

Then he thought of how he had built up his west-side business: the risks he had taken and how it was poised to break into the big money. He had enough working capital now to do what X did: buy the product directly and eliminate all the middle men. He knew suddenly that X's play was more than a move to get another victim for his sick obsession with child pornography. It was nothing less than an attempt to eliminate the competition at its most vulnerable moment, before it got big.

"That's just what he wants—for me to leave the country," he said aloud. No, nobody would force Primo out, not now when he was poised for the bigtime. *One more year,* he thought, and he would be able to retire anywhere in the world: the image of a villa in southern France shimmered in his mind. He could get Chucho to do all the dirty work and keep himself at arms' length. It was just a matter of money. How much would Chucho want—five or 10 K? He'd offer him seven. He'd drive straight to Chucho's trailer tonight and get everything set up. It was just a matter of picking up the girl and driving to the cabin in Ventura. Chucho could handle it.

Primo flew past a well-lighted gas station. His mind jumped back to the smoke-filled room and the critical moment in the game. He had read the "tell" right. It was just bad luck that X got the ace on the last card.

Then it hit him. His body went cold, and the nausea returned with sudden force. He slammed on the brakes, skidded to a stop on the shoulder, shoved himself up and over the side of the car, and retched violently on the pavement. *It was a setup. I was taken.* His photographic memory replayed the last card; he saw how Mickey's hand turned slightly to hide the bottom deal. He realized the drunkenness and rage was an act, a diversion, a con. He remembered reading somewhere, "The easiest person in the world to con is a con."

When the sickness left, an ice-cold resolve settled in his soul. He would do what he had to do to survive, and then he would get even. Yes, somehow, he would get even.

8

Rough seas
Make good sailors.

Archie had been on the witness stand for hours testifying in an ugly divorce case. It was his worst possible nightmare come true: the husband's lawyer had subpoenaed him and his confidential records. Every other time he had been able to talk them out of it by pointing out that there was as much dirt on one partner as the other; but not this time. No, this burr head went to trial. And just as Archie had said, the wife's lawyer was gleefully countering with all the muck in Archie's files going the other way. The worst of it was that the court order overrode his confidentiality agreement. Sure, the couple had signed a waiver at the start, acknowledging this very possibility, so Archie wasn't vulnerable to a lawsuit. It was the ethics of the thing that tied his stomach in knots. Then, just as the husband's lawyer rose for re-direct with an evil gleam in his eye, the scene changed.

Now Archie was on the smoke-covered deck of an English Navy frigate. The acrid smell of gunpowder hung in the air as the cannons belched fire, smoke, and deadly shot. The frigate stood yardarm to yardarm with a French ship. Strangely, Archie couldn't hear the cannons roar, yet he could feel the deck shudder whenever they fired. *I must have gone deaf from the long bombardment,* he thought. Grappling hooks were flung and the order passed: standby to board. Archie gripped his cutlass and tried to push down his fear.

Suddenly an audible voice startled him awake: "Archie!" It was Luella's voice, or was it his mother's voice? No it was Luella's. He lay in a cold sweat in the darkness, eyes wide open, seeing nothing, trying to figure out where he was and what had just happened. She had spoken with the assertive tone she used whenever she asked him to do something around the house—not aggressive, but not to be denied either. Her voice was so real that he looked beside him in the bed.

She wasn't there. He looked at the bedside clock. The big, red, digital numbers said 4:33 AM. Still disoriented, he turned on the reading lamp, put on his glasses, and squinted at his new Classic Wooden Boats Calendar.

Let's see. It's Monday....Monday, January 17, 1994. Luella has been with the Lord these many years. So the voice, what was that?

It always took Archie a long time to come fully awake...some days as much as an hour. Not this morning. As his senses returned, he realized there had been more going on than Luella's audible voice. He also sensed what he knew to be the Lord's presence. Archie didn't believe that the dead could commune with the living. His faith was that only God can cross the barrier between this world and the next. Or, better said, there was no barrier for God. His love transcended time and space, life and death, and the hereafter.

On the other hand, Archie remembered grief-counseling cases— his own clients and some cases in the literature—where the surviving spouses reported vivid visitations from the deceased. These usually happened nearer the time of death, however, and Luella's passing was well beyond the normal range for such experiences.

So what did it mean? Was God trying to tell him something? Would the Lord talk to him through Luella's voice? His gaze returned to the wall calendar, which said it was Martin Luther King Day. Did it have anything to do with that? Or was it last night's enchilada coming back to haunt him?

Archie gave up trying to solve the mystery, but he couldn't shake the effect the voice had had on him. He was wide awake, certain he would not get back to sleep, not with all the adrenaline surging through his old body. He decided to make the best of it. *I'll get up and have sunrise devotions on the deck.*

Archie laid out the warm outfit he used for winter sailing. The key was layers of clothes so you could adjust your body temperature if the sun came out. He put on a flannel shirt, corduroy pants, and then over that a navy blue, heavy sweatshirt with a comfortable hood. On top of

178

all that he laid out his windbreaker, his fleece gloves, and his Mariner's ball cap. He had been a fan when they lived in Seattle and kept the cap for sailing because of the nice compass rose logo. He also laid out his heaviest Mexican blanket for a lap robe. As an afterthought, he tossed the portable phone on the growing pile near the sliding glass door. Archie liked to be prepared.

He reheated a cup of yesterday's coffee in the microwave and fixed his usual breakfast of eggs and toast. By the time he grabbed his Bible and prayer list, there was light in the eastern sky. Archie could tell without looking at his watch that the sun would rise sometime during his prayers. He couldn't say for sure yet what kind of a sunrise it would be, but based on last night's forecast he was betting on "red sky in the morning, sailor take warning!"

The little deck alcove was sheltered from the wind and, with all his clothes and lap robe on, he was ready for the refreshing January air. He first read a chapter in John's gospel and a chapter in Isaiah. Then he started to pray. He thanked God for waking him to pray, and asked if there was any meaning to the dream and the audible voice. He waited a minute or two, got no sense that the Lord was speaking or showing him anything more, and went on with his prayer list. He prayed for Nancy first, then through family, and then his various church ministries.

He had put Shanti and Danielle under friends and came to them next. He recognized the sinking feeling he had when he prayed for Danielle's salvation. He'd had it many times before when he prayed for his clients. It came after he had tried every intervention he knew and nothing worked—he had come to the end of his professional rope. Then he would turn the case over to the Lord. "I can't do it. You have to take care of this one yourself," he would say.

The recollection gave him a glimmer of hope because often when he did that, some solution would appear, or some event would occur to change the person or their life—usually something that Archie never would have thought of, much less been able to pull off. He prayed this way now for Danielle's salvation.

"Lord," he prayed, "I've tried, you know I have, and it seems like I'm just making it worse, almost like I'm inoculating her against the gospel instead of giving her a hope for it. Father, would you take this soul on Yourself? I know You love her, and I know You can do it. And I believe if Danielle comes to faith, Shanti will be right there too."

Archie's prayer for Danielle and Shanti ran out of gas at that point. He paused, sighed, and went on with the rest of his list, fighting against discouragement.

Sonny was an early riser. All his years of ranching had branded it into his psyche: up at first light, no matter what. Buck was always eager to see his master, knowing their first duty of the day was Frisbee on the beach now that there were no cows to herd.

The morning of the 17th was no different. Sonny usually went out in his bare feet. He liked the feel of the cold sand. He started throwing the Frisbee as soon as they hit the loose stuff. By now Sonny had become proficient at throwing it straight and long; Buck mastered his end after the first catch. Sonny timed the workout to one-half hour, not for the dog—he would have gone all day—but for his tennis elbow. He also alternated throws left- and right-handed to avoid the inflammation. He couldn't throw it as far left, but the dog seemed to like the short-long variation. They worked their way down to the surf and carried on there until the time was up.

"OK, boy, time to go home."

The dog dropped his head, staring at Sonny to show he didn't like it, but soon shifted gears into exploring the beach, covering a huge space as he loped in a circle around Sonny's track back to the house. Sonny saw him sniff and dig at something in the sand about 50 feet ahead and then pick it up. The dog made a beeline trot for his master, holding something in its mouth. He dropped it right in front of Sonny and began whining and making false starts toward the house.

Sonny had worked cattle with Buck for years on the ranch and knew the dog was trying to tell him something. Sonny bent over and picked up the object, brushing off the sand. It was a doll. "My gosh, Buck, is it the vaquero doll I gave Shanti for Christmas?"

Sonny knew Buck could tell by the scent, but he wasn't sure if he knew the word *doll*. "Is this Shanti's toy, Buck?"

180

Buck replied with a single bark and a twist of his head. Then he lowered his head and backed crabwise a few feet toward the house.

"You want to take the doll to Shanti?"

Buck jumped into a trot and began casting oval-shaped circles around Sonny, cutting close to him on the back of the circle, running far out on the side closer to home.

Sonny had seen him do this to get the cattle moving. He wondered if he didn't go himself whether Buck would give him a nip on his calf the way he would a stubborn heifer. *Wouldn't put it past him,* Sonny thought.

Just then Buck swung very close to Sonny's leg. Sonny was sure he would have gotten a nip if he hadn't moved forward.

"Ha, ha, all right, boy. We can go to Shanti's house. She'll be glad to get her doll back."

Sonny liked doing spur-of-the-moment things. It made him feel more alive to just go with whatever was on. He broke into a grinning jog, nearly matching Buck's enthusiasm for the task ahead.

Chucho was up at first light in spite of the beer hangover. While he waited for the coffee water to heat, he thought about the little party he had had just hours ago with Esmeralda Sanchez, a high-class prostitute he could never have afforded before Primo gave him the 5,000 in advance. Primo had offered him seven, but Chucho insisted on 10, five before and five after delivery, and got everything he asked for. He had sensed Primo's vulnerability from the start of the conversation last night and knew he could push for more. Anyway, he would have been happy to let Primo do his own dirty work if he had refused; kidnapping a child was definitely a 10,000-dollar job.

Chucho had spent around a hundred of the cash and had stuffed another 400 in the front pocket of his jeans. He liked the feeling of having it on him. He had hidden the rest in a rat-proof metal box in his *banco*—a hole he had dug in the dirt under the trailer that he went to only in complete darkness. He thought of the wad of bills directly under his feet; it was the most money he had ever had. He got 10,000 once for an assassination in Sinaloa, but that was pesos, not dollars. He thought it strange that Primo had chosen to move into this kind of action and stranger still that he was to drive the girl, unharmed, to a cabin in the Ventura foothills. What had Primo said? "She mustn't have a mark on her." He wondered why in passing, but ultimately it didn't really matter. He liked the money and, perhaps even more, liked the idea of having some leverage on Primo when he made his move to take over some of the action. If Primo didn't like it he would take it all. Chucho felt that Primo, for all his dash and charm, was a lightweight compared to some of the bad hombres he had worked for in Mazatlan, and soon Primo would find out he was a lightweight compared to Chucho.

He sipped the scalding, bitter coffee. He figured his English would be good enough in a few more months to make the move. Primo wouldn't know what hit him.

Chucho took his coffee and an empanada into the bedroom. He pulled out what he needed for the job—some rags would do for a gag and soft restraints, a pillowslip for a hood, and the highway map Primo had marked for him. He checked the loads in his .357 magnum, screwed the silencer into the barrel, and slipped it into the back of his jeans under the wide belt he always wore. He checked himself in the mirror: the loose-fitting surfer shirt completely hid the gun in the small of his back. He pulled a Dodgers baseball cap over his eyes and put on one-way reflector sunglasses. He figured that was enough to get him in and out without recognition. *We all look the same to them anyway*, he thought.

He finished his breakfast and headed for the '75 Oldsmobile Primo had given him. It was a huge tank of a car with a big trunk, perfect for this job. Among his other talents, Chucho was a pretty good mechanic and had the big V-8 running better than he thought possible for such an old beater. He put a blanket down in the trunk so the girl wouldn't get dirty and tossed a second blanket in on top of it. He knew he could pull it off without hurting her, but if she arrived dirty they might think otherwise. The day before, he had rigged the trunk with a fresh-air vent.

Chucho drove the few miles over to the house in Venice he knew so well. He had enjoyed spying on Danielle and had spent many hours beyond what was required lusting after her. *What a woman,* he thought. He drove on in silence, going over how he would pull off the job. He knew the little girl was an early riser and liked to play in the backyard. It would be easy to slip in through the back gate, bundle her up, and be gone before anyone knew what happened.

He had only two concerns: the big, ugly dog and finding a parking place close by. He hoped to stop in the alley near the gate where there was a slight widening of the lane. Otherwise he would park on the street at the end of the alley. There were too many commuters to risk blocking someone in the alley. As for the dog, if she got into it, he would shoot her. The caffeine and adrenaline kicked in at about the same time as he swung the big Olds into the alley. He said nothing as he rolled by the gate and saw that the parking space he wanted was occupied by a motorcycle. He rolled on down to the end of the alley, looking left and right for a parking space and found one about halfway down the block. It was farther than he wanted, but it was better to park legally than risk getting in trouble with a traffic cop for double-parking.

He eased the big car into the space, went to the trunk, and pulled out the blanket. He figured if he wrapped the girl up in it, any onlooker couldn't be sure what he was carrying. He dropped the rags in the middle of the blanket, left the trunk closed but unlatched, and walked down the alley. He reached the gate, listened for a moment, and let himself inside.

As he had expected, the girl was playing with her dolls on the back porch of the big house. The dog was lying asleep some 10 feet away from her and off to his left. *The old dog must be deaf,* he thought. He drew the gun, clicked off the safety, and moved quickly toward the girl.

Shanti heard a foot on the deck. Thinking it was her mother, she didn't look up from her intense play, but continued her dialogue: "I don't want to, and you can't make me."

"Oh yes I can."

Just then a calloused hand clapped over her mouth.

Munchie was going deaf, but there was nothing wrong with her sense of smell, and something foreign had entered her world. She didn't know it was the smell of beer seeping through the man's pores from the drinking he had done into the early morning, but she knew it wasn't right. She lifted her head, saw the man holding Shanti, and shot for him with a terrible squealing, growling sound that terriers make when they are going into battle.

Chucho had laid the gun down on the deck to open the blanket. But since he anticipated trouble from the dog, he kept his gaze fixed on her as he grappled with the child. When the dog lifted her head and began to run, he stooped down, picked up the .357, and dropped her with one shot. Her lunge brought her to Shanti's feet, where she lay motionless, blood pooling from the wound in her chest.

Up to that point, Shanti wasn't sure what was happening to her and had only made small sounds of distress as she struggled with an adult she couldn't see. Now, however, the sight of her precious dog shot at her feet set off a terrible wail of agony, fear, and rage. She began fighting the stranger with all her strength.

The moment Danielle heard Munchie's high-pitched growl, she looked out the window and saw the struggle below her. She grabbed the aluminum ball bat and flew down the outside stairs, making little sound in her bare feet. She crossed the lawn in two strides and aimed a hard swing at the assailant's head.

184

Chucho stood up with the gagged Shanti under his left arm when he saw Danielle running toward him with the ball bat. Her staggering blow struck his right shoulder. Searing pain shot through him as he dropped the girl and rolled toward the gun. He was able to grab it by the barrel just as Danielle aimed another swing. His right shoulder felt numb from the first blow, but the next grazed harmlessly off his back as he rolled into Danielle's legs. His lunge knocked her down, and in the same motion he whipped the pistol over the top. It made a strange, thunking sound when the heavy butt struck the side of her head.

She lay motionless as he struggled to his feet. He stood over her, cursing her, the gun hanging in his left hand, his right arm throbbing.

Shanti, wailing through her gag, threw herself at his knees. He reached around, grabbed her, and this time finished the job of binding her in the blanket. As he carried her out of the gate, he looked back at the woman and dog, lying a few feet from each other. They were dead or unconscious, he didn't care which.

Sonny found a parking place right in front of Mrs. Johnson's house—a commuter pulled out just as he arrived. "Well, here we are, boy," he said to Buck. "Do you want to give the doll to Shanti?"

Sonny held the doll out to Buck, who immediately took it gently in his mouth. Sonny jumped out his door and was almost tripped when the dog ran by him. Sonny pulled the latch string on the front gate, letting them into the yard. Buck trotted ahead and Sonny ran behind, not wanting to miss the expression on Shanti's face when she saw Buck bringing her the doll. He anticipated telling the story of how they found the doll.

As he came toward the back of the house, he looked up to see if Mrs. Johnson was up yet. He saw her sipping her tea in the window of her breakfast nook at the side of the house. He waved and shouted, "Hello, Mildred," but she evidently neither saw nor heard him.

Suddenly Buck came running back to him without the doll, whining and making starts toward the backyard.

"What is it, boy?" Sonny said as he picked up his pace. "Mother Mary, have mercy!" he cried as he surveyed the scene in the backyard.

Buck worried back and forth over the two fallen figures, giving Danielle licks in the face, but not getting so close to the pool of blood around Munchie.

Sonny dug out his handkerchief, dipped it in Shanti's plastic water toy, and threw himself down beside Danielle. He wiped the blood away from the gash on her head. "What happed here, darling? Where's Shanti?"

Danielle gripped his arm weakly and tried to focus. "Shanti… kidnap…get her…" Her head fell back, eyes rolled upward.

Sonny sprang to his feet and ran to the back door of the house, yelling "Mildred, Mildred!" at the top of his lungs.

Mrs. Johnson jumped to her feet when Sonny slammed through the screen door. She waved and turned up her hearing aid.

"Mrs. Johnson, thank God you're here. There's not a moment to lose. Someone's kidnapped Shanti, knocked out Danielle, and shot Munchie. Buck and I will go after Shanti if you take care of the other two. Call 9-1-1, tell them you've had a home invasion and a kidnapping. Get a patrol car and an ambulance over here now!"

As he was speaking, Sonny ran backwards out the door and into the yard.

"Of course, Sonny, go find Shanti. I'll take care of Danielle." At the best of times the 90-year-old's head shook and her voice quavered whenever she spoke…more so when she was excited. Her mind, however, was as sharp as a tack. Her adult children laughed at how she was always several steps ahead in any conversation, setting up jokes at every opportunity. Now she moved as fast as she could for the back door.

Outside, Sonny turned quickly to Buck. "Find Shanti, boy! Find Shanti!" and gave him the hand gesture to search.

Buck, who had been sniffing around the yard while Sonny was talking to Mildred, made a beeline for the back gate and pawed and whined at it. Sonny threw it open, and the two of them raced down the alley. They came tearing around the corner where the alley met the street just as someone put an Olds in gear.

Border collies are working dogs, known for their speed and endurance. But their most unique quality is their intelligence. Some say they have the problem-solving ability of a school-age child. Buck followed the scent trail to the parking place and saw the car driving away. He realized he couldn't stop the car. Instead of running futilely after it, he turned, barked a single bark at Sonny and began his false start routine toward the Land Rover parked in front of Mrs. Johnson's.

Sonny saw the dog's behavior, figured Shanti was in the Olds, and didn't break stride as he sprinted behind Buck past the now-empty parking space and around the corner to the Rover. They ran the stop sign and careened around the corner just as the Olds made a right turn a few blocks down. Sonny floored the Rover and ignored the speed limit signs. If he picked up a patrol car, so much the better.

To cover any sound coming from the trunk, Chucho turned on the car radio already set to his favorite Mexican music station. However, the morning of the 17th there wasn't a station in L.A. broadcasting music. Chucho realized in seconds that something momentous had happened as much from the pressure in the newscaster's voice as the words he spoke.

"The quake occurred at 4:30 this morning, in the San Fernando Valley about 20 miles west, northwest of Los Angeles. Registering 6.7 on the Richter scale, the quake caused the strongest ground motions ever instrumentally recorded in an urban area in North America. It goes without saying, the resultant damage has been a cataclysm of biblical proportions. Buildings have collapsed, freeways are twisted like pretzels; hospitals, schools, and apartment buildings are destroyed or severely damaged. Because the quake occurred at 4:30 AM, however, preliminary reports suggest few lives have been lost, although hundreds, perhaps thousands are injured. For those of you hoping to commute this morning we are going to our traffic-control reporter in just a moment, but I can tell you nothing is moving in the Valley. If you are planning to drive anywhere from Thousand Oaks to Burbank, go back home and phone your office."

Chucho looked at the map Primo had given him. There wasn't any way to get to the cabin—neither the I-5 nor the coastal route—that didn't involve some travel through the valley. He picked up his cell phone and called Primo. As it was dialing, the traffic reporter confirmed that all possible routes were closed.

Primo answered the phone on the first ring.

"Boss, do you have your TV or radio on?"

"What kind of a question is that? Do you have the girl?"

"Of course I have her. No problem at my end, Boss," Chucho lied. His shoulder throbbed and hand shook as he held the phone on his partially disabled right side and drove with the good arm. "There's been an earthquake and the roads to the cabin are all shut down. Turn on the TV and see for yourself."

Primo clicked the remote with the sound off and surfed through a few channels. Everyone was broadcasting emergency quake reports. He came to one with a map of road closures and saw there was no way to get to the cabin. If he had been dealing with anyone else, he would have called X, told him the situation, and asked for more time or another arrangement. But nobody called X. No one had his unlisted number. Primo's choices were limited, but doing nothing and giving X an excuse to kill him was not one of them.

"Where are you now Chucho?"

"I'm just driving around the neighborhood with the girl in the trunk." Chucho didn't say he thought he was being followed and was "driving around" to elude his pursuer.

"All right. Meet me at the gate to the marina in seven minutes. We'll take her to Ventura in the *Cobra* and make our way to the cabin from the back side."

Once in the Beamer, Primo called a client in Ventura—a car dealer who owed him a favor—and asked him to leave a car at the Ventura marina. He would be using it for just a few hours and bring it back before evening.

Primo sped to Marina del Sur and found Chucho behind the wheel of the Olds near the gate. Primo heard the Spanish broadcast of the earthquake news go dead just as he reached the car. He realized that the phone conversation with Chucho had not been in Spanish, and now the clarity of Chucho's English made him feel uneasy. He brushed away his vague apprehension, however.

"I've thought of a way to get the girl on the boat, without arousing suspicion," he whispered in Chucho's ear. "Hide on the floor behind the front seat, then follow us. *Comprende?*"

Going quickly to the back of the car, Primo heard Shanti's muffled cries and said, "Is someone in here? Just a minute, I'll get you out." He opened the trunk and saw the girl gagged and bound. Shanti was blinded by the light when Primo opened the trunk. "Oh, you poor child," he said, as he took out the gag and untied the restraints around her wrists and ankles.

Shanti began talking a mile a minute. "Primo! We have to go to my house. A bad man hurt my mommy and shot Munchie. We have to go there right now."

"Listen, Shanti, I have a better idea. The *Cobra* is right over there. Look—you can see her. There's a radio on board; we can call the police and an ambulance. and they will get to your house faster than we can! Come on."

While he was talking, Primo lifted the little girl out of the trunk of the car, closed it, and began carrying her toward the gate.

She looked at him. "I can walk by myself."

"Of course you can, sweetheart," Primo said, putting her down but holding firmly to her hand.

As they approached the gate, Shanti got her bearings. She was one of those kids who had a great sense of direction, always remembering landmarks. She realized that Archie's apartment looked right down on the marina; she tried to pick out the right window. All of the windows looked the same, but she knew it was on the top floor and figured it was near the end.

Hey, is that Archie sitting on his balcony? She was not surprised to see him there. Since he had plucked her from the sea, she'd secretly believed he would always be there for her when she most needed him.

Suddenly Archie jumped up and stood at the railing, holding a phone to his ear. Without hesitation she pulled her hand from Primo's, turned, and ran back up the ramp.

"Archie, Archie!" she shouted as she ran. "A bad man hurt my mommy and shot Munchie!"

Archie was finishing his intercessory prayers when the phone rang. He found it right beside his chair. "Hello."

"Shanti's been kidnapped! Danielle's knocked out! Munchie's shot!"

"What?" Archie shot to his feet, his heart pounding.

"I saw the guy, Arch. He's driving a '75 Oldsmobile, but he kept doubling back and I lost him just a minute ago. He might have been heading your way."

Archie stood at the rail of his balcony, looking out over the marina. Suddenly he heard his name. He looked in the direction of the voice. He saw a little girl running up the ramp. It was Shanti! She ran right into the arms of a small dark man with a baseball cap and sunglasses. He picked her up in one arm and awkwardly clamped his other hand over her mouth.

"Sonny, listen to me, Shanti is here, at the marina. Where are you?"

"Just blocks away, Arch, but—"

"They're here. A small dark guy with a ball cap and sunglasses is carrying her down the ramp and...Primo is with them!"

"I never trusted that weasel. Wait 'til I get my—"

"Sonny, there's not a moment to lose. Meet me at the gate to the docks as fast as you can."

"I'm on my way!"

Mildred got the screen door open and looked out on her backyard. "Oh dear, oh dear," she said as she surveyed the bodies. She turned quickly to the wall phone near the back door. All her phones had hearing impaired assists. She dialed 9-1-1.

It rang several times before a woman's voice said, "9-1-1 operator."

"Hello, this is Mildred Johnson. I live at 271 Gardena in Venice. I'm calling to report a home invasion. My renter is knocked unconscious, bleeding from a head wound, her dog is shot, and they have kidnapped her four-year-old daughter. Could you send an ambulance and a patrol car at once please?"

"Yes, ma'am, I'm calling the appropriate dispatchers as we speak. But I'm afraid they are backed up. We are working on a 75-minute delay right now with the chaos the quake has caused. Do you know basic first aid?"

"Yes dear, I do."

The operator picked up the quaver in Mildred's voice. "How old are you ma'am?"

"I'll be ninety-one next week."

"Is there anyone you can call to help you care for the injured while you wait for the ambulance?"

"Yes there is—my friend from church, Mrs. Samos."

"I suggest you get her to help you. Now give me a name and description of the four-year-old."

As soon as Mildred finished the 9-1-1 call, she phoned Nicky. Nicky Samos was only 78 and could still drive. She picked Mildred up every Sunday morning to attend the early service at first Methodist in Santa Monica. They also went to other church activities together and occasionally got out for a movie or lunch.

"Nicky, something terrible has happened to that nice family that lives over my garage. You know, Danielle and Shanti."

"What happened?"

"I don't have time to explain it all to you now, dear. I'll fill you in when you get here. Park in the alley beside the gate. And bring your first-aid kit."

Mildred grabbed her own first-aid box from its place in the kitchen, two tea towels, a sports injury ice pack she kept in the freezer, and a couple of "back porch" blankets, tossed everything into a shopping bag, and headed for Danielle and Munchie. She eased Danielle's twisted legs into a more comfortable position, grunting with the exertion, and put a blanket over her. She took the bottle of alcohol from the kit, poured some on a clean tea towel, and began wiping the blood away from the contusion on the side of Danielle's head.

"You poor dear," she murmured as she cleaned the wound.

Danielle, startled at the sting of the alcohol, came to a groggy level of consciousness. She recognized Mildred's voice and tried to speak. "Shanti...taken..."

"I know, dear, they've taken our precious girl. But Sonny and Buck are in hot pursuit, and I've phoned the police. Now you rest easy." Mildred's voice quavered.

"But I have to..."

"I know, dear, you want to go after your little darling. You can help find her when you're feeling better, but right now you're in no shape to move."

The back gate opened and Mildred's friend Nicky came into the yard. "What on earth? Oh my goodness, Mildred, what happened here?"

"Nicky, am I glad to see you. We had a home invasion. They kidnapped Shanti, shot Munchie, and hit Danielle over the head. You see what you can do for that poor dog. I'll carry on with Danielle."

"Oh my goodness," Nicky repeated as she hustled over to the dog. "Did you call 9-1-1?"

"I did, but they said there would be a long wait. Everybody is busy with the earthquake."

"Oh my," Nicky said as she bent over the dog. The bleeding had slowed, but there was already quite a large pool of blood. Nicky held her hand in front of the dog's nose and felt for a pulse at her throat. "She's still breathing!"

"Good. Dogs are pretty tough. I hope she'll pull through."

The two elderly ladies worked steadily over their charges, doing what they could. After cleaning Danielle's wound, Mildred rigged a way to hold the icepack on her head and then held the injured woman's hand and prayed a silent prayer. She looked at her watch. It was still a long time before the ambulance would come, too long.

"Nicky, what do you say we load these two in your car and take them to the hospital ourselves?"

"I'm up for that, but Santa Monica General is being evacuated. It seems a fault line runs right under it, and the old building couldn't handle the shaking. The news said it's chaotic over there—patients in the parking lot, nurses running everywhere."

"Well, we could take them to my G.P. His office is in a wood frame building and should have done better in the quake." Mildred, like most Southern Californians, knew that wood-frame houses were more flexible than masonry structures.

"Well, it certainly seems like a better idea than just sitting here. But how are we going to get them to the car?"

"My children made me buy a wheelchair after my fall last year. I never have used it, but it should get the job done for Danielle. There's a wheelbarrow in the garage for Munchie."

The two elderly women managed to get Danielle up and into the wheelchair and tied her in with one of Mildred's shawls. They dumped the wheelbarrow on its side, rolled the dog in, and then managed to right it again. They pulled and pushed the wheelchair to the side of Nicky's SUV and, with a little help from Danielle, managed to get her in. They loaded Munchie into the back and headed for Mildred's doctor's office, minutes away.

Archie and Sonny arrived at the marina gate at almost the same time. The two ran down the ramp together while Archie tried to fill Sonny in. Archie was winded, sprinting from his balcony. "Go to gas dock...find...fast boat...gassed up....They boarded...*Cobra*...going out!"

Sonny, not winded, suddenly ran ahead. He tore around the gas dock corner and saw Chad chatting with Charlene, the gas attendant who was hanging up the hose. Beside the dock lay the *Dolphin*. Chad and the attendant looked up as they heard the boys pounding down the dock.

"Shanti's been kidnapped!" roared Sonny.

"Cast off your lines," shouted Archie.

Chad turned slowly and watched the boys run past him to the lifeguard boat he had just gassed up. "What's happening, boys?" Chad asked mildly.

"There's not a moment to lose!" Archie said, gasping for breath.

"Shanti's been kidnapped," rasped Sonny again.

It was the fierce look in Sonny's eyes that got Chad moving. "We can get into action," Chad said as he took control of the boat, trying to think of a way to cover his behind with the Lifeguard Commander. "We'll say I took you guys out for a ride-along, but the boss isn't going to be happy I left my guards on the dock."

"God bless you, Captain!" Archie said as he shot Sonny a hard look. He knew Sonny was about to say something about stupid bureaucrats, but he caught Archie's meaning and bit his lip. Archie shoved off from the dock and Chad pulled clear.

"The *Cobra's* slip is on one of the inside docks. There might be time—there has to be time," Archie said.

"OK guys, but fill me in as we go. If this really is a kidnapping, I can get a lot of help out here in a hurry."

Archie and Sonny told Chad the story quickly, in the grimmest tone. They finished their account just as the *Dolphin* popped into the main channel. Chad had Archie look forward port and starboard while Sonny kept watch astern in case they had beaten the *Cobra* into the channel. There was lighter-than-usual weekday traffic, but no sign of the *Cobra*.

"I'll hold at the T," Chad said, "where we can see north, south, and east back up the channel."

As they approached the T, Archie noticed white water coming over the top of the rock wall. "Quite a swell."

"Yeah, northwest swell running eight to 10 feet; be a big surf day at Malibu," Chad said, grinning. His surfer smile faded when he saw Sonny's fierce profile beside him. "We've had quite a few rescues last couple of days," Chad added.

Archie contemplated the problems the sea presented. It would be hard for the *Cobra* to make a fast run in this, but at the same time if they didn't pick her up soon she would be much harder to spot, hidden in the troughs. If they could find her, Chad should have an edge from handling the *Dolphin* on the surf line. But now they cleared the east-west channel and all three men strained to pick up the electric blue boat.

"There!" Archie, shouted, pointing up the north channel. "About half a mile out, it looks like the *Cobra*."

Chad put the glasses on her and picked up the name on the stern at the top of a swell. "It's her all right. Athletic-looking guy at the wheel and a little dude in a ball cap beside him."

"Yeah," Sonny growled. "It's them all right."

The three men already had their life jackets on but, seeing spray coming over the western wall of the breakwater, Chad wanted more insurance. "Sonny, reach in that compartment under your elbow and grab each of us a safety harness. We're in for a rough ride." Chad studied the *Cobra* crashing through the swell quartering off her port bow, white water flying. "I don't think they see us yet, but they will."

Chad handed the glasses to Archie and gunned the engine. The three men fell silent as the chase began, all of their energy riveted on the fleeing boat. They got their safety gear on and hooked their lines to the available ring bolts with 200 yards to go before they hit the full swell.

Chad was sure the *Cobra* could outrun the *Dolphin* on flat water, but her speed advantage was taken away in these conditions. Now operator skill gave him the edge. He could already see that the *Cobra* wasn't being well handled. You had to develop an anticipatory feel for quartering into swells like this at high speed. It had taken him years of practice to properly time the course corrections, slipping the oncoming swell by turning slightly away and then correcting course again on the way down the back of each wave. As well, you couldn't lose your focus for a moment, as each wave was slightly different, a few a lot bigger. He had seen the wreckage of guys overpowering into stuff like this. He had heard all their stories of how the operator made a seemingly harmless mistake, how a cascade of events started, and how it ended in one form of disaster or another. He, on the other hand, had been reading rough seas, slipping crests, and making rescues in the worst conditions for years. *After all, it's when you've got "conditions" that people get in trouble and we have to go to work*, he thought. He knew Archie liked a good blow too, but a sailboat with its deep keel and pressure on the sails was more stable than a powerboat in these conditions.

Chad's calculations were interrupted. "We don't seem to be gaining on them," Sonny said. "Are we gonna catch 'em'?"

"Oh, we'll catch them all right," Chad replied after he had maneuvered around a particularly gnarly crest.

Archie didn't like the way Sonny was pressing Chad. He had seen Chad in action and was certain he knew a lot more about what he was doing than the two of them ever would. He didn't want Sonny's impatience wearing on him. So he tried to explain to Sonny. "Chad here has made a living going out in the worst conditions. Let's let him handle the boat. Come below. I want to talk with you about what we might do when we catch her."

Chad exhaled audibly when the two were out of the con. "Amateurs," he said to himself. However, he had too much going on to stew over Sonny's insult and whether he could or couldn't catch the chase was immaterial. He had planned all along to call in the Harbor Patrol. He keyed his mike.

Danielle had been groaning and holding her head for the last three blocks.

"Turn in the second driveway on the right and park behind the office," Mildred said to Nicky. Then, to Danielle she added, "Hang on, dear. We're at my doctor's office. You're going to get the best care. Park right beside the door, Nicky."

Nicky stopped in the RESERVED FOR DOCTOR space, jumped out of the car, and pulled the wheelchair out of the back. Munchie looked no worse; she hadn't bled through the bandages and was still breathing. The ladies loaded Danielle into the chair and wheeled her into the waiting room. The waiting patients gawked and gasped at the bloody bandage on Danielle's head.

Mildred made her way to the receptionist. "Good morning, Ruthie."

Ruthie couldn't see Danielle around the corner of her alcove.

"Good morning, Mrs. Johnson. You don't have an appointment this morning; how can we help you?"

"Ruthie, we had a home invasion," Mildred said in a loud, quavering voice. "Danielle here has a serious head injury and needs immediate attention. Her dog, Munchie, in the car outside, has been shot."

Ruthie stood and leaned forward so she could see Danielle. "But Mrs. Johnson, we aren't set up for emergencies, and we certainly are not equipped to handle dogs. You should take Danielle to the nearest ER, and as for the dog...."

Ruthie had a reputation with Dr. Hazim's patients of being tough as nails when it came to disrupting his schedule. The patients in the waiting room heard what was being said, looked at Danielle, looked at each other, and blasted into the conversation. "You can't turn her away," shouted one. "Ruthie, she could be dying," yelled another. "What about the Hippocratic oath," cried a third. "Take her first," said a fourth.

Mildred tried to explain to Ruthie that the earthquake had shut the ER down, but couldn't make herself heard over the din.

Dr. Hazim drove as fast as he could from SMG to his office. He had done all he could for his patients in the parking lot and anticipated a waiting room full of less acute, well-paying clients. He had borne the chaos of doing parking lot medicine with an élan that went above and beyond his usual excellent bedside manner. Truth be told, he found the chaos exciting and a welcome break from his routine.

The SUV with the open back door, parked in his reserved space, took him aback, however. A small thing after the chaos at SMG, but stealing his space was a personal affront. He had to park a few paces away, but as he walked briskly past the vehicle the sight of the bloody, comatose dog swept away his rising indignation. Imagining more earthquake injuries, he sprinted the few feet to his personal entrance. He immediately heard shouting voices—his receptionist's the loudest—somewhere inside. He abandoned his usual routine—checking messages, reviewing the day's schedule—and went straight through to reception. He popped into the room and nearly collided with one of his oldest patients, Mrs. Johnson.

"Dr. Hazim, am I glad to see you," Mildred said, her head shaking side to side. "My renter, Mrs. Jackson, has a head injury. We brought her here because..."

Hazim looked over Mildred. "Danielle!" He rushed past Mildred and knelt beside the wheelchair. "Danielle, what has happened to you?" He began a preliminary examination while, at the same time, firing orders. "Nurse Remple, take Mrs. Jackson into the nearest examining room. If there isn't one available clear one. Ruthie, change the outgoing message on the answer machine to: 'We're responding to the quake emergency, leave a message.' Then find the driver of that car outside and take the dog to Abdul's veterinary office down the block. I hope the rest of you understand you will have to wait a bit longer."

"We do, Doc!"

"Do your best!"

"Don't worry about us!" came back to him in a chorus. Dr. Hazim turned to Mildred. "Mrs. Johnson, Danielle is a former patient—that is, her daughter was. She will receive the best care."

"That's the spirit, Doctor," Mildred said. "You take care of Danielle and Munchie; I will take care of the bills."

Things calmed down quickly, although the people in the waiting room insisted on being informed of every development. A preliminary X-ray showed Danielle's skull was not fractured, but Hazim said she definitely had a concussion and would have to be kept under observation. Dr. Hazim was on the phone in his office, trying to find a hospital bed for her, when Nicky returned from the vet and found Danielle and Mildred in an examining room.

"Dr Abdul took Munchie straight into surgery. I asked him to call us here as soon as he has any news. I just had to come back and see how Danielle was doing."

Danielle opened her eyes. "Dr. Hazim said I'm going to be OK, but Shanti..." She broke down.

Mildred took her hand, "Sweetheart, the best thing for us to do for Shanti is to pray for Jesus to take care of her. Come on, Nicky, let's pray."

It seemed surreal to Danielle—everywhere she went, she was surrounded by Christians. But praying for Shanti was something she surely could do. She closed her eyes and as Mildred led off praying aloud, she shaped her own silent, deeply felt petition.

Primo knew he was being chased; the following boat was the only other to leave the breakwater headed north. As well, the pursuer was stuck right on his course and was throwing a huge bow wave, proving he was pushing it. Primo was dimly aware he was driving too hard, but he had no choice. To get caught now with the girl on board meant life in prison. The *Cobra* shuddered, however, as she took a wave very hard and green water poured over the deck, some as far as the cockpit.

His boating safety instructor's voice echoed in his head. Every day he would start the class with the same mantra. "The captain's first concern at sea is"—he would pause and wait for the class to finish with—"THE SAFETY OF HIS CREW AND SHIP." But Primo failed to remember that his teacher also said, "Classroom knowledge of what the sea can do is one thing; experience of it is another." And Primo was short on rough sea experience. Like most boaters, he didn't go out if the seas were high, and he ran for port ahead of any sudden squalls. This was the first time he had left the shelter of the breakwater with big seas running.

On the second crest of a smaller set of swells Primo risked looking back at his pursuer. *Not gaining,* he thought. *Maybe even farther back, yes farther back.* A half smile was on his face when he turned forward again. Then, in the distance, he caught a glimpse of something that made his blood run cold. It was just a glimmer of lights dead ahead, intermittent red and blue lights. He swore bitterly as he stood up for a better look. The view from the extra height confirmed his worst fear: Harbor Patrol. He'd had a run-in with a Harbor Patrol boat a few months ago. He'd had to pay a stiff fine for passing too close to some surfers off Malibu waiting for outside waves. One of them had a two-way and called him in.

Now panic gripped him. He couldn't help taking a second look at the pursuing boat as well, but when he made the quick turn his trick knee locked up. His body involuntarily bent forward with the shooting pain. But his biggest mistake was taking his eye off the incoming swells, something a boat operator of more experience would never have allowed. As so often is the case, the last of the small set was followed by a steep wind wave that was breaking at its crest. Instead of turning well away, quartering into it and slowing a bit, the *Cobra* plowed her bows deep under the green water.

The sudden deceleration threw Primo forward at an awkward angle. He struck his temple on the compass bulb in the middle of the dash. His brain exploded with light and pain. His body pulled involuntarily back and away. He felt himself falling, falling into total darkness. The dead-man switch clipped to his shirt popped out as it was designed to do. Its coiled cord sprung free and fell under his body. The *Cobra* stopped, dead in the water.

Chucho had gone below to check on the girl moments before Primo hit the wave. He too was thrown forward, but in the padded cuddy neither he nor the child were injured. Chucho made his way back to the cockpit. He looked down at the unconscious Primo and swore bitterly. This job had gone bad from the start.

From the crest of a wave he saw the *Dolphin* approaching their stern quarter, and from the next crest he caught sight of the distant blue and red lights of the Sheriff's boat coming straight at them. Chucho knew nothing about operating the boat; he saw it was certain they would be caught. Still, if he could dispose of the evidence before they got too close, he could say they never brought the girl on board. He recalled seeing the anchor chain in a compartment in front of the V berth. If he could wrap it around her and throw her over the side, there was a chance they would get off.

He made his way forward and began pulling the chain back into the V Berth. It was still shiny, he noticed, having never been used.

Chad saw the *Cobra* nearly bury itself in the wave and then suddenly go dead in the water. He eased back on the throttle slightly to make a less violent passage over the remaining swells that separated the two boats.

Sensing the change in motion, Sonny and Archie popped back out of the cabin.

"Why are we slowing?" Sonny asked.

"The chase just went dead in the water. We'll be there in minutes."

"We have to board her, Chad," Archie said.

"Hold on now. Those guys are probably armed and we aren't. I don't have clearance to put two civilians in harm's way. Anyhow, I've got the Harbor Patrol on the way. They are trained and equipped to handle this."

"It says. 'LIFEGUARD' on the side of this tub in two-foot-high letters," Sonny growled. "Is your job saving people or not?" Sonny pressed his face as close as he could to the much taller man.

Chad came right back at him. "They will shoot you to pieces if they have automatic weapons; we wait for the Sheriff."

Before Sonny could escalate the conflict further, Archie squeezed between them. "Now Sonny, tell the Captain you meant no disrespect. You don't want the bosun to have to shake out his cat."

Sonny remembered the necessary hierarchies at sea and said, "Sorry Captain, I forgot myself."

Then Archie turned to Chad. "Captain, I dread what might be happening to that little girl. I understand that normally you have to make decisions in a crisis based on what you know rather than on speculation. In this case, you're pretty sure you would be putting Sonny and me in harm's way if we board and we have far less information about Shanti's status. But sometimes speculation has to override what we know when the risk is horrific and that's what we face here. I've worked with child-abuse survivors for 30 years," he said, gauging the shrinking distance between the two boats. "I can't stand by, not knowing what's happening to Shanti." As Archie spoke he felt his words were inadequate, stilted…even futile. He wanted to say more but stopped his plea suddenly.

Chad took a quick sideways glance at Archie and Sonny. He wasn't particularly good at reading people, but only a fool could doubt their resolve. Normally, in a situation like this, a police helicopter would already be overhead, ready to drop boarders into the water while another officer covered their assault from the air. But there was no chopper available today; they were all diverted to the quake. He thought of putting Archie on the helm and boarding himself, but that opened another can of worms of uncertainty and complications. In the end, Chad agreed with Archie's risk assessment, and he knew delay was the lifeguard's enemy. Chad's problem was department regulations: how could he get them on board and not lose his job?

The three of them went on in silence. The two older men were now resolved that boarding was Chad's decision to make and his alone. Archie prayed Chad would say it's a go. The *Cobra* wasn't more than a few seconds away when Chad broke the silence. "Either of you take basic first aid?"

"I did," Archie said.

His heart leapt as Chad gave him a quick nod and keyed his mike. "Harbor Patrol 7, this is Lifeguard 22, over."

"Pete here, go ahead, Chad."

"The speedboat, *Cobra*, is dead in the water about five miles northwest of the Santa Monica Pier. The operator looks unconscious. Maybe he hit his head going under a gnarly wave. I'm going to put a couple guys on board to stabilize his condition and secure the vessel. Let me know your ETA as soon as you can, over."

"Roger 22, we're getting close."

Chad slowed the *Dolphin* as he neared the *Cobra*. "All right. You boys unhook but one hand for the boat; we're going to pitch like a cork once we lose headway. Get whatever gear you're taking with you and then wait on the swim platform. And kick all the fenders over before you get out there."

"You're doing the right thing, Chad," Archie said as he and Sonny pushed the fenders over the side.

Chad frowned and said nothing. Putting two civilians aboard in these circumstances wouldn't play well with Commander Ortega. Still, the reason to board was following procedure. He would have to sell the idea that he had to send the old guys because there was no one else available, given the crisis on land. It fell under the heading of Resource

Management in the manual. It was thin, very thin; but it was something.

Archie and Sonny had discussed boarding earlier while Chad was getting them close. Their plan was simple: Archie would jump into the cockpit; Sonny would rush the forward hatch. They would find Shanti, free her, and convince her kidnappers their situation was hopeless— Archie's idea. Or somehow they'd overpower them—Sonny's preference. One thing they agreed on: get Shanti to safety at all cost. Archie held a loaded spear gun and Sonny a heavy oxygen tank as they stepped onto the stern swim platform.

"It's going to be touch and go, boys, so get ready to jump," Chad yelled as he spun the *Dolphin* in a tight circle and began to back the remaining few feet to the *Cobra's* stern.

The boats rolled wildly as they lay broadside to the swells. Archie and Sonny jumped for the *Cobra* just as they touched. The speedboat had no swim deck; each fought for a handhold to pull himself aboard. Archie slid down into the cockpit. Sonny stayed low as he sped forward on the pitching deck, carrying the oxygen tank in one hand, holding on to whatever he could with the other.

Chucho heard something thump astern. He dropped the anchor chain, picked up the .357, and made his way through the cuddy into the cockpit.

Archie held the spear gun pointed low at Chucho's legs; Chucho's .357 hung at his side. At this range neither would miss.

Archie felt a surprising calm come over him and an urging to speak to the man in front of him in Spanish. *"Deje cayer la pistola. Es su unica esperanza,"* Archie said. *"La Polecia estaran aqui en minutos."*

Chucho hesitated. Then a tremendous boom sounded from the bows. The entire boat shook as Sonny smashed the oxygen tank through the forward hatch.

Chucho's eyes widened. *"Mentieras!"* he said to the old man in front of him.

Archie saw the gun coming up and the barrel blossom fire just as he triggered the spear gun aimed at Chucho's legs. All Archie wanted was to buy Sonny some time. He had weighed the cost of killing in violence before at Active Pass. Better to die here than to have to live with another man's blood on his conscience.

Chucho shot to kill. He took dead aim at Archie's heart, but a sudden lee lurch made him shoot slightly high and right. The .357 slug hit Archie's shoulder, spun him, and knocked him down. He heard a scream as the spear plunged into Chucho's thigh. Chucho's second shot missed everything as the shock of the spear wrecked his aim completely. He doubled over in pain and looked disbelievingly at his leg, now covered with his own blood.

On the ranch Sonny was accustomed to things moving when he laid hold of them. He had never studied the laws of physics but over the years, he had developed a fine, intuitive sense of mass times velocity when it came to busting things loose. Smashing the forward hatch with one blow of the heavy oxygen tank seemed a natural thing to do. He flipped the shattered hatch cover out of his way and then dove headfirst into the opening. His desperate face stopped its descent inches from Shanti's, who looked right back at him with huge eyes.

"I found you, I found you," he kept repeating as he quickly removed the turns of anchor chain from her torso.

"I knew you would come," she said. He pulled her to him with one arm and then, in an unbroken motion that only a bronco buster could accomplish, lifted them up and out and launched backward, free of the deck, into space and the sea.

A second later Chucho opened the V berth and swore as bitterly as a man from Sinaloa could. He turned and dragged himself through the cuddy back toward the cockpit. With each movement paroxysms of pain shot through his leg where the spear had lodged. He tried to hold it steady without success. He screamed again as a wave pitched him, spear first, into a bulkhead. He gritted his teeth and pulled himself into the cockpit. His breath came in short rasps, and he was shaking uncontrollably as the shock began to wear off and the full force of the searing pain in his leg took hold. He saw Primo out of the corner of his eye, awkwardly slumped over the bench behind the wheel, still unconscious.

Chucho's full attention turned to the cause of his agony: the old man lying in the cockpit sole now awash with blood and seawater. He stood over the fallen *viejo*, the magnum .357 hanging at his side.

As quickly as Archie and Sonny jumped to the *Cobra*, Chad stood the *Dolphin* off a few boat lengths. His attention was now divided three ways: the boarders facing the probably armed kidnappers; the sea, which could cause mayhem if the two boats came together; and the advancing Sheriff's boat. He kept one eye on the *Cobra*'s deck and one on the incoming swells. In a lull between big waves he clipped a 50-foot floating line to a ring buoy and attached the bitter end to the stern Sampson post. He checked his radio, still on channel 52—the one he and Pete had agreed to use.

"Come on Pete, get here," he said just as the radio crackled.

"Chad, this is Pete, over."

"Pete, got an ETA for me?"

"Axel's dead reckoning puts us there in under two minutes, over."

"Roger, two minutes." Chad wanted to look for the approaching red and white but never took his eyes off the *Cobra* or his sixth sense off the building sea. He saw Sonny raise the oxygen canister and smash the hatch cover. He heard two quick gunshots, a scream, and saw Archie go down. Then Sonny and the girl were off the deck into the water.

Chad shouted "Sonny!" and tossed the ring buoy. In seconds he had towed the two of them far enough away to make a pistol shot difficult in the rolling sea. Chad pulled them hand over hand onto the *Dolphin*'s swim platform. He pointed Sonny to towels and blankets and shot back to the controls. He saw the red and white Sheriff's boat bearing down on them.

He looked hard at the *Cobra*'s cockpit and keyed the mike. "Pete, this is Chad. Go right to the speedboat, I've got the little girl on board and one of my boarding party. But I still have one of my boarders on the chase and the two perps. Shots fired, Pete. Repeat, shots fired."

"Roger, Chad, we're going right for her. Roger shots fired," Pete said.

On board the Sheriff's boat were Deputies Pete Maras, his partner, Axel Gonzales, and Richie Calk, a recent academy graduate on his first training run. They had checked out an oil spill in a marina up north and were the closest unit available to respond to 22's request for Harbor Patrol assistance.

The three men saw the two boats ahead of them, wallowing in the swell. Pete headed for the *Cobra*.

"Get ready, Richie. This is going to be interesting," Axel said while he tried to size up the recruit.

Richie was clearly feeling sick from the race through the following sea.

Axel put a 12-gauge pump on Pete's dash and held another in his left hand. "Get out your piece, Richie, but don't start shooting unless we do, OK?"

Richie, smiled, squinted, and said, "I'm tight with that, Axel." He drew his .38 police revolver and checked the loads.

"Not a bad training run, hey kid?" Axel said, smiling thinly.

"I'm stoked," Richie said. "This is Richter!" But his darting eyes told Axel that he was not as confident as he was trying to appear.

"Just don't start shooting unless I do."

The two men kicked all the fenders over, then silently waited, their attention glued to the *Cobra*, as Pete slowed and turned for a stern boarding. None of them could see any activity on board. They were within a couple of boat lengths when Axel saw a figure emerge from below deck. His pant leg was soaked with blood, and he had a gun in his hand.

"Pete, gun!" Axel shouted.

Pete keyed the loudspeaker: "This is the Harbor Patrol. Drop the gun and put your hands over your head."

The words, bouncing off the water at 110 decibels, startled the man. He looked up. He saw the red and white boat with SHERIFF in big black letters on its freeboard. He saw the three officers in their forest green flak jackets and realized he was looking right down the muzzle of two large bore shotguns.

"This is the Sheriff. Drop the gun," Pete repeated, this time in

Spanish.

The boat rolled. Chucho dropped the gun.

9

Only a fool
Goes to sea
For pleasure.

"That went well," Axel said dryly, "but now comes the tricky part." Axel and Richie took turns covering the perps while they put on rubber gloves. Axel handed Richie the shotgun. "Keep your line of fire clear, kid, and whatever happens, don't shoot me."

Axel grabbed the first-aid kit, a pocketful of zip ties, and stepped onto the swim platform. Pete backed the sheriff's boat down to the wallowing *Cobra*. Axel barked his shin getting on board but otherwise made it safely into the cockpit of the pitching speedboat. He took a quick look around as he moved to the perp standing as ordered with his hands on the windshield. Axel didn't like what he saw—two men down and the well awash with blood. He kept out of Richie's line of fire as he pulled the perp's hands behind his back and zip-tied them together all the while reciting his Miranda rights in English and Spanish. Then he had the guy sit on a locker and zip-tied him to the locker latch. He rolled the big unconscious man over, tied his hands behind his back, and then to some hardware on the other side of the cockpit.

He keyed his two-way radio on his lapel. "Pete, I found the dead-man switch under one of the perps, so I think we can get this thing underway. Send Richie over with the bolt cutter."

Axel finished his triage of the three injured men while Richie ran below for the bolt cutter. The older man would get first intervention: his age and the location of the gunshot wound made him the most critical. Axel could see he was having trouble breathing, and there was some foam in the blood. *Must have nicked the left lung.* The good news was he had fallen on his left side.

Just then, Richie and the bolt cutter came aboard.

"Richie, find some blankets to cover these guys up and prop the older fella so he can't roll over. We have to keep the blood out of the good lung. Then, as soon as you can, plug in the dead-man switch and see if you can get this thing fired up."

"Excellent!" Richie said, looking at the three huge engines in the back.

"I'm working here, so don't get any ideas about opening her up," Axel warned. "Find a speed where we minimize pitch and roll. I'm guessing 10 knots."

"Aw, Axel, you're no fun."

The older, injured man opened his eyes.

"Hey old-timer, how you feeling?"

"Not so good," the man said. "The little girl, is she..."

"She's fine, on board the 22 with Chad and the other gentleman. I'm Deputy Sheriff Axel Gonzales, and this is Deputy Calk. What's your name?"

"Archie Douglas."

"All right, Mr. Douglas, we're going to get you stabilized and into port as quick as we can. I'm going to put an oxygen mask on you here so you can breathe a little easier. How old are you, sir?"

"I'm 67."

"Are you allergic to any medications?"

"No."

"Have a heart condition?"

"My doc says I have the blood pressure of a 20-year-old."

"Well, good for you, Archie. Do you have any other injuries?"

"I must have hit my head when I fell—it is pounding."

Axel could have used a few more facts, but didn't want to tire him. He cut away Archie's shirt around the wound. He could see the small entrance wound and relatively small exit wound, indicating that the bullet hadn't hit any bones. He cleaned the wound with sterile water, then applied pressure bandages front and back to slow the bleeding. He rigged a sling for Archie's arm to immobilize the area as much as possible. He moved Archie's feet and legs more athwartships to minimize the effect of the roll, which had greatly lessened since Richie had got them underway. Finally he put a blanket under Archie's head and wedged a couple of boat cushions around him to keep him from rolling over.

"It's very important you lie on your left side, Mr. Douglas, just as you are. We don't want any fluid getting into your good lung, OK? Richie, keep an eye on Mr. Douglas; make sure he stays in this position."

Axel moved to the spear wound. The perp was shaking hard, so Axel put another blanket around him. As he did he noticed the contusion on his left arm—it was swollen to almost twice its normal size. "Looks like somebody gave you quite a thump, *amigo*."

Chucho swore under his breath in Spanish but said nothing more.

Axel explained that he was going to have to cut the spear near the leg with the bolt cutter so he could wrap the thigh with a bandage to reduce the bleeding. When Chucho seemed to not comprehend, he repeated what he said in Spanish and Chucho said, "OK."

Axel moved on to the unconscious big man. "Richie, tell Pete we're winding up BLS, confirm three need immediate medical attention, and ask him where we are taking them."

Richie got on his two-way while Axel bent over the big boat operator. *No cuts, no bleeding, one bump on the temple. No clear fluid coming out of his ears. Pupils are equal and reactive but still out like a light.*

The boat operator jerked awake when Axel held the smelling salts under his nose. He immediately started groaning.

"I'm Deputy Sheriff Gonzales, and you are under arrest." Axel finished the recitation of the Miranda rights, then asked the perp his name. He wouldn't—or couldn't—answer. "All right big man, you know where you are?"

"I'm on my boat."

"And you know who I am?"

"Harbor Patrol." Axel finished examining him and moved up beside Richie at the wheel. "The big guy is oriented times three, he should be all right. But we have to get the other two in quick. You're doing a good job handling the swells, kid. Take her up to about 15." He keyed his lapel mike. "Pete, any idea where we can go with SMG shut down?"

"Roger, Axel, I just got off the line with the hospital at Marina Del Sur. Their ER is standing by, ready for one gunshot wound with a pierced left lung, one spear in the thigh injury and one concussion."

"I thought that place was for plastic surgery."

"Well, apparently they do have an ER as well. They are taking up the slack for SMG—Dispatch says some of the doctors and nurses from Santa Monica are helping out. I'm not sure how we're going to get them from the dock to the hospital; all the ambulances are tied up with the quake, but I'm working on it. "

Pete's dispatch found two detectives from the L.A.P.D. Child Exploitation Branch of the force's Sex Crimes Unit who were very interested in interrogating the perps. He also discovered their ride was a nice new mini-van and, under the circumstances, got them to agree to transport the perps and Archie to the hospital as long as the Sheriff's Department would guarantee they wouldn't get any blood on their new upholstery. It was just a matter of covering the interior with plastic tarps. The detectives could get the wounded men to the ER in no more time than it would have taken an ambulance crew. By now, every emergency response officer in the county knew there was a lot of improvising going on after the quake and looked the other way as regs went out the window.

Pete had a sheriff's deputy standing by at the dock to quarantine the *Cobra* for CSI to do their thing as soon as they got in. Pete was satisfied they had done all they could do. Now everything depended on getting them there in time, and it looked like Richie knew how to handle a boat.

Dr. Hazim returned to the room just as Danielle, Mildred, and Nicky were finishing their prayers.

"In Jesus' precious name, amen," Mildred said. "Doctor, we said a prayer for you."

"Allah be praised," he said. "I need all the prayers I can get. I have good news, ladies. I have found Danielle a bed at Marina Del Sur Hospital. I have visitation rights at MDS; thus I can be her attending physician. There are no ambulances available. Therefore, one of my nurses and I will drive her over in my Jaguar. You ladies can follow in the SUV."

"Dr. Hazim, that is above and beyond," Mildred said.

"Not at all, not at all, Mrs. Johnson. They are transferring some of my patients from SMG to MDS as well, so it makes perfect sense for me to go over now to reassure them."

"Thank you, Doctor," Danielle said weakly.

"It is my privilege to care for you, Danielle," he said.

Dr. Hazim had phoned ahead to expedite Danielle's admission to the hospital. Because he and an RN were accompanying her and because the Emergency Room was swamped, they had agreed to take her right through the ER to an available bed.

Dr. Hazim pulled into the hospital lot, where ambulances, police cars, and private vehicles were bringing in the injured in a steady stream. A police officer who was directing traffic stopped the Jag about a hundred yards from the hospital entrance. Because of the quake, the hospital disaster plan was in effect: the ER triage unit, supported by the ambulance crews, was doing preliminary exams right in the parking lot.

Dr. Hazim and Nurse Remple helped Danielle into Mrs. Johnson's wheelchair and began making their way through the controlled chaos. Hazim's high spirits returned as he exchanged hellos with some of the nurses and physicians he knew.

"I've got an extra gown for you, Doc," one of them said.

"Jihad!" Hazim shouted back with a wild, happy look, and a fist shot skyward.

None of the docs or nurses looked up from their grizzly tasks of probing, palpating, evaluating, and occasionally swabbing, sterilizing, and bandaging the cross-section of humanity laid out in front of them, but all of those from Santa Monica General cracked wry smiles and one of them—a nurse—said "Jihad indeed" as she recalled Hazim's personal definition of his middle name: holy war against illness.

The doc who had extended the invitation and who knew nothing of Hazim's nickname shrugged and shook his head. Hazim, ever the gentleman, said, "I'll be right with you, Dan, as soon as I get this patient settled in."

The ER entrance was blocked open and patients on gurneys, in wheelchairs, or sitting and standing lined the hall. Dr. Hazim caught the eye of the ER receptionist he had reached earlier; she handed him a clipboard with all the forms.

"You know the drill, Doc. Anything you can't fill in today just leave blank; we'll catch up another day."

They started down the crowded, noisy hallway toward the elevator when the air was pierced by a high-pitched voice shouting, "Mommy, Mommy!"

Suddenly Shanti's slender arms were wrapped around Danielle's neck and she, in turn, held her precious girl close, both gushing tears and babbling incomprehensibly at once.

Dr. Hazim tousled Shanti's head and explained to Nurse Remple, "I have no idea how she got here."

"Archie and Sonny rescued me *again* and Archie's been shot!" Shanti pointed down the hall as she spoke.

"Is he here?" Hazim asked.

"He's right over here, Doc," Sonny said, walking up, "and he's in a bad way."

"Nurse Remple, take Danielle on up to the room on the chart and stay with her. You know the protocol for head injury. Show me where he is, Sonny."

The two men hurried down the hall and around a corner.

The first thing Archie saw when he came out of the anesthetic was Sonny's concerned face. "The doctors say the surgery went well, Arch."

"That's good," Archie mumbled.

"Apparently the bullet passed right through without hitting anything hard so it caused the least possible damage. It did nick the top of your left lung, but that's the worst of it."

"Somebody must have been praying for me," Archie said weakly.

"You're telling me. Hazim said it hit just that far from your heart." Sonny held up his thumb and forefinger just inches apart.

"Sonny, what happened out there after I went down? There's a blank space between the time I was shot and when the deputies started patching me up. And how did you end up in hot pursuit of these villains?"

Sonny filled in the parts of the story Archie didn't know, adding as many details as he could think of. Archie was delighted that Buck had a part in it and was particularly interested that Primo and Chucho had been turned over to the Child Exploitation detectives. He waved a feeble hand to slow Sonny down and began to speak, "Jesus said, 'If anyone causes one of these little ones to stumble, it would be better for him to have a millstone hung around his neck and to be drowned in the depths of the sea.' "

"Amen!" Sonny rejoined quickly.

"You're going to get religion yet," Archie said, managing a weak smile.

"I just hope those bleeps don't get off on some technicality. They deserve the worst."

"Shanti is safe—that's the main thing."

"Yeah, it is." Sonny smiled at his old friend. "I have to get home for a while, but I'll look in on you later. Anything you need? Anything I can get you?"

"Do you see my glasses anywhere?"

Sonny made a quick search of the room and couldn't find them.

"I have a backup pair in my dresser, first small drawer on the right. The case is blue-gray. It's going to be unbearable here if I can't read."

"Sure Arch, I'll pick them up for you." Sonny grabbed Archie's keys and headed out the door. "Oh, I almost forgot. Danielle is here too, just for observation. She got hit on the head."

"How is she?"

"Well, let's put it this way: she's in a lot better shape than you are."

Captain Otterlink's office was on the fifth floor of the new wing of the L.A.P.D. downtown complex. It was normally lit by fluorescent ceiling lights, but Otterlink found them oppressive and sprung for a halogen lamp in the corner and another on his desk. They gave the room a warmer feel than the rest of the cubicles outside. The two detectives from Child Exploitation, Jedediah Lincoln and Charlie West, had requested a meeting and Otterlink—head of the Sex Crimes unit—figured they had been making progress with the perps from the arrest at sea.

"So, what have you got, boys? Are the perps talking?"

"They are, Captain, oh yes, they are." Detective Lincoln spoke first. "We did the interview with the little one in Spanish. Says his name is Aurillio Rodriguez, an undocumented alien. He has rolled over on the other perp, one Primo Carreta. The D.A. says we have a strong case—kidnap, intent to commit child exploitation, intent to commit child pornography, assault with a deadly weapon—and forensics has a pile of hard evidence already. We can put Carreta away for a long time, and Rodriguez faces deportation as soon as we are through interviewing him. But it's what Carreta is telling us that we thought we should see you about."

"Go on."

"Carreta says he can give up a major player in cocaine and child pornography. Says the guy is in deep cover: goes by the alias X and nobody—not even his own people—know his real name. Carreta says he will give X up if we hold Carreta in protective custody and then let him leave the country. He claims he can give us enough that we can put this X away forever, break up a huge drug-import business, and a child pornography ring."

"X, huh—is that like Malcolm X?"

"No, Triple X, like the porno rating."

Otterlink looked at Lincoln and West. They could tell from the tiny shake of his head they had said something that he found interesting. *Thirty years on the force*, he thought, *and this is the first perp who named himself after a porno rating*. "What has Carreta given you so far on this X?"

"Remember the Coast Guard bust a few weeks ago off the coast of Ecuador—they seized 14 tons of cocaine?"

"Yeah, I read about it in the *Tribune*."

"Well, Carreta says he knows for a fact that was X's cocaine, and he says it was just one of many shipments."

"You got my attention," Otterlink said. For the first time in the meeting he scratched a note to himself on a desktop pad. "How does he know?"

"He says he was at X's cabin in Ventura the day it went down. X was drunk and belligerent and one of his sidemen told Carreta it was because he lost a big shipment of cocaine in a Coast Guard seizure off the coast of Ecuador."

"What's the perp's connection to the big player? Does he work for him?"

"No, Carreta runs his own small-time operation in Venice. He sat in on X's poker game once a week at X's cabin in Ventura. He says he lost a bundle in one of the games and when he couldn't pay up, X gave him a choice of bringing the little girl or he would kill him."

"So how's he going to give him up?"

"Carreta says X has deep cover, but he can blow it. He claims he has a clear set of X's prints, says there is a big money trail, and he gave us a license plate number that we got a hit on."

"What kind of a hit?"

West picked up the narrative. "Jed and I ran a stakeout in front of Valley Productions, in the Golden Triangle. The plate Carreta gave us matched a limo we shot a few weeks ago. The vehicle is registered to Global Productions Ltd., an offshore company we are checking out."

Lincoln jumped back in. "He told us X has warehouses full of unlaundered cash and he can put us onto his money man, some ex-poker dealer from Vegas. And, Boss, we matched some of the kids on the videos he named with photos from missing persons—we suspect they murder the children after they use them."

Otterlink looked up from his scribbling, frowned, and took a deep breath. "Boatloads of cocaine, warehouses full of money, the kidnapping and murder of innocent children," he said and went back to his note-taking.

"The other thing that comes into play here is neither Rodriguez nor Carreta has a record," West said. "The D.A. figures Carreta will get a break for that."

"So we catch and release a minnow and land a whale," Captain Otterlink said.

"There is one wrinkle in the deal." Detective Lincoln had left the bad news to the last. "Carreta says he won't appear in court. Says he will stay in protective custody here until we close the deal on X, then he wants to leave the country. He is certain that X will kill him if he can find him and says X has the resources to do it."

"Do you think he will give us everything he has as the investigation goes forward?" Otterlink asked.

"Based on his cooperation so far, I'd say yes," Lincoln answered.

"Will he ID photos and pick people out of a lineup?"

"He ID'd X's limo and said he would do whatever we want, as long as he doesn't have to go out on the street," West answered.

Otterlink tapped his pen on the desktop, pondering his decision.

"The DA figures if we can find that kind of cash and get the money man to testify we can put X and his organization away forever, and if we follow the money trail, Carreta's testimony would not be necessary," West said.

"This is going to have to go higher than department," Otterlink said. "I'll have to arrange a conference with the Chief, Narcotics and Missing Persons, and somebody higher up in the DA's office." Otterlink wrote himself more notes. "And you know the Feds will want in on this. For now, tell Carreta I want more, a lot more before I'll even consider it. I want those prints, a positive ID, and X's real name for openers."

Lincoln smiled. Otterlink knew how to do business.

"All right," Otterlink said, "give me everything you have so far in writing."

"Here is our written report, Boss; we got Larissa to type it up in department form," Lincoln said.

"Good work, men. Let's stay on top of this one."

Archie hated being in hospital. He hated being cooped up, hated the food, and hated not being able to go sailing whenever he wanted.

However, he was as weak as a kitten and his shoulder hurt. He knew without asking that this was going to be a long stay, so he purposed to make the best of it and he got a lot of help. Nancy was an RN and could visit whenever she wanted, which was all the time. She helped out in the Del Sur ER right after the quake, but all that had calmed down; now she took advantage of being laid off and was at Archie's bedside day and night. The other thing that made Archie's stay more bearable was the incredible amount of news he had missed being literally at sea during the first hours of nonstop coverage of the quake.

Nancy brought the local papers in every morning and read all the stories aloud. "Oh my goodness, Archie, here's an article about SMG," Nancy said, getting quite animated. "I know all the people they are quoting."

"Read," Archie said.

"January 17 at 4:31 AM Santa Monica General was shaken to its foundations by the Northridge Earthquake. Unknown to most west L.A. residents, a fault line runs right under the hospital."

"Tom Jackson practically predicted this when I visited him at U.C.L.A. a few weeks ago," Archie said. "Fascinating, read on."

"The 6.7 quake plunged the hospital into darkness as electrical lines were severed. When the emergency lights came on, the on-duty staff was greeted with spouting water leaks, broken glass, and fallen debris. The most distressing signs of the quake, however, were visible cracks in walls. Ralph Ireland, chief of engineering at the hospital, immediately instigated disaster plan procedures."

Nancy lifted an eyebrow. "That must be why I got paged just before five."

"You got called in to help, didn't you?" Archie said, smiling proudly at Nancy.

"Yes, I helped evacuate the ward. Oh, listen to this: *'Head Nurse Latoya Wilson'*—Latoya's my good friend," Nancy said, getting even more animated.

218

"Is she?"

" 'Nurse Wilson prepared to evacuate the children's ward on the second floor.' "

"That's my ward—where Shanti stayed. We will have to read this to Danielle and Shanti when they come down for their visit this afternoon."

"Indeed we will."

Nancy read on:

"Nurse Wilson and her staff carried, wheeled, and walked the children out into the parking lot. Wilson said, 'Now I know how the Pied Piper felt.' "

"Oh, that's so like Latoya. She always has something clever to say!" Nancy added, then went back to the article.

" 'The scene in the parking lot reminded me of some of my experiences in Viet Nam,' Ireland said. 'People crying out, nurses giving shots, and the whole scene lighted in this eerie way by the backup system. Those nurses earned their pay that night.' It was quite exciting, and the children for the most part responded very well. In a press release yesterday hospital administrators said they thought they would have to permanently shut down due to the extensive quake damage. All 1700 staff were laid off. It is the first time the hospital has been closed since its opening in 1942. However, the hospital board has already committed to rebuild and turn Santa Monica General into a state-of-the-art facility."

"Amazing," Archie said. "And no one was hurt?"

"Nothing in the article about that, Arch, but oh dear, here is another column with the latest update on the death and injury toll. Oh dear...oh my..."

"Read, dear, read aloud!" Archie said.

"Sorry darling, I'll summarize: the Northridge Quake is now considered one of the costliest disasters in U.S. history. Property damage is now in the billions of dollars, with over 10,000 damaged structures and counting, 20,000 displaced persons, 1500 serious injuries, and...oh dear," she said, looking up at him, "57 deaths."

The two of them were pondering this grim report when there was a light knock on the open door.

"Jimmy!" Archie cried. "Come in, come in. Good to see you."

"Here's a place for you to sit, Pastor Jim," Nancy said, moving out of the chair closest to Archie and into one at the foot of the bed.

"No, no, don't trouble yourself, Nancy. I can't stay long; I'm on my way to a prayer meeting. I just had to stop by and tell you what I found out yesterday." Jim stood by Archie's bedside. "It was one of those connect-the-dots experiences. But first things first: how are you today, Archie?" Jim said as he put his hand on his old friend's good shoulder.

"No better, no worse; but give me the news, Jimmy. The nastiest thing about being in here is the boredom, and there's nothing like news to fight it off." As he spoke, he reached down to the hospital bed's tilt control lever to move himself to a more upright position.

Nancy smiled fleetingly at his animated face, her enjoyment overshadowed by her concern for his overdoing it. She said nothing though, thinking instead, *Once we are engaged I'll be more forthright with him about health issues.*

Jimmy was primed to tell his news. "Tricia and I were going over my sermon series for the next few weeks—which is something else I want to talk with you about. In the middle of our meeting I got a call from Steve Cantrel, a pastor friend in the Valley, who insisted on being put through. His church is in Sylmar, about six miles northeast of the epicenter."

"I know something about Sylmar," Archie said.

"I know you know," Jimmy said, grinning. "But here's what you don't know. Steve said the quake completely—and he repeated *completely*—destroyed the Golden Triangle. Pornographic video production in Sylmar is no more!" Jimmy paused to see what effect his news would have on his listeners.

A cold sweat broke out on Archie's forehead, and his pale complexion turned a shade paler.

"Archie, you don't look well. Should I call the nurse?" Nancy asked.

"No, no! What else did he say?" Archie asked, his gaze fixed on Jimmy.

"He said all three porn production buildings were razed to the ground. He drove by each of them and there is nothing but rubble. Everything is destroyed—equipment, master tapes, all crushed beyond repair. He's sending me a copy of one of the Valley papers. Apparently the owners vowed they would leave the Los Angeles area and never return. They got a quote from one of the porn moguls saying, 'This should make the religious right happy.' "

"Ooch...awe," Archie said, looking out the window.

"There's more, as I think you know, Archie. Here's the connecting-the-dots part. I hang up and I'm sitting there with Tricia. Of course she wants to know what was important enough to interrupt our meeting. So I tell her. You know how perky she is; always has something to say. Well, not this time; she just sat there, looking stunned. So finally I said, 'What's going on?' It was then that she told me about the Anaheim Worship conference, how you guys prayed for the region out of Haggai, chapter 2..."

"I will once more shake the heavens and the earth, says the Lord Almighty," Archie interjected, looking very grim.

"That's the verse. Tricia said the guy leading the prayers interpreted the passage as a shaking up of the church. Nobody thought it meant you were praying for an actual earthquake. Anyway, Steve Cantrel says there's this guy up in Sylmar called Wild Bill—an ex-biker Christian."

"Actually, he's a Christian biker," Archie said.

"Right, that's what I meant. Steve said Wild Bill was holding a praise-and-prayer vigil right in front of Valley Productions—or what's left of Valley Productions—to thank God for destroying the whole thing. So what do you think, Archie, Nancy? What do you think about all of this?"

Archie said, "Ooch" and Nancy, "Oh my" at the same time. They thought a long time before they spoke.

Jimmy was content to wait for a while but finally said, "It's a tough one, isn't it? I'd be willing to bet that suffering is the most frequently raised objection to our faith. We claim that God is both good and all powerful. So our critics say if God is good, He wouldn't tolerate suffering, and if He is almighty, He would be able to prevent it."

"Well, first of all we can't rule out natural cause," Archie said. "The Golden Triangle sat right on a major fault line in one of the most likely areas in the state for violent earthquakes. At the same time, there is no doubt that 1200 intercessors prayed fervently through Haggai chapter 2 that night in Anaheim—not to mention what Wild Bill and his crew have been asking the Lord to do—and it's no stretch to say we got what we prayed for. It wouldn't be the first time that God surprised me with His answer to my prayers."

"The destruction of pornography production fits the biblical pattern of God actively judging sin in this life," Nancy added. "The problem is the 57 deaths and 1500 seriously injured we just read about. Probably none of them had anything to do with pornography. Archie and I have been praying every day for the families who lost loved ones," she said, looking at Archie.

"Some of the suffering we endure is a result of our own sin," Archie said. "And innocent people suffer as the result of someone else's sin. But in this case, if we accept Wild Bill's direct cause-effect explanation we are left with the appearance that our loving God allowed innocent death and injury as an acceptable part of carrying out His judgment on the porn industry. It seems a bit off to me."

"Theologians and philosophers have debated the problem of suffering forever, and no one has come up with a good answer. Even the Bible doesn't address the issue systematically," Jimmy said.

"Still, we have to grapple with it," Archie said. "We can't just say 'oops' and carry on." All three were silent for a moment, then Archie went on. "I guess what has worked for me in tragedies in the past is I have always had faith that God would work through them. Suffering is never good in itself, but God uses it for good. I've seen people come to salvation as a result of tragedy. I've seen Christians grow and mature in character as a result of it. When I lost Luella, I grew in faith, although it took a long time."

"I lost my first child," Nancy said softly. "He died only a few hours old. At the time, I thought it was so unfair. But it has helped me so much in my work—to understand how other people feel when they suffer loss."

Archie reached for Nancy's hand. He thought of his own girls and imagined how painful it would be to lose a newborn.

The three of them sat silent for a time. Then Nancy said, looking lovingly at Archie, "The text that I held onto through the darkest times was Romans 8:28, where Paul tells us: 'In all things God works for the good of those who love him, who have been called according to his purpose.' "

The verse and Nancy's story had quite an effect on Jimmy. He swallowed hard. "In a way, that brings me to my second reason for coming over this morning. There is one good thing that has already come out of this tragedy: the response of so many people to others in need. My office has been flooded with reports. So I got the inspiration a few days ago to do a 'Heroes of the Faith' sermon series. That's what Tricia Knox and I were planning when Steve called. The idea is we videotape interviews with Christians who responded to others in need over the past few days and then tie it into how Jesus responded to our need. What do you think?"

"Ah, Jimmy," Archie said, chuckling.

"Sounds like a good idea to me," Nancy said. "What's the joke?"

"Jimmy will do just about anything to fire up his sermons. Some of us think it's great the way he brings in current events. Others have called him shameless for taking advantage of what's happening in the community."

"Hey, I point my critics to the Master. I'm just imitating Him. Jesus not only used events of the day, He even created teachable moments by performing outstanding miracles. Anyway, Archie, I would like to interview you as part of the series. What do you say?"

One of Archie's character strengths was a genuine humility. He shied away from anything like self-promotion, but Jimmy came prepared for his reluctance. "Come on, Arch, you will be just one of six in the series. I guarantee people will respond to Christ as a result of this. I can feel it already. It's a gamble we have to take," Jimmy said, giving Archie a knowing look.

But Archie wouldn't bite; he pursed his lips and shook his head imperceptibly, trying to remind Jim that topic was confidential. Of course, Jimmy could tell Nancy how Archie had helped him with his addiction and he did without hesitation.

"Arch helped me overcome a gambling addiction years ago, Nancy. I bet on sports events, football, baseball, flats—that's horse racing—just about anything. I had a tab with a local bookie, the whole nine yards. But since Archie helped me, the only thing I gamble on now is the Lord's work. Ha, ha."

Before Nancy could reply, Archie said, "Well, if you interview me you should interview Nancy, too. She was in on that evacuation of Santa Monica General. Show him the article, sweetheart."

"Oh, Archie." Nancy blushed as she handed Jimmy the open paper.

Jimmy scanned the article and grinned. "Done and done! I'll have Felix bring the videocamera here whenever you like."

Jimmy knew how to close a deal; he was an evangelist after all.

That afternoon Danielle and Shanti came down for a visit. Danielle was still being held for observation for the concussion, but had no symptoms other than a persistent headache. Her white head bandage, however, made her look like a war casualty.

Archie and Danielle chuckled about who looked worse. It was no contest about who felt worse.

After a few minutes, Archie noticed that Shanti was much more subdued than usual. "Is Shanti acting differently since the events of Monday?" he asked, not wanting to say too much in front of the child and give away that he was worried about post-traumatic stress disorder.

"No, she seems to be herself. I just told her you needed peace and quiet, and there would be terrible consequences if she upset you."

"You're being quiet for me?" Archie asked as Shanti moved to his bedside and took his good hand.

"Yes, Archie," she replied in a muted voice.

"Well, actually, Danielle," Archie said, still looking at the little girl and squeezing her warm hand, "boredom is the worst of being here. And diversion makes me forget about the pain. So as long as you don't jostle the bed or whack me in the shoulder, I would like it very much if you would be your delightful self, Shanti."

Shanti turned to her mother and had a long whispered conversation with her hand cupped over Danielle's ear. Archie caught a few words, but couldn't make out what they were saying. He could tell from their looks that something was up, but no amount of cajoling would get them to tell him more than, "You'll see soon enough!"

"All right. I'll be waiting," Archie said. "How are you managing childcare, Danielle? You're in here, and Tom must be unimaginably busy with the aftermath of the quake."

"Tom asked his mother to come up from Long Beach to take care of Shanti. I thought it would be best if Shanti could stay in her own house, so Mrs. Jackson is staying over at my place and Tom crashes there too whenever he sleeps."

Archie could tell Shanti liked her grandma visiting as soon as the subject came up. "Lucky girl," he said. "You get to have your grandma with you all the time, don't you?"

"Yeah," she said, smiling. "Grandpa is coming over tonight, and he's bringing pizza!"

"Oh, I didn't know that," Danielle said. "They do spoil her."

"All grandparents are like that," Archie said. "Anyway she needs a little spoiling after what she's been through."

Archie didn't have to wait long to find out what Danielle and Shanti were plotting.

At the start of visiting hours the next morning, he and Nancy were just getting into the newspapers when Danielle, Shanti, and Sonny swept into the room and closed the door behind them. All three of them wore red plastic noses and had the wild Doctor Bobo look in their eye.

Sonny also carried a medium-sized duffle. He set it carefully on the floor, unzipped the zipper, and out jumped Buck.

"Ladies and gentlemen," Shanti said, projecting her voice, "I give you Buck the wonder dog, the smartest dog in the world."

Danielle and Sonny stood at the sides of the room, making goofy faces while Shanti ran the eager dog through his paces: sitting, rolling over, playing dead, and then finding a hidden toy in various places throughout the room. Normally Archie would have worried about the violation of countless hospital regulations, but the combination of weakness and painkillers induced an unfamiliar letting go and he purely enjoyed the show.

Afterwards Sonny put Buck back in the bag and made his way out undetected.

With all the quake news Archie was eager for a visit from Tom. He got his answering service and left a message.

Tom returned the call in just a few minutes. "How are you?"

"I'm recovering. The tedium is the worst of it."

"I would love to stop by and catch up. Maybe I could bring some of the preliminary data on the quake. Would you find that interesting?"

"I would like that above all things."

"Great. Well, it's against my religion to work on Sunday, so I'll stop by after early mass. How would that be?"

"Perfect!" Archie hung up.

Nancy had family commitments on Sundays. Now he wouldn't be alone.

Tom covered the small metal folding table next to Archie's bed with a heap of documents, and the two men greeted each other as warmly as Archie's many aches and pains allowed. "Arch, I've been thinking about this all the way over, and I wondered if I could sort of consult you professionally before we get into the quake data."

"Of course, Tom. Just fire away, and I'll send you a bill in the morning. Ha!"

"Well, it's about Shanti and Danielle and all the trauma. Not just the physical stuff—I guess in that department Shanti is fine, and Danielle seems a lot better than a few days ago. I'm more worried about the psychological issues...you know, post-traumatic stress and all that. I mean, Danielle seems more down than I have ever seen her, and Shanti...well, it's weird with her. She just keeps bopping along like nothing happened; yet what she has been through has to have traumatized her. So I figured you, being a psychologist, would know what I can do, what to look for, stuff like that."

"Of course. I'll help in any way I can." Archie reflected back on similar cases he had worked on. "Well, let's start with Shanti first. There are several factors in her favor. First of all, the way she is processing is perfectly normal for a four-year-old. Second, the trauma only happened once; it's not a continuous story of abuse or neglect that continued over years of her childhood. Those are the ones who need years of therapy." Archie paused for Tom to comment or question.

"This is all good, Archie. I'm already feeling better."

Archie went on. "Third, she wasn't raped or in any way sexually molested, thank God. That is also much more difficult to heal. Fourth, the men who hurt her were not people close to her—not parents or siblings or friends."

"God forbid!" both men said simultaneously.

"Fourth, Shanti is a strong, assertive person and probably has the sand to bounce back from this."

"Good stuff, thanks," Tom said.

Archie carried on. "Now as far as what you can do: make sure she feels secure, loved, and cared for. Don't go overboard and smother her; a little extra time, attention, and affection will do the trick. Oh, and one other thing. Sometimes children her age can work through their feelings by reading a story not unlike the traumatic event that happened to them. You could probably find just the right book in the children's section or describe the event briefly to the librarian or book seller. They might know just the one. You or Danielle read the book to her at the right time, a little farther away from the kidnapping...say a few weeks from now...and let her interact with the story as much as she wants. The book gives the child a narrative to follow that takes her through her feelings. Something she isn't old enough to do on her own yet."

"Yeah, that makes sense. I'll definitely do it. What about Danielle?"

"Right. Part of what we see in mood change could be no more than the result of the concussion. At the same time I imagine she must feel pretty upset about everything that has happened, especially as far as Shanti is concerned."

"She's always been the best mom to Shanti," Tom said.

"I tell you what, Tom. She stops in to see me every day. I'll keep a lookout for any chance to talk this through with her. And you do the same."

"She does seem softer with me; maybe she would open up. Thanks. Archie. Thanks so much."

"My pleasure."

"So," Tom said as he moved over to the heap of files on the side table, "are you up for some quake analysis?"

"Oh my, yes," Archie said, looking eagerly at the pile.

"You sure you're strong enough to carry on?"

"Boredom is my enemy, not fatigue."

"All right, all right," Tom said, opening the top file. The young seismologist left the issue of Archie's endurance behind and was lost in his own narrative. "In '71 most of the serious damage was done by uplift, but in this one, ground-shaking inflicted the most damage and over a much wider area. It is, in fact, the hardest ground-shaking recorded in a metropolitan area. Think about the amount of damage…if we hadn't been tightening building codes for 23 years."

Archie nodded, not wanting to break Tom's flow by saying anything.

"There's no question that the upgrades prevented total collapse. Besides the shaking, the whole area has been uplifted in places. There is a dome-shaped pattern of uplift—at the epicenter as much as 20 inches higher—that will probably affect the area's water systems."

"How do you measure these changes?" Archie asked.

"The preliminary data is coming from GPS reports."

"Amazing."

"Oh, everybody is in on this one, Arch. Ummm, remember how we said the day you visited me at U.C.L.A. that the area is very stable—that's why we expect big, violent quakes?"

"Yes, I do recall that."

"Well, here is an interesting thing. JPL—that's Jet Propulsion Lab, in Pasadena—JPL says the quake has slowed to almost nothing already, very few and very small aftershocks. The consensus is that the lower crust where the quake began must be cold and hard instead of gooey. So this explains why this area builds so much stress before a quake happens. There isn't any movement until the pressure gets big."

"Fascinating," Archie said.

"We also have preliminary data that the Granada Hills continue to lift as a result of the quake. We are talking inches at a time here, and in this business, that's a lot. You know how the quake has damaged the entire infrastructure of the basin: railroads, water systems, electrical lines, not to mention buildings. Here is one area where I have a lot of data—freeways. We have tried to focus here preliminarily because we can't get at the other stuff until we have restored the highway system. Here, look at this photo of a crushed support column on the 10."

"The Santa Monica Freeway—that's a long way from the epicenter, isn't it?"

"Right, but this is pre-'71 design. See how the column pushes outward at the top? What we do now is encase the concrete column in steel so that didn't happen to the columns built after '71."

"Why weren't these columns retrofitted?" Archie asked.

"It's quite an undertaking, when you consider all the freeways and bridges built before '71. We were working on it. Here, look at this picture of the westbound Santa Monica between Venice Boulevard and La Cienega."

"Look at that," Archie said, pointing to the total collapse of the structure in several places.

"Here's the kicker—this section was scheduled for column retrofitting this month!"

"Isn't that amazing? So if the quake had happened a few months from now, that section would still be standing."

"More than likely. Altogether there were about 2,000 bridges in the epicentral region; of these only six failed and four others are so badly damaged that they will have to be replaced. However, these failures occurred on some of the busiest freeways in the world: most notably the Santa Monica, and the 5, and 14 interchange. Now look at this photo: these Mission Gothic, flared columns, designed in '76, performed unexpectedly poorly. The bigger upper portion forced failure at the base of the flare. Now we're going entirely with straight, steel encased columns."

Archie began to flag a bit and needed a break from Tom's presentation, if not a complete adjournment. Archie leaned back against his pillow. The movement caused a sharp pain in the shoulder, and Tom noticed Archie's grimace.

"Need a rest? Want to take a break?"

"Yes. The spirit is willing, but the flesh is weak."

"OK, Arch, I could stop by next Sunday; I'll have more data."

"That would be superb."

"I meant to tell you. I saw Chad, the lifeboat operator, this morning at early mass."

"He's a good kid. Does he attend regularly?"

"Yeah, he says he does and he says to give you his best. He plans to stop by to see you sometime this week."

"That would be great. I'd love to hear his version of what happened."

Archie was able to nap after Tom's visit, something his discomfort had prevented up to now. He awoke to see Danielle sitting beside him. He realized it was the time she usually visited, and he was glad to see her. However, she sat with her head bowed uncharacteristically. Archie couldn't tell whether it was the posture or the bandage or actual weight loss, but she seemed somehow smaller.

"Hi Danielle, how you doing?"

"Not good, Archie, not good." As soon as she looked up and spoke, tears started down her cheeks.

"Dear, dear, what's wrong? Is your head hurting again? Have you told the nurse?"

"No, it's not that. My head is better." She wiped away some of the tears. "Tom stopped by; I guess right after he was here with you and told me everything you said about Shanti. Archie, it's my fault that she was traumatized. It's all my fault. I will never forgive myself." With this the tears abated somewhat as some of the old hardness returned.

Whether it was just fatigue or a conditioned response from so many head-bangers with her, Archie went blank. *Oh help me, Lord,* he prayed. *I mustn't fail her now.*

Just tell the truth rang in his head.

"Danielle, I so much want to help you, but my mind is a complete blank."

"Oh, you poor dear," she said and grabbed his free hand, the one not hooked up to the IV, and held it tight. "I put you here, Archie. It's because of me you almost got killed and Shanti almost...." She couldn't finish saying what had almost happened to her precious daughter.

Archie noticed the tears flowing again, but what really got his attention was the excruciating pain shooting from the hand Danielle grasped so firmly. He didn't know how it happened, but in the exchange of shots—gun and spear—in the *Cobra*'s cockpit, he had jammed the very fingers she held so desperately. This was the first time Danielle had been so vulnerable, and he feared any reaction to her grip, any pulling back, might end the blessed encounter.

God help me, he cried inwardly. Whether it was the pain or answered prayer, his mind suddenly cleared. "There is a terrible cost to forgiveness."

"What do you mean?"

"When you were doing Bible study with Nancy, did you ever talk about forgiveness?"

"No....yes.... I don't know."

"I have personal history with how hard it is to forgive. I don't think I ever told you how my first wife died, did I?"

"No."

"She was murdered by drug dealers."

"Oh, Archie!" Danielle clamped onto his injured hand with both of hers.

Now the pain was too great to control. Archie's arm involuntarily jerked at his firmly held hand.

"What's wrong?" Danielle said, pulling back.

"Nothing, nothing, I...my nose itches," Archie said.

After he had rubbed his nose what he thought was a convincing amount of time he carefully rested the hand on his bandaged shoulder; from time immemorial doctors and nurses had made clear to every visitor: this region was untouchable.

His fingers still throbbing, he went on as if nothing had happened. "It was at night, we had just anchored in a remote bay in the Gulf Islands, Canada. The criminals wanted our boat for their own purposes and, without warning, shot both of us. I was on deck when they came alongside. The first shot knocked me overboard. My life jacket saved me, and I was later rescued by a Vietnamese family who was fishing in the area. Luella wasn't so lucky."

Danielle listened and watched Archie with riveted attention.

It was the first time he had told the story in such detail to anyone. "A lot more happened later between me and them, but the point here is that my faith said I had to forgive them. It took me years to do, and even now it still comes up and I have to pray through it again. But Danielle, the hardest thing was to forgive myself."

"Why?"

"Because I lived and she didn't."

Danielle gasped with full understanding. Now the tears flowed down both their faces; neither could speak for some time.

"I need to know how you do it, Archie. How you forgive yourself?"

Before Archie could answer, the partially closed door swung wide open and Shanti burst into the room, followed at a more dignified pace by Tom. "Mama, Mama—you have to come see what Daddy brought us. There's one for you and one for me and they are up in your room!"

"How wonderful darling, I'd love to," Danielle said as she returned Shanti's hug.

"Danielle, have we interrupted something?" Tom asked, noticing her red, swollen eyes.

"That's O.K., Tommy," Danielle said, getting up. "Archie and I have all the time in the world to talk. Right, Archie?"

"Yes of course. We can pick this up any time."

10

We have this hope
As an anchor for the soul,
Firm and secure.
HEBREWS 6:17

Pastor Jim Mitchell knew how to work the phones. When Tricia said she had Commander Ortega on the line, Jim picked up immediately. Jim enjoyed the community relations aspect of his job. He liked talking with people who were not members of his congregation. Jim had a real gift of evangelism. He was willing to talk about Jesus anywhere, anytime. With Tricia's help he had most of the pieces in place for the upcoming "Heroes of the Faith" sermon series: six video interviews lined up and a dozen other details in place. His preliminary interview with Sonny Milan had uncovered another principal player in the offshore action—the lifeguard boat operator Chad Gier.

Over the past several years, Pastor Mitchell had faithfully taken his turn on the pastoral support team for the local police, fire, and lifeguards and, as a result, had gone with Chad's commander to console a drowning victim's family the past September. Commander Ortega expressed deep gratitude to Pastor Jim for his presence at the visit and attended the service at Westside that Jim arranged for the family, who had no church connection.

"Commander Ortega, this is Pastor Jim Mitchell over at Westside Community Church."

"Ah, Pastor Jim! How are you?"

"Very well thank you, and you?"

"Just fine, Pastor."

"Commander, I'm doing a 'Heroes of the Faith' sermon series starting this month. We are tying the sacrifices that so many people made in the aftermath of the quake with the sacrifice our Lord made for all mankind."

"Oh yes, I see. That sounds appropriate."

"Yes, indeed. Well, I thought it would be good for our church to give public recognition to the good work you and your department do, so I was wondering if you would be willing to come to Westside on a Sunday morning and give some kind of commendation to one of your lifeguards in front of the congregation."

"Well, I might be able to do that. Which lifeguard are we talking about?"

"Chad Gier. He was the boat operator in that recent rescue at sea of the kidnapped little girl, Shanti Jackson."

"Yes I know. I have been reading his written report. You know, Pastor, I have a bit of a problem because Gier did a good job in one way, but at the same time he violated multiple department regulations: leaving his crew behind, taking those senior citizens out in an angry sea, and then putting them aboard a vessel with armed and dangerous men."

"I'm sure it's put you in a tight spot."

"Yes, but at the same time, I know what it's like out there. You have to make decisions on the spot. How is the older fellow doing—the one who was shot?"

"Archie is my good friend and mentor, and I can assure you he is recovering nicely."

"Ah, he is your friend." Ortega paused and Jimmy waited. "Well, if the community is honoring Chad for what he has done, how can we do any less?"

"Wonderful, wonderful. Now I want you to know we will have a news reporter covering the story. We can't allow a television crew in the sanctuary, but there's a reporter from the *Tribune* who is following this story and she will be attending that Sunday."

"A news clipping might be a helpful piece of evidence of community support in Gier's file."

"Excellent. I'll make sure you get a copy. Now I'm also wondering about all the others who played a part in this rescue. Is there anything we could do to recognize them?"

"Well, we do give honorary lifeguard awards sometimes."

"Oh, that would be perfect," Jimmy said, scribbling a note for Tricia.

"Yes, that would not be out of the ordinary to do. I tell you what: I'll give some thought to what sort of commendation I might give Gier and get back to you."

"Thank you so much, Commander Ortega, and may God bless you richly."

When Ortega hung up the phone, his concerns with Chad Gier's performance at sea dimmed in the glow of Pastor Mitchell's blessing.

Later that day Chad Gier sat in front of Commander Ortega ready for the worst. Ortega had a reputation of being a fair but no-nonsense commander and headed a well-run organization. He also had a deep, rumbling bass voice that could put the fear of God into anyone when he was upset.

"Chad, do you have any idea how many department regulations you violated in this recent action? What were you thinking?" Here Ortega paused, seeming to add up his marginal notes on Chad's written report.

Chad knew that any answer he might give would only make the reprimand worse. He waited in silence.

"Violation after violation," Ortega went on. "However, I will note in my report that the earthquake created serious personnel and equipment shortages that forced you to, ummm, innovate. Also, it has come to my attention that the community wishes to recognize your part in the rescue of the little girl, and I have chosen to follow suit. I will be presenting you with a commendation at Westside Community Church in a few weeks. You will be able to attend?"

"Oh yes, sir! Just name the day and I'll be there."

"Very well, you may go now on one condition: promise that you will go by the book from now on."

"Oh, I will, sir. I have no intention of having anything more to do with innovations."

After Chad left, the Commander felt sorry for him. Chad had been promoted as high as he could go as a lifeguard and would go no higher. He was a good kid and very able. He had passed for fireman but had little chance of getting hired. He had been turned down in interview after interview around the L.A. basin. Since affirmative action, the various fire departments hired minority group members or women first.

Pastor Jim wanted to videotape Nancy and Archie at the same time, but Tricia couldn't make everyone's schedules fit. As it worked out, Jim had already run Nancy's video and presented her with an award on the first week of his six-sermon series and still hadn't taped Archie. Jim's approach was to show the clip and preach the same sermon at all three services, but have the live awards ceremony at the 11 o'clock. Archie was reluctant to go through with his interview and questioned Nancy closely on what went on in church.

"Well you know, dear, how uncomfortable I was with the whole thing," Nancy said, touching the side of the hospital bed. "But it was very tastefully done. They used just snippets of the interview with me interspersed with clips from the TV news coverage of the hospital evacuation. Then Tricia Knox—lovely girl—gave me a bouquet when Pastor Jim had me stand briefly. The whole thing lasted just a couple minutes as a preamble to Jim's excellent sermon. He talked about how the nurses at SMG were prepared years in advance for such a crisis and how well that training and experience served us in the evacuation. In the same way, he said, Jesus was prepared for His mission of salvation before the creation of all worlds. I must say the whole focus was on Jesus, and in the end I was happy to be a part of it. Oh, and I was deeply touched at how many people raised their hands to give their lives to Christ."

Archie felt somewhat reassured by Nancy's report, but he didn't entirely trust Jimmy to do the same thing with him. He knew Jimmy was willing to do outrageous things to promote the gospel. When Jim and Felix arrived later that morning to tape Archie's interview, his reluctance was at its lowest ebb, however, as a result of Nancy's recent report. Felix, the cameraman, was very good at disappearing into the woodwork with the camera running. He had a cover over the "on" light so the subject couldn't tell if it was running or not. As well, Jimmy was especially good at doing these interviews, putting the subject at ease and asking leading, open-ended questions. He obviously enjoyed what he was doing, which further disarmed Archie's suspicions.

When it was over, Felix rushed off to his next appointment, but Jimmy lingered with Archie. "Arch, you're looking better today. Any idea how soon you will be out of here?"

"Dr. Hazim says I finish the course of IV antibiotic in two more days. Then I hope I can go home. I told Hazim the sea air has curative powers, but he said so do antibiotics."

"Sonny and I can care for him at home," Nancy added.

"Good, good, well, you know Tricia has the whole church praying for you."

Then Nancy said, "Jimmy, you know we don't do altar calls at First Presbyterian, but I must say the idea of public commitment that I saw at Westside last Sunday has a powerful appeal."

The comment stimulated a flurry of theological discussion: the importance of each individual making an informed decision; the major role of the Holy Spirit equipping you to give your life to Christ; the decline of those denominations that had moved away from evangelical theology; the growth of those that embraced it and so on. At one point Archie remembered something from his early days as a Christian. "Have you ever seen a spontaneous altar call?"

"I've heard of them, and I'd give anything to be there when it happened," Jimmy replied.

"I don't have a clue what you're talking about," Nancy said.

"Well, I saw it happen back in South Dakota, when I was still a baby Christian. Luella and I were invited to a meeting on the reservation by Roger Crowfoot, who was conducting the revival. Roger, a holiness preacher, was known for going on for two hours, but on this occasion he was only about 30 minutes into his message when the people, and it seemed like just about everybody there, got up, and started coming forward." Archie paused, reflecting on just how it happened.

The other two waited eagerly for him to continue.

"It was most amazing. Luella and I got there late—made a wrong turn—and had to sit in the overflow room. Even there people started coming forward right in the middle of his talk and knelt down in front of the television screen. At first I thought they had no sense of decorum at all; then I saw the camera pan back and people all over the main hall were coming forward too."

"Amazing. What was he preaching on?" Jimmy asked.

"That's the thing, Jimmy. He was preaching on Acts 16:30: 'What must I do to be saved?' When the people came forward, they were crying out, many of them very loudly. Now old Roger—he looked ancient—was a little hard of hearing." Archie looked at Nancy. "You know how it is with me." He smiled. "Well, Roger could hear the voices but couldn't make out the words. Then a younger man came to him on camera—one of his aides, I suppose—and in the overflow room at least, you could hear this funny conversation between the two of them. 'What are they saying?' Roger asked the young man in a frustrated tone. The aide replied nervously, 'Roger, they are saying, *What must I do to be saved?*' Roger paused, then said, 'I can tell them!' and swung right into his altar call, skipping the remainder of his message."

Archie grinned. "And Jimmy, you know how hard it is to get a preacher to do that. Ha, ha."

"Now let me clarify," Nancy said. "These people came forward without invitation, in the middle of his talk?"

"That's right," Jimmy said, unable to restrain himself. "Sometimes the Holy Spirit just takes over a meeting, and if you have any sense at all, you follow His lead just the way Pastor Crowfoot did."

Jimmy hung up the phone and jumped to the door to call Tricia Knox, his administrative assistant, from the next office. "Tricia, come in and shut the door. I just got off the phone with Archie; he gets out of hospital next week for sure, and I want to run this by you. Now, first of all, this whole thing has to be a complete surprise for Archie. If he gets wind of what I'm planning, he'll never show up. That's why I figure we have to put him in the third slot. The longer we wait, the more likely he is to find out what's afoot."

"Sure Jim, top secret," Tricia said.

"All right. What do you think of this?" Jimmy went on. "We show the video—it's ready, isn't it?—we show Archie's clip a week before he actually comes. That way we get the whole congregation in on the deal. Does that seem right to you?"

"Brilliant."

"Now, do you have the music lined up?"

Tricia glanced at her notes. "I was able to get the sheet music for Archie's favorite nautical medley and the four mariachis from the Spanish-speaking service are excited about sitting in with the band. I also am pulling in a couple other horn players we use for the Christmas pageant and a piccolo player."

"Excellent, excellent. OK, so I'm going to show the two-minute clip this Sunday and make some kind of announcement about how we are going to honor all these people who had a part in Shanti's rescue the next Sunday," Jim said as he scribbled notes to himself. "So let's see..." He looked at his wall calendar. "That gives the band 10 days to get ready. Is that enough time?"

"Yeah, plenty. They are all good sight readers, and I must say, I have never seen them so motivated. I just want to clarify one thing: your plan is to tell Danielle Jackson, Sonny Milan, and the others to come to support Archie; they are not supposed to know they are getting an award too?"

"Right. We surprise them at the last minute. That reminds me: it's all on with Commander Ortega."

"Oh my goodness, Pastor Jim. I think you are about to outdo yourself."

"Yeah, we'll have to put our flak jackets and helmets on after this one I'm sure."

"I don't know. Everybody likes Archie; you might be surprised at how this goes. Also, do you want the overflow room prepped?"

"You think we'll need it?"

"I'll get the custodial team on it. No harm in being ready."

That Sunday, a week before Archie was to appear in person, Jimmy previewed the story for the congregation at all three services. Carlie Simpson, an enterprising, young reporter for the *Tribune,* had not only gotten the story right, she managed to distill it to 500 words. Jimmy had the article reproduced, with the paper's permission, and handed it out with the church bulletin. It had a picture of Archie all bandaged up in hospital and another of Munchie and Buck—Munchie swathed in bandages and Buck looking keenly right at the camera. There was also a sidebar with an account of Archie's first rescue of Shanti and a beautiful shot of Sonny in the tiny *Mira Flores.* Then, just before his message, Jimmy introduced Archie's video clip.

"I'm going to show you a preview of one of next week's 'Hero' award recipients. It's somebody many of you know—one of our deacons and my mentor, Archie Douglas. Now, did everybody get the *Tribune's* synopsis of the story? Did you all read it? Good, good. All right, so we're going to run this clip and then I'll tell you more of what's going on next week."

The lights dimmed, and Archie appeared on the big screens to the right and left of Jimmy. He looked thin and small propped up in the hospital bed, and his sailor's tan had faded to almost nothing. The most arresting feature, however, was the large white bandage over his left shoulder. His overall appearance caused more than one gasp and a lot of murmuring among his friends. Jimmy's calm, even cheerful, interviewer's voice off camera seemed to reassure Archie's friends that he looked worse than he felt and Archie's own evenly modulated voice confirmed it. As well, the congregation giggled and Pastor Jim grinned whenever Archie called him "Jimmy."

The high point of the video for Jim came when Archie responded to Jim's question about heroism. "Jimmy, I'm no hero. Not at all, I'd call myself cautious."

"But how do you explain it, then, that you risked your life to save that little girl?" Jim grinned from ear to ear, anticipating Archie's final response. Jim had thought Archie was the greatest for years, but these recent events put his esteem for the old gentleman into another category altogether.

The camera kept rolling as Archie thought back, tried to get into his frame of mind during those critical moments. Finally he said, "I don't know, Jimmy. I guess I pretty much forgot about myself. All I could think about was that brave little girl, how much I loved her....I had to do all I could to save her."

As the lights came back up, Pastor Jim said, "So here's what's up for next week: we are going to give awards to no less than eight people who had important parts in the rescue at sea at this 11:00 service; they are all mentioned in the *Tribune* article. Even the two dogs in the story are getting awards, although neither will be appearing in church. Phil Kirk, a pet store owner in the congregation, is donating a year's supply of 'Dog Treats' for Buck and Munchie. The vet tells us that the dog that was shot is going to recover. What else do you need to know?"

The congregation was really into this and Jimmy knew how to get the most out of it. "Archie's friends from the Saturday night crowd and today's earlier service agreed to gather out in the commons to welcome him and since they could never fit in here with all of you, they will watch the proceedings from the overflow room. The band is going to play a medley of nautical tunes and Commander Ortega from the lifeguard unit involved in the rescue will be here to give the awards. It's going to be a great day for the community, so bring all your friends and neighbors, especially those who are not Christians. But here's the deal, we hope to....No, we have to make it a surprise. Those of you who know Archie will agree he would never show up if he found out what we are planning. So top secret, amen?"

"Amen!" they almost shouted back.

By the next Sunday Archie had been home for four days. He wanted to go to church and was pleased that Nancy and Sonny had agreed to drive him over. He could have walked to the car, but Dr. Hazim said he would approve of the outing only if Archie used a wheelchair—he said the internal injuries needed a few more days of inactivity to stabilize. Archie reluctantly agreed, but his physical condition was not his main concern, it was Jimmy. He phoned Jack McClelland, fellow deacon and fellow sailor who ushered at the 11:00 service, to find out how last Sunday's message went. He knew Jack was a steady, conservative kind of guy, and Archie suspected Jack didn't much care for Jimmy's shameless promotions.

"So Jack, how did the 11:00 service go last Sunday?"

"It was fine, Arch. Jimmy preached well as usual, and I think five people raised their hands for the altar call."

"I'm particularly interested in the hero award thing. To be frank with you, Jack, I'm worried that Jimmy is cooking up some kind of extravaganza for this morning. So how did he handle the fireman last week?"

"Everything in good order, Arch. Pastor Jim did a two-minute live interview with the fireman—who came in his dress uniform. There was some polite applause, but nothing over the top, all in good order, and then Jim rolled into his message."

"Thanks for the info, Jack. I guess I'll see you in a couple of hours."

Jack hung up, relieved that he hadn't had to lie to Archie about what was planned for this morning.

There was a bit of a scene about using the wheelchair, but head nurse Nancy Hollings had dealt with grumpy patients before. Once she spoke to him in her authority-filled voice, Archie got in.

As they approached the church Sonny said, "Hey Arch, with you in the chair, we can park in one of those handicapped stalls right at the front door."

"That's putting a positive spin on it," Archie said.

Sonny pulled into the lot and, sure enough, the handicapped stall closest to the door was vacant. He quickly parked the car, pulled the chair out of the back, and Nancy got Archie into it without further incident. Everything seemed normal as the three of them headed for the door to the commons along with other people arriving.

Archie looked at his watch. There were just a few minutes to get to their seats. Jimmy always started on time. Archie decided to make the best of it, saying over his shoulder as they reached the door, "It's good to be going to church even in a—"

He never finished the sentence. A throng of people lined both sides of the commons five deep, all the way from the front doors to the sanctuary entrance. The moment Archie appeared they all began clapping—a few even cheering—and everyone looked at him with beaming faces.

Archie did not return their joy. *It's Jimmy! Jimmy arranged all of this! Oh, he's shameless, shameless!* Then a sudden gust of greetings swirled back and forth as Danielle, Shanti, Chad, Dr. Hazim, even Mildred Johnson and her friend Mrs. Samos joined the procession toward the sanctuary doors. Archie wanted to bolt, but it was too late— the little group's momentum carried him inexorably forward. Just before the sanctuary doors, prettily dressed little girls presented bouquets to the ladies while other church members gave gift certificates to all of them. Phil McClelland handed Archie a large card with a spectacular aerial photo of a five-masted schooner. Her great array of sails aloft and alow and her long bow wave white against the blue water arrested Archie's attention. *She really is cracking on*, he thought. Inside the card was a beautiful, hand-written note entitled *Paul's Voyages: Sailing Is Biblical.*

Archie's perusal of the summary of Paul's three missionary journeys in the book of Acts was cut short as Phil bent near his ear and said, "You're a good sport to go through all this. Charlotte and I thought, when you're feeling better, you might like to take this voyage with us. The *Sun Clipper* here makes almost all the stops Paul did."

Archie was feeling nothing like a good sport, but before he could respond more than grabbing Phil's sleeve, Tricia Knox appeared and addressed the group. "I know you all think this presentation is for Archie, but in fact each of you is being honored for heroism today just as Nancy was honored two weeks ago. Pastor Jim would like all of you to proceed right down the center aisle and up on the stage for a brief awards ceremony just before the sermon."

As Tricia spoke, Archie heard—yet he could hardly believe it—a piccolo coming from the sanctuary playing the opening bars of "Jack's the Lad." Tricia quickly led them all into the packed-out sanctuary. Every seat was taken in the 1400-capacity hall, and people were even standing at the back. A 15-piece band spread across the stage. Archie immediately recognized his four friends from Don Pepe's mariachi band. Juan and Miguel, the violinists, joined the piccolo on the melody. The band played the lively tune flawlessly as the group came down the aisle of the packed hall.

The combination of seeing his Latino friends on stage and knowing his comrades-in-arms would get fair recognition today began to lift Archie's foul mood. As well, it was a happy crowd—all standing, smiling, clapping in time, and reaching out to give a pat on the back as the procession passed. It became apparent to Archie that somehow Jimmy had gotten the whole congregation in on the deal, but how? The last of Archie's grumpiness evaporated; the nautical music filled his heart with too much joy.

When the procession reached halfway down the aisle, Luis and Paco stood up and played a trumpet fanfare—the opening bars of "See the Conquering Hero Comes." Archie couldn't believe the full-brass sound they were able to pull off with two trumpets, one trombone, and one French horn. *The synthesizer must be augmenting the sound,* he thought. They played the sheet music perfectly. Archie anticipated that they would close with "Rule Britannia." He forgot that he often choked up during it.

When they reached the stage, Archie refused to go up the ramp in the wheelchair. "I'll walk from here Sonny," he said.

Nancy's intense conversation with Danielle made her a second too late to prevent his escape. At the top of the stairs Jimmy greeted each one with a firm handshake, and Tricia lined them out facing the congregation. Archie was about to say something to Jimmy, but he saw Commander Ortega—looking very nautical in dress uniform—standing just behind the pastor's left shoulder. The sight left Archie speechless.

Then, just as they were all toeing the line in good order, the drummer made a perfect, tight roll, and the band moved together into the majestic opening bars of "Britannia." *What an amazing homage to O'Brian, to sailors, to honor and nobility,* Archie thought.

244

Archie felt a lump in his throat and tightness in his chest. Now a rising fear accompanied the rising joy: would he break down in front of all these people? But the harder Archie fought for self-control, the greater the pressure in his chest. Finally the combination of his two heart's delights—nautical music and church—was too much for him. To his utter horror, tears began streaming down his face.

Pastor Jim came quickly to his side, however, and was a great help toward recovering his dignity.

"Don't worry, Jimmy, I'll get even," Archie said, shaking his finger in Jimmy's face.

Jimmy roared with laughter.

This whole time Tricia Knox had been watching Archie closely, wondering if the music would have the same effect on him here that it had that day in his living room. "You have to read the books to understand," he'd said to her, waving at the O'Brian bookcase and wiping away the tears with his other hand. The music always stirred him deeply with the courage and nobility of the British Navy's desperate battles during the Napoleonic wars.

Tricia wondered now—as Archie cried in front of God and everyone—if perhaps they had gone too far. Her nascent guilt eased when she saw Pastor Jim put his arm around his dear friend. She saw Archie poke a finger at Jim, then the two began laughing. Well, Archie was laughing and crying at the same time.

At just that moment the band began the closing measures of "Britannia": one ritard with augmented chording from the lower brass; then a second ritard and crescendo as the mariachis all climbed into their instruments' upper registers. This culminated in the final chord which they held, and held, and held, and held, then finally ended with a thundering bass drum roll and perfectly timed cymbal crash. It ended just in time for Archie, who was beginning to lose his composure again.

The greatest martial music in the world—at least that was Archie Douglas's opinion—had an effect on others besides Archie too. Although the group on stage couldn't hear it with the band playing fortissimo behind them, the cheering had started somewhere in the middle of the final note's eight bars. When the band stopped, the cheering continued. It's not often that people get to cheer in church. At first many were a bit reserved, but their inhibitions faded when they saw the effect it had on the people on stage, especially Pastor Jim.

Jim nodded enthusiastically, then shot both arms over his head, striking an awkward Rocky pose. The cheering went well beyond any level of decorum one could imagine and left Jim without any doubt: he would get complaints on Monday. But Jimmy had no worries today. Even his worst critics were cheering on their homeboy and his little band of brave friends.

A city block away, a passerby heard the cheering. He stopped to listen and said aloud: "It seems to be coming from that church over there." He stood still and listened again. "No, it can't be. Must be an NFL broadcast."

Inside the church the full-throated cheering had quite the opposite effect on Archie that the music had. Now completely sober, he looked around at the others. Danielle seemed a bit stunned, and Shanti was trying to hide behind her mother's skirt. Archie fully realized, and hoped everyone else would, that it was really God who was the hero of the recent action off the coast; His fingerprints were all over it. As Archie stood, head bowed in front of the congregation, he lifted his palms up in front of him and looked up to heaven. In his heart, Archie gave all the glory to God.

There was another crescendo in the cheering, then Jim raised his hands and brought the meeting to order. Jim introduced Commander Ortega, who gave each one, starting with Shanti, an "Honorary Lifeguard" navy blue T-shirt from a stack that Tricia held for him. He shook each hand and said "Honorary Lifeguard" after their name.

As Commander Ortega was making his way down the line, Sonny leaned over to Archie's ear and asked, "Is this church?"

"Yeah," Archie answered. "Westside is heavily involved in the community."

246

When they came to Chad, Tricia handed Commander Ortega an official-looking document instead of a T-shirt. He turned to the congregation. "Well, we can't make Chad an honorary lifeguard because he is a lifeguard. But we can nominate him for 'Lifeguard of the Year.' " He gave Chad the letter and shook the amazed young man's hand.

The crowd applauded warmly as Tricia led the group off the stage, and Jimmy thanked Commander Ortega for coming. When they got to their seats, Shanti tugged her mom's sleeve. "Mama, Mama, what does it say, and who are these men in the picture?"

"It says, 'Honorary Lifeguard, West L.A. Ocean Lifeguard Association.' And the smaller letters down here say: 'The Highest Calling is Saving a Life.' "

Between the lettering on the back was a black-and-white picture of 10 smiling men wearing old-fashioned swimsuits. This Danielle also interpreted.

"And the little circle on the front?"

"Well, darling, I guess that is a life ring, with two paddles, and there are the ocean waves and I suppose some kind of a float. The words are the same as the back. And this one is an award for Munchie."

The year's supply of dog treats pleased Shanti immensely and Buck's like reward was the high point of the proceedings so far for Sonny.

Jimmy liked soft lighting in the hall when he preached so people could have a sense of privacy as they communed with God. The lights came down as Pastor Jim began his message. He was usually smooth on stage, but not today. He made a couple of false starts, then croaked, "Give me a minute."

The congregation loved it. Someone shouted, "Take your time Jimmy," and everyone laughed; it looked like "Jimmy" was gaining traction.

The laugh helped him gain composure. It wasn't so much what had gone on so far in the service that was getting to him now, it was the anticipation of what he was about to do. He knew God had given him a powerful message, and since it was the last service he could let it go its full 40-minute course. "We're running about 10 minutes late today; if we're over at the end, those of you with little children feel free to go to the nursery at the usual time. Next week we continue this sermon series with another very interesting guest from our local community. As well we will be blessing and sending Pastor Marlin Fair and his wife, Clarisse, to Costa Rica. They have accepted a call from a small church there, and we're sure they are going to do a great job."

Archie had always wanted to explore the islands off the West Coast of Panama and then go through the canal into the Caribbean. He wondered if Nancy would be up for a honeymoon trip on the *Dawn Treader. We could visit Pastor Marlin in Costa Rica and then go on down the coast,* he thought. *I guess I'll have to ask her to marry me first,* he said to himself, chuckling at his backwards logic as he reached for her hand. The two of them were happy to listen that way as Jim carried on.

"We began our 'Heroes of the Faith' sermon series in response to the many heroic acts following the recent Northridge Quake. We have been looking into the question: what is heroism? Two weeks ago we looked at Nancy Hollings' story of the evacuation of the children's wing at Santa Monica General Hospital. Nancy said she was just doing what she had been trained to do, doing her duty. We noted that preparedness is often an overlooked element in heroism. I just mention that because Nancy is here again this Sunday, supporting her friends who were a part of today's story.

"This week we're looking at the question: What motivates people to risk everything to save someone else? At the moment of truth—the moment when you decide to risk all, to run toward danger instead of away from it—what goes through your mind? Danielle ran right into the butt of a pistol to save her daughter; four-year-old Shanti tackled a grown man to save her mom."

At this, Shanti and Danielle gave each other a hug, and Nancy put her arm around the two of them with tears in her eyes.

Jimmy went on. "Sonny and Archie risked their lives to save their little friend—Archie with a gunshot wound to prove it. Dr. Hazim said the bullet was only a few inches from Archie's heart. What made these people run toward danger instead of away from it? Let's go back to last week's video where Archie described his state of mind at the moment he risked his life."

"So that's how he did it!" Archie said to himself, but so loudly the regulars sitting in front of him gave each other knowing looks. In all the excitement Archie had forgotten about the video.

Pastor Jim held up his notes. "Here's the quote: 'I don't know, Jimmy, I guess I pretty much forgot about myself. All I could think about was that brave little girl, how much I loved her...I had to do all I could to save her.' "

He put the notes back down and looked out at the congregation. "Archie wasn't thinking about himself. He could only think about his friend Shanti and what she was going through. His entire focus was on her suffering; his compassion overrode any concerns he had for his own well-being. Our natural survival response tells us to run from danger. But sometimes, as in the case of these heroes, love compels us to run towards it. So it was with our Lord Jesus Christ who, though being God, did not hang back, did not cling to His secure place in heaven, did not try to protect Himself in any way, but for us He became a man. For us He died a terrible death on the cross.

"You see, Archie, Sonny, Danielle, and Shanti risked everything because of love for each other. The Bible tells us God so loved us that He gave up His only Son for us. God *so* loved He knew He would have to pay the ultimate price: the life of His Son. God places the highest value on every soul—the value of His only Son. Men, women, children...there is no gender bias, no racial bias, no cultural bias. When it says God so loved the world it means every man, every woman, and every child."

Jimmy paused and then seemed to Archie to speak extemporaneously. "You know what all these brave folks did for Shanti will be remembered a long time in our community, but what Jesus did for all of us will be remembered to the end of time."

Jimmy went on to give his usual concise summary of the gospel message: how all have sinned, how there are consequences to sin both temporal and eternal, and how Jesus bore the punishment for our sin in His own body on the cross. "This is where Christianity starts, in the agony of the cross." He went on to point out that each person has to decide for themselves whether Jesus is who He says He is. But if a person does believe in Jesus—believes He is the Son of God and accepts that He died for his sins—that person can start a new life in Christ that will last for all eternity."

Jimmy was about 20 minutes into his sermon now, and Archie felt it was going well. Archie also sensed an electric attentiveness in the congregation.

Just then Jimmy stepped out from behind the lectern. Somewhat out of the glare of lights, he was able to make eye contact with people in the assembly. "I prayed that I could speak to every heart this morning," he said with complete sincerity and more than a little passion. "For love of you, Jesus left His Father, left a place of perfect peace, left all the riches of heaven. For love of you He was beaten and finally tortured to death. For love of you He is here now, pleading with you, 'Let Me save you from this life that you have made for yourself. Let Me give you My life in exchange for yours.' Oh, won't you come to Him this morning? Listen—if you hear Him calling you, don't wait for me to finish. Come and meet Him right now."

Back at the podium, Jimmy paused and looked down at his notes. *Has he lost his bearings?* Archie wondered. Then Archie heard a stirring beside him, turned, and saw people moving into the aisles. Many of those closest to him were weeping. One man in a biker jacket was sobbing.

God in heaven, it's a spontaneous altar call! Archie looked back at Jimmy; saw the surprise on his pastor friend's face as he leaned out of the spotlight, trying to figure out what was going on. "Ooch, come on Jimmy, it's a spontaneous altar call," Archie whispered. Now Archie saw the look of surprise turn to one of recognition and finally resolve.

Jimmy glanced in Archie's direction.

"Remember Roger Crowfoot!" Archie mouthed.

Jimmy nodded almost imperceptibly, gathered himself, and launched the formal altar call, skipping over the second half of His prepared sermon.

"It was probably better than the first half," Archie murmured happily to himself.

"Now some of you here are saying, Jimmy, I believe Jesus is calling me to Himself this morning, just as these folks are saying by coming forward. If you have been running from that call, or if this is the first time you heard it and understood what it means to you, come and join them. If you don't have a personal relationship with Jesus Christ, but would like to have one, come forward now."

He looked again at the heroes' section. "Danielle, Shanti, Sonny, and Archie all risked their lives in the last few days, I figure you can risk coming up here. Prayer counselors, you come on up too and maybe we could have a little music."

Another wave of souls moved into the aisles. Jimmy met the keyboard player partway across the stage. "You realize this is going to take some time with all these people up here?" He nodded and looked at the growing numbers just below his feet. "Go with something tender, worshipful," Jimmy said as he turned to go down into the press of people.

Westside usually reserved the walk-up altar call for Easter, using the raising of hands for other Sundays. Normally, for the walk-up, the moment Jimmy called people forward, the prayer counselors eased out of their seats all over the hall and headed forward; this made it easier for the guests to go up, since everyone going forward looked the same. Then, as the guests arrived at the front, the counselors were already there to lead them through the "I'm sorry, thank you, and I welcome you into my heart prayer," sign them up for follow-up, and give them one of the packets of information and a New Testament.

But today, as the counselors arrived at the front, they had to work their way around and through the throng that was already two and three deep. This was a big altar call even for Westside, a church known to be seeker-friendly. Archie fully expected Jimmy to call for additional help and, sure enough, he returned to the mike and asked for the off-duty prayer counselors and all the staff to come forward.

Archie was so taken up by the crowd at the front he didn't notice Shanti's animated conversation with Danielle or Danielle's tear-stained face until the two stood up and, hand in hand, began to squeeze by him.

"She wants to go forward," Danielle said to him, "and to tell you the truth, it seems right to me, too."

Archie was flabbergasted. "But..."

"Archie, after I was knocked on the head, I prayed with Mrs.

Johnson. I told God that if he would save Shanti a second time, I would give my life to Jesus."

Archie sat in stunned disbelief as first Shanti and then Danielle moved past his wheelchair and, hand in hand, turned toward the stage. All he could think of was how poorly he had answered Daniel's adamant arguments, but now the only argument was in his head: *She doesn't really understand what she is doing!* a whining voice said.

God will teach her all she needs to know, when she needs to know it, a calm voice replied.

Her decision was made under extreme duress; it won't last!

God often works through the crisis moments in our lives—when our attention is focused on what's really important, the calm voice said.

Perhaps it was the "what's really important" that brought Archie back to the reality that the two were making their way well down the aisle. "Nancy! Sonny! Tom!" he hissed. "Danielle and Shanti are going forward. Lose not a moment and wheel me up there, Sonny, will you? And Nancy, you should be there beside Danielle, and Tom, you with Shanti."

While Archie was still speaking, Sonny sprung around behind him, kicked off the brake, and started the chair down the aisle. The other two passed them going forward. At the front Jimmy made a beeline for Danielle and Shanti and personally led them through the prayers. Nancy was right in there too. Tom and Archie silently, tearfully gave the greatest thanks.

Father, Archie prayed, *if this isn't the fulfillment of the Anaheim prophecy it is good enough.*

Then some of the words of Simeon's prayer—one he had unsuccessfully tried to set to music—came to him: *"Sovereign Lord, as you have promised, you now dismiss your servant in peace. For my eyes have seen your salvation, which you have prepared in the sight of all people..."*

Epilogue

Eighty-seven souls came to faith that day at Westside, and another 42 renewed their commitment in both the main hall and the overflow room. Some attributed the "revival" to Pastor Jim's anointed, albeit foreshortened, preaching; others to the wakeup call from the recent quake. Whatever the reason, the third "Heroes of the Faith" Sunday went in the record books as Westside's biggest altar call ever.

Paul's Voyages

First Missionary Journey
1. *Seleucia to Cyprus Acts 13:4*
2. *Paphos to Perga 13:13*
3. *Attalia to Antioch 14:21-26*

Second Missionary Journey
1. *Troas to Samothrace to Neapolis 16:11-12*
2. *Berea to Athens 17:14-15*
3. *Corinth to Ephesus to Caesarea 18:18-22*

Third Missionary Journey
1. *Troas to Neapolis 20:1, 5*
2. *Philippi to Troas 20:6*
3. *Assos to Mitylene to Samos to Miletus 20:13-16*
4. *Miletus to Cos to Rhodes to Patara to Phoenicia to Tyre 20:38-21:3*
5. *Tyre to Ptolemais to Caesarea (Jerusalem) 21:7-8*
6. *Paul taken to Rome, shipwrecked at Malta 27:1-28:16*

About the Author

RICK CAMPBELL writes what he knows; he brings years of diverse experience to this novel. He was a Peace Corps volunteer, a Southern California hippie, a devotee of an Indian guru, and, after getting saved in 1982, a lay worker in his home church, one not unlike Westside in this story. Rick earned his Ph.D. in psychology in 1975 and practiced counseling for 32 years. In 1996 he wrote *Gaining Spiritual Ground: A Practical Guide to Sanctification,* a self-help book that sums up what he learned throughout his Christian counseling career.

Rick is an avid sailor. "It's when I feel most alive; God is out there," he says. For 15 years he has cruised the Pacific Northwest, one of the top sailing destinations in the world. Now that Rick is retired (although you never really retire from church work), he and his wife, Anne, spend weeks in the spring, summer, and early fall gunkholing in the Gulf and San Juan Islands. He has passed on this love of sailing to his three daughters and their families.

"I wanted to write a book about sailing, but the characters took on a life of their own and it turned into a whole lot more," Rick says. He is working on a prequel and a sequel to *Sylmar.*

For more information:
www.oaktara.com

Printed in the United States
206609BV00002B/28/P

9 781602 900455